"We can't do this. Must forget it ever happened," she insisted, her breathing still labored.

"Forget it? The bloody hell I can forget it." Garrett took one long stride and reached for her.

Wyn slipped away. "We have to," she said. "Have to make sure it never happens again."

"Wyn!"

She evaded him, taking running steps back into the glow of lantern light. She turned as she pulled open the hatch, looking back at him over her shoulder, sorrow and regret clear in her eyes. "It can't," she said. "It can't."

Before he could stop her or ask for an explanation, Wyn was gone, slipping through the hatch, headed back to the safety of the stateroom she shared with her widowed friend, leaving him alone with the increasing whine of the wind and the echo of longing he'd heard in her voice....

Dear Reader,

This month, we are very pleased to be able to introduce Silhouette Yours Truly and Special Edition author Beth Henderson to our readers with her first historical for Harlequin, *Reckless,* the story of a young woman, accused of being a jewel thief, who is rescued by a mysterious baron intent on clearing her name. *The Literary Times* calls Beth Henderson's writing "fresh and creative," and we hope you'll agree.

Rae Muir, whose first book, *The Pearl Stallion,* made *Affaire de Coeur*'s Top Ten List for 1996, is back with *All But the Queen of Hearts,* a lively Western set in Nevada Territory with an unsinkable heroine whose determination and skill in the kitchen finally win the heart of her reluctant hero. Also keep an eye out for Laurie Grant's new Western, *Lawman,* the fast-paced sequel to her 1996 release, *Devil's Dare,* about a lonely lawman who rediscovers love in the arms of his childhood sweetheart.

And for those of you who enjoy the Regency era, Taylor Ryan's *The Essential Wife* is the delightful story of a dashing nobleman who suddenly finds himself in love with the penniless heiress whom he has arranged to marry out of pity.

We hope you'll look for all four of these wonderful books, wherever Harlequin Historicals are sold.

Sincerely,

Tracy Farrell
Senior Editor

Please address questions and book requests to:
Harlequin Reader Service
U.S.: 3010 Walden Ave., P.O. Box 1325, Buffalo, NY 14269
Canadian: P.O. Box 609, Fort Erie, Ont. L2A 5X3

Reckless

BETH HENDERSON

Harlequin Books

TORONTO • NEW YORK • LONDON
AMSTERDAM • PARIS • SYDNEY • HAMBURG
STOCKHOLM • ATHENS • TOKYO • MILAN
MADRID • WARSAW • BUDAPEST • AUCKLAND

ISBN 0-373-28970-7

RECKLESS

Books by Beth Henderson

Harlequin Historicals

Reckless #370

Silhouette Special Edition

New Year's Eve #935
Mr. Angel #1002

Silhouette Yours Truly

A Week 'Til the Wedding

BETH HENDERSON

began writing when she was in the seventh grade and ran out of Nancy Drew books to read. It took another couple of decades, and a lot of distractions and procrastination, before her first book appeared in print.

That happened in May of 1990, and since that time she has written romantic-suspense, historical, young adult and contemporary romance under a variety of names for a variety of publishers.

Although a native of Ohio, Beth spent twenty years in the West, living in Tucson, Arizona and Las Vegas, Nevada. During that time she sampled a number of professions and has been a copywriter and traffic director in radio, done print display advertising and been a retail department manager. Now returned to her hometown, she is thrilled to be a full-time writer and loves to hear from readers. Her address is P.O. Box 262, Englewood, Ohio 45322, U.S.A.

To my aunts,
Catherine Hemme Ocskasy
and
Marjorie Daniels Schemmel

Prologue

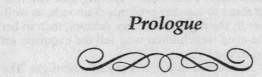

San Francisco, 1879

With the heavy brocade drapes drawn, only a sliver of moonlight entered the room. It was enough to catch the gleam of cut stones and to silver the rich setting as the necklace dangled from the dark-gloved hand.

The thief smiled, a small, self-satisfied curving of the lips, and admired the piece. The diamonds were as clear as water and nicely matched. They had been hoarded away in a vault at the bank for years, nearly forgotten by the family, before Oswin Hartleby had remembered them. His first wife had been a rarity in San Francisco society for she hadn't cared for ostentation. But Hartleby's second and much younger bride liked to flaunt his wealth. To please her, he'd spent a fortune having the diamonds made up in a glittering necklace and matching earrings. The gold for the setting had come from his own mines.

Nearly played out mines.

Of course, no one had known that until life with a wife forty years his junior had been the death of old Hartleby. There were some who claimed that, married to the coldly beautiful Hildegarde Keyes, Oswin's last years had been joyless. It was the young widow who wasn't smiling now.

Hartleby's will had been read the day before and the news
had sped about town, running rampant through the parlors.
Oswin Hartleby had left few bequests and astonishingly
high debts.

Old fool, the thief thought in derision, then grinned
widely in amusement. *Poor Hildy.* Having lost her husband, she was about to lose her precious diamonds, as well.
If not to a thief in the night, or hungry debtors, then to her
prickly middle-aged stepchildren who felt the exquisite set
should remain in their care.

The stones shimmered in the thin ray of moonlight. The
necklace was a gaudy trinket in many ways. It reeked of
new money, lacking the taste that came with inherited
wealth.

It was much admired in San Francisco.

If, by some chance, the widow didn't weep for it, there
were a good many other covetous women in the city who
would.

The necklace dropped into a dark bag with a slight tinkle
of sound and was joined by the matching earrings. There
was little else of interest in the jewelry box to add to the
cache. Although they'd been married nearly five years,
Hildy had received promises from Oswin rather than more
baubles. The thief closed the lid quietly and walked silently to the window. More moonlight spilled into the
room, outlining the dark-clothed form as the drapes were
parted. If there had been another in the room they would
have seen a figure of average height but little else. A silk
mask covered the lower section of the thief's face, a cloth
cap disguised both the color and length of the robber's
hair. A shapeless sack coat and baggy trousers hid any
trace of build. To all intents and purposes it had been a
shadow that had retrieved the diamonds from the wall safe
in Hartleby's house.

If any of the sleeping residents heard a sound in the
master suite, they put it down to Oswin Hartleby's ghost.
Now that he was gone, his young widow had moved her

personal belongings to a more cheerful room down the hall.

The thief moved quickly, letting the drapes fall closed, returning the room to its peaceful slumber. Outside the night grew attentive to a shadow's needs. Tendrils of fog stretched from the sea to shroud the moon. When the veil was complete, the thief slid from hiding, hastening to take Hartleby's diamonds to their new home.

Chapter One

The slap echoed in the parlor.

A lone beam of sunlight shone through the bow window, falling on the intense young couple who stood frozen in the center of the room. It burnished the pale flaxen locks of the woman, and brought a brighter sheen to the rose fabric of her afternoon gown and the multilayered train that spilled away from it across the fading patterns in the Oriental rug. The man's dark-suited back was turned away from the day, his expression temporarily masked by shadows and the tawny, rather rakish side whiskers that framed his lean cheeks.

The woman was the first to recall her lines, words she had heard other women speak, words she had never thought to utter, especially to this man.

"How dare you," Winona Abbot rasped. Her hand stung sharply, a physical reflection of the blow Deegan Galloway had dealt her ego.

"I love you," he answered simply. "I made a mistake and…"

"A mistake!" Wyn swung away from him. Crossing the room, she snapped open the pocket doors. Moments ago they had turned the front parlor of her family's Nob Hill mansion into a private haven for lovers. Now that same sanctuary felt like a prison that confined Deegan and her in each other's company.

"You don't understand, Wyn," he said.

She wheeled back to face him, the rich fabric of her train whirling with the motion. "Oh, I understand only too well. It was never me you cared about, Deegan. It was my dowry. After all," she snapped, her usually soft tone harsh with sarcasm, "there is so much a man can accomplish with a quarter of a million dollars."

He stood his ground on center stage, the imprint of her hand still clear on his face. "With you it was never the money, Wyn. Never."

If he meant to pacify her with the compliment, the effort was a failure. Her deep green eyes, dark lashed and mysteriously foreign against her fair coloring, flashed with indignation. The delicate curve of her chin tilted upward in a challenge. "So you admit it. You are a fortune hunter."

Deegan drew a deep breath, the air hissing through his clenched teeth. "I wish to God I knew who told you about Leonore Cronin."

There was a part of her that wished she had never learned of his perfidy, as well. But she had, from Leonore's own lips. "Did you think she and I didn't travel in the same circles, Deegan?"

"I thought," he said, "that you would understand when I did the girl a kindness..."

Wyn's brows rose at the inappropriateness of the term.

Deegan plowed on as if he hadn't noticed. "...and danced attendance on her last night. She looked so miserable sitting with the chaperons along the wall. I merely asked her to dance."

"I see. And was it then or on a previous occasion that you poured honeyed love words in her *shell-like* ears?"

She noticed Deegan had the grace to look embarrassed at hearing his own words thrown back in his face. How many times had he praised her own beauty using the trite phrase? How many times had she fallen happily into his arms, her maidenly reserve melted by his murmured praises of her charms?

At twenty-five, Wyn had thought she knew the wiles of men well enough not to make herself a fool over one of them. She had been wrong.

Wyn turned her back on Deegan, unwilling any longer to gaze on his handsome features. She had believed she loved him and yet had never been sure of him, never trusted him. That being so, the pain of his deception should not be this sharp. Wyn rested her brow against the highly polished molding around the door. "Oh, Deegan," she whispered in anguish, "tell me true. Was this gallant behavior begun before or after you discovered Leonore's father made his fortune in Nevada silver? Did you know she is his sole heir?"

When he didn't answer immediately, her heart broke a little more.

"Wyn…" Deegan took a step toward her, his hand touched her shoulder.

"Don't." She didn't want him to lie to her anymore, wouldn't tempt him to do so for the sake of a relationship that, for her, no longer existed. Wyn straightened her shoulders, gathered her courage. "I think it would be best if you left."

Deegan's hand fell away. "You aren't being fair to me, Wyn," he said quietly. "I love you. You love me. I would think you'd be pleased that I played Galahad for your little friend."

Played Galahad. Is that what he called the hours he'd spent with Leonore? According to the desolate girl, he had called on her with flowers, had whispered tender words, had squired her on rides through the park, had in every instance shown that he was courting her. In Leonore's eyes Deegan had done everything except formally ask for her hand. Earlier that day when they had both chanced to visit the same home, Leonore had burst into tears when Wyn was teased about her own relationship with Deegan Galloway. Flinging the accusation that Wyn had set out to steal her fiancé, Leonore had run from the room, leaving an embarrassed silence behind her.

"Please, Wyn. Forgive me," Deegan pleaded softly.

How could a woman forgive unfaithfulness? It was the ultimate insult and Deegan had compounded it by being unfaithful to two women at once.

Surreptitiously Wyn regarded him, her gaze dispassionate. Once she had thought his brown eyes to be beautiful, an almost feminine feature in his otherwise masculine face. But now there was a desperation in them when they met hers. Rather than eliciting tenderness and compassion, the emotion hardened Wyn's heart. Leonore had looked that way before fleeing earlier that day. Wyn would never forget that moment, or the man who had caused the younger woman such pain and disillusionment.

"I think you'd better go, Deegan," Wyn said.

Long after he'd collected his hat and stormed out of the house, Wyn continued standing at the front window, staring out unseeing over the city, remembering.

They had met at a ball, introduced by her elder brother. Wyn had thought the men were business associates. She certainly saw Deegan at all the Nob Hill parties. She had begun to look forward to his attendance on her, to his tenderly whispered compliments, to his growingly insistent kisses.

She had been so close to succumbing to Deegan's wishes. He had wanted her. Her, not her dowry, even if she had flung that accusation at him. Compared to the fortune Leonore Cronin would inherit, the sum settled on herself appeared minuscule. Fool that she was, she had thought he cared for her. His protestations of love had been many, always followed by kisses guaranteed to undermine a maiden's resolve. As she weakened, Deegan grew bolder until she had begun to crave the stolen minutes, the clandestine caresses, with the passion of an opium eater. Wyn grew flushed at the memory of the time they had spent together, longing for what she would no longer have and embarrassed that she had so forgotten herself in sampling those forbidden delights.

The future of which she had dreamed would no longer become a reality, for with Deegan went her last hope. While her friends had found mates and married, she was still alone, a spinster, on the shelf, overlooked or forgotten when it came to love.

The truth was difficult to admit. She was an acclaimed beauty, an heiress. With those lures to attract a mate, why had she not been able to find a man who drew her?

Even Deegan, handsome and charming as he was, hadn't managed to do that. She had been tempted...only tempted.

The sun slipped into the western seas unnoticed. The sky grew dusky and lamps came to life in the nearby homes and along the sloping streets. Unseen, a maid came to attend to the gas jets in the hall, only to creep silently away from the parlor rather than disturb Wyn. It was only when the front door swung shut and impatient male footsteps sounded in the entryway that Wyn came out of her reverie.

"What the devil are you doing in the dark?" a man's voice demanded.

Wyn turned from the window at the first bark of her older brother's voice. "Oh, hello, Pierce. Back already?"

He tossed aside his hat and fumbled for a match in the pocket of his coal black frock coat. "Already? I stayed at the shipping office an hour later just trying to catch up on various matters. I've got a train to catch tomorrow, if you recall."

The match scraped to life. A moment later the room was filled with the soft glow of light. Pierce adjusted the gas jet on the wall then dropped full length onto the plump cushions of the sofa. "Don't you know it's damn cold in here, Wyn?"

"Is it? I hadn't noticed."

He glanced at her, a frown of concern drawing his dark brown brows together over his straight patrician nose. "Not coming down with something, are you, Ace?"

Wyn shrugged. "Do you want a fire?"

"Lord, yes. But first, tell me what's wrong."

"Nothing. I've just been thinking." Wyn gathered her narrow skirts and sank companionably to the floor near him. "Do you still need financing for the new ship?"

Pierce pushed off one shoe then the other. The sound of each falling was hollow against the tongue-and-groove wood flooring. "Let's just say the bank is anxious. They'd like a payment since we're running behind schedule on building the *Nereid*. Are you going to light a fire, or do I have to do it?"

"I'll do it. Have you got another lucifer?" He fumbled in his pocket again and passed her a match. Wyn leaned forward on her knees to light the fire. It had been laid on the hearth earlier by a maid in anticipation of the damp San Francisco evening. "Just how much does the bank want?"

"More than I feel comfortable discussing," Pierce admitted. Although he had become titular head of the Shire Shipping Line in the past year, Wyn knew her brother had moments when he doubted his ability to run the family business.

The flame caught the tinder and ate greedily along the underside of a log. Wyn sat back on her heels and leaned one arm along the sofa cushions where her brother lay stretched out. "On my last birthday, you and Pop arranged for me to have some money of my own," she said.

"Your dowry, Ace. Besides, you'll need it to reel Galloway in."

"Mr. Galloway has proven to be a cad," Wyn said tightly.

Pierce sucked in air between his teeth. "Worse than me, huh?"

"Infinitely worse than you."

He shook his head sadly. "Damn, and I thought I held the record. I guess you found out about the mouse."

"Leonore Cronin? Yes, I did. Do you mean to tell me, you knew he was courting her and didn't tell me?"

Pierce snorted. "La Cronin didn't have a chance against you, Ace. And so I told anyone willing to give me odds on the outcome."

Wyn sighed. "If you had a wager on it, I can understand why you didn't drop a hint. What was my standing in this particular race?"

"Hell, you were the favorite, of Galloway and of the betting books."

"Thank you for the kind compliment, brother dear," Wyn murmured, her spirits beginning to return. Having the matter reduced to the level of a sporting event put things in a different perspective, making it appear ridiculous for her to continue railing against fate.

"I'm sorry I lost you your wager."

Pierce sighed deeply. "You know I've always been a rotten gambler. Let's hope I'm a better businessman."

Wyn smiled warmly at him. "You are, much to the astonishment of the business community. Tell me truthfully, Pierce. Is the *Nereid* bankrupting you?"

"Truthfully? Nearly. That's why I'm leaving for Boston tomorrow to oversee the final construction. It means changing my schedule. I won't be able to sail on her maiden voyage as planned. However, a personal appearance on my part now should soothe the bankers. Our Shire cousins are careful administrators in the Eastern office, but they don't see the *Nereid* as a necessary expansion of our business."

"The Shire Line has always carried passengers," Wyn said. She held her palms toward the fire, suddenly aware of how cool the room had become. "And each year we've ordered larger ships to be built."

"Maybe it's just me," Pierce said. When Wyn made a discouraging noise, he laughed. "Okay, it's the expense. We've never gone in for steamships before, and the *Nereid* is more than just that. She's a luxury liner, designed specifically for passenger business rather than shipping."

Wyn stared into the fire and came to a decision. "Pierce, I want you to take my money. All of it."

He sat up abruptly. "Hell, no!" His stockinged feet hit the floor with an emphatic thud. "I do have my pride, Wyn. Pop and I worked it all out when I decided to take over the Shire office. Rather than divide the company up into shares, I bought each of my siblings out. That money is yours, Ace. It belongs solely to you and your future husband."

"I'm not going to have a future husband." Wyn took his hands in hers and gazed up into her brother's concerned face. "Don't you see? This is the perfect solution. I do believe in your plans for the *Nereid.*" At his doubtful expression, she squeezed his hands. "All right, it's you I believe in, Pierce, in your dreams for the line. I want to invest my money back into it. Think of it as a loan. You can pay me interest, dividends, whatever you want to call it."

He wasn't convinced. "And if indeed I do bankrupt the company with this scheme? You'll lose it all, Ace."

"Then you can take care of me for the rest of my life," she assured him brightly. "I'm not worried. The point is, you need to pay the bank something on account and I want to tie my dowry up so that it is no longer a lure for fortune hunters."

Pierce still looked doubtful. "You haven't thought this through, Wyn. I know it sounds good to you at the moment. Hell, it sounds like a godsend to me and you know I'm a proven cad who'll leave you high and dry like I did…"

Wyn pressed a hand to his lips, silencing the grim reminder of the girl he'd nearly wed.

"You won't let me down, Pierce. I know you won't. I can't say the same about any other man and since I can't, the best thing to do is never marry."

He removed her hand from where it sealed his mouth. "Don't gammon me, Wyn. You're a beautiful woman. There'll be lots of men who want you whether you've got a dowry handy or not."

A smile crept to her lips. "Are you going to take my money?"

"Hell, yes, I'm going to take it. I'm not that noble. But I'll do so on one condition only. Since I can't be there, you've got to be the family representative aboard the *Nereid* for her maiden voyage," Pierce insisted.

Wyn cocked her head to one side. "Can I take Hildy with me?"

Pierce's brows rose in mock surprise. "The far-from-sedate Widow Hartleby?"

"She's on the verge of a decline," Wyn divulged.

Pierce's mobile brows snapped together over the bridge of his nose. "Probably more so over the loss of her diamonds than over old Hartleby's demise. However, since you can't exactly travel alone—"

"You prude," she accused.

"Where my sister is concerned? Damn right, woman. I suppose Hildy is a better solution than hiring a companion."

"She's nearly a pauper," Wyn said.

"I'll arrange her passage, but that's it," Pierce insisted.

Wyn surged to her feet and, plumping down on the sofa next to him, hugged her brother fiercely. "It's a deal. You are the best of relatives no matter what the others say."

Pierce's frown darkened even more. "And what exactly *does* the rest of our family say, my dear Winona?"

The bellboy caught the coin, his eyes widening in surprise as he recognized the denomination, and responded by giving the man who'd tossed it a snappy salute.

Amused by the youth's enthusiasm, Garrett Blackhawk smiled as he pocketed the telegram the lad had presented and closed the door of his suite at the Palace Hotel.

The boy was his second welcome interruption of the evening. The visitor sprawled in the comfortable chair by the fireplace had been the first, delaying Garrett's dressing for the dinner party he wished to avoid. The delivery had delayed Deegan Galloway's pitch.

"Forgive the intrusion, Dig. You were saying that you're persona non grata in Frisco?" Garrett asked, dropping with careless elegance into another chair, his right leg thrown loosely over the padded arm. He was in his shirt-sleeves, evening trousers donned, starched shirtfront and collar in place, tie still dangling loosely around his neck. Although the clock on the mantelpiece was a constant reminder that he was late, Garrett made no attempt to rush his unexpected guest. Instead he reached for the cigarette papers and bag of tobacco on the table at his side and began rolling a smoke.

Deegan sighed deeply and buried his nose in a snifter of brandy before answering. "I was merely hedging my bets, Garrett. There's no way around it. I've got to marry a woman with money or seek employment. Either one will have to be done in another city. Between them, those two women will make it impossible for me to succeed here."

Blackhawk deftly sealed the edge of his cigarette and soon had obscured his face behind a screen of smoke. He'd heard it said that he fit his name well. Some insisted that, like a hawk, there was a predatory gleam in the obsidian shadows of his eyes, and a hunter's alertness in the tall, tapered frame of his body. His hair was sable in color, luxuriant in texture, and frequently tousled. Although born an English gentleman, of late his skin had been warmed to a primitive bronze by the sun of three continents. The craggy lines of his face could have belonged to a Spaniard, a Bedouin or a Mayan, and, at one time or another during his travels, Garrett had found it prudent to assume the identity of each in turn. He was careful in his choice of companions, allowing very few to know him well. Deegan Galloway was one of the specially chosen permitted to see the man beneath the mask.

Garrett drew deeply on his cigarette, savoring the taste of tobacco on his tongue, enjoying the slight euphoria of the smoke in his lungs. "You have my abject sympathy," he assured Galloway.

"Sure and it isn't enough," Deegan drawled in an ex-

aggerated brogue, then abandoned the affectation, returning to his normal speaking voice. "I came begging a grub-
stake as you very well know."

Blackhawk reached for his own glass of brandy, adding
the lush body of the wine to the tally of sensory delights
he planned to sample over the course of the evening. His
current company was pleasant, and the brisk dampness of
the San Francisco air reminded him sharply and depressingly of home. It was one of the reasons he was anxious
to leave the city. Business kept him a temporary captive.

A hardwood fire burned on the hearth, efficiently warming the hotel room. It reminded him of nights before the
huge fireplaces at Hawk's Run in Shropshire, only there
the heat would have been supplied by locally mined coal.
The estate might well be as distant as the moon for all the
thought he'd given it over the past two years.

"If you want a position that will take you far away,
you're welcome to become my secretary and take up residence at the Run," Garrett offered. "It would be a favor
that would enable me to stay blissfully distant from the
place."

Deegan chuckled. "Trying to turn me into an Irish peas-
ant? You forget I'm an American, born and bred. My da
was the potato eater. Although your largess is appreciated,
I'll stay on this side of the Atlantic. A monetary handout
will be more than sufficient, my friend."

Garrett grinned in response to Galloway's request. "At
least you know your limits. I notice you didn't ask for a
loan."

"Lord, no." Deegan swished the brandy in his glass,
watching the liquid swirl. "You'd never get it back, and
well you know it, old chap."

Garrett took another soothing draw on his cigarette.
Rolling his own had become a habit, one picked up out
of necessity during his travels. It made him feel self-
sufficient, perhaps a ridiculous affectation, but one he had
no intention of giving up. "Did you love her?"

"Who?"

He'd known Deegan long enough to recognize when his friend was evading something. "Whichever. You said there were two women."

Deegan tossed off the last of his brandy. "Devilish greedy bastard, aren't I? Most men would be content with winning one heiress." He reached for the brandy decanter on the table between them. "What makes you think I loved them?"

"Not *them*, just one," Garrett clarified. "Do I need more than the fact that you rarely drink?"

On the point of refilling his goblet, Deegan halted. Garrett blew a series of smoke rings while his friend struggled silently within himself.

Deegan set the decanter down and pushed his empty glass away. "It's the situation, not the woman. Besides," he insisted lightly, "you know I love money more than I could ever love any woman."

It was interesting how a man could lie to himself, Garrett mused as he drew on his cigarette. Interesting how he could believe the lie. "Tell me about her anyway, Dig," he urged.

Deegan slumped deep into the cushions of his chair, stretched his legs out and grinned. "Not believin' me, are ye, laddie," he said. "The lady's not for me. Knew it the moment I set eyes on her. She's so beautiful, so graceful." The artificial lilt dropped from Deegan's voice, replaced by a quality that could only be described, Garrett felt, as dreamy. "It was like seeing an angel to watch her dance," Deegan continued. "She glides, my friend. Glides. And when a man waltzes with her it's akin to floating right in the clouds."

Garrett smiled faintly. "Sounds to me as if Cupid's sunk his arrow deep." He drew a final lungful of smoke and leaned forward to toss the butt of his cigarette into the fire.

"Hmm," Deegan murmured thoughtfully. "Doubtful, my lad. How could I be when she deserves someone like you?"

Caught exhaling the smoke, Garrett choked. "Bloody

hell, Dig," he gasped when he could breathe once more.
"You don't have to kill me to get into my wallet."

"My point exactly. I get by on my wits..."

"Such as they are," Garrett grumbled, uneasy at the
turn the conversation had taken.

"But you, my friend," Deegan insisted with a wry grin,
"have the magic touch. You seem to make money by
merely thinking about it. Little did I know when I rescued
you from that strumpet in Sonora..."

Garrett got to his feet with languorous grace. "I'll be
damned if I'm going to sit here and listen to your insults,"
he said, leaning toward the mirror that hung over the mantelpiece and turning his attention to the involved process
of fixing his tie. "You rescued me? That isn't how I remember the event. If memory serves, there was a lynch
mob after you when you barged into my bedroom."

"All in your perception, my friend. As I was saying..."

"And loving the sound of your own voice," Garrett
added under his breath. It had been a decidedly nasty
shock to have Deegan turn the conversation on him. If
there was something he didn't need in his life right now
it was a beauty with ethereal habits. That kind of woman
belonged to the life he abhorred, the life that would claim
him once more in the distant future.

Gliding and floating. Garrett fumed silently as he looped
the narrow band of black silk into a crisp bow. Deegan
may claim he wasn't in love with the woman, but he
wouldn't convince anyone else with talk like that.

Deegan was listing the physical attributes of his goddess
now. Garrett wished he hadn't drawn the man out. If only
he'd turned Dig away earlier instead of welcoming him as
a savior. If only he'd made a stir when the telegram had
arrived, the whole mess would have—

Telegram.

"You remember where I put that blasted wire?" Garrett
demanded, interrupting Deegan in midsentence. Something
about hair of spun gold.

"In your pocket," Deegan supplied. "Now her eyes are…"

Garrett stopped listening again. "Why do I have such cursedly abominable taste in friends?" he asked.

"You mean me," Deegan said, far from insulted. "It's your money, laddie. It attracts rogues like myself."

"Meaning if I had my wits about me, I'd stop finding ways to make more of it," Blackhawk growled. The paper he'd received from the bellboy was creased from his own careless handling. Absently Garrett smoothed it out. "You might be interested in this, Dig. I've been waiting to hear from a man in Cheyenne. I'm thinking of investing in a cattle ranch in Wyoming Territory."

"Spare me," Deegan pleaded. He reached for the cigarette materials and was soon tapping tobacco along the length of the small square of paper in his hand. "No doubt a week from now you'll be camped in some forsaken spot staring deeply into a complacent cow's brown eyes. Cattle." He sighed in resignation. "Who would ever have believed a civilized Englishman would prefer the face of a longhorn to that of a beautiful woman?"

"I don't," Garrett said, at last opening his message. "Beautiful women always rank ahead of a cow, although the cow will give me less trouble." He scanned the telegram quickly, then read it again more slowly before crumpling it in his hand.

"The bloody hell." Barely audible, the words were rough to the ear. Garrett followed them with a few well chosen curses from three other languages. The crushed telegram shot into the fireplace, caught flame among the coals and was soon reduced to curling black ash.

Deegan halted in the act of lighting his cigarette. "Trouble?"

Garrett's jaw was stiff with suppressed fury. The future had galloped in on fleeter hooves than he had expected. Mentally he called himself every kind of fool. Had he really believed the burdens he'd carried for so long would remain at bay even for a few more months?

Well, he'd had two years of hard-won freedom. They would have to suffice him a lifetime. A cold, bleak lifetime.

It took a moment for Deegan's quiet question to register. Garrett remained standing, staring down at the hearth, at the smouldering black remains of the telegram. "My father is dead."

Silence stretched between them, and the sounds of the hotel around them seemed to magnify. Garrett was conscious of the rattle of a wheeled trolley cart in the hallway, of the sound of running water through the plumbing, the footfalls of a guest in the room above. Outside on the street, a man yelled an obscenity at another driver, wheels rumbled, a horse whinnied.

"Your father. I'm sorry," Deegan said.

"Not half as sorry as I," Garrett noted wearily. "It means I have to go back, take on the responsibility of being head of the family."

More importantly, he knew, it meant facing the accusations again. Dear Lord, it was more than any man should be pressed to endure.

Garrett forced a wan smile. "Why don't you return at one tomorrow, Dig? I'll arrange something with my bank for you, but I don't think I'll be a very companionable bloke tonight."

The facade of the carefree adventurer was no longer present on Deegan's face. "If there's anything I can do, you have only to ask," he said. "I'm not quite as shallow as I'm made out to be. I stand by my friends when they need me, Garrett."

"I know, Dig. I know."

Chapter Two

Although the day had been sun filled, around midnight the damp chill turned into a cold rivulet of rain that coursed down the back of Garrett's neck. He had been walking the city streets ever since Deegan left. It had taken but a moment to scribble his regrets to his host of the evening, sending a bellboy off with the message. He hadn't bothered changing clothes, but had shrugged on, over his evening attire, the long vaquero's duster he'd worn in Mexico, and added a battered, broad-brimmed slouch hat. His outward appearance blending with a thousand other men in San Francisco, Garrett trudged through the muddy streets, his mind far from his surroundings.

It had taken his solicitors in London months to find him. If he hadn't become interested in the cattle ranch and contacted them, the firm of Hafner, Horrigan and Long would still be searching. He'd been carefully avoiding them for a long time, but now the ever-restless trace of his journey was at an end. Of necessity he would be in touch with the solicitors frequently, his travel plans limited by the thin binding lines of the telegraph that linked him to their office.

Garrett worked his way along Kearny Street, his footsteps aimless. According to the wire, his father had died six months ago. What had he been doing the day Stewart

Blackhawk was interned in the family crypt? Garrett wondered. Had he been in South America yet, in the Amazon jungles? Or had he reached Mexico at that time? The memory of one carefree day was gone, no longer a time that he could pinpoint to a particular event or place.

Six months. The delay in reaching him served as a reprieve, no matter how short. Various business interests would supply the excuses he needed to delay a month, two at the most, then he would have to shoulder his responsibilities at Hawk's Run once more.

He'd tried so hard to outrun them, to distance himself from both the good and the bad. And the whispers.

The rain was more mist than storm, making it a match to his mood. It dampened the streets as much as the wire had dampened his spirits. Coach lamps created glowing fingers of light on the glistening pavement and highlighted where puddles had begun to form in the depressions. The drizzle discouraged even the braver souls from walking the streets. Those men who did scurried for shelter quickly, heading into the warm, brightly lit doorways of various saloons and private gambling clubs, and the more dimly lit and even warmer parlors of the bordellos. A more perfect night for grieving was difficult to envision. If, that is, he could grieve for the man he suspected had not been his father.

Garrett's legs ate the distance, taking him away from the city proper and into the shadowy lanes that comprised the Barbary Coast. Rain dripped from the bent brim of his hat, dampened the waxed length of his duster, and still he strode on as sure in each step as if he had a particular destination in mind.

His thoughts were thousands of miles away in another land. What were the Salopians saying of him in the local tavern now? he wondered.

Ever since his dark head had made its appearance among the fair-haired residents of Hawk's Run, there had been rumors concerning his birth. A nursemaid had been dismissed for spreading the tale that he was an elfin child, a substitute left when the brownies stole the true golden-tressed heir. Despite the fact that black-haired ancestors were visibly present among the oldest of the portraits in the family gallery, the levelheaded gentry whispered that he was a bastard, the child Antonia Blackhawk had cuckolded her husband with as his own. Although he'd spent many a rainy afternoon staring at the paintings, Garrett had never recognized his own features among the host of dark ancestral faces.

Matters had not improved as he grew taller and broadened, his form that of a muscled athlete rather than of a fine-boned scholar like his diminutive father. Stewart Blackhawk had been an academician, brilliant when it came to translating ancient Greek poetry, inept and uninterested when it came to running his estate, cooly distant and silent when it came to Garrett's doubts and questions concerning his birth.

With the family debts mounting, Garrett had left the halls of Cambridge and made his dark features a familiar sight in the meadows of Hawk's Run. He had worked alongside the tenants for plantings, for harvests. Yet the whispers continued, reviving tales of wizardry that brought fertility back to tired fields.

In the City of London it was no different, for men there jokingly claimed he bewitched weak investments into profitable ventures. It was even said, more seriously, that he had blinded Stewart Blackhawk to the truth, for the man never commented on the validity of his eldest son's birth, an oversight the grown Garrett recognized as neglect rather than belief. Sometime during his childhood, Garrett had begun believing the rumors himself simply because his father had never eased his son's mind over his legitimacy.

Members of society read a wealth of mystery and intrigue into Stewart's silence on the subject as well and whispered all the more. And so, assaulted by suspicion on all sides, Garrett had set out to be exactly what they termed him. He had adopted the qualities of a chameleon, changing with his environment, one moment the mystic who communed with supernatural folk, the next the arrogant upstart who flaunted the Blackhawk name.

He had learned much in playing these parts. He'd discovered he was a natural deceiver, a man who could don the face of an actor, who could adapt to any situation and find something to claim as his own in every outcome.

Or he did most of the time, Garrett admitted silently. In Cairo his so-called powers had been impotent, and Sybil had paid the price for his pride. It had been a tragic and most humbling experience.

He had grown as a result, had learned that he hated what fate had made him. What fate was forcing him to become once more.

He was back to living a lie. The life he had enjoyed as a ragged Bohemian adventurer the past two years had disappeared, leaving in its place a man who of necessity must become the epitome of the unruffled British aristocrat.

In other words, he was going to be a bloody damn hypocrite.

The rivulet inching down his neck grew more uncomfortable. After extended stays in Egypt, along the Equator, and in Sonora, he was used to the unrelenting rays of the sun and had forgotten the chilling trials of a cloud-ridden climate.

Rather than be miserable, Garrett decided in favor of shelter. The saloons of the Barbary Coast were somewhat drier than the streets, although they smelled worse. The company was more rowdy than convivial and the whiskey was vile enough to take paint off a house. It was better than being alone with his thoughts, and being with strangers meant, if he could not check them, at least he could keep those thoughts to himself.

He nearly changed his mind when he entered the nearest door. A combination of scents assaulted him, of which cheap whiskey, cheaper perfume, cigar smoke and sweat were the most recognizable. The whole was overlaid with the taint of mildew.

"Why, hello, handsome," a woman greeted throatily.

She sashayed up to him, hips swinging, breasts bobbing. Her smile was a smear of rouge, and her eyes were fanned with runny streaks of kohl. She posed briefly, one hand propped on a cocked hip. The garish purple of her gown was mirrored in bruised circles beneath her eyes. The smile she gave him was tired, and as falsely brilliant as her brassy-colored hair.

She could easily have been a reflection of his own soul—worn, tawdry and devoid of hope.

"Lookin' fer a little fun tonight? Somethin' ta warm yer blood?" she purred.

"A drink, I thought," Garrett said, making no effort to hide the upper-crust edge of his accent. The need to hit something was strong, and past experience had shown that in a low-class saloon the sound of his accent alone increased the possibility of a brawl.

"A drink, is it?" a man's voice demanded in a heavy Irish brogue. "Well, squire, ye've come to the right place." A disheveled, extremely wet man launched himself away from the support of the door behind Garrett and staggered forward, making shooing gestures at the woman. "Get along with you, lass. The squire and me's got business ta discuss."

Miffed at his interference, the woman turned her shoulder to the newcomer. "Ya'll remember me, won't ya, handsome? I'll be around when this boyo passes out." She stared hard at the man who stood swaying at Garrett's side. "He looks like the kind that always does," she added in disdain before moving toward another prospective customer.

"Cheeky little tart," the man growled after her retreating form. Beads of water had formed on the rim of his narrow-brimmed bowler. The shoulders of his suit coat were soaked through and the lapels were limply turned up in an effort to keep the rain from further dampening his wilted shirt collar. "Now then, squire. 'Bout our business." He pitched to the side, stumbling over his own feet.

Garrett nearly staggered himself when the Irishman fell

against him. "What business might that be?" he asked, steadying the man upright once more. "The return of my wallet and watch, perhaps?"

Rather than take offense at the accusation of theft, the man grinned widely. "Yer've been snaffled afore, have ye, squire?"

"By better men than you," Garrett said. "Shall we adjourn to the bar and see which of us pays for the drinks with my purse?"

The man chuckled. "I like you, squire. 'Struth. Oh, look will you, I've mussed the front of yer lovely coat." He brushed hastily at Garrett's duster, removing imaginary soot. "Perhaps I could put yer right of a special little brew. Highly recommend it."

The barkeep probably did store a "special little brew" behind his counter guaranteed to knock a customer out, Garrett mused. If a man accepted, he would wake up at sea, shanghaied more efficiently than any man who'd ever been impressed by the Royal Navy.

"Whiskey," he said when they reached the bar. "Neat."

"I'll have the same as me friend here," the dripping man declared. While waiting to be served, he leaned back against the scarred bar top, the heel of one shoe hooked companionably on the brass foot rail, and grinned widely on one and all. His clothing created puddles on the floor, the runoff sending out small rills that fed into the spittoon channel beneath the bar rail.

Garrett waited until they'd been served and his damp companion had unabashedly paid for the drinks from the wallet he'd lifted from Garrett's pocket. "That's the most atrocious accent I've ever heard," he said.

"It's dead to rights, my lad," the other man vowed, his voice pitched low, the brogue abandoned. "Buzzed it from me da himself."

Garrett studied the smoky glass the bartender had slid before him and the strong liquor within it. He wondered briefly if he'd been smart to follow the western creed of allowing a man his anonymity when it came to the past. Particularly when it came to the man who had become his traveling companion over the past few months. "Why are you following me, Dig?"

Another man pushed next to them and called for a bottle. Deegan shrugged back into character and reached for his own tumbler. "'Tis a mortal sin fer a man to be forced to drink alone, squire." He took a sip of his whiskey and grimaced. "Holy Saint Patrick! But that's a fine elixir," he declared hoarsely.

Since Deegan's eyes had begun to water, Garrett ordered soda water before sampling his own shot.

Deegan toasted the other patron as he moved away from the bar, then turned back to Garrett. "If you had another friend handy I would have left you to your own bloody devices," Deegan continued in an undertone. "But you don't. That leaves you a choice. We can make a night of it in this charming little groggery or find a more appropriate setting to get soused. Either way you're going to tell me what's bothering you." He held up a hand, halting any attempt Garrett might make at a rebuttal. "And don't tell me it's your dear old da's demise."

Garrett stared at the whiskey in his glass, considering his words. It would be so much easier to let Deegan remain nothing more than the companion of his Mexican adventures. With the loss of two heiresses in a single day, and dwindling finances, Galloway had his own problems.

In a corner a man shoved to his feet, angrily upsetting a table over his companions. A woman shrieked as one of the men leapt forward to seek revenge.

Garrett ignored the building melee, no longer in a mood for a fight. "Let's get out of here," he suggested. "I warn you, Dig, it's an ugly tale. Melodrama at its worst."

Manfully Deegan tossed off the rest of his whiskey. "I'm fortified," he assured. "And who might the actors be?"

Garrett ducked in a reflexive move as a chair sailed across the room. "The cast includes myself, of course, my brother Ellery, and a beautiful innocent named Sybil Tilbury.''

Deegan signaled the bartender and tossed greenbacks onto the bar. ''Two bottles of yer finest rotgut,'' he said. ''The squire's spinnin' me a fine tale as he sees me safely home. Were you wishin' after the return of yer wallet, yer lordship? It seems to be a trifle empty.''

A dazzling parade moved past the window where the shadow crouched, dark clothing blending with the natural shadows in the garden. It was fortunate that the night was damp. It kept the revelers indoors and made observation so much easier.

The women in their jewel-colored gowns were unaware of the threat. The men in their onyx black suits never sensed the danger. They talked, flirted, danced, drank— unaware that another watched.

Gowns of watered silk, bedecked with lace, ruffles, ruching and ribbons, were on display, the carefully draped aprons caught up and drawn back into elaborate cascades that drew attention to a woman's form. Trains trailed or were held outstretched to whirl with the steps of a dance. The elegant ebony tailcoats of the men moved in sync with the gowns, sailing with the rise and fall of the music, and occasionally a flash dazzled as lamplight caught the glitter of gold or silver threads woven into the pattern of a waistcoat. It was the moving, glowing fabrics that had life, not the people. Yet, at the moment, it was the people who held the watcher's attention.

The stiffly starched fronts of the shirts held the prey at attention, and the corsets squeezed the soon-to-be bereft into improbable shapes. Weskits and waistlines strained across expanding torsos, clear evidence of the comfortable life-style enjoyed by the guests.

Candles and gas jets fought for prominence, creating pockets of alternating light and dark. The light was sought by women anxious to display a new bauble, a new gown, a new beau. The dark was the habitat of lovers, of stolen moments, of stolen caresses and murmured lies.

The shadow watched them all, carefully noting which of their jewels the ladies wore. The garnets of one guest were nice but could never compare to the bloodred rubies of another. The watery glint of aquamarines flashed by as a gallant swung his partner in an enthusiastic polka. A new debutante paused near the window, the light falling softly on her gently curved neck and the modest necklace of matched pearls that graced it. The possibilities were endless. It was so difficult to make a final choice. So delightful to plot the method by which to reap.

A man glanced out the window, his eyes seeming to meet those of the thief. He started away, looked back, then signaled to one of the waiters, motioning to the window.

The shadow melted away moments before two men with lanterns arrived to comb the garden for intruders. The thief waited just out of sight, enjoying the chase. Fools, that's what they all were. It was so easy to play this game.

"You see anything?" one of the searchers called out.

"Hell, no. I think Stokes was seeing things. Had a bit too much champagne punch, if you ask me."

"I don't know. Claims he saw someone peering in from the bushes."

"A cat most like."

The shadow waited. So it had been Elmer Stokes who had raised the alarm. He would pay for that. What bauble had his wife worn? Had it been the jade or the fire opals? Did it matter? The victim had been chosen.

The parlor door barely closed behind Wyn before Hildegarde Hartleby tossed aside the latest copy of *Demorest's Monthly Magazine* and gazed excitedly on the folded newspaper in her guest's hand.

"Not another robbery!" she breathed, sinking dramatically back onto the sofa, one hand pressed to the string of jet beads that lay against her breast. "What was it this time?"

Wyn tossed her friend the news sheet and reached up to unpin her plumed walking hat. "Don't you mean *who?*" she asked.

Hildy refrained from reading the story. "Let's make it a game," she urged. "If I know *what* was taken, I wager I'll know the *who.*"

Wyn unbuttoned her light coat and tossed it casually over the back of a chair. Since the pernicious state of Hildy's finances made it impossible to pay wages, she had lost both housekeeper and housemaid. Those friends who came to visit the young widow quickly learned to make themselves at home.

"You must admit, Wyn, there is no one who knows the contents of the jewel boxes of our set better than I do," Hildy insisted. Her soft brown hair was arranged in playful curls that spilled from a knot at the crown of her head. Despite the deep mourning color of her gown, there was nothing mournful about the flush of excitement in Hildy's cheeks as she leaned forward in anticipation. "I used to make lists of my favorites and give them to Oswin hoping that he would visit the same jewelers," she admitted. "If anyone can match the pieces with the person, it's me."

"All right," Wyn agreed, reclaiming the newspaper and settling into the deeply cushioned chair across from her friend. They had played together in the school yard as children, and had attended their first ball arm in arm. Young men had clustered around them both, vying for favors. As inseparable as they had always been, Wyn had still been stunned at the news Hildy had whispered one evening soon after their presentation. She had promised her hand to Oswin Hartleby, a wealthy man nearly forty years her senior. "But, why?" Wyn had demanded. "Because I'm tired of being just comfortable," Hildy answered. "I want to be rich." Her wish had been granted, if only for a handful of years.

Wyn scanned the newspaper until she found the story about the most recent theft. She had come to visit Hildy nearly every day since her bereavement, making an effort to cheer her friend's lonely hours. Hildy had always been a social gadfly and the constraints of widowhood had depressed her nearly as much as the loss of the Hartleby fortune.

"Here it is." Wyn rustled the paper, making a production of refolding it. "The thief walked off with opals," she announced.

"Hmm." Hildy tapped a finger against her lips in thought. "Cordelia Earlywine or Olympia Stokes."

"There's more."

"More?" Hildy's eyes widened with pleasure. They were a deep sapphire blue and surrounded by long, curling lashes.

"Diamond cravat pin, diamond shirt studs."

Hildy jumped in her seat. "Stokes!" she shouted.

"If it were possible," Wyn said as she tossed the newspaper aside, "I'd wager on your ability to pinpoint the robber's victims using nothing more than a description of the missing jewelry."

"Perhaps there is a future for me with one of those detective agencies," Hildy suggested. "Do you think Mr. Pinkerton would hire me?"

"Only if you could name the thief as easily as you do the victim," Wyn answered.

Hildy sighed. "Well, that I can't do. If I could I'd have my diamonds back." Petulantly she leaned back into the cushions of the sofa, apparently no longer interested in the robbery now that the latest victim had been identified. "Have you heard from Pierce?"

Wyn stretched her feet out, studying the toes of her shoes where they peeked from beneath the dark green pleats that trimmed the hem of her skirt. Her brother had been in Boston a month and in that time she'd received two letters, both assuring her that her money was being put to excellent use. Earlier that day a telegram had arrived. "He's on his way back. The liner is nearly finished. We sail in three weeks."

Hildy bounded back up, squealing with excitement before sobering once more. "Oh, but, Wyn! Whatever shall I wear? I refuse to traipse around in funeral black. Oswin has been dead three months, which is quite long enough to mourn him in my opinion. I have resolved to travel in half-mourning."

Deciding she would prefer to delay hearing how Hildy intended to finance a new wardrobe, Wyn tried changing the subject. "Did you write to Rachel?"

Three years before, Hildy's sister had made the coup of the social season by marrying Sir Alston Loftus and moving to his ancestral home in England.

"Oh, Rachel and Lofty will be expecting us," Hildy assured, casually unconcerned. "I told them in my letter that we'd be on our way before they could reply, but there's a standing invitation. Now..." She resettled on the couch, her expression changing to one of serious intent as she reached for the magazine she'd abandoned earlier. "I've been thinking," Hildy said, and quickly leafed to the fashion section. "Oswin only left me the use of the house, so I can't sell it, but his will wasn't as specific about the furnishings. If I sell off the heavier pieces, I should be able to get at least a decent start on a new wardrobe. Enough to travel with at any rate."

"What if the Hartlebys object?" Wyn asked.

"I won't tell them," Hildy said, dismissing her late husband's middle-aged offspring. "Will you be using your dressmaker before we leave? What do you think of this pannier overskirt? Too overdone?"

Resigning herself to the planning of her friend's wardrobe, Wyn moved over next to Hildy on the sofa and was soon discussing the merits of bunting for a lightweight excursion costume.

Pinkerton operative Magnus Finley hung back as his suspect paused at the corner to let a freight wagon rumble by. It wouldn't do to be discovered. It had taken weeks of intensive field investigation and paperwork to get the case to this point. He couldn't afford to lose it all now through a careless step.

The dray passed, the horses trudging on down the street, hooves dropping in weary thuds. The driver's face was as long as those of his team, his expression just as dull. He made no effort to hurry the animals but sat hunched forward, his hat pushed to the back of his head, the reins dangling in his hands.

The suspect waited until the wagon was well past before attempting the street. Magnus continued following without crossing. He was fairly sure of the final destination. He'd dogged the same footsteps along this same path for a week now as the suspect spent a good deal of money. The largess manifested appeared to indicate that the jewels had been sold rather successfully.

Which was extremely odd since none of the known fences in the city claimed to be aware of a recent sale.

If the thief had found a buyer, it wasn't just the Stokes woman's opals that had changed hands. The Hartleby diamonds were still unaccounted for, as were sets of various other precious and semiprecious gems.

Numerous operatives had been put on the job as one robbery followed another. Clients ranging from weeping widows to blustering businessmen had descended on the Pinkerton office demanding results. The local police had not reclaimed the jewels nor had they indicated progress in learning the thief's identity. But Finley thought he'd discovered a vital clue. Until he could prove his suspicions, he was playing his cards close to his vest.

The suspect entered the expected doorway, the shop of a valise and trunk maker. Finley settled in the mouth of an adjacent alley. He knew from experience that it would be an hour or more before his quarry left.

The door swung open and closed a little later as a young boy emerged, hastily pulling on a sack coat and donning a cloth cap. He gave a quick glance up and down the roadway before heading toward Market Street.

Finley snapped open his pocket watch and consulted it.

He began to think about dinner, considering various restaurants where he could eat and still keep one eye on the person he trailed. There had been no deviation in the suspect's schedule in the seven days Finley had been on the job.

A cab rattled up, the wheels clattering noisily, the horse's hooves striking the pavement sharply. The boy from the shop hopped down from the back of the vehicle and dashed inside. Moments later he returned, struggling with a small trunk. The shop door swung open again as Finley's suspect and the shop owner emerged and stood watching as the baggage was wrestled aboard.

The boy tugged on the brim of his cloth cap when a coin exchanged hands. The suspect took a warm leave of the luggage maker then murmured a direction to the cab driver and climbed into the interior. After his employer returned to his work, the shop boy remained gazing after the retreating vehicle, a look of longing in his face.

Caught without transportation to follow, Finley went in search of information. He crossed the road, staring down the way as the cab rounded a corner neatly and was lost from sight. "Somebody's in a might hurry," he remarked to the boy.

"Train ta catch," the youngster said wistfully.

"Wonder where to?" Finley mused. "Sacramento, I'll bet."

"Further," the boy insisted. "Headin' ta the East ta get on a ship."

Finley shrugged as if in wonder and moved on. He'd barely put the corner of a building between himself and the boy when he took off at a run.

Chapter Three

To Pierce Abbot
Shire Shipping Line
San Francisco

Brother dear,

You may run up the flags and pop the champaign. Loath as I am to admit it, you win our wager. The Boston relations are indeed deadly dull. How a social butterfly like yourself ever managed to retain your sanity in their company for an entire month is quite beyond comprehension. Undoubtedly they were the true impetus that kept your nose to the proverbial grindstone.

Hildy and I did enjoy one bit of excitement during our blessedly brief sojourn. Someone nipped off with the family sapphires.

My own modest cache of gems remained untouched, possibly because it is so modest. No, I don't regret selling off the better stones at the last minute to keep you flush with the bank. I believe in your scheme as I always avowed.

Besides, the boat is quite a delight and I will enjoy the profits more than an untouched dowry or all the gemstones in the world.

The captain made us quite comfortable. I've been proclaimed the reigning BELLE for the maiden voyage—who better qualified than this confirmed old spinster?

Shall report all the dazzling details of the trip upon docking in Liverpool.

Your loving sister,
Wyn

Aboard the Shire Liner *Nereid*
Boston Harbor
Eve of Departure

Garrett stood at the ship's rail, sable wings of hair whipping to blind his sight as he stared out over the vessels bobbing in the sun dappled bay. The majority of passengers lined the *Nereid*'s rails, where they could wave excited farewells to friends and relatives. He had taken a stance away from them, savoring his privacy for a brief while longer. Soon the ocean liner would ease away from the pier, leaving the tainted city skyline far behind. However, the social conventions that it represented would sail with them, the state preserved intact, neatly compartmentalized by the price paid for a ticket. His own place among the elite was guaranteed, if not by the location of his stateroom, then by his name and the honored invitation he had received to dine at the captain's table.

He had Deegan to thank for that. Garrett grinned grimly. He would have his revenge on his friend later. For now he was content to stare out to sea, his companions limited to the squawking gulls. His loyal and determined Patroclus was no doubt among the first-class passengers making up to yet another heiress.

There was an autumnal bite in the breeze. It wafted inland off the choppy waters calling to the primeval core of a man and drawing forth the memory of ancient passions in his blood. Although the New England air carried a different scent and taste on its currents, Garrett remembered having felt this particular call before. It had been when he'd taken ship from the shimmering, parched sands of Egypt, running from the fears and impotency he'd felt there. He had stayed at Sybil's side for three long, sleepless days as her spirit lingered in her fevered, emaciated body. The day he left Sybil and North Africa behind, there had been a pleasant Mediterranean breeze filling the ship's sails, healing his battered soul with a promise of hope. Back then the world had lain open and new before him, a host of untasted adventure available, and his for the sampling. This time Garrett felt as if Neptune's wind had snatched away that brief hope, and was searing his soul rather than healing it.

He'd kept his mind on other details in the weeks since receiving the wire from home. Consulting with bankers, he'd arranged backing for the mine he'd visited in Brazil and the railroad he'd helped survey in Mexico. Deegan had pitched in, making travel arrangements, writing letters, to all intents and purposes assuming the duties of a secretary. But, although he was doing the work of one, Galloway refused to officially accept the post when it was offered once more. He preferred to remain a companion, albeit a nearly constant one. Within a week, they'd been on a train bound for Wyoming Territory, and from there, along the steel rails to Boston town.

In all, it had taken seven weeks to put his affairs in order. Garrett wished it had been longer. He still wasn't prepared to face a life at Hawk's Run.

Perhaps he never would be.

Once he'd thought of this voyage as his last reprieve. The final chance he would have to be the man he wished to be. The arrangements Deegan had made destroyed that hope.

"Damn, but you live under a lucky star," Galloway had announced upon their arrival days earlier in Boston.

Having nursed depression over his future with the better part of a bottle of whiskey the night before, Garrett hadn't felt particularly lucky. He'd managed to crawl out of bed and dress, but the drapes in the hotel suite remained tightly closed against the light of day. He barely squinted at his friend before closing his eyes again and covering them with his arm. "I'm quite sure that star fell on me last night," Garrett said.

"So happens I've got a friend who runs a shipping line," Deegan rambled on enthusiastically. "I checked in with Pierce's office here and they've got berths available on a steamer pulling out on its maiden voyage."

"Just what I deserve. A coffin in steerage," Garrett groaned.

Deegan went to the window and threw the drapes open to let the sun spill in, bringing with it glorious pain to Blackhawk's already throbbing head. "Hell, no," Dig had insisted. "I told them who you were and got the Shire Line's equivalent of the President's Suite."

His destiny was beyond recall now. His trunks had been delivered aboard the *Nereid* earlier that day and were resting untouched in the elaborately decorated stateroom. Rather than enjoy the comforts his station in life afforded, Garrett had opted for an isolated corner of the deck in the hope that the breeze would renew his spirit.

Since it had turned traitor, he watched a pair of gulls ride the wind currents.

They looked stationary, as if they were toys suspended by strings, their wings spread wide, their bodies dipping occasionally as the master puppeteer manipulated wires to give them a semblance of life.

Fate was his puppeteer, Garrett mused. Deegan was the current stage manager, pushing him to assume the mantle he had shunned in the past. The estate itself would complete the transition, closing all doors behind him. There would be few moments like this in the coming days, the coming years. He had a part to play. His lines were rusty from disuse, but he'd been born for the role. Bred for it. The richly appointed stateroom, the hand-tailored clothing, the seat at the captain's table—they were the props, they set the stage. From this day forward he was no longer a man like any other; he was Blackhawk of Hawk's Run.

The gulls tired of their game. One folded back its wings and dove into the water only to emerge with dinner in its beak a moment later. The other bird fluttered out among the anchored fleet of merchantmen and soon disappeared from sight.

The steam-powered engines had come alive during his reverie, Garrett noticed. They sent a thrumming through the ship that translated itself through the boards of the deck. There was no turning back now. No chance to lose himself. He was committed as never before.

The crowds at the rails nearest the dock sent up cries of excitement, of pleasure, of farewell. With the roar came a shift in the air. The weight in his soul lightened briefly. He'd misjudged Neptune after all. Perhaps if he stayed on deck long enough, the breeze would continue to offer his heart this temporary surcease.

If the brief miracle was the providence of the wind, that is.

Underlying the tide of distant, raised voices was the soft, nearby whisper of silk. The pungent aroma of the bay was replaced by the subtle scent of spring flowers.

Even without the sensory clues, he was aware of the woman's presence. He had felt her arrival.

She stood the length of two deck chairs away, her stance nearly a replica of his, her forearms resting on the ship's rail as she gazed out at the dancing waters. A ridiculously flamboyant Gainsborough hat was pinned securely over her spilling flaxen curls. The stiff breeze had spun out a few strands so that they tossed like loose ribbons around her shoulders. She was tall and slender, her figure enhanced by the narrow cut of her suit, the fitted jacket, long waistline, draped apron and green-striped fabric all obviously chosen to draw a man's appreciative eye.

She sighed with obvious pleasure when the ship pulled away from the dock.

Her eyes were closed when she lifted her face toward

the bay breeze. Bright, wind-whipped color touched her cheeks, her lips parted as if she anticipated a lover's kiss. She breathed deeply a moment, savoring the taste of the air. And with her action, his interest was further pricked.

It had been weeks since he'd indulged his carnal appetites and the matter of selecting a willing partner had always been a most enjoyable part of the game. A journey of eight days lay ahead of them. Dalliance with a lovely woman would ease the despair in his heart. Or at least keep it at a distance until they reached England.

This one was a remarkedly beautiful woman. Incredibly long, dark lashes lay like unfurled ebony fans against her rice paper skin. They were exotic and at odds with her breeze-tossed blond tresses.

When her lashes lifted, it was to reveal eyes the shade of thickly wooded pine forests, mysterious, shadowed and intriguing. They widened in surprise, clouding with confusion, when she realized Garrett was staring.

"I hope I haven't intruded on your thoughts or disturbed your solitude," she said.

Her voice was cultured, her accent that of the western American coast rather than the eastern from which they sailed. There was a faint throaty purr in her tone that reminded him of a contented feline. Or a satisfied mistress.

"Not at all," Garrett assured. "My official claim on this section of decking has yet to be filed at the assay office."

Her amused smile started a pleasant tightening sensation in the pit of his stomach.

"My appearance was timely then," she said.

"Most, from my view," Garrett agreed. "My own company was becoming a bit of a bore." He nodded toward the hallooing of the crowd. "No one to see you off?"

She shrugged and stared out over the water again. "It's doubtful they could even find me in the crush."

Because she wore gloves he had no inkling as to whether she wore another man's ring. He guessed that she was traveling without a male escort, for any man would be a fool to let this beauty out of his sight.

"Besides," she added, her voice growing nostalgic, "I'm one of Trident's hedonists. My grandfather was a ship's captain and I seem to have inherited a love for the feel of the wind on my face and the taste of the sea on my tongue."

She was a most unusual woman, Garrett mused.

There were many lovely ladies littering his past. His success in London had not been tied solely to financial transactions. Before he'd gone to Egypt in Sybil's wake, he'd cut a bold swath through the ballrooms of the elite, seducing many a lovely guest or sultry hostess during the movements of a dance, rutting amongst many a cuckolded peer's lace-edged sheets. There had been little pleasure in any of the affairs. He'd been labeled the black-hearted Blackhawk before his arrival and had merely played each scene as it was written.

None of the beauties in the past could be compared to the lovely, disheveled woman who dallied with him at the ship's rail, not even Sybil.

The wind drew a long strand of her flaxen hair across her face. It brushed her cheek, teased her nose, caressed her mouth. When it eluded her grasp, Garrett took the opportunity to close the distance between them. Without asking her permission, he trapped the errant lock between his fingers.

It was the texture of finely spun silk threads and glistened with a sheen more akin to moonlight than sunlight. Her hand grazed against his when they both moved to secure the curl beneath her hat.

"Perhaps I'd better do this," she said.

If they'd still been alone, he would have been tempted to rip her ridiculously large picture hat away, to free her pale golden tresses so that they entangled in the wind. Then he could bury his hands among the glorious strands and turn her face up to his. But they were no longer alone. The *Nereid* was nearing the mouth of the bay and other passengers were strolling the decks, invading what had once been his preserve alone.

His alluring companion tucked the tangled curls back beneath her hat. White, even teeth worried a corner of her bottom lip as she worked. Despite the crowds, Garrett nearly gave in to the compulsion to draw her close and kiss her. Savor her.

"There. Much better," she announced brightly. "Thank you for coming to my aid, sir."

"It was an honor," he avowed, forcing himself to look away from her lips. "But the name isn't Galahad, it's Blackhawk. Garrett Blackhawk."

Galahad. Wyn paused as the name sounded an unwelcome echo in her mind. Deegan had dredged up that particular knight of the Round Table in conjunction with his courting of Leonore Cronin. The Galahad of legend had been pure, noble and unselfish. That description hadn't fit Deegan and she doubted the high-minded ideals would settle any easier on Mr. Blackhawk's broad shoulders. At least he had disclaimed any resemblance to the knight.

He was attractive, too, although perhaps a bit forward. When his eyes had lingered on her lips, she'd felt breathless. There had been a singing in her blood, and an excited fluttering beneath her ribs that she hadn't felt since Deegan Galloway had enthralled her senses.

Garrett Blackhawk made her feel that way with nothing more than a look.

What a frightening and thrilling sensation!

And how comforting to know that she no longer had money with which to tempt the man. No doubt he had recognized the expensive tailoring of her clothing and equated that with wealth, which she would have again if each voyage the *Nereid* made was profitable. That was in the future though. For now, she felt safe.

"It is a pleasure to meet a fellow traveler, Mr. Blackhawk," she declared. "I'm Winona Abbot."

She offered Blackhawk her hand and was faintly disappointed when he didn't play the gallant and place a kiss on her wrist or on the back of her gloved hand.

Instead his fingers curled around hers, his grip firm and businesslike. It lingered long enough for her to experience another delightful chill of awareness.

"Winona," he repeated, his voice appearing to caress each syllable of her name. "It's quite unusual and beautiful. Like its owner."

Wyn smiled to herself. Oh, yes, he had definitely staked a claim. There wasn't a man alive who could deal with a woman honestly. They felt the need to flirt, to cajole, to compliment. Well, this time she would enjoy the experience but she wouldn't be hurt when he was revealed as a cad.

If only she didn't find these roguish bounders so attractive.

"In the language of the Sioux Indians, *Winona* translates to *firstborn daughter*," she explained. "Or so I've been told. And what about you, Mr. Blackhawk?"

His smile was rakish but perhaps she only thought so because his coloring was so dark, his skin so warm, his eyes so bold. He was as tall as her brother Pierce, a fact that appealed to her. Due to her own above-average height, she often met men eye-to-eye. With Blackhawk her eyes were level with his lips. It had to be the reason her gaze returned to linger on them so often.

"The Blackhawks are Saxon rather than Sioux, despite certain similarities in name imagery," he said. "We had a strain or two of Celt creep in before the Conquest but there hasn't been much culling from other bloodlines since then."

His voice was a pleasant baritone, yet not overly deep. It was the crisp way he pronounced some words and yet seemed to linger over others that drew her. It wasn't just that his tone differed from that of American men. A host of English men materialized each season in San Francisco, many on the lookout for wealthy wives. Blackhawk's voice was similar to theirs and yet it wasn't. Perhaps the difference was that his words were more a caress than a sound.

What a fanciful thought!

"Would you care to tour the deck with me, Miss Abbot?" he asked.

Fanciful or not, his voice was blatantly sensual. She felt it to the tips of her toes.

Wyn shook her head. "I'm sorry, but I already have an engagement."

"Later, perhaps."

"Perhaps."

When she made no immediate move to leave, he closed the scant space between them even more until the hem of her skirt brushed the toes of his boots. He took her gloved hand and raised it in his. Wyn was barely conscious of her surroundings when at long last his lips brushed audaciously over her fingertips.

The breeze was fresher now that they were at sea, but the passion in Blackhawk's eyes held the chill at bay, and warmed her. His hair was as dark as his name implied and lay in tumbled splendor over his brow. She recognized the work of a master tailor in the cut and fit of his dark suit, and of an artist in the design of his boots. Deegan had dressed as dapperly, though. Clothes were part and parcel of a fortune hunter's trade.

"What are you thinking, Miss Abbot?" Blackhawk asked, recalling Wyn to the present.

She gave him a considering look. "I was wondering, Mr. Blackhawk, if you play whist."

Hildy was busily sorting through her belongings when Wyn returned to the suite of staterooms they shared. With her new status as a Shire Line stockholder had come the privilege of boarding the ocean liner the evening before. Wyn had thought she and her friend already settled, their trunks unpacked, their gowns hung neatly in the clothespress, the few personal belongings they'd brought scattered around the trio of linked cabins.

"Have a nice stroll?" Hildy asked, without turning her head. A number of her new gowns were tossed negligently aside, covering divan, chairs and ottomans in the parlor. She held a gown decorated with silver tissue before her and considered her reflection in a cheval mirror.

Wyn closed the hatch, carefully securing it behind her. "There was a lovely breeze off the port side," she said. "Since the captain was occupied with putting to sea, I managed to enjoy myself without his running commentary." Of course, she admitted silently to herself, the encounter with Mr. Blackhawk had greatly enhanced the minutes she'd spent on deck.

"That's the burden you must bear for being the lady of his choice this voyage, dearest," Hildy reminded. "You yourself told me there is always a *belle* on the voyage. If I didn't have other plans, being fawned on by a man in uniform would appeal strongly to me."

Wyn walked through the archway that led to her sleeping quarters, unpinning her hat as she went. Two long strands of hair dangled over her shoulders. She touched one briefly recalling how Garrett Blackhawk had rescued it from the wind, imprisoning the contrary lock between his long, elegantly tapered, masculine fingers. Rather than refix the knot at the crown of her head, Wyn pulled the rest of her hairpins free and let the curls spill loosely down her back. "Plans? What sort of plans?" she called out to Hildy.

Her friend appeared in the hatchway, an elaborate gown over each arm. "In which of these do I look the most attractive?" she demanded. "The silver or the deep lavender?"

Hair brush in hand, Wyn glanced back over her shoulder. "Don't tell me you have a new prospect in mind already?" In Hildy's vocabulary, a *prospect* meant an available, marriageable man.

"I cornered the purser while you were communing with nature," Hildy said. "I gushed compliments about the ship until he regaled me with a list of viable names."

Wyn sank onto the stool before her dressing table and worked at the tangles in her hair, half envying her friend's single-mindedness. Perhaps she should adopt it. If her requirements in a husband were only half as mercenary as Hildy's she would soon have a home of her own, then children about her skirts.

And a lifetime of winter in her heart.

It was better to remain alone.

"By all means, make it the lavender then," Wyn advised. "It nearly gave the meat packing magnate in Chicago apoplexy when you wore it to dinner at the hotel."

Hildy held the dress against her curvaceous form and peered past Wyn to her reflection in the ornately framed mirror that hung over the dressing table. "Quite a staid little man, wasn't he?" she mused. "Hopefully I'll have better luck this time. The steward tells me we have a member of the British aristocracy aboard and he will be eating at the captain's table with us tonight."

"A duke perhaps?" Wyn suggested.

"A baron. Not a very exalted rank, but I understand he's wealthy."

"Perhaps he knows your brother-in-law. You could ask him as a conversational opening."

Hildy exchanged the lavender for the silver gown and considered her image in the glass a second time. "And totally destroy the good baron's interest? The Loftus family connection is the last thing I should mention. You're right about the lavender. Lord, I hate being in mourning, even half mourning. Are you wearing the *terre-verte?*"

"Not if I'm going to stand near you," Wyn said brushing through another wind-born tangle. "Besides, I have no need to dazzle anyone. As the only Shire Line family member aboard, I'll have the captain's undivided attention even if I dress in sack cloth."

"Well, you are the Belle," Hildy said. "Oh, but I did learn a bit of distressing news."

Thinking the ship had developed a problem, Wyn put her brush aside and turned to face her friend. "Don't tell me one of the grand saloon chandeliers is loose."

"Don't be ridiculous," Hildy scoffed. "The ship is perfect. It's the quality of the passengers that is at fault."

The rakish dark face of Garrett Blackhawk flashed in Wyn's mind. He was probably only one of many fortune hunters aboard. Hildy surveyed her reflection a last time, considering how to make her conquest. Yes, Wyn reflected, there were a good number of mercenary passengers aboard, and they were not all male.

Hildy tossed her gowns over the end of Wyn's bunk and perched on the lid of her largest trunk. "If I'd discovered he was aboard before we sailed you could probably have had him tossed off," she said and assumed a thoughtful expression. "Do they still keelhaul people?"

This was serious indeed. "Not aboard a Shire ship," Wyn answered, "and never to a paying customer."

Hildy sighed. "Well, perhaps Deegan didn't pay for his pas—"

Blood rushed to Wyn's face. "Deegan? Deegan Galloway?" she demanded in a tight voice.

"I don't believe he noticed me," Hildy admitted. "He was engaged in conversation with a very pretty girl and a mountainous woman whom I took to be her mother."

Not only was he aboard, he was dallying with another heiress! Wyn surged to her feet, fuming and confused at the tumult of emotions his name raised in her breast. Had Pierce arranged this? She recalled clearly that he'd placed a wager on Deegan's success in winning her. Pierce's disreputable conduct in the past lead her to believe in the likelihood of the scheme. He'd probably sought Deegan out before leaving San Francisco months ago and arranged everything.

Well, he'd read her heart wrong if he believed she would fall readily into the perfidious Mr. Galloway's arms again.

Wyn strode angrily around the cabin, unaware that Hildy was unnaturally quiet.

Had Pierce actually used her eagerly offered money to appease the bank during construction of the ship, or had he merely *told* her that he had? If it was still nestled in the vault of the Bank of California, she was going to cheerfully murder her older brother.

"I wonder what he looks like?" Hildy murmured.

No, she would torture Pierce first. She would see about acquiring thumb screws from a moldering dungeon and—

"What?" Wyn snapped, halting in mid stride.

Hildy looked up, her face still contemplative. "I was just wondering what the baron looks like," she repeated.

"Fat and balding probably," Wyn said, her voice bordering on a growl. Didn't Hildy realize the complications Deegan's presence presented?

Hildy shivered theatrically. "Oh, I hope he isn't," she said with a sigh. "I'd enjoy an improvement over Oswin, in looks, age, and money."

Especially money, Wyn thought ruefully. It had come as a nasty shock to Hildy to find the man she'd married for his wealth had died nearly a pauper. Apparently her friend had yet to learn her lesson. There were other things in life that mattered more than a healthy bank account.

As if reading her thoughts, Hildy sighed again. "I do wish I had my diamonds rather than the paste copy to wear. The baron will probably notice the difference. Those of noble birth tend to be more educated in these matters than Americans are."

Spoken like the true snob Hildy was, Wyn decided with disgust.

"What do you think the baron will think is my most attractive asset?" Hildy asked seriously.

In resignation, Wyn sank back down on the dressing stool. She had suggested Hildy accompany her on the voyage to restore her widowed friend's spirits. Deegan Galloway could be dealt with successfully later. For now, it was Hildy who needed her whole attention.

Wyn pasted a bright smile on her face. "Your charm," she declared staunchly. "It will stand you in good stead once you are a baroness."

Hildy laughed softly and leaned forward to hug Wyn. "You're lying but I love you for it," she said.

The porthole framed a portrait of early evening. Flamboyantly painted shadows in various shades of purple appeared like bold brush strokes across the eastern sky. The stateroom suite was located on an upper deck and, to Wyn's mind, afforded some of the most spectacular views available. How lovely it would be to escape to the bow of the ship and watch night gather. The heavens would sparkle in their full glory and, when the moon rose, the ocean would metamorphose into a gleaming reflection of the vast universe above.

But as an Abbot aboard a Shire ship, she had responsibilities.

"Perhaps we'd best change for dinner," Wyn suggested. "You wouldn't want another lady to attach your baron before we arrive."

"If another woman so much as looks at him, promise me you'll help me toss her overboard," Hildy said, her tone of voice making Wyn wonder if her friend was actually serious rather than theatrical. Obviously, bringing a man with a title up to scratch meant a lot to Hildy. If that was the case, Wyn vowed silently to do whatever it took to make Hildy happy once more. Perhaps in doing so it would mollify her conscience over the way her blind attachment to Deegan had inadvertently hurt Leonore Cronin in San Francisco.

"I do wish the purser had been able to give me a few details about the baron's appearance instead of being insidious," Hildy said as she gathered her gowns from the bed.

Wyn began working loose the buttons of her form fitted jacket. "Perhaps he hasn't met the man," she offered.

The fabric of Hildy's evening gowns rustled softly, brushing against the flounces of her day dress as she crossed the room. "No, he said he met all the truly important passengers as they came aboard. But all he would tell me was that the baron's appearance was quite appropriate to his name."

Wyn turned her attention to the fastenings of her cuff. "What is his name?"

"Nothing spectacularly strange sounding." Hildy paused in the doorway a moment. "It's quite plain and distinctly Anglo-Saxon really. It's Blackhawk."

Chapter Four

Preferring to spend as little time as possible in his suite, Garrett changed for dinner and retreated to the gentlemen's smoking room where he plied a steward with silver for information. It took only a single clandestinely passed bribe to learn the direction of Winona Abbot's stateroom, and that she represented the Shire family aboard the liner.

The news cheered him immensely, for it meant they met on far more equal footing. Both were not only financially comfortable, they were wealthy. Even though Deegan had handled the arrangements for their trip, Garrett's nose for business had led him to make inquiries about the Shire Line before actually boarding the luxurious steamship. What he'd heard had impressed him. A number of shipping companies had folded when pitted against the sailing expertise of the White Star Line and Cunard, but the Shire Line had held fast, cutting a niche of their own in both the Atlantic trade and that of the Pacific. Considering that luxury liners had been making the crossing regularly since the *Great Eastern* launched in 1859, a good twenty years previous, he was rather surprised that the *Nereid* was the Shire Line's first attempt to corner a share of the first-class passenger trade. Perhaps they had dallied, learning from the mistakes of their competitors. He wondered idly if the Shire and Abbot families had considered issuing stock, tak-

ing their shipping business out of the realm of a closed
company, opening it to investors. A block of Shire stock
would work well with his other investment interests. As
soon as things were settled on his family's lands, he'd
check into the matter, escape to London and—

Garrett nearly laughed out loud. Considering the way
his associates in London treated him, London was anything
but an escape. It would be little more than a brief reprieve
from the oppressiveness of the Blackhawk estate.

That destination, thank God, was still more than a week
away. A week in which he intended to immerse himself in
the delightful pursuit of Winona Abbot. This would no
doubt be the last time he could trust a woman to see him
as simply a man rather than as Blackhawk of Hawk's Run.

Unless, that is, his wretched reputation was known by
someone aboard, which, considering a good many of the
passengers enjoying the luxurious accommodations were
British, was quite possible. It was only a matter of time
before news of his past escapades buzzed in the plushly
appointed saloons, flitting first in the men's lounges before
flying fleetly to that of the ladies', where it would be tattered even more thoroughly. Perhaps even embroidered
upon.

It certainly had been in the past.

Ah, his wretched past.

When she learned who he was, would it change the way
Winona Abbot looked at him? The memory of her darkly
lashed deep green eyes lingered in his mind as strongly as
the vision of her shapely form teased it.

It was only their first day at sea. Surely word would not
spread this quickly. Surely he could remain anonymous for
a brief while longer. Until she learned who—what—he
was, Garrett intended to enjoy every moment he could
steal with Winona Abbot.

It was a simple matter to lie in wait for her when it drew
near to the hour for dinner. Fortunately, she was alone
when she left her stateroom, rather than accompanied by
her companion. The helpful steward had given him a

name, but all Garrett recalled now was that the other woman was a widow, nothing more. She, after all, hadn't been the subject that held his interest. He was relieved the widow appeared to be keeping to the cabin rather than join the company in the dining room, for sharing the blond beauty was not on his itinerary.

Winona didn't notice him lurking in the shadows near the companionway. Her attention was on a contrary button on the wrist of her long ivory glove. Even with her head bent, Garrett found she was far more beautiful than his memory had painted her. No longer tossed by a sea breeze, her flaxen locks were upswept to a knot that spilled artful curls to tease her creamy shoulders. Delicate drop earrings danced as she moved, the cut of the crystal stone catching the light of each lamp she passed along the darkly paneled corridor, creating quickly flashed prisms of color. She wore no other jewels, but Garrett was too entranced to question why. His attention was drawn instead to the neckline of her bodice as it dipped low over a bosom that was both full and cleverly concealed by a swath of fine pale blue tulle. Silk a scant shade deeper molded to the rest of her torso, accenting her narrow waist, and swept in a shimmering apron around her generous, womanly hips. Fabric cascaded behind her in a graceful train, rustling with every gliding step she took. As he watched, she finished with the button and bent slightly to catch up her train before descending the stairs.

Garrett waited until she lifted her slimly cut skirts before he stepped forward. The delay allowed him a glimpse of her delicately turned ankles and high-heeled satin slippers.

He doubted there was another woman aboard to match her for beauty and grace.

She noticed him just as the ship dipped slightly, gently tipping the deck upon which they stood. Ever alert to opportunity, Garrett took advantage of the situation.

"Good evening, Miss Abbot," he murmured, slipping his hand beneath her elbow to steady her. The scent of her perfume teased his senses, a mixture of rose water that hinted of vanilla and clove. Its effect on him was erotic, titillating. And yet when she looked up at him, her very expression was one of innocence. "It is *Miss* Abbot, not Mrs.?" he pressed.

She didn't pull away from him but paused, as if considering whether to accept his escort or not. Rather than answer his question, she posed one of her own. "And it is *Baron* Blackhawk, rather than Mr., is it not, my lord?"

Garrett grimaced wryly. Obviously he had been too wicked in the past to merit a respite from fate now. "Found me out already?" he asked as the deck righted once more.

Winona seemed little aware of the ship's movement. "You needn't feel flattered," she said lightly, and proceeded down the staircase. "I did not go seeking the information, sir."

Far from appalled at whatever rumors she had heard about him, she appeared to be far more miffed that he hadn't told her of them himself. Garrett grinned to himself, pleased she cared that he hadn't. "I am crushed," he murmured.

"Yes, I can see you are," she answered dryly. "Why didn't you tell me you were titled, my lord?"

"Actually, it was to avoid having you call me *my lord* in just that tone of voice. I'd much rather hear you use my first name, which, if you recall, is Garrett," he said.

She stepped away from the touch of his hand as they reached the bottom of the stairwell. The glow of the setting sun reached them through the glass of a nearby porthole, casting a pink glow around her, coloring her cheeks a warm, blushing peach.

She turned slightly to face him, her chin lifting in resolution. "I think not. I'm sorry if you got the wrong impression of me earlier on deck," she said. "I really am not interested in a shipboard romance, or a brief flirtation. You would do much better to set your sights on another lady if dallying is your goal, my lord."

"And if it isn't?" he asked.

"Forgive me if I doubt your word, but what other reason might you have for lying in wait for me?" When he didn't answer immediately, she smiled knowingly. "Believe me, sir, where men are concerned, I am far from an innocent as to their intent when they seek me out."

"You would convict me without a trial? My dear Miss Abbot, surely that goes as much against an American's grain as it does an Englishman's," Garrett insisted. "Do you not believe that I enjoyed your company this afternoon and wished to continue our conversation?"

She shook her head slightly. He was pleased to note the corners of her mouth still curved upward in amusement. "What I believe is that you don't enjoy taking *no* for an answer, my lord."

The hatchway to the outer deck swung open. "Ah, my dear!" a voice greeted loudly, interrupting her. Although Garrett had only met the man once upon boarding, Captain Kittrick's gravelly baritone was quite distinctive. "Thought I'd come along to see you safe to our grand galley. I see someone else's had the same idea, though, eh, Baron?"

Garrett held back a snarl of frustration. "Quite," he agreed, allowing his voice to drop into the sarcastic drawl he had perfected in London a lifetime ago. "We shan't have to duel over who wins the honor of escorting the lovely Miss Abbot, shall we?"

Winona's eyes widened in surprise then clouded with a hint of confusion at his metamorphosis from determined flirt to bored aristocrat. Garrett couldn't blame her. He hadn't even been conscious that he was doing it. Donning the role on cue had become so natural over the years.

Kittrick chuckled as if he'd heard a great joke. "A duel? By George! You'll find me quite game—ha-ha. What shall we use? Shuffleboard cues? Ha-ha."

Before Garrett could respond, Winona slipped her gloved hand onto Kittrick's proffered arm. "Nonsense, Captain," she insisted lightly. "Lord Blackhawk was merely asking for directions to the dining room. I'm sure he won't mind tagging along behind us."

She glanced back at him over one shoulder, issuing him a steady green-eyed challenge. "Will you, my lord?" she purred.

Although Hildy and, no doubt, the captain believed Blackhawk was wealthy, Wyn maintained her belief that he was nothing more than a fortune hunter and thus a cad. She had surmised it earlier, and had seen no evidence that he was anything else yet. But he was an awfully attractive one. She only hoped that Hildy would see past his handsome exterior to the true man beneath. That she would realize he was not the man she had hoped he would be.

Such would not be the case, though. Her friend's breathing would be just as erratic when Blackhawk was around as her own was at that moment.

If only he weren't so...so...

Dangerous.

Yes, that was it. There was nothing in his appearance that could not be found just as attractive in a dozen other men aboard. It wasn't the way the midnight black of his evening wear fit him. It was obviously the work of a master tailor. It wasn't the breadth of his shoulders or the leanness of his build that pulled her eyes to him so often. Other men were as well of feature and form. No, it was something else. Something she had simply not managed to isolate as yet to explain why she thought him splendid.

He was most definitely that. The color of his coat and trousers was a continuation of his natural coloring, adding to the illusion that he was a reflection of his namesake, the black hawk. Was it simply his superficial resemblance to a hawk that gave him the aura of a predator himself, inclining her to believe he was as dangerous to court as would be the predatory bird?

Wyn was not surprised when Blackhawk chose to pick up the verbal gauntlet she'd tossed. "I would be honored to arrive on your heels, Miss Abbot," he vowed, his deep voice still harboring the newly acquired sardonic edge. Rather than trail behind though, he fell into step at her side. "However, I find it very inhospitable of the good captain to keep you all to himself."

Kittrick chortled. "Jealous of me, are you, Baron?" He patted Wyn's hand on his arm. "Well, you see, I have first call on this lovely lady. She's my chosen belle for the voyage."

"Not an easy choice to make, I'll wager," Blackhawk said. "There are so many other lovely ladies aboard."

"That there are," the captain agreed readily. "But I've an eye for the special ones."

"You do at that," the baron murmured, casting Wyn another glance of approving admiration.

She laughed softly. "Thank you, my lord, but I can do without blatant compliments. You had best find another ear in which to feed them."

"And if no other appeals to me?"

"I'm sure a good number of them will," Wyn assured him. "Simply the knowledge that you are a lord—"

"A very minor one," Blackhawk interrupted. "So minor, the state barely deserves notice."

He was far too intent upon singling her out for a flirtation. Wyn wished she had followed Hildy's course in remaining in the press of passengers at departure. If only she hadn't been alone at the rail earlier, he would be as much a stranger to her as he was to the rest of the *Nereid*'s company. If only Hildy hadn't decided that having a baron aboard suited her plans for the voyage perfectly. She must find a way to discourage him before Hildy misread the whole situation. Her friend's emotional state was too fragile at this time to recognize that Wyn was not encouraging him.

Although to *not* encourage him was difficult. Very difficult.

He leaned closer to her as they walked, his voice dropping to a confiding rumble that made Wyn regret her vow to help Hildy find romance this journey. "Believe me,"

Blackhawk murmured, "a good number of people have gone quite out of their way to avoid noticing the baronage in the past."

"Indeed? But I sincerely doubt they are among our companions on this voyage," Wyn persisted. "Do you not agree, Captain?"

"Humph," Kittrick said. "You see, sir, you are our sole personage, you might say, on this trip. There's a good bit of money traveling with us, but it's not the inherited kind, if you catch my drift."

"Neither," Blackhawk said, "is mine."

"Still, that's not how folks will see things," Kittrick continued. "And, you being a single gentleman, the ladies will be atwitter. We've a number of families with marriageable daughters sailing with us and the purser's planned at least one grand ball before we dock. Two if the crossing is smooth."

Wyn smiled at Blackhawk. "You see, my lord? You will be quite merry without adding me to your string of conquests."

"Will I now?" he asked, lifting one dark brow in patent disbelief.

"Can't help but be," Kittrick said with a chuckle. "Can't say I envy you though, sir. It's a hard life for a man dealing with bevies of beautiful women demanding his attention. Damned hard life."

Wyn was glad that their leisured steps down the long paneled inner passageway at last joined another corridor and they began to encounter other guests. It enabled her to slip free of the captain and his now-captive lord. She lingered only long enough to enjoy the sight of the enthusiastic Kittrick taking great pleasure in introducing the baron to his fellow passengers, then she slipped into the dining room.

Although she had seen it the evening before, the intricacy of detail in the room still left her feeling stunned. The area appeared vast upon first sight, the bulkheads rising the height of two full decks before arching in a shallow dome over the room. Elaborately painted friezes rose above rows of portholes, the style and subject matter a distinct reflection of her older brother's flamboyant taste. For a change Pierce had exercised a hitherto unknown sense of good taste. She had feared to see furnishings that rivaled those chosen by a whorehouse madam. She did, after all, know exactly where Pierce tended to spend his spare time.

Instead of a blur of scarlet, the room was tastefully decorated. An unknown artist had created massive portraits of two ancient sea gods. It was easy to recognize the Roman god of the sea, Neptune, with his spear, surrounded by ships, sea serpents and mermaids. The mermaids were lush creatures. Definitely Pierce's choice. The Greek god Nereus was lesser known but, having fathered the sea nymphs known as the Nereid, his appearance in the frieze was de rigueur. He was banked by a host of his lovely daughters. Very lovely daughters.

Pierce definitely needed a new direction in his life.

The long dining tables had been set in advance, their tops covered with gleaming white linen, each place setting a picture of perfection, from glistening china to delicate crystal to highly polished silver flatware.

A number of the luxury-class passengers were already seated at their assigned tables or picking their ways through the crowded room in search of their places. The captain's table sat at the head of the room, far from the double-doored entranceway, directly, she noted, under the complacent gaze of Nereus himself. The company there would number ten, four on either side of the board with chairs at both head and foot, as well. Some of the captain's other guests were before her, already seated where the stewards directed. There was an older couple, so obviously married they had begun to resemble each other in feature, a very pretty, very young woman who was obviously their daughter, and a dapper but solemn-faced young man.

Choosing not to wait for Hildy—who planned to make an entrance—or the captain, Wyn began picking her way toward her own place. Briefly she wished it could be at one of the other tables rather than in the very visible chair at the captain's right hand.

She'd barely taken two steps when a startled male voice gasped nearby.

"Wyn."

Wyn closed her eyes briefly, letting the sound of Deegan Galloway's voice wash over her. He still said her name with a lilt that hinted at adoration. It had once sent pleasant chills skittering up her spine. This time she felt nothing and, as a result, bereft that the sensation was missing.

"Wyn," he said again, his voice sounding a bit thunderstruck as well as awed at her appearance. "What are you doing here?"

She opened her eyes, turned to stare at him coldly.

A faint rush of color flooded what was visible of his face beyond his tawny side-whiskers. He'd added a dashing mustache since she'd last seen him. It enhanced his appearance, she thought. When his devilish smile curled beneath it, female hearts would melt en masse. Except for hers.

Deegan's eyes shifted as he glanced nervously aside. "I mean, I thought you were still in San Francisco. How does it happen you're aboard the *Nereid?*"

"I could ask you the same, Deegan," Wyn said. "More to the point, I'm wondering what you are doing in this dining room. Considering the state of your finances, I would have thought steerage the limit of your travel funds."

He flinched. "That's cruel, Wyn, even if I did deserve it. As it happens, I'm traveling with a friend of mine."

"Female, I suppose," Wyn snapped, incensed despite herself. "I hope she can afford your tastes."

Deegan actually grinned with pleasure. "Well, *he* can, at any rate. It is a bit difficult, you and I stuck on the same ship. I swear, Wyn, if I'd had any idea that you were sailing on this pleasure palace, I'd have booked with another line. I chose a Shire ship out of loyalty and affection for your family, believe me.''

It was difficult to be spiteful over his actions after such a declaration. ''Thank you,'' Wyn murmured, albeit reluctantly. ''But I'm sure that you will agree, the less we must deal with each other during the voyage, the more pleasant this journey will be.''

An expression of shifty unease flitted across his face. ''Well, there may be a difficulty in avoiding each other. You see...'' His voice trailed off as he glanced away, back toward the wide entranceway and the crowd of richly dressed people congregated near it.

Wyn wasn't to be distracted though. She kept her eyes firmly on his face, determined this time to see the real Deegan Galloway, and not be seduced into thinking him a different man than he was.

''Yes?'' she prodded.

''You see,'' Deegan bleated, still scanning the crowd for someone. Obviously a party to rescue him from the awkwardness of their encounter, Wyn decided. ''My host is a fellow who draws the limelight, and, er, even standing on the outskirts of it as I am...''

Wyn gave an unladylike snort of disbelief.

''...I doubt you and I will be able to escape rubbing shoulders because...''

The interruption didn't come from among the gathering at the door. It sneaked up on them from the rear.

''Excuse me,'' one of the stewards murmured. ''Miss Abbot? Might I show you to your chair?''

Wyn jumped at the chance to end her unwelcome conversation with Deegan. ''Certainly,'' she agreed, rewarding the uniformed attendant with a brilliant smile as she took his arm.

Her smile dimmed considerably when the man addressed Deegan, as well. ''Would you mind coming along, too, Mr. Galloway?'' he asked respectfully.

Deegan gave Wyn a weak smile of apology before answering. ''Yes, of course.''

"We will begin serving shortly," the steward assured them both, leading the way to the captain's table. He held Wyn's chair, allowing her time to arrange her skirts and train before taking the seat. "Is there anything I can get for you at this time?"

Wyn just wished he would leave, taking Deegan with him. "Nothing, thank you."

The steward turned to Galloway. "And you, sir?"

"Just point out my place and leave it at that," Deegan said.

The steward looked taken aback a moment, but recovered swiftly. "I'm sorry, sir. I thought you knew. You are just here." He gestured to the right.

Wyn's heart sank.

"We've seated you next to Miss Abbot, sir."

Magnus Finley slipped into the dining room with none of the fanfare a good number of the guests appeared to demand. He, unlike them, preferred his presence to be overlooked. While the price of his passage had given him the luxury of hobnobbing with the wealthy, it had also been modest enough to allow him to go unnoticed by them. His assigned seat was located a decided distance from the captain's table, yet allowed him an excellent view of the guests gathered there. It had taken a bribe to secure this particular chair, but he felt it well worth the expense, one that would no doubt come out of his own pocket rather than company expenses, since he had decided not to take Captain Kittrick into his confidence. From his observations thus far it was already apparent that, if apprised of his mission, the blustery captain was more likely to make a slip that would tip off the suspect Finley had gone to such trouble to follow all the way from San Francisco. Kittrick wouldn't have taken kindly to the suggestion that one of the passengers chosen to sit at his table was an alleged jewel thief.

In all honesty, it wasn't a single passenger that Finley had his eye on. While his own investigation led him to favor one suspect over all others, the reports of various Pinkerton agents had made it advisable to add other names to his list. Especially when it was discovered that all of them were sailing aboard the *Nereid*. It had only been that afternoon that he had learned the suspects would be gathered together at the captain's table that evening.

The situation led him to hypothesize a new theory: it might not have been a single thief who had lifted jewels in San Francisco, or added to the cache in Boston, but a team of clever thieves, each able to vouch for the other, to cover the other's tracks when capture threatened.

As the last of the glittering passengers made their way to the tables, Finley kept an unobtrusive eye turned to the table at the top of the room. He hoped to discover a clue— a series of clues—that would allow him to narrow the scope of his investigation before the ocean liner docked in Liverpool. Even though he would be contacting police officials in Britain for assistance in apprehending the thief, if he still had more than a single suspect to follow, Finley doubted he would be taken seriously. Especially since the whole case currently hung only on suppositions, educated guesses based on the fact that these suspects had had the opportunity to commit each of the crimes, rather than on the evidence of a witness to the thief's escape or of a fence trying to extricate himself from involvement in the series of crimes.

There was nothing solid about the case yet. Nothing that would hold up in a court of law. Unless he had an out-and-out confession, in the presence of witnesses, Finley feared the case would drag on, that the agency's clients would lose confidence in the Pinkerton office and withdraw, leaving him frustrated with the knowledge that the criminal had been the only winner in the drama.

They all looked like winners now. The guests gathered at the main table were amongst the most glittering. His own tablemates appeared tacky and lacking in both grace and taste when compared to the captain's chosen few. While the woman across from him was gowned in expensive finery, her dress was too frilled and her gems were of an inferior grade. The man at her side sampled his wine with a shopkeeper's profit-conscious expression rather than with the appreciation of a true aficionado. The guests on either side of the couple were cut from the same mold, eager to be a reflection of the class to which they aspired and from which they were held back by their own antecedents.

Nearly all the people he watched at the far table belonged to a different breed. The very naturalness of their movements, choices and actions, set them apart even though Finley suspected their bank accounts on the whole were inferior to those of the guests at his own table. It was their financial resources that had occupied him of late as he studied reports for patterns he could use to prove a motive for involvement in the now long series of jewel robberies, or as proof that profit had been gathered from the sale of one of the stolen items.

He had not yet found what he was seeking. But he would. Finley was sure of it. The clue he sought was awaiting his notice, perhaps had already been gleaned and not recognized for its impact as of yet. If such was the case, he knew from experience that only time would allow it to rise to the surface.

The stewards arrived laden with tureens of soup. Finley watched them deftly maneuver among the waiting guests, tilting their trays to avoid spilling the broth when the deck tilted slightly beneath their feet. His mind wasn't on the dexterity of the crew members though, it was on the information he had gathered on the passengers whose names headed his list of suspects: Deegan Galloway, Winona Abbot and Garrett Blackhawk.

Chapter Five

It ranked as one of the worst evenings of her life, Wyn decided as she watched the soup imitate the ocean, moving from side to side in her shallow bowl. Not only was Deegan seated on her right, his placement forcing her to speak civilly to him when table etiquette so demanded, but Garrett Blackhawk occupied the chair directly across from hers so that she felt his glance on her frequently. It made Wyn nervous since Hildy was at her most bubbling effervescence on his left.

Why must he continue to be so contrary and single her out over all the ladies at the table? If not with his attentions, then with his eyes? She'd particularly chosen her gown because it paled in splendor next to Hildy's. Miss Suzanne Carillo, who looked to have only recently lengthened her skirts and put her hair up, wore a gown far more rich and attractive than hers. While Blackhawk didn't appear to have noticed Hildy's daringly cut dress or Miss Carillo's elegant one, Wyn didn't think there was a single thread of her own ensemble that hadn't fallen under his approving scrutiny. Nor had he missed the fact that his study left her flustered.

Perhaps that was *frustrated*, Wyn corrected herself waspishly. Either way she would have been in a far pleasanter frame of mind if Hildy weren't involved. Or if he were anything but the fortune hunter and con man she believed him to be. Why was it that she was always attracted to the wrong type of man? Hadn't she learned anything in her disastrous past?

As if she didn't have enough on her plate of problems, there was Deegan to deal with, too. When his foot brushed against hers beneath the table, she was transported to another world, an aeon ago, when such touches had been considered intimate, precious, stolen caresses. She could feel the heat of his body next to hers, smell the scent of his cologne, both so familiar.

And yet, she didn't feel any of the same sensations that had once assailed her when in his presence. In its place was this all too intoxicating awareness of every gesture Deegan's friend Garrett Blackhawk made.

His friend! Another unhappy coincidence. It had been nearly as much a shock to learn that Blackhawk and Deegan were traveling companions as it had been to learn that Blackhawk was Hildy's baron. Now that she considered the matter though, Wyn was inclined to believe the two men belonged together. They were both handsome, charming and unconscionable liars. One had only to listen to the farfetched tales they told over dinner to realize the last. They were fortune hunters. Dazzling young, unsuspecting women was part of their trade.

How had they come to be aboard the *Nereid?* Had they pooled their funds, plotted their current course, determined to, between them, seduce at least one wealthy young woman into plighting her troth before the ship reached England? Which of them would it be who requested the captain perform a wedding service while still at sea? And who would be the victim bride? Miss Carillo? Her parents doted in equal measure on the unscrupulous pair. The fact that the Carillos merited inclusion at the captain's table was like waving a red flag before the likes of such men. Only passengers of a certain status were awarded the pleasure of Kittrick's company. More often than not, that status was given to the very wealthy. Or the titled.

No wonder Blackhawk was claiming to be a baron! It enabled him, and Deegan as his associate, to be placed in a position that allowed them to meet only the richest women aboard, be they young heiresses or lonely widows.

Hildy's pursuit of the baron would no doubt slow down his courtship of the impressionable Miss Carillo, but Deegan would have all the opportunity single-minded determination could afford. She should warn the young woman's mother.

Wyn glanced to where the lady in question sat, her face aglow as she surveyed the guests. It seemed doubtful that Mrs. Carillo would give due merit to any warning issued by another woman. She was too enthralled to be among the elect company.

Which meant the Carillos' money was new money. They would squander it in Europe, likely buying whatever they wished. Wyn had little doubt that a husband for their daughter headed the shopping list. It had been the reason a good many wealthy American families had gone abroad.

And if such were the case, the Carillos might as well take Deegan, Wyn thought. At least he wasn't as bad as some of the cads she had had the misfortune to meet.

"Would you care for more wine, Wyn?" Deegan asked.

"No, thank you," she murmured coolly.

He grinned at her fondly, then turned to his right to offer the same service to the blushing Miss Carillo. The young woman's murmured answer was lost as her mother tossed table etiquette to the winds and leaned forward to claim his attention.

"This is all so exciting!" she gushed. "I do wish you would tell me of the adventures you and Lord Blackhawk shared in the Amazon, Mr. Galloway. I know Mr. Mosby is interested and my precious Susanne is quite breathless in anticipation, aren't you, my dove?"

Mr. Mosby looked disconcerted. Miss Carillo colored even more brightly in confusion but leaned a bit nearer so as not to miss one of Deegan's dulcetly dropped words.

"In Mexico, my dear lady," he corrected. "I haven't

the stamina that a trek up the Amazon entails. Dealing with bandits in the mountains of Sonora was quite chilling enough."

"Bandits! Good heavens!" Mrs. Carillo gasped. "However did you get involved with them?"

Wyn listened with half an ear as Deegan spun out a tale that she was quite sure he made up as he went along. Since he worked Blackhawk into the scenario, she wondered if the two men would meet later to coordinate their stories.

Blackhawk, she had found as the captain drew him out, told just as hair-raisingly improbable tales, a good many of them featuring Deegan as his companion in arms. Of course, he was far less sensational in the telling than the dramatic Galloway. She felt it had something to do with the baron's delivery. The adventure, when retold in the careless, drawling affectation he had assumed at the captain's appearance earlier, took on the mantle of a tedious trial endured with a stiff upper lip. She was quite sure that, like Deegan's tales, not a single word bore the least resemblance to the truth.

"You hid from savages in a cave overnight, *then* in the morning discovered a fabulous vein of gold ran directly above your head?" Hildy demanded, her blue eyes sparkling with excitement as she gazed at Blackhawk. "Did you immediately file a claim, my lord?"

"Bother the gold," Captain Kittrick snorted. "However did you escape the savages?"

Wyn sampled her soup and let the conversation wash over her.

She should have been prepared. Having Blackhawk at the captain's table practically insured that the company would be agog. She'd seen her keenly republican neighbors in San Francisco become overnight royalists when a traveler with an old-world title arrived in the city. It had happened again that evening as the captain made the introductions. He'd barely let Blackhawk's name trip from his tongue before Mr. Mosby, the young man seated next to Miss Carillo, had stammered that he'd heard of the baron. Even Blackhawk's sardonically lifted eyebrow had not stemmed the flow after that. Eyes aglow with something like hero worship, Mr. Mosby had asked about a mine in Brazil. That had put Mr. Carillo in mind of a rumor of a rail line Blackhawk was said to have been involved with founding somewhere in Mexico. Mrs. Carillo remembered hearing a friend tell of an incident involving the Blackhawk name in Egypt a few years ago, although she had not been able to bring the details readily to mind. Hers had been the only statement that neither Blackhawk nor Deegan had seen fit to expand upon thus far.

By the time the final course arrived, Wyn had ceased to listen to the fantasies that held the rest of her dining companions enthralled. It was with a decided start that she realized Kittrick was addressing her.

"I'm sorry. What was that, Captain?"

He chuckled good-naturedly. "I was just suggesting that you partner Lord Blackhawk for a hand or so of whist after dinner."

Against her better judgment, Wyn's eyes flew to meet the baron's. His glinted with mischievous humor. And why not? She had given him the very means to single her out earlier. Her weakness—whist! Oh, why had she ever mentioned the game to him?

The captain turned back to Blackhawk. "You won't find a better partner, sir. Played a round or so with her last night and, I can tell you, the lady is a deadly serious gamester when it comes to cards."

"*Deadly* is certainly the right word," Deegan agreed, grinning affectionately at her. "I've always made it a point never to bet against Wyn. At least, I did after she and her partner wrung me dry at a card party in San Francisco."

Wyn remembered the occasion well, the evening they first met. The evening she had begun to dream foolishly about the future.

She knew better now. The future could stay nebulously distant and unknown for all she cared. Never again would she tempt her heart with such dreams, even if, whenever

Blackhawk smiled faintly at her, that traitorous organ appeared primed to dream in spite of her resolutions.

His dark gaze was on her now, causing the unwanted awareness to seep through her veins, warming her.

"Cleaned your pockets, did she?" the baron drawled. "Amazing."

Wyn met his amused look with an arch one. "You would not think so, my lord, if you had played cards with Mr. Galloway often."

"Ouch." Deegan flinched theatrically, as if struck a blow.

Mr. Carillo chuckled. "Sounds like you're just the kind of fella I like at a card table, Galloway. Not as a partner, of course."

While the others, including Deegan, laughed politely, Blackhawk's mouth curled in a thin smile. Despite the walls she'd been building to protect herself from him, the slight lift of his lips made Wyn feel as if she'd been running downhill, out of control. She couldn't catch her breath. Couldn't hear the conversation around her for the pounding of blood through her veins.

"It seems you have unplumbed depths, Miss Abbot," Blackhawk drawled, his voice moving over her, through her. "Will you give me the pleasure of a game this evening?"

As much as she longed to do just that, she daren't. Not with Hildy looking on. Hildy, who knew her so well and yet would read the situation all wrong.

Blackhawk was definitely not the man for her friend, but Hildy would discover that soon enough. In the meantime, flirting with a decidedly attractive man such as he would cheer Hildy immensely. There was only one thing she could do, Wyn decided.

She folded the linen napkin in her lap, and lifted her chin determinedly. "No, my lord, I won't," Wyn said. She pushed her chair back. "If you'll all excuse me? It has been a long and tiring day and I'd like to go to my cabin."

Three hours and innumerable games of patience later, Wyn wished she hadn't lied. Why hadn't she simply said she preferred to have another lady as her partner at the card table?

She dealt three cards to herself, turning the topmost over. Nine of clubs. She placed it on a ten of hearts, moved an eight of diamonds into place, and proceeded to stare at the rest of the card layout unseeingly.

She couldn't have told that big a lie, Wyn admitted to herself sadly. Not and gotten away with it. Too many people knew that she detested having a woman for a partner at whist. Only the evening before at dinner with the captain, she'd denounced her sex as able players. They lacked the competitive spirit, the dedication to detail, the concentration that men tended to bring to the table. Well, most men. Admittedly, there were some terrible male players. Her brother Pierce, for one. Still, she could have stood a woman partner if only to escape being matched with Blackhawk. Or she could if Hildy and Deegan had not been present. They would no doubt have shouted with laughter if she'd even suggested a partnership with another woman. Both knew her far too well to believe such a preposterous tale.

Three more cards slipped quickly through her fingers. Absentmindedly Wyn snapped an ace on the table, dealt more cards, finished one sequence of alternating red and black cards, and began another in midrun with a six of spades.

She should have claimed to be ill. No, Hildy and the captain would have fretted over her, insisting that the ship's doctor examine her and douse her with a vile-tasting concoction. Wyn sighed deeply.

It took nearly a full run through the cards in her hand before she found a card to play. Another three before she admitted that the game had bested her. Again. Rather like fate had been doing since the *Nereid* put to sea.

Wyn swept the cards together, stacked them, shuffled

them, her mind slipping backward in time to debate options she could have followed.

She had nearly decided that an insincere but sorrowful-sounding confession of having promised to play with another set of passengers would have worked—despite the fact that she knew only those passengers who sat at the captain's board—when Hildy swept into the stateroom suite and spun in a circle, her arms outstretched in happiness.

"He's perfect," she announced. "So perfect, I can scarcely believe my luck."

Wyn abandoned her cards with alacrity and turned in her chair. "So you managed to get the baron all to yourself? Did you partner him at cards?"

Hildy pirouetted again, her narrow lavender skirts flaring slightly with the motion, then sank gracefully onto the divan. "No, with Mr. Mosby, actually. Lord Blackhawk declined joining our table, or any other, saying he preferred to watch and assess our skill."

The arrogance of the man! Wyn fumed at the picture Hildy's words painted.

Her friend didn't sound insulted by the baron's attitude though. Perversely she seemed even more enchanted by it.

Well, she would, Wyn admitted silently. Hildy was a snob at heart, believing herself better than most of her acquaintances. Still, she was a dear friend who had been through a traumatic time, losing her husband to death, his fortune to the tradesmen, and even her diamonds to an unknown thief.

If happiness could be found with the despicable baron, even temporarily, then Hildy had her blessing.

"And did he choose a player worthy of being his partner tomorrow evening?" Wyn asked.

"I've no idea," Hildy admitted. "I was so intent on playing my best, I didn't even notice when he left the card room. Which reminds me..." She fished in her beaded purse a moment then waved a handful of greenbacks in Wyn's direction. "Mr. Mosby and I swept to victory with ease over the captain and Mrs. Carillo. Mr. Mosby is such a gentleman. He insisted that I keep all our winnings to myself.''

If she recalled correctly, Wyn mused, young Mr. Mosby was the sole recipient of his grandfather's enormous fortune, one built, like Astor's, on the fur trade earlier in the century. The money Hildy gloated over was, no doubt, insignificant to him. She was pleased that Hildy was glowing, and a bit surprised that her friend hadn't redirected her interest from Blackhawk to the clearly besotted Mr. Mosby. His fortune certainly fit her friend's requirements. He was a few years younger than Hildy, Wyn guessed, which would cause some talk. But then, nearly everything connected with wealth did. If only he were not so sadly lacking when it came to a manly bearing. He was short of stature and a bit too fleshy to be considered handsome by even the most kindhearted people. He had a pleasant, if retiring, personality, and a warm smile. It had simply been his misfortune to be seated at a table with Deegan and Blackhawk, two splendidly tall, robust men. By comparison, Mr. Mosby appeared an extremely poor specimen of manhood.

Hildy was definitely overlooking him at any rate.

"It doesn't matter though," Hildy announced, pulling free the ribbon that encircled her upswept curls. "I would much rather not be partnered with the baron. It makes carrying on a flirtation with a man so difficult if he dislikes the way a woman handles her cards. If I do nothing more than watch his play, then when he thinks of me it will be as a pleasant diversion, not as the woman who misused her trumps."

Which, Wyn admitted, her friend did frequently. It was certainly the reason she avoided having Hildy as a partner.

"I didn't expect you to wait up for me, dearest," Hildy said, sitting upright as she plucked pins from her now tumbling soft brown hair. "I fully expected you to be fast asleep by now."

Wyn played with the belt of her wrapper, carefully

avoiding meeting Hildy's eyes. "So did I," she lied quickly. She never felt more alive than she did when at sea. She'd only been waiting until the ship quieted for the night, for the passengers to seek their berths. For the time when the promenade deck could be hers alone.

"All I did was toss and turn though. Playing patience hasn't helped, either. I was considering taking a turn along the rail before you arrived."

Hildy smiled softly. "And possibly meet Deegan during your stroll?"

"Good gracious, no! Never!" Wyn vowed vehemently.

"He still cares for you. I could see it in his expression whenever he glanced your way," Hildy said. "I thought it was incredibly romantic."

"Inconvenient, you mean. Hildy, he lied to me."

"Well, Oswin lied to me."

"It isn't the same," Wyn insisted.

"It certainly isn't. Deegan is young, vital, virile, and Oswin was none of those things. He most definitely was not in love with me, and Deegan is demonstrably in love with you."

Wyn busied herself with gathering the cards. "Deegan fancies himself in love with any woman with sufficient wealth to supply him with a comfortable life-style. Besides," she said, tapping the deck together neatly, "I don't want a man who loves my bank account more than he does me."

Hildy laughed merrily. "You are such a romantic, dearest. But that's probably why I love you. Promise never to change."

It wasn't herself that she was worried about though, but Hildy. She was the one who was vulnerable. She was the one who would be hurt if she allowed herself to fall in love with Garrett Blackhawk. If only Hildy could see him for the actor he was.

Wyn got to her feet and crossed the room to kneel next to her friend's reclining form. "Promise me you'll keep

your eyes open and not leap blindly into anything," she pleaded.

Rather than take her seriously, Hildy laughed again. "Oh, Wyn," she admonished. "You are such a dear. But there is no reason for you to fret over me. I'm well able to take care of myself."

If only she could believe that, Wyn thought. But she couldn't.

"Join me for a walk along the promenade deck," she urged. "It's a lovely evening."

"It's cold and damp and the wind is blowing," Hildy countered. "You go ahead, but before you do, would you unhook me?"

The moment the dark figure slipped through the hatchway onto deck, Garrett breathed a sigh of relief. He'd been waiting for over an hour now, sure that Wyn Abbot would not be able to resist the lure of the sea any more than he could.

She was cloaked from head to foot, a hood drawn up to hide her pale hair. In the dark she blended with other shadows that flickered to life in the dancing glare of a single lantern. He himself had taken care to stay out of the meager circle of light, preferring to linger in the deeper shadows, invisible to any who came along. Or relatively so. If she had arrived a minute earlier she would have seen him, spotted the glow of his cigarette in the night as he took a final drag on it. The butt had sailed like a small shooting star over the rail only seconds ago, caught by the brisk wind that had sprung up to starboard, and he had returned to anonymity in the dark.

Few had ventured forth that evening. As the games in the card room broke up, a couple of men had sought the deck, indulging in a last smoke before retiring. A few women had peered from the companionway then scuttled back, away from the chilling bite of the North Atlantic night.

It was cold. Damn cold. He'd turned the collar of his

dinner jacket up and kept his hands buried in his trouser
pockets for most of his vigil. Now that she had appeared,
his thoughts had warmed decidedly and he no longer felt
uncomfortable.

Neither, apparently, did Wyn.

Wyn.

Garrett grinned to himself. He liked her pet name. It
was a taunt, challenging him to do just that—win her. And
win her he would.

Oblivious to his presence, she moved slowly toward the
rail, the fabric of her cloak and skirt molded to her long,
slender limbs by the building fury of the wind. Garrett
enjoyed the tightening of his own body in response to the
blatant display of her hitherto hidden charms. He fought
back the desire that rose in him to rush to her side. Delaying instead, he feasted on the simple sight of her at the
rail, allowing Wyn a few brief moments of the solitude
she sought.

Earlier the sky had been studded with a million stars
but, along with the wind, clouds had begun to arrive, veiling the bright spots of light. The sea had grown choppier,
too, but not enough to send him back to the lush cabin he
despised. Garrett wished, not for the first time, that Galloway would trade cabins with him, taking the ostentatious
grandeur in exchange for the modest stateroom Deegan
had booked for himself. Dig had been adamant. As much
as Garrett hated the reminder, he was now the head of his
family and needed to adjust to his new role long before
they arrived at the gates of Hawk's Run. The elaborate,
spacious suite was the stage upon which he must accustom
himself to perform from now on.

He wasn't a peer tonight though. He was a man in pursuit of a woman. The most intriguing woman he had yet
to meet.

The wind tore at her hood, pushing it back as she stared
up at the nearly hidden stars. Long strands of hair, pale as
moonlight, whipped from their bonds to perform a primitive dance of their own making. Wyn brushed back a ten-

dril that blinded her briefly. Garrett thought she smiled softly as she did so. Was she, like he, remembering their encounter earlier that day?

The memory alone was enough to set him on the course he had chosen when she had flown from the dining table. Her excuse had been flimsy, trumped-up, blatantly false. He knew it wasn't an evening of cards she was avoiding, but him. And he wanted to know why.

But not until he had held her in his arms, kissed her. Proven to himself, and to her, that she wasn't as unaffected by him as she had tried to appear.

A fresh gust snatched the edge of her cloak back, making it flare behind her like a giant wing unfurled. Garrett snagged the fabric and drew it snugly around her as he stepped near.

She glanced up at him, startled by his sudden appearance. "Oh, good evening, my lord."

"Garrett," he said. "Remember?"

"I recall only that you requested I call you that, not that I agreed to do so," she admonished lightly.

Her nearness made him feel reckless, more so than he ever had during his wandering the past two years. But then, time was running out for him.

Garrett slipped his arm around her waist and drew her close. "Do so now," he urged huskily. "Because I have every intention of calling you Wyn."

"And I suppose there is nothing I can do to stop you?" she asked, pushing a wayward lock of wind-whipped hair away from her face. It returned, as if drawn to the softness of her lips.

As was he.

Garrett stroked the curve of her cheek with the back of his fingers, traced the path the strand of gold forged along the contours of her mouth. "Nothing," he said, and tipped her face up to his. When his lips covered hers, Wyn leaned into him, shivered slightly, her lips breaking with his after only a brief touch but lingering so near her breath was a caress in itself.

"Garrett," she murmured. "We shouldn't be doing this."

"I've wanted to do just this," he whispered. "And this." His lips feathered across her eyes.

Wyn sighed with pleasure. "And this," she said, her mouth gliding to his again for a slightly longer kiss. She pulled away far too soon to suit him. "We should fight it though," she insisted. "It isn't right to—"

He swallowed her halfhearted protest, slanting his lips over hers, deepening the caress until her lips parted, tempting him to make the kiss even more intimate.

Garrett groaned with longing. Slid one hand up her spine to bury it in her streaming hair, supporting her head as she tilted it back even further, her body melting against his.

"Wyn," he said. "Wyn."

As if the sound of her own name had broken the spell, Wyn pulled back, pressing her hands flat against his chest to separate their bodies by inches of space. "No, this is insane," she insisted, gasping for breath.

"It bloody well is," he agreed. "Wonderfully insane. Come back with me to my cabin where we can continue this in comfort."

Wyn shivered. Garrett wasn't sure if it was with pleasure over his suggestion or because the wind showed every sign of turning into a veritable tempest. Either way, he enfolded her, holding her a captive within her cloak, his arms providing warmth. "You're cold," he said. "The sooner we get inside, the better. The gale is rising and—"

Wyn chuckled softly. "A gale? You mean Trident's breath? This is minor."

It wouldn't be for long, Garrett knew. "Still, my breath is much warmer," he said, set to cajole her into his bunk. "As are my hands. My lips." He kissed her again, slowly, thoroughly, this time allowing his tongue to steal past her lips. The hands that had pushed him away turned to grip the lapels of his coat as she clung to him. When her tongue met his timidly, then more boldly, Garrett forgot the danger of the building storm and lost himself in the sensation.

Again, it was Wyn who regained her senses first. She broke free of his arms, putting five feet of decking between them this time. She was breathing heavily, he noted, although he could barely hear her gasps over the sound of his own and the wail of the rising wind. It grabbed her cloak once more, whipping it high and nearly free behind her.

"We can't do this. Must forget it ever happened," she insisted, her breathing still labored.

"Forget it? The bloody hell I can forget it." He took one long stride and reached for her.

Wyn slipped away. "We have to," she said. "Have to make sure it never happens again."

"Wyn!"

She evaded him, taking running steps back into the glow of lantern light. She turned as she pulled open the hatch, looking back at him over her shoulder, sorrow and regret clear to read in her eyes. "It can't," she said. "It can't."

Before he could stop her or ask for an explanation, Wyn was gone, slipping through the hatch, headed back to the safety of her stateroom, leaving him alone with the increasing whine of the wind and the echo of longing he'd heard in her voice.

Chapter Six

The *Nereid* had steamed from the stormy seas by dawn. Wyn nearly regretted the efficiency of coal power since she no longer had the excuse of bad weather to keep to her cabin. The day was still overcast, the gray skies smoother versions of the gunmetal gray waves. It was only while standing at the taffrail that the scene varied, for the speed of the liner kicked up a wake of churning white water.

Wyn resisted the urge to linger. It was all too likely that Garrett would look for her at the rail and, after the wanton way she had acted the evening before, Wyn didn't think they could treat each other as chance-met companions.

Perhaps they never had been that. Even at their first meeting, there had been a promise of intimacy between them. Now they had taken a step closer to being lovers and she still knew nothing about him. Furthermore, she suspected that what she *had* heard about him was untrue, that he was a player playing a part.

Crewmen from the galley arrived with buckets of scraps, the remains of the elaborate breakfast buffet enjoyed by the luxury-class passengers. More passengers drifted to the taffrail to watch as the garbage was tipped over the side, immediately drawing the fish that schooled around the ship to the feast.

Wyn eased out of the crowd, turning away from the sight of frenzied feeding, and found herself nearly in Deegan Galloway's arms.

"Wyn!" he greeted, his hands gripping her upper arms lightly. "I was hoping to run into you."

He was dashingly handsome with the breeze stirring his tawny side-whiskers and his soft brown eyes glowing as he looked down at her. The newly grown mustache made him appear even more rakish than she had thought him in San Francisco. Unlike the other men, rather than wear a boater or derby, his fair hair was uncovered, subject to the caprices of the wind. His frock coat and trousers were a pale buff color and immaculate, his westkit a pattern of brown stripes. The whole turnout was clearly the creation of a master tailor. Deegan's shoulders had always been broad, his form pleasingly masculine, but there was something different in the way he carried himself now. Something that had nothing to do with keeping his balance at sea. There was a new dignity about Deegan Galloway.

Her heart did not lighten at his appearance but tightened with resentment. She had been so close to making a mistake over him. So ready to believe that her future lay with him.

Wyn waited coolly until Deegan dropped his hands away from her person. "I can't say I was hoping to run into you, Mr. Galloway."

He shivered theatrically. "Brrr. And I thought the wind was freezing last night."

Wyn slipped around him, striding away as quickly as her narrow skirts allowed, the chocolate brown dyed ostrich plume in her English straw hat dipping and dodging with each step she took. She wished she had chosen a different ensemble, but the tan Norfolk jacket and deep brown silk pleated and tied-back skirt had always been one of her favorite costumes. It was ill fate that made it appear that she had dressed in complement to Deegan's clothing.

His long legs quickly ate the distance she tried to maintain between them. "I know I deserve your contempt," he wheedled, falling into step at her side, "but it's a small ship…"

It was 532 feet long and 52 feet wide. Graced by three funnels, the *Nereid* also carried over an acre of auxiliary sail on her three masts. With officers and crew of nearly two hundred, first-class accommodations for 450 and 600 third class, the vessel was anything but small.

"…and we can't help but run into each other often, especially since we've both been honored by the captain's invitation at meals," Deegan finished.

Wyn stared straight ahead, refusing to look at him. "A gentleman would make an excuse and find a different table rather than continue to harass a lady who has shown she no longer requires his attendance."

"I never claimed to be a gentleman, Wyn. I thought that's what you liked about me," Deegan said.

It had been. Once.

"So," he continued, "you can't expect me to simply fade into the woodwork."

"Far be it from me to expect such a thing," Wyn snapped waspishly. "After all, you and your friend are on his ship to make your fortune, aren't you?" She stopped walking and turned on him. "Why not simply say what you mean, Deegan? You don't want me to warn Miss Carillo's family, or any of the other wealthy passengers about you and your phoney baron."

"Warn them?" He irritated her by smiling, clearly amused by her reading of the situation. "Warn them about what, Wyn?"

"About what!" she gasped. "About your mercenary intentions, that's what. Do you really believe I can sit by and watch a sweet child like Suzanne Carillo fall in love with you?"

Deegan's grin widened. "That, my dear, sounds suspiciously like you're jealous."

If they'd been alone, Wyn knew she would have struck him again. Bother the fact that her hand would sting. It

would give her even more satisfaction than slapping his face had a few months earlier.

"And it sounds to me as if you need to drop sail on that wind-filled ego of yours," she countered.

His lips continued to curl in a teasing manner. "You know, there is one way to insure that I don't steal little Suzanne's heart. You could—"

Wyn spun on her heel and strode angrily away.

Deegan jogged after her. "I was kidding, Wyn. Honestly. I know how you feel about me. I know I ruined any chance of winning you. I just wish you could forgive me enough that we can at least *seem* friendly during the voyage."

"Friendly!" Wyn nearly strangled on the word. She lengthened her stride.

"Pretend to be," he said, keeping pace easily. "It's only for a week. After that, you'll never see me again."

"I thought that before," she reminded him, "and look where we are now. But I suppose *that* bit of fate can be laid at Pierce's feet, can't it."

"Just because he's a friend of mine? It's the reason I chose a Shire ship."

"No!" Wyn glared at him. "Because he put you up to this. Told you I would be aboard the *Nereid*. Told you to press your suit again."

Deegan looked puzzled. "Why would he do that?"

Why did men continually do things guaranteed to bring women to the point of physical violence? Wyn wondered. "Because of his bet," she said between tightly gritted teeth.

The stunned expression on Deegan's face lasted only a few seconds before dissolving into one of laughter. "He actually bet that I would wed you?"

Her tone rivaling the chill of an iceberg, Wyn kept her eyes focused on the bow of the ship. "You find that funny?"

"Only that Pierce thought my success was such a sure

thing," Deegan admitted. "If only I'd known, I could have saved us both a lot of trouble."

"Trouble," she repeated. "Is that all it was? Trouble? You broke Leonore's heart, ruined our friendship—"

"I broke Leonore's heart but not your own, Wyn?"

She let the observation lie unanswered between them. "As I was saying," she continued, "you ruined my friendship with Leonore and—"

He interrupted again. "You were never more than nodding acquaintances. Why do you think I thought you'd never find out about her? She was my ace in the hole. I was that unsure of my chances with you."

Farther along the promenade deck, Wyn spotted the all too familiar form of Garrett Blackhawk leaning on the rail. As she watched, Hildy slipped from the warmth of the companionway and buzzed with the single-mindedness of a honeybee directly to his side.

Wyn pulled open the nearest hatch, determined not to be a spectator to her friend's wanton forwardness.

Or watch jealously as Garrett smiled lazily down into Hildy's lovely deep blue eyes.

Deegan held the hatchway open, waiting for Wyn to precede him into the dim interior of the ship. "Can we put the past behind us, Wyn?" he asked softly.

Unsure as to whether the hurt she was feeling was solely due to Deegan's actions in San Francisco, or fueled by this new, unwelcome awareness of Garrett Blackhawk, Wyn found herself helpless to fight back emotion.

She paused a foot inside the passageway, resentment washing over her unchecked. She could feel Deegan at her back, the remembered heat of his body only inches from hers. It had been early spring when they met. The company had been select that night, an evening of dancing and cards in the home of a Nob Hill neighbor. As always, she had chosen cards over dancing but after she and her partner triumphed over Deegan and his at whist, Galloway had asked her to favor him with a dance in compensation. The strains of a waltz enveloping her and Deegan smiling down at her in his arms had nearly made Wyn forget cards altogether.

His courtship had been heady after that night, the pace fast, frantic, fascinating. She had surrendered to the thrill of it, not only looking forward to his kisses but looking for opportunities when they could steal away at a party, be alone together, be in love.

What a fool she had been. How blind.

"No, we can't, Deegan," she said wearily. "You were despicable then, and you are now. And, if you so much as look like you are playing up to Miss Carillo or any of the other wealthy women aboard, I will most certainly make it a point to tell them exactly the kind of man you are."

He stiffened. "I'm not looking for a rich wife on this voyage."

She wasn't to be deterred. "Helping your friend the baron find one then," she countered.

"Don't pile my failings at his door, Wyn."

"Why not?" she demanded, glaring up at him. "Aren't you both cut from the same cloth? Tell him my warning goes for him, too, Deegan. I can't countenance either of you using a Shire ship as your personal hunting ground."

"Bad for business, is it?" he quipped. He wasn't entirely successful in wiping all traces of resentment from his voice. She was glad he wasn't as adept an actor as Blackhawk appeared to be. Perhaps he really had cared for her once.

"Please, Deegan. Don't joke about this. I'm deadly serious," she said.

"As am I, Miss Abbot," he answered stiffly. "As am I."

Garrett found Deegan alone in the smoking room, nursing, in lieu of luncheon, a bottle of the Shire Line's best Irish whiskey. Rather than interrupt his friend's reverie, a decidedly unhappy one judging by his glum expression, Garrett helped himself to a tumbler from behind the bar and fished out his pouch of tobacco and cigarette papers.

It wasn't until he'd rolled two smokes and helped himself to a healthy swig of alcohol that Deegan appeared to notice he was no longer alone.

"You're missing a free meal," Deegan said.

"Considering the price I paid for those echoing staterooms, it is doubtful if the word *free* applies to anything on this trip. See it rather as my poor attempt to evade the persistent Mrs. Hartleby," Garrett drawled. He offered Deegan a cigarette and availed himself of the tinderbox on the table between them.

Rather than light his own cigarette, Deegan tipped more whiskey in his glass and swallowed a good measure of it. "She despises me," he said.

"Pretty little Miss Carillo?"

"Wyn."

"Wyn," Garrett repeated. He closed his eyes, pressing thumb and forefinger to massage the bridge of his nose as he sank lower in the armchair. "I had assumed you knew her through her brother, but that's not quite right, is it."

"No," Deegan admitted. "In fact, I had to lie in wait for her brother Pierce at his favorite gambling club to strike up a friendship. I needed an excuse to be at the same entertainments she was and being his boon companion afforded me the opportunity."

Garrett could guess what came next. "You fell in love with her."

Deegan grinned wryly. "With her fortune at any rate. I wasn't alone in that."

"Having met her, I can bet the competition was sharp," Garrett said.

"It was that. If only I had been patient, I might actually have swept her to the altar. But I panicked and made a mistake." Deegan finished off his glass of whiskey and reached for the bottle.

"The bloody hell," Garrett groaned. "She's the goddess?"

Deegan put the whiskey bottle down. "Is that what I

called her? Hell, I must have been even more drunk than
I am now.''

''You weren't,'' Garrett said, and moved the whiskey
out of his friend's reach. Deegan didn't appear to notice.
''And now she despises you. Wouldn't you say that was
a logical progression?''

''She thinks I'm on this ship to find my next victim,''
Deegan mumbled as he placed the cigarette between his
lips and reached for the box of matches. Striking a lucifer,
he let the flame draw toward the tobacco as he inhaled
deeply. Garrett doubted Deegan took much pleasure from
the cigarette. He seemed to be moving by rote rather than
by reason.

''She thinks you are doing the same,'' Deegan added,
letting the smoke stream slowly from his lungs.

Garrett drew deeply on his own cigarette. ''Interesting,''
he mused. ''What have I done to merit the label of fortune
hunter?''

Deegan shook his head slightly. ''I'm not sure. She
thinks you aren't a real lord, either.''

''Does she.'' Garrett mused on the idea, uncommonly
pleased with Deegan's news. ''And, tell me, Dig. How do
you feel about the lady?''

Deegan exhaled a fresh cloud of smoke. ''I told you
back in Frisco,'' he said. ''She's not for me. Why?''

Garrett ground out his cigarette and stretched his legs in
front of him, digging his heels into the darkly patterned
weave of the Oriental rug. Elbows on the padded arms of
his chair, he slumped down into the cushions. ''Oh, no
particular reason,'' he said, a slight smile playing at the
corners of his mouth. ''But it appears Miss Winona Abbot
needs to learn not to leap to conclusions. And I do believe
I'm just the chap to teach her.''

Wyn spent her afternoon in the ladies' saloon, enduring
the chatter of the women over the card table. Given the
choice of running into either Garrett or Deegan on deck,
she had resigned herself to whist with the ladies.

The room itself had been decorated to appeal to the feminine eye. Or at least a man's idea of what appealed to a woman. Rather than the dark paneling found in the men's smoking room, the bulkheads here were covered in delicately patterned silk featuring dusky roses and soft blue morning glories against a pale pink background. The rugs continued the rose and tendril patterns, enlarging upon them and deepening the color. Islands of comfort had been created with circular sofas built around ceiling supports. Gas lamps shaped to resemble a morning glory's trumpet supplied a warm glow in dark corners. To spread natural light in the wide cabin, mirrors were placed where they could best catch and reflect the endless sky as seen through curtained portholes.

There were only a few tables for cards, but it appeared that the majority of women gathered in the saloon simply to gossip as they worked erratically on embroidery, tatting or knitting.

Mrs. Carillo was one of the few who fancied cards, but not above gossip, Wyn soon learned.

A single hand of cards was dealt and played before Wyn's partner, a shallow-faced, indifferent player, leaned toward Mrs. Carillo. "My dear lady," she gushed, "you can not keep us in suspense any longer. Tell us all you know about your mysterious partner at dinner."

Considering that Hortense Carillo commanded the chair near the foot of the table, her *partners* at the table were the ship's doctor and her husband. It took Wyn a moment to realize Mrs. Carillo's friend meant neither of these two.

Mrs. Carillo dealt out thirteen cards to each player, pretending to concentrate on the game. "I don't know who you mean, Trudy Woodrow," she insisted before raising her eyes to the table at large, "unless you are referring to his lordship."

"I understand he's only recently come into the title," Mrs. Carillo's partner submitted. "Did you tell us what the trump suit is, Hortense?"

"Hearts," Mrs. Carillo said.

"How appropriate," Trudy declared, and sighed theatrically. "I swear, if I wasn't married to Mr. Woodrow, my own heart would flutter like a hummingbird's wings just being near the baron."

"I would watch your sweet Suzanne around the man, Hortense," Mrs. Carillo's partner advised. "She is at such a susceptible age."

"Oh, but he has such a romantic past," Trudy insisted. "A girl can't help but be attracted by it, isn't that so, Miss Abbot?"

Wyn chose a card from her hand and led the play. "I really wouldn't know, Mrs. Woodrow."

"Clubs!" the woman on Wyn's left exclaimed in disgust. "Oh, you leave me no option, Miss Abbot. I must trump you already at this point." She'd barely played her card before turning back to Wyn's partner. "I must admit, the baron is quite an attractive man. But so is his secretary, that dashing Mr. Galloway."

"Fiddle," Trudy said, snapping down a six of diamonds.

Wyn foresaw an endless afternoon of very indifferent play and wished she had not stubbornly stayed away from the card room the evening before.

"What woman would fall in love with a mere secretary when his wealthy and handsome employer is at hand?" Trudy continued.

"Not I," the woman on Wyn's left declared. "Do you know, I heard that the baron paid for his suite in cash?"

"No!" Trudy gasped. "But the cost of his rooms must have been enormous."

Wyn knew to a penny what the luxurious suite had cost Blackhawk. The fact that he had paid in cash reinforced her belief that he was in search of a rich wife. Her experience with fortune hunters had shown that men like Deegan and Garrett used windfalls from a run of luck at the card tables to buy themselves into a setting more conducive to deceiving a prospective bride's guardians. The truly wealthy arranged their travel through agents who used bank drafts rather than cash.

"As Mr. Carillo tells it, the baron can well afford to buy the ship if he wishes," Hortense Carillo announced. "He has a Midas touch, they say. No matter what he invests in, profits follow."

"I heard he owns diamond mines in Brazil."

"Nonsense." Mrs. Carillo snorted in derision. "I don't believe they have diamond mines in Brazil."

"Fought a duel with a duke over a faithless duchess..."

"My dear!"

"Was wounded by bandits while laying rail lines in Mexico and saved a sheik's life in the Arabian desert!"

Wyn's mind drifted as the women gossiped. Her attention didn't need to be on the cards. She doubted if anyone was paying attention to their play. When a trick was won, it was purely by accident.

Surely, she thought, no one could possibly believe the tales that were told about Garrett. They were all too improbable. No man in his right mind went seeking danger, and, if the stories about him had even a grain of truth in them, that was exactly what he had done. The bored aristocrat who had sat opposite her at dinner hardly appeared the man to risk his life in pursuit of adventure. Even as he had related them, Wyn had doubted the authenticity of his tales.

But that man was a different one from the man who stole her breath away with his reckless kisses. And yet, they were one and the same.

"You are so quiet, Miss Abbot," Trudy Woodrow admonished as Mrs. Carillo's partner swept up the final trick. "Surely you have an opinion to contribute when it comes to our notorious baron."

Wyn gave her a weak smile. "I'm afraid I haven't been attending to the conversation. I have a touch of headache and..."

Baron Blackhawk as a subject for discussion was dropped immediately as home remedies were hastily offered. Wyn took the opportunity to escape the saloon, promising to try each recipe in turn. But rather than return to her stateroom, she fled up the nearest companionway bound for the highest point on the ship.

Captain Kittrick beamed at Garrett as he guided him around the narrow confines of the wheelhouse. "I know it is difficult to believe," Kittrick said, "but the *Nereid* can do seventeen knots or better."

"Or better," Garrett murmured, forcing himself to sound impressed. He was far more interested in keeping Wyn Abbot in sight. He'd had the fortune to glimpse her flight earlier and had followed at a distance. Her trail had led him straight into the captain's clutches.

"We're making wonderful time," Kittrick announced. "Seeing the wind was in our quarter, I've had the sails raised, you see, to augment the engines."

At the rail that encircled the narrow deck around the wheelhouse, Wyn had her eyes lifted toward the billowing sails. She had removed the feathery concoction that had adorned her fair locks earlier, grasping the flimsy hat between her hands as she communed with Neptune.

"Lovely young woman, isn't she?" Kittrick said, dropping his voice so as not to be overheard by those members of his crew who shared the narrow cabin with them. "Don't blame you for dogging her footsteps, Baron. Not in the least. Would myself if I was younger and didn't have the ship to see to. Doubt if she'd have me, though. As I hear it, the lady has turned down scores of suitors over the years."

"Has she?" Garrett asked lightly. "No doubt she has her reasons."

"Keeps them to herself, then," Kittrick said. "Still, a man can't help but admire her. Not only because she's a beauty, but because she isn't in the normal run of things, woman wise, if you get my drift. I mean, how many ladies are willing to let the wind tangle their hair like that?"

Few, Garrett admitted to himself. Watching the long

strands that had torn free of her hairpins, he itched to capture them, crush the sweet-smelling locks in his hand, smooth them back into place before drawing her near.

She would come, too. Willingly as she had done the evening before. If she thought him a fortune hunter today, she had no doubt thought him one when she returned his kiss last night. She had fled because she feared herself far more than she did him.

It wouldn't do to allow Kittrick to read even a hint of his thoughts though. With an effort, Garrett turned away from the enticing sight of Wyn at the rail. "I didn't realize passengers were welcome to roam this section of the ship," he said.

"They aren't," the captain said, and chuckled. "But Miss Abbot is an exception. As are you, my lord. At least, at this moment. Why do you think I headed you off so quick, hey?"

Garrett gave his practiced, thin-lipped smile. "Quite," he murmured. "I've worn out my welcome now, have I?"

"Certainly not."

Having perfected the art of dissembling, Garrett knew a polite lie when he heard it. "I must be going at any rate," he announced, and lifted his pocket watch from his vest pocket. "As I thought. Nearly time to dress for dinner. If you'll excuse me, Captain?"

Kittrick waved him off, but didn't wait to make certain he'd left the wheelhouse area before sending a crew member out to recall Wyn from her solitary reverie. Garrett slipped down the companionway, taking a moment to scout out his surroundings. A row of closed hatches stretched away from him, clearly officers' quarters. Silently Garrett turned the handle of the first one.

It hadn't helped, Wyn admitted to herself. Trident had failed her. There had been no lifting of her spirits as the salt-scented breeze whipped at her cheeks. No cleansing away of Garrett Blackhawk's face from her mind. Or of his touch from her memory.

Notorious, the women had termed him. He was no doubt that, but in which of his roles? She had met him barely twenty-four hours ago and already knew him to be an actor, and therefore, a man who lived a lie.

And yet she could not stop thinking about him. Could still fancy the taste of him on her lips.

The ladder to the wheelhouse was steep, but Wyn refused the aid of the blushing crew member the captain had sent to escort her to the main deck. She sent him back to his post before lifting her narrow skirts with one hand, and descending slowly.

Compared to the rest of the ship, this section was quiet. The whisper of her skirts sounded loud in the lonely corridor. Wyn took a handful of steps along it before sensing that she was no longer alone.

"Good afternoon, Miss Abbot," Blackhawk greeted as she turned to face him. His deep voice thrummed through her as thoroughly as the steam engine thrummed the decks. "If I didn't know better, I'd think you had just spent an hour dallying with a lover." When she didn't answer, he gestured to her falling, tangled hair. "But I do know better."

"The wind," she said.

"As you say," he murmured. "The wind. A cruel lover, the wind. It has burned your cheek."

As if mesmerized, Wyn stood rooted to the spot. "It has?"

Garrett stepped nearer until he was standing so close she fancied she could hear the beat of his heart. He brushed the curve of her cheek with the backs of his fingers, the movement feather light along the contours. "Come," he urged. "I'll show you."

She was helpless to do otherwise. Or so it seemed. Perhaps the hours she had spent thinking of him had conjured his presence now. If not, they had certainly drained her of the will to resist either his cajoling tone or the warm, glowing look in his eyes.

She had thought he would lead her back to the deck,

escort her to her stateroom. Or his. Instead he drew open
the nearest hatchway and ushered her into the narrow confines of one of the officers' cabins. Wyn's gaze went directly to the built-in bunk.

"You're fortunate," Garrett said. "The fellow who
lives here is vain enough to own a mirror."

"A mirror?"

"Turn around," he urged, and placed his hands on her
shoulders to guide her. "See? A bit too bright for a chaste
young woman, wouldn't you say?" Again he brushed his
fingers lightly along the windburned redness of her cheek.

Wyn watched him in the mirror, watched as he continued the caress down along her jaw, along the high, tight
collar of her jacket. Her hands tightened on the brim of
her discarded hat, crushing the straw.

Garrett lifted one tangled lock of her hair and rubbed it
between his fingers. "Personally, I like you this way," he
said. "But I would make one improvement."

"And what would it be?" Wyn asked, her voice barely
audible.

He met her eyes in the mirror. "If Neptune were a decent lover, he wouldn't have overlooked these." Using her
captured strand of hair, he brushed the end of it over her
lips.

Although she was sure she was hardly breathing, Wyn's
mouth went dry. "And how should Neptune have treated
them?"

"Tenderly," Garrett said. "Passionately."

The sight of his sun-darkened hand against her paler
skin was erotic. His touch was intoxicating. Barely aware
of the consequences of her request, Wyn let the tip of her
tongue dampen the full rise of her bottom lip. "Show me,"
she whispered.

He was in no hurry. Once more he guided her, his hands
at her waist this time as he turned her to face him. When
his head dipped toward hers, her crushed hat fluttered free
and forgotten from her hand to the floor. She closed the

gap between their bodies, slipping her arms around his neck and her fingers into the glossy sable of his hair.

"First, tenderly," Garrett murmured, his lips touching hers, moving along them in a sensuous glide.

"And then?" Wyn asked, her voice little more than a breathless sigh.

"And then," Garrett said. In an instant the sweetness of his kiss changed, caught fire, searing more than just her lips. And, as if she were nothing more than a candle brought too close to his flame, Wyn felt herself melting against him in an unconscious request for more.

"Ah, Wyn," he rasped. "Beautiful, beautiful Wyn."

"Don't talk," she murmured, reveling in the sensations his touch brought flaming to life. "Just kiss me."

"Gladly." But he did so only briefly before drawing back to smile down into her face. Hands cupping her wind-reddened cheeks, he let the pads of his thumbs slide over her now-swollen lips. "Now you look thoroughly compromised," he said softly.

The choice of words was as effective as a drenching by an icy North Atlantic wave. Wyn turned to stone in his arms. Her hands dropped away from him.

"So that is what this is all about."

His expression alone told her he realized he'd made a mistake. "I only meant that the picture is complete."

"That I now look as if I'd spent the afternoon with a lover?"

She'd nearly done just that, Wyn realized. If he had continued to kiss her, she wouldn't have had the will to resist if he'd carried her to the bed.

"That is what you implied earlier, isn't it?" she demanded.

When he didn't answer, she pushed away from him and bent quickly to retrieve her ruined hat. "I was wrong about you," Wyn said. "I knew you were a cad, but you're actually far worse."

Garrett leaned back against the bulkhead and folded his

arms across his chest. "I wasn't alone in this cabin," he reminded. "And I wasn't the only one enjoying myself."

Wyn could feel her cheeks burning, and doubted the brightness could be attributed to windburn alone. "Oh, you...you...scoundrel!" she flung at him. In a single motion she yanked the hatch opened. She wasn't sure, but she thought she heard Garrett's low chuckle follow her as she fled.

Chapter Seven

Garrett's laughter died along with the echo of Wyn's running footsteps in the corridor. He could almost taste the bitterness his burst of self-deprecating humor left on his tongue, it had been so overpowering.

He'd been brilliant. He'd planned to prove to her that she wanted him despite the prejudice she'd formed against him. And he had been successful. So bloody successful that, when she'd turned to liquid fire, he'd forgotten why he had hunted her, trapped her, and had stepped into the snare himself, loath to leave her.

The more he was with her, touched her, tasted her, the more she became his opium. She was heaven and she was hell. He wanted to put her from his mind, forget her. And yet he couldn't. He wanted to feel the satin texture of her skin beneath his fingertips, wanted to taste again the nectar of her mouth and the sweetness of her response. Needed to feel the passion that smoldered just beneath her ladylike exterior waiting, or so it seemed, for the tinder of his embrace.

Garrett ran a hand over his jaw and back to knead the suddenly stiff muscles at the nape of his neck. Oh, he'd been brilliant, all right. So much so that he had a feeling the person who'd been taught a lesson in the unknown officer's cabin that afternoon hadn't been Wyn Abbot.

* * *

Wyn dashed through the main door of her stateroom suite and leaned back against the panel, as if barricading it. Her heart pumped quickly, loudly, in her ears, a reminder of how caught up she had been. Or was it because she feared Garrett would follow her and further mesmerize her? She touched the puffy, sensitive curve of her lip, reliving the moment when her will had ceased to exist, leaving her with nothing more than the desire to stay pressed close to him, returning each kiss, each caress.

She had always prided herself on using common sense when alone with a suitor. Had always remained in control of the situation, and of herself. There had been stolen kisses in shadowed corners, in starlit gardens and in the sheltered seclusion of carriages.

None of them had been anything like the intoxicating moments she had spent in Garrett Blackhawk's arms.

Why was she acting this way? Hadn't she mistrusted him from their first meeting, recognizing that he was not what he appeared to be? Hadn't she planned to steer clear of him, not simply because she believed him to be of Deegan's ilk, but because Hildy had singled him out? Why was it that her mind reasoned out a logical course, then forgot all about it when he stood before her?

His smile was no more appealing than that of other men. Nor were his features more comely. Deegan's were far more attractive, as was his manner. But Blackhawk was a far more despicable man than Deegan had ever been, for, when pressed, Deegan had never professed to be anything more than a man in search of a wealthy wife. Garrett allowed everyone to believe he belonged to the privileged class, that he was rich beyond measure. She couldn't blame others for believing the sham. He was very convincing in the role. But the captain and their select group of passengers had not seen the man he really was. The one who loomed from the shadows to entice her senses. There was nothing of the bored aristocrat in that man, only the foolhardy recklessness of the born adventurer. The Garrett

Blackhawk who kissed her was a man who would dare anything simply for the thrill he derived from the exercise.

He belonged to a different era, one where new lands awaited discovery, pirates roamed the seas, and the choice of life or death ofttimes was dependent upon the strength and ability of a man's sword arm.

Garrett was out of place in the modern world. The wonders of science had destroyed the world of the swashbuckler. Vaccines now prevented epidemics. Mr. Bell's telephone made it possible to contact people around the city without leaving home or office, and the oceanic telegraph lines made it possible to contact people around the world nearly as quickly. Electricity was beginning to replace gas in the lighting of both homes and streets. And, just as the transcontinental railroad had replaced the sailing ship as the means of traveling from one coast of America to the other, now vessels with coal-fed, steam powered engines were replacing the majestic clipper ships as the means of reaching other continents.

Was it any wonder that Garrett Blackhawk assumed an actor's mask as he moved among those who belonged in this new world?

And was it simply the fact that he didn't belong in it that fascinated her so?

"Oh, dearest!" Hildy exclaimed, stepping from her stateroom into their shared sitting room. "Your complexion! What have you done to it?"

"My...?" It took a moment for Wyn to understand her friend's question. "Oh, the wind. I—"

"Don't tell me," Hildy urged. "I know you well enough to guess. You really don't have an ounce of sense at times, Winona Abbot."

Her mind still puzzling over the ill logic of her response to Garrett, Wyn was inclined to agree.

Hildy sailed across the room, the skirts of her scarlet dressing robe billowing behind her. The ways of society might force her to wear the somber shades of half mourn-

ing in public, but in private, Hildy had no intention of
conforming to such strictures.

No matter what her personal preference was, Hildy was
single-minded in her determination to present the proper
public picture. Clucking her tongue in disapproval, she
studied Wyn's burning cheeks and passion-bruised lips.
"A lady," she informed Wyn, "is supposed to know better
than remain out in the weather. You know how disastrous
the elements are to delicate skin."

"It's just a touch of windburn," Wyn said.

"A touch! Dearest, you haven't seen how chapped you
are. Why, if I did not know better, I would swear that you
had forgiven Deegan Galloway and enjoyed a secret tryst
with him."

Wyn felt more color flood her already reddened cheeks.
It had been exactly what she had done, only not with Deegan. She had, after all, enjoyed every touch, every caress,
every moment up until she'd realized Garrett had been
doing nothing more than playing yet another scene.

Hildy didn't appear to notice her blush. "I know you
couldn't have, though, for Mr. Galloway spent the day
secluded in that horrid smoking room," she confided.
"But, come with me. I think if we set to work immediately, we can disguise the worst of the damage with an
application of cream and a careful dusting of powder.
However, I would definitely advise you not to wear the
gown with the pink sarcenet netting this evening. Rather
than enchanting, I'm afraid the effect would be quite disastrous!"

Wyn wore her *terre-verte,* while Hildy donned her silver
gown, all the while bemoaning the loss of her diamonds
which, she was sure, would have been the pièce de résistance to her toilette. The simple silver locket and earrings
she wore in place of the Hartleby diamonds fell far short
of her expectations.

Wyn slipped the crystal bobs she'd worn the night before in her ears without a pang of regret. The matched set

of opals that had once complemented the watered deep green silk of her gown had been sacrificed to the altar of debts her brother had accumulated in building the *Nereid*. If all went well with the cruise, and those that would follow, she could always replace her jewels. Replace her whole wardrobe. Those things all lay in the nebulous future. In the much too immediate present she was far more concerned about coming face-to-face with Garrett at the dinner table, far too busy devising ways of avoiding him at the musical soiree the purser had planned for the passenger's enjoyment in the grand saloon later that evening.

She hated Garrett Blackhawk, Wyn told herself. He had bemused her senses, made her forget the vows she had made to herself, and then he had laughed when she realized that he was trying to maneuver her into an untenable position. Or what would have been an untenable position for any other woman. She was made of sterner stuff, Wyn knew. It would take more than being discovered alone with a man, in a flagrante delicto position, to feel that nothing short of marriage would protect her good name. More than one man had already attempted such a ploy, and, to his great disappointment, found his acceptance among the upper crust of San Francisco society gambled away instead. Garrett Blackhawk would find there were no longer opportunities to pursue such a goal. If the officer whose cabin he had appropriated had returned and discovered them, it would have been a matter of her word against Blackhawk's. The officer, if he valued his position with the Shire Line, would not have backed the blackguardly baron.

The difficulty now lay in discovering a member among the *Nereid*'s company who was not enamored of Blackhawk and his supposed position. Hildy, she knew, had every intention of clinging to Garrett. Deegan was his friend, and if the gossips had it right, Blackhawk's secretary, which, since Garrett was obviously not a real baron, was simply another of the untruths the two had foisted on the company. Miss Carillo had proven shy when he addressed her, but since she had also shown a preference for

Deegan's company, Wyn decided it was best to rule her out as a boon companion for the evening. Mrs. Carillo doted on Blackhawk, her husband was eager to pry information concerning investments from him, and Mr. Mosby had not yet overcome an adolescent tendency to see Garrett as some kind of romantic hero. Neither, she had to admit, had the captain, although his years far outdistanced those of young Mr. Mosby.

She would have to look farther than her own table for companionship then. But where?

When she and Hildy went in to dinner, Wyn paused a moment to scan the room. The other tables catered to larger numbers of guests than did the captain's board. Each was headed by either a ship's officer or an honored guest. Was there one among them she could count on to not fall under Blackhawk's spell?

Wyn's gaze flickered over one face after another, until she came to that of an unassuming man seated at a table in the far corner.

Garrett listened politely to the babble around him. The overzealous Mrs. Hartleby stood nearer to him than the crush of passengers and stewards necessitated, droning on about something. He paid her not the least bit of attention, although his stance appeared to indicate that he attended her every word.

He was far more interested in the puzzled expression on Wyn's lovely face. Rather than rush immediately to the table, she had paused just inside the entrance to the dining room, her eye caught by something—or someone.

He followed the direction of her glance and found nothing—no one—of particular interest. The passengers were busily taking their places in expectation of yet another feast, the men politely assisting the women. None showed the least interest in Wyn, although her gaze continued to linger on that particular sector of the room. As no one returned her look, Garrett was at a loss to know which guest had taken her fancy. It irked him to find he was studying each of the men in turn, evaluating them as potential rivals.

As if realizing that she had lingered too long, Wyn pretended to adjust the wrist loop that allowed her to lift the spilling fabric of her train out of harm's way as she moved through the crowd. Garrett watched her graceful approach, amused that she was careful not to look directly at him. Her attitude didn't surprise him. He knew from Deegan's experience, if nothing else, that the lady was very good at holding a grudge.

"Good evening, my dear," Captain Kittrick greeted, holding her chair for her. "Can we count on you to play us a little song or two this evening?"

While Wyn demurred, declaring herself an indifferent performer on the pianoforte, Garrett glanced back at the table that had held her interest.

And found himself looking directly into the face of a stranger.

The man in question covered his interest quickly, his gaze drifting almost leisurely to the huge portrait of the god Nereus on the bulkhead behind the captain's chair. Garrett wasn't deceived though. The fellow had pretended ignorance rather than meet Wyn's eyes earlier, but he was far from uninterested in what she did.

He wasn't rival material. Garrett guessed him to be in his early forties. His brown hair was cut in a common manner, as were his evening clothes. His face while far from handsome was equally far from downright ugly. It was a pleasant face, but so much like that of other men aboard, that Garrett took special note of each feature, so that he would know the fellow again, no matter what the circumstance.

"Ah, Miss Carillo," the captain murmured with evident pleasure. "Without insulting the other lovely ladies, I believe I can say without a doubt that you have quite put them in the shade this evening."

Garrett joined the company in politely complimenting the young woman on her looks, but his mind was caught up by something far more intriguing than little Suzanne's toilette. Why, he wanted to know, was Wyn Abbot under surveillance?

The pearls were a soft pink, perfectly matched, and spilled in twin strands over the girl's still-budding form. They mirrored her innocence, seemed to reflect the soft blush of her cheek.

They were too perfect to ignore, the thief decided.

Or perhaps it was simply that, as richly decorated as the ship was, the company itself was stiflingly stiff. To steal the pearls would stir things up. Make things exciting, dangerous, since everyone would be under suspicion.

This was nothing like it had been in San Francisco, or Boston, or any of the other cities in between. In the homes and various hotel rooms where other trinkets had been stealthily acquired, the police had tended to investigate the known criminal element of the city in their search for the perpetrator. They had never suspected the identity of the true hand to have plucked the gems from within their velvet nests.

The thief smiled softly, careful to conceal the reason for the amusement from those nearby. Where would the investigation begin once Miss Suzanne missed her pretty little baubles? Would the captain descend into the bowels of the ship to search the depressingly drab residents in steerage? Would he interrogate the members of his own crew? Would he have the courage to search the quarters—the persons—of those wealthy enough to rub shoulders with him each evening?

It was worth the chance of capture just to see what would happen. Well worth it.

Garrett stood with his back to the highly decorated bulkhead, feeling as if he were back in Mexico protecting his back from ambush. He had certainly avoided receiving a bullet in the back then, and now, although the chance of such a thing happening aboard the ocean liner was slim indeed, but he had not managed to avoid the ambush.

It was led by Mrs. Carillo, who bore down on him with a gaggle of her particular friends at her heels. "My dear Baron Blackhawk," she simpered. "I hope you don't mind, but I promised a few people that I would introduce them to you."

"Indeed," he said coolly. There was no reason he need make it easy for the woman to proceed. Besides, he decided, catching the knowing glance exchanged by two of her cohorts, his reputation had preceded him. They might thrill to tales of his exploits, but he was all the more intriguing because he snubbed nearly one and all.

What was it about Americans that made them decry the class system of the Old World, then worship at its shrine themselves?

Not all Americans, of course. Dig's manner toward him hadn't changed. When she finally realized that his title was real and not assumed, would Wyn's attitude change? Having been met at dinner with responses so frosty they rivaled those delivered by a royal duchess, Garrett didn't think it would. She was furious with him whether he was the scoundrel she believed him to be, or the peer he was in unfortunate truth.

"This is Mrs. Trudy Woodrow," Mrs. Carillo said, cutting, with an imperious wave of her hand, a path through her gathered friends down which the selected neophyte was to approach him.

"Your lordship," a thin, overdressed woman said, dipping in a rusty curtsy. "And this is my daughter."

There were always daughters.

Miss Woodrow was a younger, slightly plumper version of her mother, but her curtsy was more practiced. Probably, Garrett mused, because of her extreme youth. He doubted whether her skirts had been lengthened more than a month or so ago.

"Enchanted," he said, although not one of his listeners could possibly believe that he was.

Miss Woodrow blushed all the same. Her mother twittered excitedly. Garrett wondered how many times this episode would be retold to acquaintances. Would he remain a minor baron in the story or would his rank progress over the years until Miss Woodrow was an ancient crone reminiscing to grandchildren about the time a prince had said she was enchanting?

The ladies had only to consult with Wyn to know he fell far short of princely manners. Or those of a baron, for that matter.

"And this..." Mrs. Carillo began as she supplanted one set of females with another.

Garrett glanced over their heads in time to see Deegan and Suzanne Carillo approach the pianofore, the guests around them applauding encouragingly. Miss Carillo's father stood to the side, beaming proudly as Suzanne arranged her skirts on the plush bench cushion.

"Excuse me," Garrett said, interrupting. "I believe my friend Galloway is about to honor us with a song."

"Your friend? Oh, but I understood he was your secretary," Mrs. Woodrow said, and earned herself a glare from her patroness.

"Secretary?" Garrett snapped. "Nonsense. The man writes an atrocious hand." It took three long strides to free himself entirely of the women's clutches. Another handful to reach relative safety at the captain's side.

"Baron!" Kittrick greeted jovially. "So you managed to escape the hens, heh? Thought I'd have to send in the cavalry to get you out." He laughed. "It took a bit of convincing to get Mr. Galloway to sing for us. What will it take to convince you to do the same?"

"Something more than I wager you can deliver, Captain," Garrett said, turning to watch the performers. Miss Carillo's fingers fell lightly on the piano keys. She was a competent player but not out of the ordinary. Deegan waited patiently, one hand resting on the polished surface of the piano, prepared to turn the sheet music when his accompanist so requested.

"And what might that be?" Kittrick asked.

"You'd have to convince Miss Abbot to join me in a duet," Garrett said. "And considering the lady has taken me in dislike, I doubt she will agree."

"Shame," the captain murmured. "I'd guess you've got a fine voice. Not like my old foghorn one. Perhaps another evening then since Miss Abbot has retired for the night."

The murmur of conversation dropped as Miss Carillo touched the final chords of the introduction and Deegan's pleasant tenor rose above the sound of the piano. "'The years creep slowly by...'"

Kittrick sighed nostalgically. "'Lorena,'" he said, identifying the song. "Always one of my favorites. I don't mind telling you, sir, that there were times during the war when hearing these sweet strains brought a tear to my eye."

Garrett wasn't in the mood to hear tales of The War of Secession, though. "Miss Abbot is ill? Nothing serious, I hope."

"No, no. She assured me it was nothing more than having overtaxed herself earlier in the day. Although, if you want my opinion," Kittrick said, and leaned nearer, "I think it was feminine pique that sent her scurrying for her quarters. Understand that she and Galloway were next to leaping over the broomstick when she changed her mind. Don't think she cares to see the way the other ladies flutter around him." Kittrick grinned. "Women, in my experience, always want what they can't have. Or do until they've got it, hey?"

Not all women, Garrett thought. He had known Sybil all her life, girlhood to womanhood, and she had never been that way. And neither, if he was any judge of character, was Wyn.

If she had slipped away from the musical soiree, it was because she was avoiding him.

Or because she was meeting someone.

Deegan finished the first verse and sailed into the second. "'A hundred months have passed, Lorena, since last I held that hand in mine...'"

"Tell me, Captain," Garrett said, his voice pitched low so as not to disturb the pleasure of those attending to the sentimental song. "Who among your officers or crew is likely to know the identity of the majority of your passengers?"

"Tatterly," Kittrick answered. "Purser. The man never forgets a name and can put a face with every name he knows. Be lost without him, I can tell you."

"And just where can I find Mr. Tatterly?" Garrett asked.

Tatterly leaned back against the rail, one elbow hooked over the top, one heel anchored on the bottommost rung. The clipping speed of the ship created a breeze that tugged at the brim of his hat, but Tatterly was an old hand who knew how and when to turn his head to keep the cap in place. He inhaled deeply, appreciatively, on the cigarette Garrett had offered him, before answering the question that had accompanied the gift.

"Common-looking sort, you say, sir? That's not an easy man to tie down."

"The captain is sure you can help me," Garrett said, taking a long draw on his own cigarette. "He looks familiar and I would much rather I knew the chap's name so that I can place him before he takes offense and believes I've cut him on purpose."

"You, sir?" the purser murmured, enjoying another pull on his cigarette. "Not likely."

Tatterly obviously hadn't observed his *Baron Blackhawk* performance very closely, Garrett decided.

"All the same, Tatterly, I'd hate to sully a promising business deal because I inadvertently snubbed one of the partners. The man has brown hair, is around forty, and looks to be in fairly good physical shape compared to other men his age."

"And where was it you saw this man, sir?"

"In the dining room. He was seated at the far-most table under a particularly luscious-looking mermaid," Garrett said.

"Ah, yes. Her. She's a favorite with the crew. Well, that narrows things down quite a bit, sir. You must be thinking of Mr. Finley."

"Finley." The name didn't ring any bells, but then he hadn't expected it to, Garrett admitted. It was Wyn who had looked both puzzled and a bit disconcerted upon spotting the elusively ordinary Mr. Finley.

"Magnus Finley," Tatterly enlarged. "If you're worried about having insulted him, I don't think you need worry much, my lord. He's not a man of business himself."

Interesting. "Inherited wealth?" Garrett asked.

The purser chuckled. "Or so he'd like you to believe. But, no, he's probably no more pocket proud than I am."

"A gambler?"

"In a way, sir."

"In what way, Tatterly?"

The purser sucked in a lung full of smoke and let it out very slowly, clearly enjoying every drawn-out moment of the action. "It's like this, sir. He's after someone."

Despite his appearance, Mr. Finley was obviously not the average transatlantic traveler. "A bounty hunter?"

"No," Tatterly said slowly, no longer easy about answering questions. "Not exactly."

"A member of the police then," Garrett pressed. Although of which nation if such were the case? And why would Wyn recognize the man if he was?

The purser grimaced as if holding back the information hurt him physically.

Garrett took a final drag on his cigarette and sent the remaining stub sailing over the rail. "Like another?" he asked.

Tatterly appeared torn. He had admitted in accepting the cigarette that he had been too busy before sailing to restock his own supply of tobacco. He had smoked the cigarette

Garrett offered down until he nearly burned his fingers at the glowing tip.

Garrett pulled out his papers and bag of tobacco. Turning so that his back was to the wind, but his actions were in full view of the purser, he tapped a portion of cured leaf into a fold of paper.

Tatterly looked on longingly.

"And what exactly does Mr. Finley do for a living, Tatterly?" Garrett asked before sealing the cigarette.

The purser hadn't answered by the time he had lit it. He hadn't wanted the smoke, but Tatterly most definitely had.

Garrett exhaled slowly, making sure that the cigarette smoke wafted around the purser's head before being snatched away in the wake of the ship's speed. "Tatterly?"

As the purser's resolve broke, Garrett tossed him the pouch of tobacco.

Chapter Eight

Wyn waited in the dark for what seemed like hours. The unfamiliar cabin was small, compact, and smelled faintly of hair oil and damp wool. Other than the shapeless dark coat that hung on a hook to the right of the entry hatch, there were very few personal items to be found. Although her search had been brief, and accomplished during the all too short life of the match she had struck, Wyn hadn't noted the usual belongings that passengers left out: discarded hats, hairbrushes, books, letters. She wasn't sure what she had hoped to find. Something to prove that she was right about the identity of the man at the far table, perhaps.

The sounds of passengers returning to their cabins assured Wyn that she would soon have the answer she sought. All it took was patience. And courage.

It wasn't surprising that she had failed to notice Magnus Finley the day before, Wyn told herself. He was a man who specialized in being anonymous. She had seen him only fleetingly in the past, exchanging a brief greeting as they passed in the hall when he came to report on the investigation he had done for her parents. How long ago had it been since the thefts at the Shire warehouse in San Francisco? Three years? Four?

What was he doing aboard the *Nereid?* If there was the

smallest hint of danger to the passengers, she needed to
know. It was her ship as much as it was Pierce's. More so
since her entire future was dependent upon the liner's success. If the *Nereid*'s reputation was sullied on her maiden
voyage to the extent that it was perceived as being a *bad
luck* ship, there would be little call for the liner to ever put
to sea again. There was no one more superstitious than a
man in the sailing trade, and finding a crew for a cursed
ship, much less passengers, would be a gigantic undertak-
ing. Although it would put a dent in his income, grounding
the *Nereid* wouldn't bankrupt Pierce, for he still had a
dozen or more ships doing business. She, however, didn't.
And, Wyn admitted to herself, although it had seemed like
a wonderful idea to liquidate everything she owned and
invest the money in the steam liner, she had not done so
entirely to tie up her inheritance. She wanted to make a
profit from it.

Now if only Magnus Finley would return to his cabin,
she could—

Wyn froze in her place. One set of footsteps had not
passed on down the hall but had paused directly outside
of Finley's cabin.

Arrogance had its place, Garrett admitted. It had taken
only a single haughty glance on his part to dampen the
joie de vivre of the men and women who had gathered
around Deegan in the grand saloon. While some looked
perturbed that he was intent upon cutting Deegan out of
their midst, most looked relieved that Garrett intended to
leave the festivities himself.

It was more difficult to convince Deegan to leave the
party. For a man who touched spirits only upon occasion,
he had made fairly good headway into a bottle of whiskey
earlier, and had topped it off with a good deal of wine at
dinner. Although Deegan was steady on his feet, Garrett
doubted his friend was in top form.

As Garrett dragged him on deck, Deegan only stumbled
once, tripping over a deck chair someone had left unse-

cured. The brisk air of the Atlantic would, Garrett hoped, clear Dig's head enough to enable him to help search the ship. Garrett had done so himself already, but unsuccessfully.

"Something's up," Garrett announced. "Wyn Abbot's not in her cabin."

Deegan glanced back toward the sounds of laughter and music at the soiree. "Wasn't she...? No, now that you mention it, I didn't see her there."

"She told the captain she was under the weather."

Deegan snorted. "And he believed her?"

"Exactly," Garrett murmured, knowing that the true import of Wyn's lie would make an impression on Deegan. As it had on him.

Deegan frowned. "But she's not in her cabin? Maybe she just didn't want to answer when you knocked."

"I didn't knock."

Deegan's eyebrows rose in surprise. Garrett expected his friend to question his action since to the company at large he and Wyn appeared as only chance-met acquaintances. He wasn't sure he had an answer so he was relieved when Deegan followed a different line of questioning. If Dig wondered at his concern, the man was keeping his council over it at present.

"The door was unlocked?" Deegan asked.

"Hardly, but you know what a resourceful chap I am," Garrett said. "I simply let myself in."

Deegan ran a hand back through his hair, the nervous action showing that he was now as worried about Wyn's disappearance as was Garrett. "I never should have taught you that trick," he said.

"But, fortunately, you did. You know her better than I do, Dig. Where could she be?" Garrett demanded.

"Walking the deck?"

"I already thought of that and made the circuit twice. There wasn't a sign of her."

"Playing cards."

Garrett shook his head. "Ladies' saloon is dark and empty."

"Lord! If that's where you looked, you were in the wrong place," Deegan insisted. "Wyn hates playing with women. She doesn't mind cigar smoke, either. Did you check the—"

"Everywhere," Garrett insisted, cutting him off. "I'm afraid something has happened to her."

Deegan buried both hands in his hair, his growing fear for Wyn's safety visibly working to strip away the effects of his overindulgence with alcohol. "Like what?"

"I was hoping you'd have a suggestion," Garrett said. "There's a Pinkerton aboard, and he was—"

Deegan sat down abruptly on the deck chair. "An Eye? Holy Saint Patrick! What's one of them doing here?"

"Judging by his actions in the dining room earlier, I'd say he's keeping a close watch on our Miss Abbot," Garrett said.

"A bodyguard? But why?" Deegan demanded. "Are you sure he wasn't watching me instead? I'm seated right next to her and my past isn't exactly blameless."

"But *she's* the one missing," Garrett snapped. "Now, do you want to comb the aft deck and steerage or the bow and first class for her?"

The hatch swung open slowly, spilling light from the companionway into the cabin. Wyn stayed where she was in the stateroom's lone chair, a prickling of unease making her whole body tense. When the glow of light crept across the planking to touch the hem of her skirt, she barely dared to breathe.

A gleam of metal preceded the man. Then he was in the room and the hatchway was sealed once more, sending the cabin back into impenetrable darkness.

She had no idea where he was. Who he was. It had been impossible to get even a glimpse of him, the man had moved so quickly.

"Would you be so kind as to light the lamp?" he requested flatly.

The matches Wyn had brought with her lay in her lap. Still, she fumbled to find one, and successfully strike it.

"Miss Abbot," he said in surprise as the flame lit her face. "I must admit, you are the last person I expected to find in my cabin."

Wyn trimmed the lamp's flame down to soften the glow of light before turning to face him. She was sure of his identity now, although in the past his voice had sounded far more pleasant. "As you were the last person I expected to see aboard this ship, Mr. Finley," she said, and paused. "It is Magnus Finley, isn't it? Or are you using a different name this voyage?"

"I'm sure you know that I'm not, Miss Abbot." He smiled faintly and glanced down at the miniature pistol in his hand. "I don't suppose I need this anymore."

"No," Wyn murmured, relaxing only after he had pocketed the small derringer. "If I was the last person you expected to see, who did you think to find?"

He let the question hang between them. She wasn't really surprised that he chose not to give her a name. "How did you know this cabin was mine?" Finley asked.

When she merely cocked her head to the side as if considering whether to answer, the corners of his mouth tweaked higher. "Think of it as professional curiosity, Miss Abbot. I'm simply interested in learning how other detectives operate."

"Other detectives, Mr. Finley? I'm merely a concerned stockholder. Not having been informed that one of Mr. Pinkerton's operatives was aboard, I could not help but wonder if I should be worried," Wyn said.

"You haven't answered my question, and, if I recall my manners, the rule is 'ladies first.'" Finley gestured to the narrow bunk. "Do you mind if I sit?"

Wyn waved her permission impatiently. "Really, sir, I hardly think we need dance around each other in this manner."

Finley continued to look amused as he brushed back his coattails and made himself comfortable.

"Oh, all right," Wyn said, capitulating. "I'm a Shire as well as an Abbot, as you very well know. Unlike other passengers, that gives me the cachet to go when and where I please aboard the *Nereid*. Knowing that the purser was busy with the musical evening, I slipped into his cabin and read over the passenger lists until I found your name. It had your cabin number noted next to it."

"Ah!" Finley murmured. "And the locked door? How did you circumvent that?"

Wyn pulled a ring of keys from her pocket. "The captain has one to fit every lock."

"And he will certainly not miss them while he is enjoying himself in the grand saloon, will he?" Finley said.

She didn't care to be reminded that her presence in his cabin was irregular. She knew it was. But stealing in to wait for him had seemed the best method to employ. Or it had at the time. Rather than admit she had made a mistake, Wyn lifted her chin in a show of bravado and forged ahead.

"Now it is your turn, sir," she reminded. "What are you doing here? Who are you following? What have they done, and are they dangerous?"

The Pinkerton chuckled. "And why must I be involved in agency business?" he asked. "Am I not allowed to enjoy a holiday from sleuthing?"

"Those are not answers," Wyn insisted. "It is difficult for me to believe you are simply on a pleasure cruise. We are a long way from San Francisco."

"I have relatives in Ireland," Finley said. "An uncle and his family."

Ireland was full of Finleys to whom he could claim clanship, whether it was real or imaginary. Wyn tried another tack. "Then it is fortunate that Mr. Pinkerton pays you such a handsome salary that you can afford to travel in the best of style."

"An unexpected windfall," he said. "It is pleasant not

to travel in steerage this trip. I have done so often when on the company's business.''

Her patience wearing thin, Wyn scowled at him. She didn't for a moment believe one of his evasive answers. ''Dear sir, I am not an imbecile. Please don't treat me as one.''

''I wouldn't presume to do such a thing, Miss Abbot,'' he assured her smoothly. ''I have the most respect for your intelligence, and for your ingenuity in breaking into my cabin.''

He made it sound as if she were a criminal for doing so. All she had wanted was to see him in private. Wyn sighed deeply. ''Mr. Finley. You can trust me. I already know there are terribly nefarious men aboard.''

His eyebrows rose in mock horror. ''Are there? You quite frighten me, my dear.''

''You know it as well as I,'' Wyn insisted. ''Why else would you enter your own cabin with a gun drawn?''

Finley shook his head sadly. ''I'm sorry. In my line of business we develop some unusual habits. Now, tell me, how are your parents? Your older brother?''

Wyn gritted her teeth. She had come in search of information and he was determined to turn her visit into a social event. ''If you dare ring for tea, Mr. Finley, I shall scream,'' Wyn said. ''Garrett Blackhawk is the man you are following, isn't he?''

''I am on holiday,'' Finley reminded.

''Well, you shouldn't be,'' Wyn snapped, pushing to her feet. ''And you shouldn't dismiss Blackhawk out of hand, either. He isn't who he appears to be.''

''And who is he then, Miss Abbot?'' the detective asked casually, standing up.

It was a question she couldn't answer. ''Please. Just do as I ask?''

''But I am—''

''On holiday,'' she finished for him in disgust and stepped past him. Finley moved around her and politely opened the hatch. Wyn paused a moment before leaving

the cabin. "Tell me, Mr. Finley. Just how did you know
there was someone in your cabin before you entered?"

"Ah, that." He smiled to himself. "I'm afraid I can't
say, my dear. It's a trade secret."

Garrett completed his third circuit of the ship without
finding Wyn. By now his imagination had formulated a
half-dozen scenarios to account for her absence, none of
them providing a pleasant ending. He had talked to every
crew member he'd encountered, every guest. In each instance he had claimed he was on a mission from the captain, but he doubted that he'd been believed by one and
all. Blast the fact that his queries would feed rumors.
Wyn's safety was all that mattered.

It was only as an afterthought that he decided to once
more check Finley's stateroom for a sign of her. He'd been
there earlier and, upon finding the door locked and a cleverly placed bit of straw where the apparently paranoid Finley had left it in the door jamb, had decided she was not
with the detective. Now he thought he might have made a
mistake.

He pictured her bound, gagged and held prisoner, although for what reason he couldn't fathom. But the fact
remained. Wyn could well be behind the locked door. She
certainly was not anywhere else.

He'd barely rounded an elbow in the corridor when he
saw the straw was no longer where he had seen it last.

Garrett inched closer, careful not to make a sound. He
was fortunate that most of the guests had returned to their
staterooms. Being found skulking on a deck two levels
below his own suite would not have been easy to explain
away.

Gas jets located high on the corridor bulkheads created
a pattern of both light and shadow, none of it deep enough
to make him invisible to anyone who might happen along.
All the same, he pressed near the wall, hoping to catch the
sound of conversation from within Finley's cabin.

He couldn't imagine Wyn being within and not making an attempt to speak.

He nearly jerked back in surprised relief when he heard her voice growl with barely restrained frustration. It was impossible to hear what was said. The liner had been constructed with great care, particularly when it came to the privacy of first-class passengers. Never having spoken to Finley, he didn't know if the man who answered Wyn was the Pinkerton or not. He sounded amused rather than threatening though. The stiffness eased from Garrett's shoulders as he relaxed. After having pictured her coshed, stabbed and raped before being thrown overboard, it was a relief to know she was alive and, judging by her voice, nothing more than piqued.

Piqued! When he had been half out of his mind with worry.

The tap of footsteps sounded in Finley's room, moving nearer to the door, the sound sharp against the deck. The sound made by a woman's heeled shoes.

Garrett eased silently away.

Finley volunteered to check the corridor to guarantee that no one would witness Wyn's retreat from his cabin. His gallantry simply irked her more. She had been so sure the detective was trailing someone, although, she admitted to herself, had Finley told her he was shadowing Garrett, she would have been sad rather than happy.

She might have warned the Pinkerton against him, but in her heart she really didn't believe he was guilty of anything more than deceiving the ship's company as to his true identity. If he wished his past to be forgotten, then Garrett was not alone in that goal. Many men had begun life anew with false names in California, and a good number of them were now respected citizens and friends of her father.

No, she wouldn't fault Garrett for that. If traveling under a false passport was his only crime, she forgave him. But if, as she surmised, he was looking to marry a fortune, it was impossible for her to stand by and let him take advantage of an unsuspecting girl.

Careful to keep her footsteps silent, Wyn slipped down the companionway, turned the corner that led back to the outer deck, and ran smack up against Blackhawk's broad chest.

"You!" she gasped, the shock of his sudden appearance making her breathless. He towered over her, outlined by a backdrop of moonlit deck and star-filled heavens. He still wore his evening clothes, but had pulled both the formal tie and stiff collar loose. His sable black hair spilled in reckless abandon over his brow, fluttering slightly in the ever-present breeze. His onyx dark eyes glittered with anger, and something more.

Something that took her breath away even as she refused to name it.

His hands closed around her upper arms, holding her in place. She had changed after dinner, slipping into a simple, wine colored merino walking dress, the better to move about the *Nereid* in the dark undetected. The fabric was much stiffer than the fine silk of her evening gown, but the heat of his palms seemed to penetrate through the material despite its thickness, to burn her skin into a nearly overwhelming awareness.

"And who was the lucky man this evening, Miss Abbot?" Blackhawk snarled. "You needn't have gone looking for a substitute. I'm more than willing to accommodate your base instincts."

Wyn tried to pull away from him. "I was visiting a lady, not a gentleman," she insisted.

Garrett's smile was far from pleasant. "Ah, a lie to sully your innocent lips," he said. "But they aren't innocent, are they, Wyn." He pressed her back into the shadows until her spine rested against the chilled planks of the outer bulkhead, then leaned into her body so that she could not move without touching him. "They are hot, demanding and wanton."

"I told you the truth," she said, but her eyes dropped

of their own accord to his lips. Her breast heaved with excitement when his grin widened, allowing a flash of wolfishly bared teeth to glint in the moonlight.

"Another lie," he murmured. "Will it sour your sweet taste, I wonder?"

"Please, Garrett," she pleaded. "Let me return to my cabin. It's late."

"Far too late," he agreed, but did not release her. If anything, his stance insured that she couldn't move. "Did he kiss you, Wyn? Did he brush his mouth against yours? So slow, so gently it was as if you'd been caressed by butterfly wings?"

Garrett's breath against her lips was just that, but warm and enticing. Thrilling.

"Please," she said, the mere action of speaking causing her lips to brush against his intimately.

"I like it when you plead," he said. "But I like it even better when you catch fire and burn out of control."

"Garrett—"

His mouth feathered against hers, teasing, tempting, eating away at her will just as it had done before. "Say it again, Wyn. Say my name."

"Garrett," she whispered. Her eyelids dipped closed as he grazed slowly, sensuously, across her mouth once more. She could taste tobacco on his lips and a hint of sea spray. Had he been waiting for her on deck again, knowing that she could not resist the siren call of the ocean night? Or the desire to be in his arms once more?

His grip eased, freeing her to flee if she so wished. When Wyn didn't move, Garrett's touch returned, his hands gliding down her arms, the tips of his thumbs brushing the outer curve of her breasts as they passed.

Her breath caught in her throat, her eyes flew open in surprise as her body responded of its own accord, moving infinitesimally nearer to him in a request for the erotic stroke to continue. When she sighed with pleasure, she could feel the satisfied smile that curved his mouth before he kissed her again. This time his lips covered hers in a silent demand for surrender.

And surrender she did, to the delicious sensations he created, if not to him. She traced a path up the rich stuff of his jacket sleeves and across his broad shoulders, the tips of her fingers sensitized to the feel of tensed, masculine muscle beneath the fabric. Her tongue met his, entwined with it, learning the exotic dance in which he led her.

So caught up in the moment was she, Wyn failed to notice a shift in the shadows as one moved.

The thief waited, listening to the sounds of the ship settling for the night. It was never completely silent aboard. There was always the creak of rigging on the masts that stretched skyward. The feel of the engines was present underfoot, sending a slight vibration through the decking. And, of course, there was the wind. The constant droning sound of the wind.

In the comfort of the luxurious stateroom, it was impossible to hear the ocean without opening the porthole. One only felt it in the rise and fall of the liner, although that was minimal when compared to the rocking of a sailing ship. The thief hoped that the slight tilt back and forth would lull the Carillos in their slumbers, making it a simple matter to slip into their cabin, and back out with the pearls.

To while away the hours until the residents of the first-class section were deep asleep, the thief opened the cleverly crafted trunk purchased weeks ago in San Francisco. It had been made to exact specifications and had not come cheaply. But, considering it carried hidden treasure, the trunk had been well worth the price the maker had demanded.

The release was simple but hidden. A touch here, one there, and the bottom lifted free. Another here, there, and a panel opened in the lid, on each of the four sides. Not one of the concealed areas was deep. The object had been to mask the trunk's true nature, to make it appear as wide and deep as any other. But besides clothing, this case carried a spurious wealth.

Rather than alert others aboard of late-night activities, the thief worked by the light of a single candle, removing one item after another, laying each piece of the cache carefully on the bunk. Rubies flashed their bloodred light and were placed next to sapphires of midnight blue. Gems both precious and semiprecious were unearthed to dazzle the eye, the gold of amber, the fire of opals, and the waterlike quality of aquamarine. Garnets followed, with various golden trinkets and assorted gems mounted in stickpins and shirt studs, until a sizable pile of glittering stones covered the counterpane.

The Hartleby diamonds were removed from hiding last, the hand that held them caressing them, warming them. As tastelessly gaudy as the setting was, they remained a sentimental favorite, booty from the virgin robbery, the thief's first one. Unable to resist their brilliance, the thief lifted the necklace so that the gems dripped like faceted ice crystals from already-gloved fingers. A simple movement sent them sparkling in the glow of the candle's flame, catching and refracting the light into a dozen rich colors.

There had been other diamonds adorning the throats of guests that evening. Moving among the crowd as one set of amateur performers after another played and sang, it had been easy to both admire and scorn the choices the frivolous women had made. Miss Carillo's pearls would be the first collected, and if all went well, other selections would follow. Perhaps the emeralds the matron from Manchester had worn, or the small, but brilliant diamonds adorning the throat of the Denver debutante. The matter could be decided later, after the euphoria of the current theft had faded and died.

The current theft, the thief mused with a wry smile. It sounded like a toast, one that should be made before every break-in. And made again at the successful conclusion.

The bell that signaled the hour and a change in the night

watch reached the thief's ears, faint but discernible to one who had been awaiting it. Carefully, each set of stolen gems was rewrapped and replaced in hiding. When the trunk was sealed once more, and the candle extinguished, the thief pulled on a dark cloth cap and slipped from the cabin to meld with the shadows.

Chapter Nine

The next morning, a knock came just as Garrett finished brushing soap along his jaw and throat in preparation for shaving. His mind hadn't been on the chore, preferring instead to dwell on the inroads he was making on overcoming Wyn's resolve. The kisses they shared had ended too soon as far as he was concerned, with Wyn returning to her cabin rather than his. He was tempted to ignore the interruption entirely, returning to his contemplation of the night before, but the insistence of the steady rap made him think again.

Especially about the benefits to be gained from employing a valet.

He'd done without one during his travels mostly because the man who had done for him in the past had been far more conscious of the Blackhawk name than Garrett was. Adventuring, he had decided back then, would be much more to his liking if he was not burdened with a stiff-faced gentleman's gentleman who felt he should dress and act as if he were in the middle of the Strand rather than in the middle of the desert or jungle.

However, the fellow would have come in handy for answering doors when he himself was engaged in the more mundane forms of grooming.

The pounding increased, demanding a response.

"Dash it! I'm coming," Garrett shouted, not bothering to wipe away the foam that covered the lower section of his face. A valet would have been shocked at the notion of his appearing shirtless, the braces of his trousers drooping in twin loops at his hips. When he yanked the hatch open, the officer standing in the companionway was equally disconcerted.

"My lord," the man said, fixing his eyes on the elaborate detailing of the walnut paneling in the stateroom behind Garrett rather than on his half-naked form. "The captain presents his compliments and asks that you join the rest of the company immediately in the grand saloon."

"He does, does he?" Garrett said, far from cordial.

"Yes, sir."

"And might I ask the reason for this request?" Garrett pressed.

The officer looked even more uneasy. His eyes shifted to another section of molding. "I'd rather not say, sir. The matter is of some urgency, though."

Garrett sighed with resignation. "All right. Will Kittrick mind if I finish my morning ablutions first?"

The man's eyes flickered to the drying soap on his jaw and away again. "I believe he can wait that long, my lord, if you hurry."

He'd barely closed the hatch when it opened again, this time to admit Deegan. "I see they are leaving no stone unturned," he commented, glancing back down the corridor at the retreating officer's back before pulling the door shut.

"Now why does that have an ominous ring to it?" Garrett asked, returning to his bedroom and the washstand. He tested the foam on his face. "Blast, the bloody stuff's already dry. Dare I risk appearing unshaven, do you think?"

Deegan lounged along in his wake. "My dear chap," he declared in an accent so stiltedly proper, Garrett wondered if Dig had been a gentleman's gentleman in his unconfessed but checkered past. "The Baron Blackhawk is, at all times, perfectly turned out."

"Thank you for depressing me quite thoroughly this early in the morning," Garrett growled, splashing water on his face. He glanced up as Deegan leaned a shoulder against the bulkhead nearby. Although his friend was resplendent in a double-breasted university coat of dove gray and darker-gray-striped trousers, the brim of the modestly crowned top hat he had tipped low over his forehead did nothing to hide the red veining in his eyes, or the pallor of his complexion. "You, by the way," Garrett said, "look like hell."

"I feel like hell," Deegan admitted. "The next time a woman depresses me, break a chair over my head rather than let me near a liquor bottle. Then I'll still have the same headache the next day, but at least my tongue will lack fur."

Garrett recoated his face and reached for his already freshly stropped razor. "If memory serves, someone did once hit you with a chair and it had no effect whatsoever on your bipedal abilities."

"It wasn't a very sturdily built chair," Deegan said, "and where would you be if I'd gone down for the count during that particular bar fight?"

"Probably still enjoying the warm Mexican sun," Garrett answered. "Did you manage to learn anything about Finley from the old friend you ran across in steerage?"

"*Nada*. Naylor's knowledge extends only to the Eyes based in Chicago and New York, and he's right apologetic about that. Didn't realize his education was so limited before, although he was very appreciative of your largess in spite of it." Deegan shifted position and combed the fingers of one hand thoughtfully through the luxuriant growth of his side-wiskers. "Running into him certainly saved me considerable time last night when we were searching for Wyn. By the way, did she tell you anything more?"

Garrett tipped his head back, carefully stroking the razor along his throat. "I haven't seen her since escorting her to her stateroom and running you to earth last night. I would suppose she intends to stick to her story about visiting another lady on Finley's deck.''

"And you have no reason to challenge her to produce a name for this mysterious and largely imaginary lady," Deegan commented.

"No," Garrett admitted reluctantly, "I don't. Any ideas about why Finley is aboard?"

Galloway smiled wryly. "Naylor asked me the very same question. Other than my paranoid belief that he's got me under surveillance, I really couldn't say. But I would bet you even money that it has something to do with Kittrick's request for an audience so early this morning."

Neither of them was any the wiser in regards to the Pinkerton's presence on the *Nereid* after joining the other luxury-class passengers in the elaborate comfort of the grand saloon.

The whole company appeared to be gathered, even those unfamiliar faces that had kept to their staterooms enduring Neptune's favorite malaise. Complexions either pale or still a bit green, the sufferers sat wilting in their chairs, frequently turning anxious eyes to the entrance hatch in expectation of the captain's arrival.

Garrett and Deegan separated, Deegan threading a path through the gathering toward friends he had made the evening before. Garrett strolled straight to where Wyn and her widowed companion stood with a skittish-looking Mr. Mosby.

"Oh, thank goodness you are here, my lord," Hildegarde Hartleby greeted, sighing deeply in relief. "Make them tell you why we were pulled from our beds so unceremoniously."

Since she waved her furled fan in an imperious manner at them, Garrett judged the culprits to be the trio of officers stationed just outside the saloon's double doors. Tatterly was among them, a sheaf of papers in hand on which he checked off passengers' names as they entered the cabin.

Garrett arched one aristocratic eyebrow. "Were you indeed, Mrs. Hartleby?'' he asked coolly, then turned to Wyn. "And were you manhandled as well, Miss Abbot?"

She was no longer the breathless naiad he'd held in his arms but had donned a disguise as proper appearing as his own. The night before, the flaxen wealth of her hair had been heavy and sweet smelling when he'd released it from its bounds and buried his hands deep in the silken strands. Now it was tightly braided and covered by a chip hat festooned with plaited Breton lace, ostrich plume and modiste-molded satin blossoms. The suit she wore was stripped of the ribbons, ruching and ruffles favored by the other women and was of serviceable English flannel dyed a deep indigo blue. She was no doubt the envy of a score of schoolmarms and governesses in such an ensemble, and the object of lectures given to young women such as Suzanne Carillo by their mothers on the appropriateness of dressing for one's proper station in life.

He thought Wyn Abbot was the most quixotically exotic creature he'd ever seen.

"Manhandled, Lord Blackhawk?" she asked. "Not by any of the ship's officers or crew."

Garrett held back a smile. So she regretted her wantonness, did she? As much as he reveled in it and looked forward to luring her into his arms again?

Her friend Hildy simpered. "Dear sir, I'm afraid you took me far too literally. We were, however, urged to hasten at a most unaccustomed pace."

"And were you hastened, as well, Mosby?" Garrett asked.

The young man flushed at being noticed and addressed. "I am an early riser by nature, my lord. But I will admit to being quite as impatient as Mrs. Hartleby is to discover why we've all been, er..."

"Rounded up like cattle?" Garrett suggested blandly.

The comment earned him a reproving glare from Wyn, and an affected laugh from the widow.

The analogy was not far from the truth, though. The grand saloon effectively corralled the cream of the company in one location, and placed a single thought in their minds: why had they been brought there?

While Hildy chatted on about the inconvenience of it all, Garrett noticed Wyn scanning the room. Looking for Finley, no doubt. Her slighter stature kept her from spotting the Pinkerton in the crush but he had no problem singling the man out. Finley had taken a stand in one of the shadowed corners, ostensibly to fiddle with the pipe he held in his hand. Garrett wondered idly if the detective actually smoked for pleasure, or simply affected the vice because it gave him the appearance of an occupation while observing others.

It was because he was watching Finley himself that Garrett noted the Pinkerton was the only other passenger whose attention was not glued anxiously to the entrance in expectation of the captain's imminent arrival. Instead, the man was keeping a covert eye on a particular member of the captive company.

Deegan Galloway.

Perhaps Dig was right to worry. But about what?

The Pinkerton's attention flickered away from Deegan, if but for a moment, when Kittrick arrived, trailing both attending officers and the emotionally wrought Carillo family. Suzanne's childishly pink cheeks were tearstained, her mater's pasty with shock, while pater's were blusteringly furious. They followed Kittrick like quail chicks, all in a row, Miss Carillo ranking just above the purser and his associates in the line.

The captain chose the head of the room for his stand, stopping next to the now closed and silent pianoforte. The room hushed, conversations breaking off in midsentence as the passengers strained forward.

Kittrick wasted no time. His previously jolly expression had been replaced by one that was unflinching and commanding. "Thank you all for cooperating, ladies and gentlemen," the captain said, his voice booming in the stillness.

"Your officers gave us no option but to cooperate," an irate man called out.

Other passengers murmured in agreement, turning to nod and whisper to their nearest neighbors. Garrett kept his own counsel.

"We'd like to know what this is all about," another passenger insisted loudly.

"You're treating us as if we were common criminals," Trudy Woodrow said. "And I can tell you that—"

"Someone aboard this vessel *is* a criminal," the captain said, cutting across her diatribe quickly.

There were a number of gasps, one of the loudest, Garrett noticed, given by the widow Hartleby. She moved closer to him as if expecting him to protect her, and clutched at his arm.

Wyn's reaction was the opposite of her friend's. She went suddenly still, Lot's wife turned to salt. Her eyes never left Kittrick's face.

"Last evening," the captain announced, the sound of his voice quieting the crowd once more, "Miss Carillo's pearls were stolen."

A woman to the front of those gathered swooned back against her unprepared companions, and slid to the jewel-toned carpet at their feet. Other women grasped at the collars of their walking dresses, as if checking that their own jewels were yet in place. A number of men puffed out their chests in outrage while others patted the pockets of their waistcoats, making sure their timepieces were intact.

"I'm sure you all realize the seriousness of this act," Kittrick continued, "and that the request I am about to make is necessary for your continued safety. While you relax in comfort here in the saloon, my officers and I wish to have your permission to search your cabins."

The babble that ensued drowned out any further announcement the captain attempted to make. Hildy's fingers turned to claws that nearly scored Garrett's arm. Her eyes flew to Wyn's, appalled and stunned.

"Surely, he doesn't mean everyone's cabin!" she cried.

"How could he think any of us is a thief? I would think the culprit would be found in the hold."

In all the hours he had spent observing Wyn Abbot, Garrett had never seen her turn a glitteringly angry gaze on Hildegarde Hartleby before, but now she did, the delicate curve of her jaw growing taut with suppressed fury.

"Do you mean third class?" she asked, her voice chillingly controlled. "Passengers aboard a Shire ship do not travel in the *hold*."

The widow was contrite immediately. "You know what I mean."

"Yes, I do," Wyn said, her manner retaining the frost. "But the act of purchasing a more modest ticket does not naturally brand a person a thief."

Garrett wished he could applaud her. Perhaps it was the rumors surrounding his own birth that had made him conscious of the fact that many of the wealthy class were quick to point an accusing finger at those different from, or less fortunate than, themselves. He had had enough fingers pointed at him over the years simply because many doubted he belonged in their ranks. Unfortunately, he also knew that the *Nereid*'s steerage harbored at least one felon. Although Deegan had not elaborated on Naylor's profession, the man was more likely than not a fence for stolen goods, if not a thief in actuality himself.

Had Naylor stolen up the darkened companionways to the Carillos' deck after helping Dig search for Wyn?

Or was the man for whom the captain searched none other than Deegan Galloway himself?

What did he know of Deegan anyway? Little. They had shared a number of adventures in Sonora. Had worked their way to the coast, he taking a position as a surveyor with a railway anxious to lay new line while Deegan hired on as a *pistolero* to keep desperados from harassing the expedition. They had guarded each other's backs when the survey team was attacked by hill bandits. In fact, Dig had saved his life a couple times over that period. Neither of them had ever made any mention of the fact, but it was why his pockets were open to Deegan, and they both knew it.

To look at Deegan now, it was difficult to picture him with a rifle to his shoulder, his every shot seeming to pick off yet another of the Mexicans who had ambushed them. But he knew Deegan was as much a master at disguising who he was as Garrett was himself.

Add to that the fact that Deegan had taught him to pick a lock, had proven a neat hand at relieving a man of his wallet, leaving his victim none the wiser. Had freely confessed, without giving details, to a less than honorable past.

And now his friend was under close scrutiny by Magnus Finley, a detective based in the San Francisco Pinkerton office.

"How could this happen?" the widow whined. Garrett found himself patting the hand that clutched the sleeve of his twill morning coat in an automatic expression of comfort. He regretted the impulse the moment she turned her tear-starred blue eyes up to him. "You'll do something, won't you, my lord?"

Wyn's gaze was cool when it rested on him, waiting for his answer. It took a moment for the meaning behind her manner to dawn on him, his thoughts were so taken up with unwelcome doubts about Deegan. When it did connect, Garrett nearly burst into laughter. A most inappropriate response, he cautioned himself, although entirely natural.

She thought he was the thief!

Finley drew quietly on the stem of his pipe, to all intents and purposes interested more in getting the aromatic tobacco to light than in the heated discussions around him. He wasn't alone in doing the unforgivable and smoking without requesting the permission of the ladies nearest him. Few of the men now puffing on cheroots, cigarettes and pipes had. They had simply given in to the need to smoke and lit up. Their flustered women were too upset with the distressing news of the Carillos' loss to even notice.

Few appeared to be aware of anything other than the blow to their self-esteem, but Finley watched, waiting, hoping to catch the one expression that would betray the culprit. On one hand he was not surprised that the thief had struck again. There was no doubt in his mind that the same hand that had stolen from the jewel boxes of San Francisco, had now lifted Miss Suzanne's pearls. The number of dazzling jewels on display in the dining room each evening were a temptation few of the light fingered could resist. What did surprise him was that the burglary had taken place only two days out from Boston Harbor. He would have expected the thief to wait until the ship was docking in Liverpool before succumbing, simply because there would be less chance of being caught red-handed.

But the thief hadn't waited. Had instead struck while the ship was at sea, knowing there would be a hue and cry.

Which meant he wasn't following a rational being, but a person bent on self-destruction.

Surreptitiously Finley checked once more on his suspects. Galloway stood apart from the others, his head bent as he comforted a lady in her distress. Blackhawk was part of a similar diorama with Mrs. Hartleby clinging to his arm. Miss Abbot stood near them, yet definitely apart, her face carefully wiped clean of any hint of emotion. Rather than pay the widow the attention she clearly craved, Blackhawk stared thoughtfully at the distant yet watchful Winona Abbot. Neither spoke, but Finley felt sure a message had passed between the two. But had it anything to do with the theft? Somehow he doubted it. Their acquaintances might be blind to the tension that sizzled between the two, but he'd been an observer of his fellow man long enough to know a mating dance when he saw one.

Even if the lady fought against it.

Finley was musing on her attempt the evening before to center his attention on Blackhawk as a scurrilous fellow in need of watching, when the man in question maneuvered

himself free of the widow's clutches and strode purposefully to where the captain stood consulting with his officers. The baron spoke briefly, his words causing Kittrick's
scowl to lighten somewhat, then stepped back to await
developments.

The captain's voice rose over the angry hum of the
crowd, proving that his career had begun with shouted or-
ders to seamen perched high above him in the rigging. It
carried strongly to every corner of the room.

"Ladies and gentlemen," he said. "Baron Blackhawk
has asked that we begin our search of first class with his
quarters. I hope you will all follow his example and be as
understanding."

Finley doubted that they would, but he also made a bet
with himself. Based on the baron's confidence in volun-
teering, when the pearls were found, he very much doubted
they would be in Blackhawk's suite. Even if the baron
proved to be the elusive thief he sought.

Confined to her cabin, by choice rather than by request,
Wyn waited to hear the results of the captain's investigation. She had no doubt that the chatter in the ladies' saloon
continued, ripping apart the reputations of those considered
most likely to have committed the robbery. Rather than
endure the gossip, much of it vicious and unfounded, Wyn
sat at the writing desk dealing innumerable hands of whist,
performing the duties of each player herself.

Hildy lingered, also, but for an entirely different reason.
Based on Garrett's chivalry that morning, she told Wyn
she thought that he was beginning to succumb to the lures
she'd cast his way. To progress to the next stage in her
campaign, Hildy announced her wardrobe needed a few
discreet changes and sat near the wide porthole, stitching
jet black, rolled satin cording along the newly deepened
neckline of her deep violet silk reception dress.

"I don't know how I can possibly ever repay you, dearest," Hildy said as she plied her needle. "Here we are

only three days out from Boston and the baron is showing distinct signs of returning my regard.''

Wyn looked up from the cards fanned in her hand. ''Your regard?'' she echoed, stunned at the possibility that her friend might be falling in love with Garrett.

Hildy chuckled softly. ''Don't act so surprised,'' she recommended. ''How could a woman not have regard for such a well-looking man?''

Blindly Wyn chose a discard from among the pasteboards, turned the rest of the cards facedown and picked up the next imaginary player's cards. ''There needs to be more to a man than an attractive face,'' she said, making an effort to sound unconcerned.

''I wasn't speaking of his face,'' Hildy murmured, ''although it would be an attractive enough one to face over the dinner table each evening.''

Wyn played another discard and moved to the next grouping of cards on the table. ''No doubt you were speaking of his purse, then. I wouldn't put much faith in its being plump.''

Hildy clucked her tongue. ''I suppose you've heard the malicious rumor that horrible Hortense Carillo has been spreading about him.''

There were a number of wild tales concerning Garrett being tossed about aboard. ''Actually, I'd be inclined to believe the man was a Bluebeard with a dozen hapless wives sequestered in a locked closet,'' Wyn said offhandedly. ''Well, perhaps their own separate closets. His manners are rather good, even if he performs them by rote. Are you sure you don't feel like a game of cards? Playing all the hands myself is incredibly boring since I win them all.''

''Absolutely not. You win them all anyway. Besides, I've far too much to do to entice Lord Blackhawk tonight,'' Hildy insisted.

Lord Blackhawk, not *Garrett,* Wyn mused. Hildy was most definitely in love, but with a title, not a man. It didn't make Wyn feel any better to realize it. At heart, she was still a traitor to their friendship for succumbing to his kisses. For wanting them to go on and on.

Just thinking about how his mouth felt as it covered hers made Wyn dizzy. The pips on the cards blurred before her eyes. A flush rose in her cheeks. Resolutely she took a deep breath and willed her wanton senses back to the slumber from which they'd stirred.

It was impossible to continue her solitary game though. Her nerves hummed with the memory of how he'd made her feel the evening before, making it impossible to pay attention to the play. To keep Hildy from seeing that she was not herself, Wyn gripped her suddenly unsteady hands together in her lap. "I wish you wouldn't rush so," she said. "I'm sure we will meet far more elegant, far more deserving lords during our visit."

"But none more appealing than the baron," Hildy countered. "The opportunity is here, Wyn. Now. Look at the company. Other than yourself, what lady among them can hold a candle to me? The timid little Suzanne? She is too young and lacks poise. Her mother is the daughter of a washerwoman. Her father is a middle-class merchant who made his fortune selling goods at impossible prices in the Colorado gold fields. What do they have that would attract a man like Lord Blackhawk?"

"A fortune?" Wyn suggested.

Hildy glanced up, her brow furrowed unhappily at the reminder that she had failings of her own that might deter a suitor.

"I'm sorry, but it's the truth," Wyn said.

Hildy bent her head over her needlework. "Perhaps as you see it," she said. "Having Deegan Galloway as a shipmate and dining partner is clouding your mind, Wyn. You believed he was in love with only you, and such proved not to be the case. Your bitterness is coloring your perception of those around you until you think every man is false."

"That isn't it," Wyn insisted.

"Isn't it?" Hildy tied off her final stitch. "I believe I

have enough satin left to make a choker yet. If you still have the amethyst brooch, would you mind if I borrowed it? I believe it will set off my new décolleté nicely, don't you?''

The brooch was the pièce de résistance, as far as Mr. Carillo was concerned. His eyes rarely left Hildy's flamboyantly exposed chest. But, Wyn noticed, Garrett seemed totally unaware of the daring cut of his dining partner's gown. Or of her presence.

''Absolutely no sign of the pearls anywhere?'' he demanded of the captain, a scowl drawing his sable brows together over his hawklike nose. ''But, surely, that is impossible. The thief had nowhere to go.''

''I know, Baron,'' Kittrick said reluctantly. ''I know. However, the fact remains. We had no success in locating Miss Suzanne's necklace anywhere.''

''More than a mere necklace,'' Mrs. Carillo trumpeted in anger. ''There was a bracelet and ear bobs, as well, all of which cost Mr. Carillo a good deal, I assure you.''

Carillo looked up from his plate. ''A tidy sum, indeed,'' he added. ''Sure you sounded for secret compartments?''

Kittrick nodded. ''Every piece of luggage has been checked,'' he assured.

''What about the cabins themselves?'' Carillo asked, before slipping a stuffed oyster into his mouth.

''I hardly think—'' Mr. Mosby began before Carillo cut him off.

''*That* I can believe if you think there aren't cubbyholes galore on this tug,'' Carillo said. ''Had to cost the Shires a fortune to build the *Nereid*, and as a result, I'd say they aren't too plump in the pocket anymore. After all, while the other ladies have dazzled us with their jewelry, I haven't noticed that Miss Abbot there wears anything but those gewgaw crystal earrings.''

As if embarrassed by her father's observation, Suzanne leaned forward to give Wyn a tremulous smile. ''I think

they are quite lovely, Miss Abbot. Were they given to you
by someone near and dear?''

Pierce had given them to her after he had pretty much
cleaned out her jewel box to finance the liner.

"My brother," Wyn murmured. "They are sentimental
favorites of mine."

"Of which I can vouch," Deegan said. "I admired them
frequently when I was acquainted with Miss Abbot in San
Francisco."

Which was a lie. She hadn't owned them until long after
she had expelled him from her life.

"In fact, I can't say I recall Wyn ever wearing much in
the way of jewelry," Deegan continued, a fond smile curving the corners of his mouth beneath his flamboyant mustache. Before Wyn could think of something to say, Deegan had turned to Hildy. "Isn't that right, Mrs. Hartleby?"

"Subtlety has always been Wyn's style," Hildy answered, neatly avoiding calling him an outright liar or con-
firming his untruth. Wyn recalled only too well the tears
her friend had shed upon hearing that she'd sacrificed a
small fortune in jewelry to appease the bankers.

"As you say, Mrs. Hartleby," Garrett said. "Miss Abbot's beauty is the sort that makes gemstones pale into
insignificance." The very tone of his voice turned the compliment into a commonplace, glib phrase ofttimes repeated
to giddier ladies in the past. It was just the sort of insincere
remark Wyn had come to expect of him when he played
Baron Blackhawk.

Wyn forced a polite smile to her lips. "Thank you, my
lord."

"Fitting tribute, sir," Kittrick commented before pinning Carillo with a pitiless glare. "And if Miss Abbot
doesn't take offense at your slur on this ship, I most certainly do."

Mrs. Carillo turned scarlet in embarrassment. "I'm sure
Horace didn't mean to imply that—"

"Most certainly did," her spouse declared, cutting

across her apology. "Facts are facts and the fact is we've been violated."

Three female voices gasped at his choice of words. "Sir!" Hildy cried, offended. Suzanne's complexion paled while her mother's grew more heated.

"'Pologize, ma'am," Carillo mumbled to Hildy, "but that doesn't give my little girl back her trinkets, does it?"

"No, it doesn't," Wyn agreed, and turned to the captain. "Perhaps if you detailed the efforts you've made thus far, sir, Mr. Carillo would feel that the investigation is proceeding."

Kittrick obviously wasn't pleased with the suggestion, but, short of refusing to discuss the matter, Wyn knew he couldn't avoid telling them so without insulting the Carillos, or having his surliness reflect badly on the Shire Line.

"I hardly know where to begin," the captain said. "We've been over every inch of the ship today, and done so more than a single time." He leaned back in his chair, toying with his wineglass a moment before continuing. "We'd barely wrung four bells when Carillo came charging into my quarters to report the theft. Not wanting to jump to conclusions, I took Mr. Tatterly with me to have a look see myself."

"And found nothing, just as we said," Mrs. Carillo inserted, her voice snippy over the event.

Kittrick's eyes flickered over her in a silent command for silence. "From there I gathered my officers, teaming them in pairs to search the crew's quarters, and then each other's. Not that I don't trust my own men, mind you, but I was taking no chances."

"Admirable," Blackhawk murmured. Unlike the flamboyant compliment he'd offered her earlier, Wyn noted he meant the commendation for approval rang true in the single quietly spoken word.

"From there we proceeded to third class. They tend to rise earlier than our first-class passengers, so it was the logical choice," the captain said.

Not to mention the most likely place a common thief would travel, Wyn thought. If the thief were common.

Garrett was far from common, and still, she felt, the most likely suspect. How often had she run into him in areas of the ship where he, by right, should not be? Passengers as a rule did not lurk in the shadows of the deck, did not invade the officers' quarters, did not materialize in cabin areas far from their own. But Garrett had done all three.

And had seduced her reason away if but briefly each time she found him.

What better reason was there for him to do so other than to prevent her from questioning his presence?

She did so now.

Kittrick finished narrating the tale of his search through the first-class passengers' cabins and quickly downed the last of his dinner wine. "Although we were unable to find the missing jewelry today, there is every indication that we'll have both the pearls and the culprit before we dock. While this sort of thing is out of my experience, Tatterly tells me we do have a man who will know best how we should proceed. He's a member of the Pinkerton—"

"Gracious!" Mrs. Carillo gasped, and fluttered her fan fitfully before her flushed face.

"Ah," her husband said, pleased at last.

Wyn felt relief herself. Finley was considered one of the best men in the San Francisco office.

"As I was saying," the captain continued, "this man is a detective, and we've asked him to look into the matter for us."

Mrs. Carillo changed her tune, sighing deeply. "Thank God. Did he say how he intends to proceed?"

"He did," Kittrick admitted. "He mentioned talking to everyone quartered on your level to learn if they had seen anyone loitering who didn't belong there."

Carillo nodded. "Who is this detective fellow? Someone I've met so far?"

"It's possible," the captain said. "Mr. Finley has a cabin on your deck, sir, only a few strides away, in fact."

Chapter Ten

Garrett slumped at his ease in the smoking room, his shoulders pressed back into the leather upholstery of a wing chair. A crystal goblet of brandy rested on the table at his side as he blew smoke rings idly toward the ceiling, the thunderous set of his brow alone keeping other passengers from intruding on his solitude. It had been an hour since Kittrick had casually mentioned that Finley and the Carillos were quartered on the same deck. An hour in which he'd done little else but question what he knew of Deegan Galloway. And of Wyn Abbot.

Dinner had progressed through the final courses, the conversation abandoning the robbery for the nonce to center around the evening's entertainment, and the ball planned for the next evening. He had answered when addressed directly, yet remained detached, his attention straying frequently to the couple across from him. Was it his imagination or did Deegan find excuses to lean near Wyn, to whisper in her delicately shaped ear? Was her response to Dig warmer than it had been, or was his own attraction to her coloring his perception? Deegan had leapt to her defense over the matter of jewelry earlier. Lying, if Garrett was any judge. Why? Despite his avowals to the contrary, was Dig in love with her?

Or was that *still* in love with her?

The idea came unbidden and unwelcomed—could it be that Wyn was not the heiress Galloway had wooed and lost in San Francisco?

Now that Garrett considered the matter, it hadn't been Deegan who volunteered the information that Wyn and his "goddess" were one in the same. He'd taken that leap himself, making the connection simply because she was unbelievably lovely and had greeted Dig coolly. Perhaps Galloway had merely chosen to let the inference stand unchallenged, uncorrected.

In which case, Wyn Abbot might not be the lady she claimed to be.

There was only one way to find out.

Once the ladies left the dining table, Garrett had eluded Deegan, and returned to his stateroom suite to dash off a quick note to the captain requesting Kittrick meet with him privately in the smoking room. He only hoped the answers the man gave were ones he wanted to hear.

Stubbing out his cigarette, Garrett picked up his brandy, but rather than sample it, he rubbed a forefinger idly around the rim of the goblet and wondered what game Wyn Abbot was playing. He had been amused earlier by her silent look, one that accused him of helping himself to Suzanne's modest treasure. He wasn't laughing now. Instead he was wondering if she had told him the truth the night before, that she *had* been visiting a lady. Or at least a lady's jewel box. The Carillos had been among the first to leave the musical soiree, and it had been quite late when he overheard Wyn in Finley's cabin. More than enough time for the Carillos to be lulled to sleep; more than enough time for a clever thief to relieve them of the pearls and rendezvous with an associate.

And who better than Finley to guarantee that the necklace and attendant accessories were not found in the inevitable search? He had already primed the way; he was nearly the only member of the company Kittrick was bound to trust, for he had told the purser upon boarding that he was a Pinkerton.

But what if he wasn't a member of that most trusted of detective agencies?

Was the theft the work of one or of a team of clever villains? And, if the latter, who was the mastermind behind their schemes?

Once more his mind suggested the obvious choice. Deegan Galloway.

Blast it! He couldn't have been *that* deceived by the blighter! But Dig fit all the requirements so well. He thought he knew his friend. They had endured hardship together, faced death together. Dig was intelligent, crafty and a touch amoral. He was also a staunch companion. It had been Deegan who took over the reins in California, arranging both business and travel arrangements when he'd been treating his despair with the medicinal aid of whiskey. Although he'd turned down the position of secretary, to all intents and purposes, Dig functioned as one. A damned efficient one.

But the facts were before him. Dig knew Wyn. Had, in fact, vouched for her identity as Shire heiress Winona Abbot. She had been within feet of the Carillos' stateroom the night before, had met with Finley, and Finley had his eye on Dig. Perhaps not as he had thought earlier, primed by Dig's own words to believe the Pinkerton was following him, but merely to watch for a signal. Add to that the presence of the apologetic but obvious felon, Naylor, in third class, and an unwelcome pattern began forming.

Had Deegan only donned the persona of the concerned friend in San Francisco because, as Baron Blackhawk, he himself possessed the cachet needed by the team of thieves to remove their booty from the country, smuggling it abroad?

Garrett lifted his glass and finished off the brandy in a single swallow. Its once pleasant bouquet turned to vinegar on his tongue. With a slight grimace of distaste, he pushed the goblet aside as Kittrick entered the crowded saloon.

The captain stood just inside the door, surveying the room with an expression of approval on his weather-lined face. He greeted various gentlemen, reminding them that they were expected in the grand saloon to cheer on the group of amateur thespians the purser had cajoled into presenting a hastily devised play that evening. Few of the men evidenced pleasure in relinquishing their brief after-dinner respite from the ladies' company; however, as they were either actors in the production themselves or related to a lady who was, attendance was de rigueur.

Deegan and the widow were among the players, as were Suzanne Carillo and many of the younger passengers. Garrett wished that Wyn was of their number. It was far too easy for a member of the audience to slip away, and, until he spoke with Kittrick, he couldn't be easy in his mind about her. That is, if he could be even then.

With a reluctant glance at their pocket watches, the last couple of men finished their drinks, stubbed out cigars or tapped pipe bowls clean, and ambled from the cabin. Kittrick looked after them a moment before joining Garrett.

"My lord?"

Garrett lifted the decanter of brandy he'd asked the steward to leave earlier. "Good evening, Captain. Can I tempt you?"

Kittrick settled in the chair across from him. "I've never turned down a dash of brandy when it was offered," he said.

Acting as host, Garrett half filled a fresh goblet and passed it to his guest. "I appreciate you agreeing to meet with me like this, Kittrick."

"It was curiosity that brought me," the captain said. "I don't often receive requests for private meetings from passengers."

"Not even the ladies?" Garrett asked lightly.

Kittrick smiled ruefully. "Alas, no. But I doubt the subject of ladies is what you wanted to talk about. Am I right?"

"In a way," Garrett admitted. He glanced to where a lone steward worked behind the bar, setting things to right once more. Assured that the man would not be able to overhear them, he leaned forward in his chair. "I'm interested in locating Suzanne Carillo's pearls."

"Ah." Kittrick rocked the bowl of his goblet back and forth. "And to what end?"

"Justice?" Garrett offered, sure that the suggestion would be laughed down. His reputation, after all, reflected a man who cared little for justice.

Kittrick didn't laugh. "And what exactly did you want to know?" he asked.

Garrett reclaimed his tobacco pouch and cigarette papers from the inner pocket of his evening coat. When he offered them to the captain, Kittrick declined with a slight shake of his head. "Forgive me," Garrett said, "but while Carillo was satisfied with the shorthand version, I thought you neglected to give a good many details earlier and glossed over the fact that your search was not as thorough as it could have been."

"And you wish to know why I was sketchy, is that it?"

"Quite. Of course," Garrett offered, "you can tell me to go to the devil instead."

Kittrick peered into the ruby liquid in his glass, watching as it swished back and forth lightly. "You tempt me, Baron," he said, glancing up, "but I'm fairly sure it would be against Shire policy to send a paying passenger elsewhere."

Garrett leaned back in his chair once more. "You relieve my mind," he murmured. "Or, I hope, are about to."

"You already know we didn't find the missing jewelry," the captain said.

"Mmm," Garrett agreed. His movements languid, he set about building a fresh cigarette.

"We searched the cabins and sounded all the trunks."

"Yet found nothing." Garrett watched Kittrick from the corner of his eye, not actually looking directly at the captain until he'd lit the cigarette and had created a screen of smoke between them. "Because none of you knew what to look for. Am I right?"

Kittrick took a quick swallow of brandy, evidencing as

little pleasure from the heady bouquet as Garrett had earlier. "Far too right. But even if my officers and I had known about mechanisms for hidden compartments, we might not have found the pearls anyway."

"You think the thief had them on his person then?" Garrett asked.

"A rather dangerous thing to do, don't you think, Baron?"

"Or daring," Garrett suggested. "Our thief took a chance and guessed right. Not one of the passengers was searched bodily, were they?"

Kittrick allowed himself a thin smile. "None of the first-class passengers, at any rate."

Garrett drew deeply on his cigarette. "So our felon is one of the elite."

"Not necessarily," the captain insisted. "As I said before, my officers could easily have overlooked a false bottom in a piece of luggage."

"But you don't think so."

"I don't *know* so," Kittrick corrected. "At this point I've turned the whole matter over to Finley. I can only hope that he learns something quickly."

"I'm sure he will," Garrett said. "If he's who he says he is."

Kittrick started so abruptly, brandy sloshed from the goblet in his hand to dampen the dark wool of his uniform trousers. "You can't mean to suggest Finley's our crook."

Garrett raised one shoulder in a careless shrug. "I'm merely saying that, while we are at sea, there is no way to check the identity of anyone aboard."

The captain tapped a finger thoughtfully against the bowl of his glass as he digested the statement. "Apparently Mr. Finley anticipated just that," he said at last. "He suggested that I speak with Miss Abbot before bringing him in to investigate. I had thought he was simply seeing that the Shire offices would cover his fee."

"And did you?" Garrett asked.

Kittrick shook his head. "While at sea, I am as much a lord of my realm as you are on your own properties."

The captain was wrong, of course, Garrett mused sadly. Once he rode through the gates of Hawk's Run, it would be the realm that ruled him.

"I had no reason to consult with Miss Abbot before taking Finley on," Kittrick continued. "I did, however, ask to see some identification that he is one of Pinkerton's men."

Something a clever thief would be sure to carry to make his masquerade appear valid, Garrett was sure. "Then tell me, Captain, how well do you know Winona Abbot?"

Kittrick laughed outright. "You are a suspicious one. Not well, I will admit, but I have no doubt of her identity, Baron, if that's what you are really asking."

"It was," Garrett admitted, taking a quick draw on his cigarette. "But only because it was my understanding that the Shire Line is based in Boston, and, judging by her accent, our Miss Abbot isn't from that fair city."

"Ah, but her mother is," Kittrick said. "Barnabas Shire opened a second shipping office in San Francisco after his daughter went to California and married. What exactly is it you're implying, Baron? You can't actually believe Winona is our thief."

"I'm simply questioning whether she is indeed Winona Abbot," Garrett said. "In light of the circumstances—"

The captain cut him off. "The circumstances, my lord, are not your concern." He set aside his brandy and got slowly to his feet. "If you'll excuse me, I have a theatrical performance to attend."

"Oh, don't be a bloody fool, Kittrick," Garrett snapped irritably. "You know as well as I do that you shouldn't be trusting anyone right now."

"And does that go for you, as well, my lord?" the captain demanded coolly.

"Damned right it does," Garrett said. "More so since I'm being such a blasted nuisance. If you're so sure Miss

Abbot is who she says she is, all you have to do is tell me why and I'll be satisfied.''

Kittrick hesitated a moment. "Somehow I doubt that."

Garrett waited.

The captain settled back into his chair. "She is the image of Marianne Shire," he said quietly. "I was acquainted with her before she married Abbot."

"You're sure?" Garrett persisted. "Memories can become distorted over the years."

"Not all memories," Kittrick murmured. "A man never forgets the most beautiful woman he has ever seen."

Which was true, Garrett knew, for Wyn's face and form would haunt him the rest of his life. "You were in love with Mrs. Abbot?"

"When she was still Miss Shire, there wasn't a man manning a Shire ship who didn't fancy himself in love with her. Some of us still are," the captain confessed and, hands braced against his knees, pushed back to his feet. "Now, I really must put in an appearance in the grand saloon. If you'll excuse me, Baron?"

Garrett took a quick puff on his cigarette and stood up, nodding shortly. "You'll keep my reservations in mind, Kittrick?"

The captain had taken barely two steps before he turned back. "You're still suspicious then? Of whom? Finley?"

"Possibly. There's one way to find out if he's on the level," Garrett said. "When he reports back to you about passengers seen on the Carillos' deck last night, if he neglects to mention either of two particular names, he hasn't done a thorough or honest job."

"And whose names might those be, Baron?" Kittrick asked, clearly impatient for the interview to be over.

"Mine," Garrett volunteered. "And Winona Abbot's."

Wyn kept to her cabin that night, fighting the longing to go on deck. She was no longer sure what it was she fought, the desire to feel the cool, salt-tinged air on her face or the need to lose herself in Garrett Blackhawk's arms. The inner battle made rest impossible no matter what the true reason. She tried reading one of the magazines Hildy had brought with her, hoping to lose herself in the impossibly tangled life of one of the heroines in the serialized novel. Unfortunately, the copy of *Demorest's* she chose featured a short story called ''His Lordship,'' the title alone bringing Garrett all too clearly to mind.

Far too clearly.

Wyn tossed the magazine aside, angry with herself for being so drawn to him. It was an addiction, this longing to be with him, to have his lips bruising hers, to have her hands buried in his thick, silky hair as she clung mindlessly to him.

Her skin felt warm just with the memory. It became impossible to sit still. She was as skittish as a mare in heat, Wyn thought in disgust, and probably far more wanton, since the minutes she spent alone with Garrett were clandestine, hidden from others.

Cherished.

Wyn kicked at the trailing hem of her dressing robe, peeved that the word had surfaced in her mind. That it was true.

Pacing did nothing to relieve the tension in her body, leaving, as it did, her mind free to relive each tender caress, each will-robbingly wonderful kiss. She tried a game of patience only to find she lacked the patience to see even a single game to its logical conclusion. It was only as dawn began coloring the eastern sky that she felt safe to steal onto deck, praying that Neptune would provide a cure for her restlessness. But fate was before her even then. As she peered from the companionway porthole to the outer deck, she recognized Garrett's broad back at the near rail. He had the collar of his dark jacket turned up and his shoulders hunched against the biting chill of early morning. His head was uncovered so that his hair lifted in the breeze, creating sable wings that she longed to smooth into place. A trail of cigarette smoke wafted away from him, toward the stern, as he stared out to sea in the direction of his homeland.

Was he thinking with pleasure of returning to England? Who waited for him? A fond family? A fiancée? Or was he thinking, as she was, of the passion-filled minutes they had spent together under a starlit Atlantic sky?

Rather than tempt fate further by intruding on his musings, Wyn stole back to her cabin and climbed under her tangled sheets, her spirit somehow at peace just for having seen Garrett. As the sun crested the distant horizon, she finally slept.

The sun was no longer in evidence due to a storm when she woke, surprisingly refreshed. She could hear Hildy rummaging around in their shared parlor, but was more curious to know the hour than what her friend was doing. She had just thrown back the covers and was feeling for her slippers when the deck tilted violently beneath her feet. Caught off balance, Wyn yelped and landed on her side, bruising her elbow against the sturdy base of her bunk.

"Dearest?" Hildy's voice called from beyond the closed hatch. "Are you all right?"

"Fine!" Wyn answered, rubbing her smarting joint. "You?"

The hatch opened to admit a disheveled Hildy. "As much as it is possible to be with the flooring shifting constantly." She pushed a loose lank of dark hair out of her face. "This is far worse than the earthquakes at home. At least then we know the jolting will stop within a few minutes."

Wyn pushed herself upright. "It's just a storm," she soothed, glancing out the porthole at the dark sky and rolling ocean. "The captain is probably charting a course around it as much as is possible."

"Yes, so the officers told us," Hildy said, clinging to the door as the deck dropped suddenly once more. "They've suggested everyone keep to their cabins until we're away from the worst of it."

"Then we're lucky," Wyn said, and climbed back into her bunk. "We've got each other to help make the time fly by. Come join me?" She patted the mattress next to her.

Her walk resembling that of a drunken sailor, Hildy made it across the tilting cabin. Careless of her dignity since they were alone, the widow hitched up her skirts and curled up on the counterpane, legs tucked beneath her. "This is just like when we were girls," she said with a smile, then sighed. "Do you ever miss those days, Wyn?"

"Yes and no." Wyn wrapped her arms around her drawn-up legs and leaned her chin on her knees. "Things certainly weren't as complicated back then."

"We thought there were so many rules, didn't we?" Hildy mused. "All we talked about was growing up."

It had been all *Hildy* ever talked about, Wyn thought. Being an adult had meant beautiful gowns, parties that stretched to dawn, and gallant men hanging on her every word. She had never mentioned falling in love or having a family.

"But really," Hildy continued, "there are far more rules to follow now that we're grown."

Wyn reached over and touched her friend's hand. "You're finding widowhood restricting, aren't you?"

"Extremely confining," Hildy said. "I swear, you'd think I was supposed to expire in the same breath as my husband the way society looks at me. I assumed there would be compassion, but behind the words of consolation people offer there's always a hint of censure. I thought it was only women in India who were expected to throw themselves in their husband's graves."

"Worse," Wyn murmured. "On their funeral pyres."

"It's ridiculous either way," Hildy said. "Did Oswin down a bottle of laudanum simply because his first wife did?"

"She didn't!"

"Probably not," Hildy admitted, and sighed. "I certainly wouldn't have blamed her if she had. The man was tediously dull. Which makes it so difficult when people expect me to miss him. Why should I? I was stifling!''

''Oh, Hildy,'' Wyn said quietly. ''I can't believe that.''

''Well, it's true. These horrid do-gooders don't have to have known Oswin personally, or know that he was so much older than I, to be snide, either. Take that uppity Mrs. Mayhew.'' Hildy resettled herself on the bunk. ''She's the woman traveling with a companion and a ladies' maid and is being escorted by her husband's male secretary? For all she's supposed to be a diplomat's wife, she hasn't a diplomatic thought in her head. You recall her, don't you? Sharp features, cuttingly proper British accent?''

Wyn nodded, although the verbal picture Hildy painted of the young matron was far from her own impression of the woman. Quietly pretty, her body rounding softly in the early months of pregnancy, she'd found Mrs. Mayhew sweet tempered and a bit shy.

''She and her companion and I were having tea with Hortense Carillo and that truly common friend of hers, Trudy Woodrow, earlier,'' Hildy said. ''I had barely mentioned Baron Blackhawk's name, inquiring if she was familiar with his family estate, when she told me it was far from proper for a woman still wearing weeds to be so much in company with a bachelor who has such a reckless reputation.''

Wyn couldn't help herself. Her ears pricked.

''Apparently, while Mrs. Mayhew decries my own curiosity about him, her companion is more than willing to gossip about Lord Blackhawk,'' Hildy continued. ''And she has the nerve to imply that I'm fast!''

''What sort of gossip?'' Wyn asked. ''At meals he's always so cool, so proper. Not really the sort of man you'd think had a past worth gossiping about.''

Hildy grabbed the edge of the bunk as the ship shuddered beneath the onslaught of the rising sea. Wind whistled around the upper decks with a bansheelike howl. Rain, at first light, began to pound more violently against the sealed porthole. Hildy stared at the wild scene, chewing worriedly on a corner of her bottom lip. "Are you sure we're safe?"

Outside, a crack of lightning was followed by the deep rumble of thunder. "Absolutely," Wyn assured her, and pulled a heavy drape over the oval window, shuttering the view. "All you have to do is keep your mind occupied. And what better way than in relating scandalous tales? Even if they are obviously not true, we can have the fun of exclaiming over them, can't we?"

"Oh, but I'm afraid they are true," Hildy insisted earnestly. "Mrs. Mayhew's companion, you see, is related to one of Lord Blackhawk's nearest neighbors."

Wyn still doubted the veracity of any such tale, but couldn't stop herself from wanting to hear it anyway. "Still," she scoffed, "what could such a stiff-necked gentleman like the baron have done to merit a reputation for recklessness?" Other than seducing stupidly susceptible spinsters beneath star-studded skies, she added silently.

Or possibly being found with stolen gemstones in his possession.

Rather than answer immediately, Hildy fidgeted with her straggling hair. "We will be out of the storm by this evening, won't we? I'd hate for Mr. Tatterly to cancel the ball. While custom decrees I can't dance yet, I would so enjoy listening to the music and watching you waltz, Wyn."

Knowing there was no way of telling when the storm would dissipate, or they would steam out of its reach, Wyn avoided answering the question. "Oh, I'm sure we'll have the ball," she assured. "If not tonight, then tomorrow. Now, stop being a tease, and tell me what you learned."

Hildy smiled faintly. "Dear Wyn," she said and squeezed Winona's hand. "You needn't playact for me. I know you abhor gossip."

"I'm willing to make an exception with the baron," Wyn said. "And if what you relate isn't dastardly enough,

I may entertain the notion of embroidering the story a bit myself.''

"You don't like him."

"True," Wyn admitted. She didn't—not when he was playing the part of the august Baron Blackhawk. When he shed the mask and was merely Garrett, the man who swept her into the shoal-filled waters of passion, she was near to loving him. "I'm not the only one, though," she said. "A number of other passengers are uncomfortable around him."

"They probably have heard about him," Hildy murmured. She glanced away again, this time to the open door of Wyn's cabin as if to confirm that they were totally alone. "He's not the true baron," she announced.

Although she had suspected his barony was false, the news still stunned Wyn. "He's not a real baron?"

"Not *the* true heir to the Blackhawk estates," Hildy corrected.

"Then who is?" Wyn asked.

"Miss Yount—you remember, the companion—says there was a second Blackhawk son but that no one has seen him in years. The belief is our baron arranged an accident so that he would come into the title unchallenged," Hildy whispered, leaning closer. "You see, the Blackhawk family have been slight of stature and blindingly blond for centuries."

Which Garrett definitely was not. He was tall, well muscled and devilishly dark.

Wyn pulled away from her friend. "I'm sorry. But even I can't believe such a ridiculous story. Who's he supposed to be? The son of a local tradesman?"

Hildy shook her head, the movement causing the single straggling lock of hair to slither over the shoulder of her deep gray silk afternoon dress. "Not at all, although I must admit I find the idea that he is a child of the pixies beyond reason. A Gypsy child, now..."

"Hildy." Wyn sighed deeply. "That only happens in novels. This isn't fiction, it's reality. Besides, as hatefully superior as he sometimes acts, I can't believe he'd kill his own brother. He just doesn't seem like that type of man.''

"I don't know," Hildy mused, the thoughtful tone of her voice making it very apparent that she was intrigued rather than put off by the suggestion that Garrett was a murderer. "You haven't heard the rest yet," she said, and further surprised Wyn by smiling in happy anticipation of the rest of her tale.

"I mentioned that Miss Yount is related to near neighbors of his?" Hildy asked. "It seems that the baron and his brother were both in love with the same girl, Miss Yount's distant cousin, in fact. Apparently they all grew up together and when the baron returned from London— oh, did I mention he went there to rebuild the family fortune?''

"No," Wyn said faintly, overwhelmed by her friend's enthusiasm for the ghastly sequence unfolding. If any of the stories had the barest grounding in truth, and actually applied to Garrett, it was no wonder he let few see beneath his aristocratic facade. Whether or not he was a real baron, she suddenly felt honored that he had let her glimpse, even briefly, the man beneath.

"Well, that's another story in itself, and I couldn't hope to remember all the names that tumbled from Miss Yount's tongue when it comes to the ladies he is said to have seduced," Hildy gushed. This time when the ship dipped at a dizzying angle, Hildy didn't appear to notice, she was so caught up in retelling the scandalous tale.

She didn't notice when Wyn went very still.

"Where was I?" Hildy asked. "Oh, yes. Sybil Tilbury. That was the girl's name. The one the brothers both loved. It seems that she was quite a talented artist and had developed a most unusual desire to see and paint the marvels of Egypt. Miss Yount claims she was thoroughly shocked when she heard her cousins were allowing their daughter to take such a frivolous journey with no one but her former governess for company. It turns out she wasn't all that alone, though, for our baron and his brother followed her.''

Hildy paused and, pulling a hairpin free, reached to refix her tumbling hair. "She must have been very beautiful to have two men follow her all that distance," she said wistfully. "Don't you think so?"

Familiar with the sometimes stifling attitude of her many brothers, Wyn found the Blackhawk men's action protective rather than lovesick. But there was something about Hildy's story that bothered her. Something to do with her careless portrayal of Sybil Tilbury. "Hildy? Why did you say the girl 'must have been beautiful'?"

"Why, because she's dead, dearest."

"Dead!"

"Yes." Hildy leaned closer, her blue eyes glittering with excitement. "That's the best part of the story, Wyn. You see, our Baron Blackhawk killed her."

Chapter Eleven

The *Nereid* steamed clear of the storm late that afternoon. The more seaworthy of the passengers tumbled eagerly from the confines of their cabins, leaving their weaker-stomached companions to languish yet in their bunks. Hildy was among those relieved when Mr. Tatterly announced that the ball would go forward, even if not in the grand manner originally planned.

Wyn, perversely, wished the purser had used the weather as an excuse to delay the festivities. To escape Hildy's frenzied combing through their combined wardrobes, Wyn stole away to enjoy a moment alone at the rail. The air seemed to crackle with energy from the storm. Although the ship had plowed free of the rough seas, the sky remained a cloud-laden pewter gray, the breeze more biting than brisk. With the sound of Hildy's voice still ringing in her ears proclaiming Garrett a murderer, Wyn's heart felt just as dismal and bleak as the weather.

It wasn't true. It couldn't be. It was nothing more than spiteful gossip, a tale invented and carried by those who didn't know him, who felt slighted by his cool reserve. If, indeed, Sybil Tilbury had died in Egypt, there was another more logical reason for her demise than cold-blooded murder because…because…

Wyn lifted her face into the wind and faced the unwanted truth. Garrett couldn't be a murderer, because she feared she was falling in love with him and, having guarded her heart so well for so long, it was impossible that she should do so with a man capable of killing either the girl he had grown up caring for, or, as Hildy had alluded, his brother.

Oh, but what if the rumors were true? He was a man who wore a mask. She had known that from the start. She had thought the player was the man the others saw, the cold, reserved Baron Blackhawk. Could she have been wrong? Was the Garrett, who had entranced her that first afternoon at sea, the true actor and she now merely another of the many women Hildy claimed he had seduced?

Before the cold could color her cheeks once more, Wyn returned to her cabin and reluctantly prepared for the gala evening ahead. She needed to look her best, not only to do the captain justice as his chosen belle, but to hide the sorrow in her heart.

Hildy was giddy with excitement, fretting once again about her lack of decent jewelry. Her ball gown pushed the limits of widowhood, being at once subdued in color and striking in design. Shimmering silk of charcoal gray clung to her figure, the narrow sheathlike skirt surmounted by jet black satin panniers that flowed into a ruched and trailing train. Rather than display her shoulders and arms, Hildy had chosen a sleeved bodice with an almost squared neckline that dipped sharply over her bosom. A single strand of jet beads encircled her throat and spilled over her breast, their glitter repeated in the dangling drops that swayed from her ears with every step she took. Wyn doubted there would be many male eyes that strayed far from her friend that night. Hildy might not be dancing, but she would have more than her share of attention all the same.

Would one of her court be Garrett Blackhawk?

He had been far more attentive to Hildy when the company convened in the grand saloon after the storm, plying her with questions about the life she had led in San Francisco, about growing up in the city and entering society. He had been in the city but briefly, Wyn had overheard him say, although the prominent men he asked after made the statement patently untrue. Unless he had merely picked up their names from copies of the San Francisco news sheets. A clever con man could easily do so without even visiting the city. Or he could have been given the names. Deegan, having spent three months in residence while he courted both her and Leonore Cronin, could have provided a list.

She had been foolish back then, and she had been foolish once more in succumbing to passion when alone with Garrett Blackhawk. She would do so no more.

And yet, when she entered the grand saloon with Hildy that evening, a pull as strong as a magnetic force drew her to meet his eyes across the breadth of the room.

He was magnificent, as always, the excellent cut of his evening clothes merely adding to his already overwhelming presence. Trudy Woodrow was twittering at his shoulder, but Wyn doubted that Garrett heard a word the woman said. His gaze drifted over her own form, pleasure in her appearance evident in the slight lift of his lips.

Next to Hildy's stunning ensemble, she had felt insipid and pallid in her sea foam green gown. Sheer tulle draped the narrow skirt, delicately held in place by creamy passion flowers fashioned from organza. More organza blended with a spill of satin to form a graceful sweeping train. The low-cut evening bodice hugged her torso and was decorated with more cleverly crafted blossoms, the decoration ending just shy of the fashionable tiny puffed sleeves. Rather than rely on her crystal ear bobs again, Wyn had fixed small mother-of-pearl earrings in place and fastened a gold locket around her throat.

The approval in Garrett's eyes made her feel like the most beautiful woman in the room, which was not the case as a glimpse at the other women's gowns quickly showed.

The most glowing form was that of Mrs. Mayhew, who was resplendent in royal blue silk, the sheer drape of fabric

across her skirt disguising the fact that she was enceinte.
A necklace, bracelet and earring set of diamonds and sapphires set off her quiet beauty to perfection. Even Trudy
Woodrow was at her best, the garnet red of her dress repeated in the tasteful arrangement of garnet stones dangling from her ears and lying on her slightly freckled chest.

"Wyn," Deegan murmured, stepping before her. "I
hope you'll allow me the favor of a dance this evening."

When she hesitated, he took her gloved hands in his.
"Can't we let bygones be bygones? I'm not suggesting we
start afresh. I'm only asking that we be friends. We were
once," he reminded.

They had nearly been more than that, yet it was difficult
to recall how caught up in dreams of a future with him
she had been. Even though she had once been ready to
marry him, what she had felt for Deegan in the past was
tepid when compared to the way she now felt about his
reckless friend. How close she had come to making a mistake. How close she danced to making yet a bigger one.

Still, she did remember how enjoyable it was to have
Deegan for a partner on the dance floor. Wyn smiled
softly. "One dance," she insisted. "And not a waltz."

"Wouldn't dream of it," he insisted. "Polka's much
more my style."

"Liar," Wyn murmured. "I'll bet Miss Carillo is praying that you request her hand in the waltz."

"Then she's out, if she is," Deegan said. "The Carillo
family is keeping to their cabin this evening rather than
join in our riotous frivolity. Seems their previously seaworthy constitutions were not up to snuff for the storm
earlier. Mrs. Woodrow conveyed their apologies to the
captain a bit ago, although she wasn't dashedly awful sorry
about their conditions, if you ask me. *Chipper* might describe her feelings though." He turned to look back to
where Trudy staunchly held her place at Garrett's side
against invasion by other determined ladies. "Damned
chipper," Deegan said.

"Ah, my dear," Captain Kittrick greeted, slipping

through the crowd. "I was afraid you would force me to lead the first dance with another partner. I hope you've worn your sturdiest evening slippers. A good number of gentlemen are eager to help you wear them out tonight. Unfortunately, we don't have dance cards so it will be every man for himself, hey, Galloway?"

Deegan chuckled. "Which is why I wasted no time in rushing to Wyn's side. And now must do so to that stunning redhead in the blue. Excuse me, my dear? Sir?"

Wyn nodded while Kittrick waved Deegan off. "Sooner I get rid of all rivals the better," he declared, then turned back to Wyn. "How did you hold up during our brief squabble with Neptune this afternoon?"

"Is that what it was?" Wyn asked lightly. "I take it the *Nereid* won the argument?"

"For the nonce," the captain said. "I'm not so sure we've outrun it entirely, but whatever we encounter later tonight will be minor compared to the tossing we took earlier. I'm hoping to wrap this shindig of Tatterly's up within short order."

"I'm not sure that's possible," Wyn said. "Those here are fairly determined party goers."

"Still, I've got a nose for these things," Kittrick declared, taking her arm and leaning closer. "I've made sure the champagne runs out," he murmured. "And if you'll do your part and claim fatigue, thus taking the dashing Mrs. Hartleby, Galloway and Blackhawk with you, I'm fairly sure the rest will declare the evening at an end, as well."

Wyn looked at him skeptically. "I'll do my best to drag Hildy away, but I don't see how my leaving will result in Mr. Galloway and the baron retiring."

"Don't you, my dear?" Kittrick grinned. "Well, fortunately, *I* do."

As the small orchestra chose that moment to play the opening bars of the first lancer of the evening, Wyn let the subject drop and moved onto the dance floor on the captain's arm.

* * *

Garrett took a final sip of champagne and set his glass aside. So far he'd watched a half-dozen men whirl Wyn about on the dance floor, but had kept distant from her himself, wondering the whole time whether he should accept Kittrick's assurance as to her identity. He wanted to. Damned if he didn't. Yet, the more he learned about her, the less he believed. Except in one instance.

"You were right, Dig," he said.

At his side, Deegan's breathing sounded labored, the result of recently having completed an energetic galop with Miss Woodrow. "About anything in particular?" he asked as he blotted his overheated face with a handkerchief.

"Wyn Abbot," Garrett answered. "She does float rather than dance."

"If only my last partner had," Deegan murmured. "I notice you've been devilishly shy of the dance floor this evening."

Garrett readjusted a cuff link, brushed invisible lint from his sleeve, to all intents and purposes interested far more in making minor adjustments to his apparel than in the activities of those around him. "Have I?"

"Not to mention uncommonly cozy with the widow lately," Deegan added.

"Extraordinary woman, Mrs. Hartleby," Garrett said, although his tone stripped all trace of compliment from the words. "A fountain of information. She thinks highly of you, by the way."

A rueful smile lifted Deegan's lips. "Does she now? Then she's changed her tune considerably since Frisco. Likely toadying up to you, old boy. What else did she say? Anything of particular interest?"

"Perhaps to you, my friend," Garrett murmured. Rather than face Deegan, he stared off across the dance floor, ostensibly observing the couples currently on the floor as they moved though the patterns of a quadrille. Having led Hildegarde Hartleby onto the subject of Deegan Galloway and Wyn Abbot, he now had details to sort through, sheaving the truth while discarding the dross of the widow's story. He needed to catch Deegan off guard. Needed to have Dig react in a manner that left no doubt as to his innocence when it came to an elaborate plot, whether it involved Wyn or someone else. "The widow says our Miss Abbot likes high-stake games."

Deegan snorted at the suggestion, his very action a defense of her. "Wyn enjoys the game, not the risk involved. She's a crack player but prefers low stakes."

"Yet, according to her friend, she's bet her entire fortune on what amounts to a single turn of the card," Garrett said. "At the moment you no doubt have more feathers to fly with than she does. Hildegarde insists Wyn is currently penniless, and since she invested everything in this ship, if the maiden voyage is tainted by an inability to discover who took Suzanne's pearls, she is likely to remain so."

"Doubtful, my lad," Deegan said. "Remember, I looked into her resources fully before pursuing her in Frisco. Wyn's income is independent of the Shire Line. Apparently the family thought it was better to keep control of the company in her elder brother's hands. He bought his siblings out a few years back and hasn't done badly for himself."

"Nevertheless, the widow says Wyn put every cent of her fortune in the *Nereid*."

"Ridiculous," Deegan insisted. "Pierce is swimming in dough, rather like yourself. He doesn't need Wyn's pittance."

"Ah, but perhaps he did," Garrett murmured. "Business can be as capricious as a woman, and Abbot's assets might have been stretched too finely."

With a final pass over his brow, Deegan pocketed his handkerchief. "The devil they are. La Hartleby heard wrong."

"What makes you think so?"

"Wyn would have said something to me."

Garrett paused before answering. "I think not."

Deegan's already flushed face burned a bit brighter. "Damn, but you're a cold bastard at times."

Continuing to stare out over the whirl of colorful gowns and midnight jackets, Garrett gave Deegan time to regain his usual aplomb. Wyn moved gracefully among the dancers, her partner in this particular quadrille set the awkward but determined Mr. Mosby.

He felt more than saw the moment when Deegan squared his shoulders with decision. "The widow's right then. I should have known it when she didn't wear the aquamarines," Deegan said.

When Garrett didn't comment, Deegan turned to him. "They were Wyn's favorites although I always thought her emerald set complemented the color of her eyes better."

"They would," Garrett agreed, his imagination conjuring the glitter of the deeply colored stones reflected in the mysteriously dark green pools of Wyn's gypsy-lashed eyes. "So you were lying when you told the table at large that she rarely wore jewels."

"*Lying* is a rather strong word for it, but, yes, I suppose I was," Deegan admitted. "What's it matter? I simply thought that, because old Hartleby left Hildy without a cent to her name and her prized diamonds were nipped, Wyn was simply choosing not to wear her jewels out of consideration. She'd do that to make the widow feel better, you know. She's loyal to the bone."

That Garrett believed. And, he suddenly realized, he was ready to concede that Wyn was who she said she was. Not on fact like any sensible man, but on faith. However, the admission didn't clear her totally of suspicion. If Pierce Abbot was desperate enough to take both his sister's fortune and her jewelry in an attempt to appease his debtors, who was to say he wouldn't suggest to her another way to keep the company solvent?

A steward paused nearby to offer them fresh glasses of champagne from his tray. Deegan helped himself to one. Garrett waved the uniformed man off. "What was that about the widow and diamonds?'' he asked once the steward was out of earshot.

Deegan sipped thoughtfully. ''You remember. It was in all the papers just before we left Frisco. Daring robbery. Fortune in stones. Hartleby died leaving a mountain of debt and in the end the diamonds would more likely than not have been sold to satisfy the more pressing duns. But the way Hildy went on at the time, even the more virulent of the bill collectors were said to commiserate with her over their loss.''

Something about the story nagged at Garrett's mind. '''Daring robbery.' 'Fortune in stones.' Those sound like the same phrases used to describe a robbery in Boston before we sailed.''

''Newspapermen haven't much imagination then, I guess,'' Deegan said. ''They probably have set phrases and headlines to use for sensational stories.''

''Sensational? Then you do remember the story.''

''How could I not?'' Deegan asked. ''It was all anyone at the docks talked about. Oh, not to an august personage like yourself, but certainly to a shifty-looking character like me. Especially since I'd very recently booked passage out of the country.''

For the first time that evening, Garrett's gaze swung away from a contemplation of the dancers. ''The police talked to you?''

''Briefly, but once I'd explained my choice of vessel, and they wired Pierce in San Francisco for verification, they let me leave.''

''I still don't see why—''

''Of course you don't, laddie,'' Deegan said, and downed the rest of his champagne. ''You were too busy nursing a hangover to pay much attention to what went on around you. If you were a sober fellow like myself you'd recall whose jewels were lifted in Boston.'' He paused a moment to lend a touch of the dramatic to his announcement. ''They were sapphires, old boy, and you won't believe the bereft owner's last name. It was Shire. Shire!''

* * *

Wyn looked longingly at the closed entrance doors, wishing it was possible to throw them open, to slip away unseen from the heat of the grand saloon. Instead she fluttered her fan before her flushed face and accepted Mr. Mosby's offer to get her a glass of lemonade. With all that was happening aboard the ship, it most certainly wasn't a night to indulge in champagne, although it appeared she was one of very few passengers of such a mind.

Considering the recent theft, she was amazed at the dazzling display of gemstones being worn that night. Clearly she was alone when it came to common sense.

She glanced at each woman in turn, mentally cataloguing their jewelry, although she was fairly sure Hildy had already compiled her own lustful list. Which of them would the thief in their midst be unable to resist? How did he make his choice? While Suzanne's pearls had been pretty, far more exquisite, expensive sets had been on display since their first night at sea. Was the selection random? Based on the needs of an unknown buyer? What reason lay behind the Carillos' theft? Or behind those that were bound to follow?

While waiting for Mr. Mosby to return, she scanned the crowd, searching for Magnus Finley. He was nowhere in sight. Where was he? What was he doing? Had he discovered anything since agreeing to investigate, if only for the duration of the voyage?

As disappointing as it was, she did agree with him that it would be impossible to continue with the case once the passengers went their separate ways in Liverpool. If only Finley could find the thief in the four days that remained before they docked.

"I am sorry it took me so long, Miss Abbot," Mr. Mosby said, returning to her side. His face was a brighter shade than it had been at the completion of the dance. Beads of perspiration dotted his forehead but he seemed unconcerned as he handed a glass to her, the low level of the lemonade alone attesting to the difficulty he'd had crossing the room without spilling it.

"Thank you, Mr. Mosby," Wyn murmured, raising the glass to her lips.

Before she'd taken more than a sip, the glass was removed from her hand and passed back to her flushed but gallant escort.

"You don't mind watching over this for Miss Abbot awhile longer, do you, Mosby?" Garrett asked. "Kittrick tells me this is the final waltz of the evening." Without bothering to ask her permission, he took Wyn's hand, tucked it into the crook of his arm and led her to the center of the floor as the ship's small orchestra began a selection from Strauss.

Wyn tried to pull away but found that with his hand firmly set over hers she was held at his side. She tugged all the same. "Did it ever cross your mind that I might not care to dance with you, my lord?"

"Devil a bit," he said. "I knew you'd want to."

"That's rather arrogant, isn't it?"

"On your part? I'll forgive you, my dear, just as long as you melt in my arms as you have done other nights."

Wyn pressed her lips tightly closed, determined not to answer him.

Garrett appeared unfazed by her silence. One arm encircling her waist, he swept her into the first gliding steps of the dance. "I missed you last night," he said.

"You make it sound as if we had arranged a rendezvous," Wyn snapped, "and you know that is false."

"Is it?" he asked.

"Yes!"

Garrett smiled down at her and tightened his arm slightly, drawing her closer still as he guided her in a graceful turn. "Perhaps not in words, but a meeting was implied in every sultry look you gave me at the dinner table."

"I did no such thing!"

"I stand corrected," he said smoothly. "You were directing them at the good captain then?"

"No, I—"

"Ah, yes. I like that," Garrett murmured, his voice dropping to an intimate whisper.

Wyn stared up into his eyes, disconcerted that the sound of his voice could affect her so. Soften her. Of their own accord, her dance steps took her nearer him.

"Do you always tremble when in a man's embrace? Or just when in mine?" he asked.

"I'm not—"

The angle of his smile alone told her she was lying.

He was right. She quivered when near him, as if she were a taut string on a violin freshly plucked.

"It's restrained anger," Wyn insisted.

Garrett chuckled lightly. "It probably is at that. Meet me tonight and we can test your theory."

She was tempted to agree. Longed to agree. "I can't."

He raised one aristocratically proud eyebrow. "Another lover's tryst arranged already?"

"Of course not."

"Then meet me," he urged.

The intentness of his gaze was enough to melt the reserve of even the most iron-willed maiden, which this voyage alone had proven she was not.

"You know I shouldn't, Garrett," she said, unable to keep the wistfulness from her voice.

Her skirt brushed that of another woman as a couple whirled too close. The man murmured a hasty apology and swung his partner away, but not before Wyn recognized the expression on the woman's face. Glimpsed it reflected in the man's. She'd seen it on many faces before, that special glow that meant the couple was in love.

Garrett's harsh face reflected another emotion entirely, one that was stronger and more driven. One that took her breath away, made her mind numb and her knees weak.

But it wasn't love.

"I shouldn't," Wyn repeated as the music drew to a close. She sank in a brief curtsy and lifted her eyes to his. Garrett kept her gloved hand in his, bowing over it, his eyes never leaving hers as he audaciously brushed his lips over her fingertips. "I shouldn't meet you," Wyn said again, "but I will."

The wind came up three hours later, bringing with it high seas that rocked the ocean liner with a far from tender hand. Wyn sat curled up on her bunk watching the view through her porthole. The night sky flickered with distant lightning, the darkness turning paler shades of gray if but briefly. She hugged her knees and wondered what had possessed her to make such a rash promise. Wondered how Garrett had reacted when she failed to meet him at the rail.

Wondered if one day her heart would cease to ache with every beat it took.

She had made her decision though. While she feared she was falling in love with him, he had shown nothing akin to a softer emotion when he looked at her, touched her. His onyx eyes burned with passion instead, which fired a burning within her body, her soul. A craving unlike any she had ever known.

But while her body urged her to follow her senses, her mind conjured up Hildy's face as a child, as an adult. She remembered the lilt of shared happiness that had rung in her friend's voice when presented with a special doll, when planning her presentation ball, when planning her wedding. When arranging for this trip. Hildy needed her in a way that was far more binding. Wyn might actually *be* in love with Garrett, but she'd loved Hildy as a friend for a much longer time.

The choice between Hildy and Garrett had been made with logic, common sense.

Why then was her heart sore over choosing her childhood friend?

Had Garrett waited very long for her before realizing she would not be joining him? Was he even yet standing in the lee of the wind, the smoke from his cigarette steaming back like a Lilliputian reflection of the vapors that flowed from the *Nereid*'s giant smokestacks?

Raindrops splattered against the porthole, gentle at first

but growing in intensity. If he still waited he would be
forced to turn his collar up, duck his dark head as he hastened back into shelter. The deck would be slick, the footing slippery.

She could hear the creak of the lifeboats swaying in their
dry berths, the whistle of the wind through the companionway as someone briefly opened a hatch nearby.

Wyn got to her feet, thoughts of Garrett driving her to
find robe and slippers, to slip out just long enough to assure herself that he was not lingering in the storm. She
eased the door to her cabin open, careful not to make a
sound that might disturb Hildy. Pierce's diligence in over-
seeing every detail of construction showed in squeak-free
hinges. The companionway outside the suite was pitch-
dark. The coal oil lamps had no doubt been blown out by
the freshened wind, although the glass flues protecting the
flames were supposed to prevent such a thing from happening.

Wyn peered into the dark, trying to see her way but
ended up using the bulkhead as a guide, sliding her hand
along it as she moved. Her trip would be so short in duration, returning to her cabin to search for a candle would
be a waste of time. The hatch to the outer deck was only
a few yards away and around a sharp elbow in the corridor.
Once there, she could peer through the porthole in the
door, or, if it was too streaked with rain to see out, push
the hatch open enough for her to see the spot in the shadows where Garrett had arranged to meet her.

Despite the workmanship of the carpenters, Neptune
managed to drive the chill touch of the wind through the
bulkheads, past the hatches, until it swirled, playful and
cold, around her shoulders and the hem of her nightdress.
Wyn pulled her robe closer and crept to the outer hatchway.

The rain had rendered the window next to impossible
for viewing, but did allow a glimmer of light to spill
through to the companionway. It was comforting to be able
to see her hand before her face once more. There was

something sinister about cloaking darkness, something that made her imagination run rampant until she wondered if she was truly alone in the corridor.

Wyn's ears pricked, straining to hear over the noise of the storm, but there was nothing but the wind, waves and rain.

Only the foolish would be abroad on such a night. Even the seamen on duty would be keeping close, huddled out of the elements in their oiled slickers. She was being ridiculous in believing Garrett might have lingered, waiting for her, in this tempest, gentle as it was.

All the same, Wyn knew she would be unable to sleep until she knew for certain that he was safe from the storm. She raised her hand to the hatch's latch, then caught a whisper of sound in the corridor behind her.

She paused, unsure that she'd heard it at first, then growing more aware that there was indeed a presence waiting unseen in the dark.

Wyn's fingers lingered on the latch as she turned slightly, peering back into the void. "Garrett? Is that you?"

A rush of footsteps answered her, then there was a whoosh of air before a hard object crashed down on the crown of her head. Wyn's hand dropped lifelessly away from the latch as she sank silently to the floor.

Chapter Twelve

Rain dripping from the broad brim of his slouch hat, the long length of his vaquero duster soaking up moisture despite its oiling, Garrett leaned back against the bulkhead and cursed womankind in general.

It was a miserable night. At any moment his teeth would begin chattering, reacting to the combined miseries of rain and icy North Atlantic wind. Now, more than ever, he missed the heat of the desert. It didn't much matter which desert, the Sahara or the Sonoran. Either would suffice. Both were equally impossible to return to. Which left him with the storm and his thoughts.

The weather was the more pleasant of the two, and it was bloody awful cold and cloying.

Hell, it was just like a woman.

Women!

Wyn had lied to him. He'd realized that an hour ago. He had even returned to his suite rather than act an ass by tarrying any longer. But the luxurious string of cabins had been too confining. Too empty. He'd only taken the time to dig out his western kit and shrug into it before returning to the deck, insulated against the worst the storm could throw at him if not against his thoughts.

They returned time and again to Wyn Abbot.

When would he ever learn not to trust women? Probably

never. They were a man's delight and his curse—more often the latter. Wyn had simply proven that she was no different than the rest of her sex, all of them cut from the same deceiving mold. She had the wiles to bemuse men, the cunning to trick them. The beauty to blind them.

Damn her beauty.

And blast her gorgeous eyes.

They haunted him night and day, whether soft and innocent, snapping and angry, or mysterious and melting. Dig was right. Aquamarines were too pale, too watery in color to do her justice. Emeralds, carefully matched and cut, of the deepest, greenest shade the mine in Brazil produced, were what she should wear. And even they would pale next to the flashing forest green of her eyes. Garrett stared into the storm picturing them, fascinated once more by memory alone.

Damn. What he needed was a smoke but, with the storm blowing, that necessitated moving indoors. He stayed right where he was. A steady stream of water dripped from the curved brim of his hat, a cross in miniature between the rush of storm run-off down a Sonoran arroyo and the spill of a waterfall in a lush Brazilian jungle. He'd witnessed both during his wandering. Nature most frightening and most beautiful.

Garrett conjured the memory of one particularly violent desert flood, picturing the turbulent, muddy waters as they had ripped through the surveyors' camp, destroying equipment and animals and men in an instant. They'd had little warning. The area they'd surveyed that day had been parched, the ground cracked and dusty, the desert plants more brown than green. It hadn't been nature they'd kept a sharp eye out for, but the local bandits. Although at rest, there hadn't been a man among them who hadn't kept a loaded rifle within easy reach. It hadn't been gunfire that split the dead of the night, but a rumble that was felt through the soil rather than heard on the wind. One minute they'd all been sitting peacefully around a campfire and the next their lives had been topsy-turvy.

Rather like his thoughts had been since meeting Wyn. Damn.

Angry with himself over the ease with which Wyn's image appeared once more in his mind, Garrett shifted position, bending his knee, putting one foot flat against the bulkhead behind him. He needed to think about something else, something other than what awaited him in Shropshire, or Wyn.

Something more frightening, more beautiful. The afternoon the natives had attacked the party of investors in Brazil qualified on both counts. He had been one of many interested in the mineral wealth of the region. Gold and emeralds his hosts had promised. They hadn't bothered to mention that one of the recent finds was in an area the local tribe considered sacred. The rain of spears and darts had taken the party by surprise. He had drawn his gun but had been unable to find a clear target in the undergrowth. When one of the guides dropped to his knees, then his stomach, and slithered through the seemingly impenetrable undergrowth, he'd followed suit. The sounds of battle had nearly died away in the distance, replaced by the more frightening rustle of the jungle, the whip and snap of plants hastily cut or pushed from a man's path. Many men's paths. He'd thought his life would end there that day, especially when the guide's trail ended at the sharp drop of a precipice. There had been a roar that drowned out the noise of the warriors trailing them and it had taken a moment or two to identify it as rushing water. Falling water. Moving cautiously to the cliff's edge, he'd glimpsed the guide's crablike scuttle from one precarious handhold to the next until he slipped out of sight behind the roaring falls. Garrett had hastened to follow. The two of them had sheltered in the cave all day, hidden from sight by the spilling fury of the water. Once the natives retreated and his adrenaline had stopped pumping, he'd thought the location one of the most beautiful he'd ever seen, the water a pure white as it tumbled hundreds of feet down to a lagoon that was mysteriously dark and green.

Like Wyn's eyes.

Oh, hell. Would she ever cease to haunt him? Did he want her to?

She was a mystery, one that begged to be solved. He doubted that enough time remained on the voyage to do so. Wondered if even a lifetime would suffice.

He was not the man to take on the task. He had problems enough awaiting him at Hawk's Run. Problems he resisted contemplating. Less than a handful of days remained until he must renounce his hard-won freedom. At least dwelling on Wyn was deucedly better than thinking about his responsibilities.

If only she had been true to her word and joined him on deck.

A bolt of lightning brightened the horizon briefly. The rumble of thunder was distant and faded quickly.

And as it did, Garrett fancied he heard Wyn call his name.

Blinding pain brought Wyn back to consciousness. Someone had touched the tender spot on her head. They probed it yet, she realized, with fingers that were tender but thorough in their examination. She moaned and tried to pull away.

"Gently, my dear," the captain murmured. "You've been away from us for a good while."

Wyn tried to open her eyes but found the effort temporarily beyond her capabilities.

"Will she be all right, Doctor?" Kittrick asked.

"Fine, fine. In fact, I would say..." Wyn didn't catch the doctor's answer. She felt him lean forward, felt her hair stir a moment before he pressed a cloth to her crown. The fresh burst of agony had her sucking in a hiss of air through her gritted teeth.

"Oh, dearest!" Hildy gasped, the gush of words sounding like a prayer of thanksgiving. A soft feminine hand grasped Wyn's and squeezed it tightly. "I was so worried!"

Wyn managed to flutter her eyes open, grimacing slightly at the brightness that surrounded her. Flames flickered in what appeared to be a hundred lamps, making the sitting room area of the suite she shared with Hildy as bright as midday. Somehow she'd come to be tucked up on the divan with Hildy perched next to her on one side and the ship's doctor seated in a chair on the other. Captain Kittrick hovered nearby, but it wasn't to him Wyn's gaze flew.

Squinting against the glare, she raised a hand to shade her sight. "What happened?" she asked.

"That," said the man standing behind Hildy, "is what we're hoping you can tell us."

At first she didn't recognize him. A cowboy's rain slicker hung open over his elegant evening wear; a damp and dripping felt hat sat low over his brow, shadowing his face, nearly disguising his concerned expression. His voice was gruff, stripped free of the artifice he usually employed, only the faintest tinge of his British accent remaining.

"I thought I heard you call," Garrett continued. "The lamps were out in the companionway. I nearly tripped over you in the dark."

Hildy glanced back at him over her shoulder, giving him her most appreciative smile. "I was never so frightened than when Lord Blackhawk burst into the suite with you limp and lifeless in his arms," she said, turning back to face Wyn. "I thought you'd been killed!"

Hildy looked anything but frightened now, Wyn thought. She looked glitteringly alive. Her soft brown hair was loose and trailing around her shoulders as if newly freed from its night braid. The front closing of her exotic robe gaped as if by accident allowing the men around her a generous view of her breasts.

Standing directly behind Hildy, Garrett was presented with the best view.

Wyn blushed, ashamed of her friend's blatant actions. She wondered just how Hildy had responded to Garrett's arrival in the suite. Had she rushed from her own cabin immediately? Or had minutes passed as she stripped off her nightgown and released her hair before donning her clinging, scarlet robe?

Hildy shivered as if in memory of the trial she had recently endured, the motion drawing all three men's attention to her quivering, lush form. "It was horrible, Wyn," she insisted. "But Lord Blackhawk assured me that you were breathing. He told me to bolt the door while he went to get the doctor and the captain, which I did, although I was sure the madman who attacked you lurked just outside ready to murder us all. I thought Lord Blackhawk was extremely brave to go back out into that inky hallway."

Garrett's foreboding frown didn't change. Wyn doubted he was even aware of Hildy's heavy-handed flattery. "The companionway was empty when I found Miss Abbot," he said. "Whoever coshed her had already slipped away."

"Do you recall at all what happened, my dear?" Kittrick asked, his usually boisterous voice considerably tempered by concern.

"Whatever were you doing out of bed anyway?" Hildy demanded.

Wyn didn't miss the slightly arch tone in her friend's voice. Considering Hildy's dishabille resembled that found in a high-priced bordello, her own high-necked cotton batiste gown and silk kimono were quite respectable.

"I thought I heard someone in the corridor," Wyn said, bending the truth slightly.

"And like an imbecile, you followed them?" Garrett snapped.

"No!" The violence of her answer made her head ache more. Wyn put a hand to her temple. "It was too dark. I couldn't see a thing."

Kittrick shook his head slowly from side to side. "Shame," he murmured.

Garrett's expression grew fiercer. "You think it was our thief on the prowl again?"

The captain allowed his gaze to rest on Hildy a moment.

"Not necessarily. Could have been a man stealing in or out of a woman's cabin."

Wyn was relieved when Hildy had the grace to blush. *Had* the presence she'd sensed in the companionway been one of the gentlemen who had crowded around her friend earlier that evening? It didn't seem possible. Not when Hildy had set her sights on Garrett.

But it had been Garrett who had carried her back to the suite. Had he also been the man stealing from Hildy's bed? The man who, rather than risk discovery, had attacked her?

Wyn frowned, thinking back. It had been dark, but not blindingly so near the outer hatch. There had been a flash of lightning not long before she was struck. A glimmer that had shown her an arm uplifted a brief second prior to the blow. An arm clad in dark fabric but made more visible by the edge of a pale cuff. She tried to concentrate, to see a face beyond the arm. Instead, Wyn saw the blur of white descending toward her once more.

She squeezed her eyes shut, her breathing quickening with a fresh onslaught of fear.

"I'm going to give you something to alleviate the pain and help you sleep, Miss Abbot," the doctor said, lifting his black satchel onto a nearby side table.

"Bless you, sir," Hildy murmured. Clasping Wyn's hand in both of hers, she raised it to her chest in a touching display of emotion. "I don't know what I'd do if something happened to my dearest friend." Her voice broke on the last word. A tear rolled down her cheek.

If she hadn't been familiar with Hildy's ability to weep on cue, Wyn might have believed the act. The captain and the doctor were certainly taken in. Rather than see the same expression of tender concern on Garrett's face, Wyn kept her eyes on Hildy.

"I recommend you keep to your cabin for the next day to two, Miss Abbot," the doctor said, measuring out a dose of laudanum into a glass of water.

"Yes," Wyn whispered, and slipped her hand free from Hildy's grasp. Playing the invalid would be ample excuse for her to avoid Garrett and would allow Hildy free rein as she stalked him. The scenes she had played out with Leonore Cronin over Deegan would not be performed again with Hildy and Garrett. It no longer mattered whether he was who the ship's company believed him to be. If Garrett was the man that her friend wanted, it was best if she distanced herself from them both.

"If you remember anything, my dear, please let me know," the captain urged. He got to his feet. "I'll arrange for your meals to be taken here in your cabin."

"And I shall stay at your beck and call, dearest," Hildy assured, "for I know how fretful you get when confined. We shall play as many hands of whist as you wish."

Despite herself, Wyn's eyes widened in consternation and she winced. She hoped those gathered put the grimace down to her head injury. The doctor certainly did, for he immediately helped her raise up enough to drink his foul-tasting sleeping potion.

"Nonsense," Garrett said. "You'll join the rest of the company, Mrs. Hartleby."

Hildy simpered up at him. "Oh, but I couldn't, my lord. Wyn needs me."

"Not if she intends to play cards," he insisted.

Wyn nearly choked on her medicine. He was quite right. Having Hildy as a partner at cards would be a cruel punishment.

"I'm sure Mr. Tatterly can concoct some form of non-strenuous entertainment for you, my dear," Kittrick assured kindly.

"Don't even think of it, Captain," Garrett said. "Tatterly has his time taken up keeping the rest of the passengers distracted. I'll send Galloway along to entertain Miss Abbot in his place."

Deegan! Wyn moaned, mumbling under her breath in defeat.

"What was that, dearest?" Hildy asked, bending near.

Garrett took Hildy's arm and drew her to her feet and away from the divan. "A snatch of Latin, Mrs. Hartleby."

His lips curled in a rueful grin. His voice had regained the edge Wyn had come to associate with his role as Baron Blackhawk. "Aimed, if I'm not mistaken, at me. *'Et tu, Brute.'* Was that not it, Miss Abbot? Quite classical of you, my dear. Perhaps I shall unseat Galloway at your side for an hour or so that we might discuss the ancients."

He didn't, of course. Wyn hadn't expected him to. Deegan arrived, as promised, the next morning. When he knocked at the sitting room hatch, Hildy had just finished pinning a stunning Leghorn walking hat over her soft brown curls and was scrutinizing her reflection in the glass. She'd filched both bracelets of satin-finished Etruscan design and a lapel watch from Wyn's meager jewel box. Her pearl gray basque fit like a glove; a matching overskirt spilled behind her in a light train. The whole was enhanced by a froth of lace at collar and cuff, again items Wyn recognized as her own. She didn't begrudge Hildy the use of her things—as a semi-invalid she certainly wasn't using them herself!

Hildy paused in her self-admiration long enough to answer Deegan's rap. With barely a nod in greeting to him, Hildy turned back briefly to where Wyn reclined on the divan, a lap robe tucked around her limbs. "Are you sure you will be all right?" she asked, clearly inquiring for appearances' sake. The jet black ostrich plume on her hat fluttered as she poised ready for flight.

"Go," Wyn urged. As long as she moved slowly, her head didn't swim. She'd managed to dress, donning a simple, loose-fitting jade housedress and, rather than disturb the dressing the doctor had put on her injury, she'd tied her hair back with a black satin ribbon. She'd accomplished it all without increasing the discomfort that lingered, an all too painful reminder of her adventure. However, watching Hildy's flighty movements made her head throb unbearably once more.

"I'll take good care of her, Mrs. Hartleby," Deegan promised, gallantly holding the hatch open for her.

Hildy smiled flirtatiously at him. "I know you will, Mr. Galloway, but I can't help but worry about appearances. Wyn is a single lady and you are a bachelor. She really shouldn't be entertaining you at all, sir."

"I'm not *entertaining* him," Wyn said. "In fact, I'll probably send him away so I can rest in peace."

"Ah, but, you see, that is exactly why I am here," Deegan drawled. "To make certain that you don't die of boredom."

Hildy lingered a moment more. "You're sure?"

Wyn reclined back against the cushions and draped a lavender-scented handkerchief over her eyes. "Go," she repeated. "Both of you."

There was a rustle of silk that indicated her friend had dashed off, probably to Garrett's side, and the closing of the hatch, but Wyn doubted Deegan had done as requested. Despite the fragrance on her cloth, she caught the headier scent of his cologne.

Wyn lifted an edge of the handkerchief and peered over at him. "There's really no reason you need stay, either."

"Certainly there is," he insisted. He doffed his top hat and tossed it aside on a chair before crossing the room to her side. "I'd go in fear of my life if I abandoned my post. If Garrett didn't come gunning for me, I'm sure the captain would." He pulled a chair and small side table within easy reach for her and made himself at home, flipping his coat-tails aside as he sat down. A moment later, a deck of cards riffled in his hands. "What do you say we avoid whist and go straight to draw poker? I'll even let you name the stakes, although, considering your current state of health, I'm willing to take your marker should you choose kisses over filthy lucre."

"Deegan."

"No? Filthy lucre it is, then."

"Deegan."

"More jewels are missing this morning," he said, his tone conversational.

Wyn sat up abruptly and was immediately sorry.

Deegan pretended he hadn't seen her grimace of pain. He continued shuffling the cards. "That Finley fellow has been turning out one passenger after another as he searches the cabins. Not making friends in the least."

Slowly Wyn pushed aside the lap robe and swung her feet to the floor, sitting up. "What was taken this time?"

"Cut?" Deegan offered. When Wyn brushed the suggestion aside, he flicked cards from the deck, dealing them both five. "You recall a particularly fine diamond and sapphire set?"

"Mrs. Mayhew?"

"The same."

"Oh, the poor lady!"

Deegan grinned fondly. "You've a soft heart, me darlin'. They're only trinkets and no doubt insured at that. You, on the other hand, had a far more lethal run-in with our collector. It might not have crossed your mind yet, but the thought has certainly been bandied about by the rest of us. You could easily have been killed."

"But I wasn't," Wyn said.

"And who should know better than I that you've got an uncommonly hard head?" Deegan gestured to the cards she had automatically picked up and arranged in her hand. "Shall we ante up or simply go on to discards?"

Wyn tossed two cards facedown on the table. "I think you mean that I have a hard heart."

Deegan dealt her replacements and took three for himself. "Some might say I got just what I deserved in courting two women at once. I'm sorry if you got hurt in the process, Wyn. It was never my intention to—"

She interrupted him. "Three of a kind. Jacks."

"You lose," Deegan murmured. "Full house. Tens and queens."

"Marked cards?"

"None other. I've played with you before," he said, "so I know I need all the help I can get."

Wyn gathered up the cards, stacked them neatly. Ran

her fingertips along the sides. "Nicely shaved," she said before beginning to shuffle. "Why'd you do it, Deegan?"

"You mean Leonore?"

She set the deck in the center of the table. He leaned forward and cut. "I like having money, Wyn," he said.

"Did you care for her at all?"

When Deegan didn't answer immediately, Wyn dealt a new hand.

"No," he confessed. "I'm a despicable bastard, aren't I?"

"Mmm," Wyn agreed. "But since you can admit you are one, you're probably reforming."

"Hell, after an insult like that, I've half a mind not to tell you the rest of our on-board intrigue." His eyebrows rose sharply as he sorted through his cards. "Now who's cheating?"

"Fair's fair," Wyn insisted, arranging her own hand. "You mean there's more to last night's robbery?"

"Robberies," Deegan corrected. "In the plural. Mother Woodrow has been trimmed of her garnets, as well. In fact, since the Woodrows are two cabins away from yours, Finley thinks you might have surprised the thief just after he'd lifted Trudy's gems."

Stunned, Wyn put her cards facedown on the table.

"It wouldn't surprise me if Finley was along later to question you," Deegan added.

"But I didn't see who it was."

"Finley thinks you might have and just don't realize it. He's already put together a few ideas based on what is known about each of the thefts. Says our man is daring, nervy. Cunning. Thrives on danger." Deegan paused. "This is without doubt the worst hand I've held in ages. I'll take four cards, please."

Wyn passed them to him absentmindedly. Daring? Cunning? Someone who sought danger? Garrett's face surfaced in her mind. He was all of those things and an actor, too. "Does Mr. Finley suspect anyone in particular yet?"

"The good Pinkerton is keeping a closed mouth, but

that doesn't mean others haven't been busily engaged in mental gymnastics over the thief's identity." Deegan groaned. "You are a vicious woman, Miss Abbot. These cards are even worse than the ones I threw away." He tossed his hand onto the table. "I concede the game."

Slowly Wyn turned over her hand, one card at a time, to show him the four aces she'd palmed and held.

"Extremely vicious," Deegan murmured. "I'm impressed. Pierce doesn't know that little trick, does he?"

"No," Wyn said.

"Remind me to look him up the next time I'm in Frisco," Deegan said. "It's always convenient to have a mark handy for a game on rainy days."

She pushed the deck across to him for the next deal. "Who do others suspect the thief is?"

"Depends who you talk to." Rather than pick up the cards, he let them lie untouched a moment more. "Carillo thinks it's someone from third class. Mrs. Mayhew's companion thinks it is Carillo busily covering up his own guilt. And then there's Garrett."

"Garr—Lord Blackhawk?" Wyn felt her cheeks redden at the near slip.

"Relax," Deegan urged, tilting his chair back on its rear legs. "He calls you Wyn, so I think you can use his given name when you're with me."

"Someone suspects him of the thefts?" she asked. Although she had her own reasons for suspecting him, it was still shocking to hear others were as suspicious as she.

"Garrett? Don't be ridiculous. As far as the ship's company is concerned, he's as pure as the driven snow. No, it's more a matter of whom he suspects that I have trouble with."

"Who is that?"

Deegan let the chair drop back on all fours. He reached for the deck of cards and let them slip from one hand to another. "This is just an educated guess, mind you, but I believe it's me."

Chapter Thirteen

Three days later, Wyn sat at the writing desk in her suite, hastily finishing the last lines of the letter she would mail upon reaching Liverpool. It was already many pages long, detailing as it did the events of the *Nereid*'s disastrous maiden voyage. She paused, stretching her cramped fingers a moment before adding the final lines.

And so, Pierce, we end this trip none the wiser. Mr. Finley has not managed to locate the missing gems, nor has he managed to uncover the identity of our mysterious thief. When we dock tomorrow, the villain will slip away with a small fortune in jewelry and we are helpless to stop him. I can only hope that news of these events does not result in a loss of passenger traffic for the Line. Only time will tell, I daresay.

On a more cheerful note, I have recovered nicely from my encounter with the fellow, and am looking forward to boarding the train for Shropshire and the Loftus estate. One of our passengers, a Mrs. Mayhew—yes, one of the victims!—tells me the countryside is lovely and that I should not miss a chance to visit the abbey ruins in a town picturesquely named Much Wenlock. She says I should bring my sketchbook when I go, which only shows you that she's not

seen my frightful attempts at drawing. I believe I will
stick to cards, thank you.

My love to everyone. Your soon-to-be-bankrupt
sister,

Wyn

Aboard the Shire Liner *Nereid*
Eve of arrival in England

Behind Wyn, the hatch opened and was slammed closed
again. Her hand jerked in surprise causing the pen to send
a shower of tiny ink polka dots spraying over the sheet of
writing paper.

"Men!" Hildy snarled. She threw down her fragile Chi-
nese ivory evening fan. It skittered across the divan and
sailed onto the floor. Hildy didn't bother to reclaim the fan
but stormed up and down the cabin, her dark gray silk
skirts swishing at every angry turn she took. "Do you
know what *that man* has done now?"

Wyn didn't have to ask who *that man* was. Hildy had
begun referring to Garrett Blackhawk by the misnomer the
evening before when he adroitly avoided being alone with
her on deck.

The heavens had been star-filled, the moon full, the Atlantic kinder for a change in the temperature of the wind
that filled the auxiliary sails, and Hildy had been floating
rather than walking after enjoying the baron's nearly constant company the past few days. She believed that his
interest was due to the changes she had made in her wardrobe. Wyn had never seen Hildy so anxious to ply a needle
before, but during the few short days they'd been at sea,
her friend's new gowns had all undergone major renova-
tions. Necklines had been dropped, trimming changed, and
hemlines shortened a scandalous half inch. Yet, when
Hildy left the dining room to stroll with Garrett in the
moonlight the evening before, she had found they were
accompanied by the Carillos and Mr. Mosby. The baron
had escalated the rise of Hildy's temper by offering his

arm to Suzanne rather than to her, leaving Hildy with Mr. Mosby for an escort.

"What has he done this time?" Wyn asked.

Hildy wrung her hands theatrically and wilted back into the soft cushions of the lone armchair. "He sent Deegan with his apologies and didn't appear at dinner."

Wyn blotted the splatters on her letter. "Did he?" she murmured lightly. She was beginning to envy Garrett the opportunity to escape her friend's histrionics.

"I thought at first that he was eating alone, like you have been doing, dearest," Hildy said. "But I happened upon a steward returning from Mrs. Mayhew's suite and discovered that he was dining with her!"

"Alone or with her companion and escort as well?" Wyn asked.

Hildy's mouth opened then shut abruptly. "I had forgotten them. Oh, Wyn, whatever am I to do? I was sure he would propose to me this evening. He's been so attentive!"

Careful to keep her eyes turned away from her friend, Wyn recapped her bottle of ink and patted the tip of her pen against the blotter. "Has he kissed you?" she asked, forcing her voice to sound casual, offhand.

Hildy's dejected sigh was nearly answer enough. "He hasn't even tried."

Despite her attempts to still it, Wyn's heart fluttered happily. Her blood sang with renewed hope and energy.

"But then these English gentlemen are far more reserved than American men," Hildy continued.

There had been nothing reserved in the way Garrett's lips had felt against hers, Wyn mused. Tender, yes, but they'd also been equally hot and demanding.

"Oh, it is just my luck to meet the perfect man only to have him turn out to be a stickler for convention," Hildy declared, peeved. "He's following the dictates of society and not pushing his attentions on a widow yet in mourning."

Wyn doubted anyone believed that Hildy was in mourning for Oswin Hartleby, even half mourning, despite her attempt to make her wardrobe appear marginally so.

"No doubt," she murmured. "Was it lovely out tonight?"

"Hmm? Oh, I barely noticed, dearest. Do you think it would impress the baron if I mentioned I'll be staying with Lady Rachel at Sir Alston Loftus's country seat? Or does that sound pompous?"

It sounded typically like Hildy. "Pompous," Wyn said. "Not to mention incorrect. As Lofty's wife, Rachel is Lady Loftus."

Hildy pouted. "I have to say something to him so he knows where to find me. Oh, do you suppose he'll be traveling on to London? I could end this silly mourning period, have Rachel's seamstress completely revamp my wardrobe and go on to the capital!" She sat up straighter, blue eyes glowing. "That is just the thing, don't you agree, Wyn?"

Knowing she had no option but to agree, Wyn nodded. "And if Lord Blackhawk isn't there, I'm sure you will steal the hearts of numerous other men."

Hildy snapped her fingers in the air. "As if I cared *that* for other men anymore."

Wyn gripped her hands together tightly on the desk top. "You love him then?"

"Love?" Hildy smiled patronizingly. "Ah, you are still a romantic, aren't you, dearest? I am more practical. He is rich. He is young. He is…well, not handsome, but certainly attractive. I've noted other women looking at him when we are together, envying my ability to hold his attention. That, in itself, is a coup. But love? I don't believe in that overrated emotion. And, if you wish to ever marry, you must rid yourself of such dreams."

It was a lecture she'd given herself enough times, Wyn admitted silently. Yet it was also a philosophy she could not follow and remain true to herself. She would wait for love or remain a spinster living on memories of the one

man she might have given her love to had circumstances
been different.

With a rustle of her skirts, Hildy got to her feet. "Oh,
I have so much to do before we dock tomorrow."

There was only one thing Wyn had yet to do, something
she had been putting off since the night of the storm.
"Would you mind if I took a last turn on the deck this
evening?" she asked. "I have so missed my nightly con-
stitutionals these past few days."

Hildy reached to her hair and unfastened the black ostrich plume pinned among her bounding sausage curls.
"Not in the least. I'll be busy packing, and should follow
your excellent example and scratch out a letter to my parents. Just promise me you won't outstay your strength,
dearest."

"I won't," Wyn promised. "I know my limitations only
too well." Far too well.

She slipped into her sleeping cabin to gather up her
cloak, forcing herself to move at an unhurried pace. It
would not do to look eager to escape Hildy's company.
Or too eager to reach the man she was sure she would find
waiting for her at the rail.

She needn't have worried, for Hildy was already in her
own cabin when Wyn returned to the sitting room. The
sounds of trunk latches being released showed that the
widow would be occupied for a good while.

Although the balmy night air seemed made for lovers,
there were few passengers on deck, most preferring, like
Hildy, to attend to their trunks that evening. All the same,
Wyn pulled the hood of her wrap up to cover her unbound
hair. She'd chosen her gown carefully and was secure in
the knowledge that, should the cape blow open, the emerald silk would help her blend anonymously into the
night.

The moon remained full and was veiled lightly in wispy
clouds. The stars glowed, twinkling like lit candles in the
heavens, their brilliance reflected in the lights that appeared to dance on each of Neptune's whitecaps. Although

she had heard that after the daring double robbery the captain had inaugurated a separate watch to patrol the ship after dark, no one challenged her. Wyn wasn't sure what excuse she could give should she be accosted. There was only one thought in her mind. It lent wings to her heels.

On other occasions it had been Garrett who stepped from the shadows to mesmerize, intoxicate her with his caress. Tonight it was he who stood outlined against the stars and sea. Wyn slowed her step, content to memorize the way he looked, his back to her, his hands resting on the topmost rail as he leaned forward. The sable black of his hair was tousled, falling forward as if teased there by the playful hand of a nereid. It was the only aspect of his appearance that wasn't rigidly correct, the only part that appeared flexible.

"You're late," he said, not bothering to turn around. "Three days late."

Wyn stayed where she was in the shadows, not even questioning how he knew she was there. "I'm sorry."

"Sorry," he rasped, giving the word an unnatural edge. "Well, then that makes everything right, doesn't it, Miss Abbot?"

She took a single step forward, reached out to him. "Garrett, I…"

He lifted one hand, the action in itself a swift command for silence. "There's no need to explain. I quite understand. I'm a rascally blighter whose only goal in life is to seduce every gullible maiden to whom I take a fancy. But then you already suspected as much, didn't you?"

Wyn dropped her arm and tugged the edges of her cape around her as if the cloth could protect her from the coolness of his tone. "Don't say such things. I know you aren't who you pretend to be," she said quietly.

"Am I not?" He turned then, but only to lean back casually against the rail as he took a prerolled cigarette from the inner pocket of his evening jacket. In the flare of the match, the craggy angles of his face looked as inflexible as those of a stone statue. "You are quite mistaken, my dear," he said, cupping a hand around the flame.

She stepped up to the rail, facing the sea rather than him. "Please don't do that."

"Objecting to my major vice?" He drew deeply on the cigarette then released the smoke from his lungs in a slow stream.

"You know what I mean," Wyn insisted. "Although I'm sure you've convinced the rest of the company that you are the Baron Blackhawk, I—"

Garrett laughed.

Wyn didn't find it a pleasant sound.

"Now if only I could convince myself of that," he murmured and took another leisurely draw on his cigarette. "Unfortunately, I *am* the cursed baron. The doubly damned baron." Self-loathing rang in his voice. "Ah, but you don't believe I am. Instead you think me Finley's elusive burglar." Garrett grinned grimly. "It's quite a delightful new role for me, but one I fear I lack the enthusiasm to pursue. I do hope you aren't disappointed."

Wyn had never heard such self-contempt in any man's voice before. The sound alone acted like a hand tightening around her heart, squeezing it painfully. What had happened to Garrett to make him loathe himself to such a destructive degree? "Please," she pleaded. "This is our last night at sea. I'd hoped we could part on better terms."

"A bittersweet farewell? How touching." He took a final draw on his cigarette then pitched the stub overboard. "Am I to be noble and simply take your hand in mine and mumble trite phrases about devotion and duty?"

He lifted her hand in his. A simple enough action, but just the sensation of his flesh against hers was as lethal as the song of sirens. Not only did her blood seem to rush in her ears, her mind clouded to everything but the moment and the man she found it impossible to resist.

If he felt the pull of attraction, Garrett gave no indication of it. One brow raised in a wicked, questioning arch. He dropped the pitch of his voice, turning it into a sensual

weapon. "What shall it be, Wyn?" he murmured, his
voice roving over her like a caress. "Poetry, perchance?"

Wyn closed her eyes, knowing she should resist him.
Knowing she couldn't.

Garrett drew her near so that the words he whispered
took on the mantle of intimately exchanged secrets. "Shall
it be lines praising your beauty, my love? A few tender,
longing glances?"

His lips moved lightly over her knuckles, the erotic sensation causing Wyn's eyes to fly open and a sharp gasp to
escape involuntarily from her lips.

"Ah, yes," he purred, "the part would definitely demand them. But I am an impatient sort. A man of action
rather than words."

Again he lifted her hand to his lips so that she felt his
breath warm and intimate against her fingers. She shivered
when, rather than kiss her hand, Garrett turned it slightly
so that he might press his lips to her inner wrist. His fingertips grazed over her cupped palm, sensitizing it, preparing it for the moment when his mouth covered it. In
the space of a single heartbeat, her breathing became labored.

"Garrett, please. I—"

She broke off, swallowing quickly when she felt the tip
of his tongue draw a damp line from the heel of her hand
to the tender mound beneath her index finger.

And as he did so, his eyes never left hers.

He knew the instant he had won. Her eyes, already so
dark and mysterious, glittered with a light that borrowed
none of its glow from either moon or stars. She trembled
slightly, the tremor doing wonders for his ego. It had been
far too long since he'd touched her, far too long since he'd
tasted her. He had feared she had triumphed over the magic
that drew them together. Something he had been unable to
do, unwilling to do. Now he knew she was as caught up
in the spell as he. That time had not diminished its power.

To keep her from learning the extent to which she had

bewitched him, Garrett hooded his eyes from Wyn. To distract her, he kissed her palm, but found himself reveling in the exotic flutter of her fingertips as they brushed lightly against his jaw. Would that he was the villain she thought him, that the world thought him. Such a man would not give a second thought to seducing her. Wyn Abbot was a trophy any man would relish. It would be so easy to lure her from her maiden's path. He'd honed his skills as a lover in the boudoirs of London's hostesses long ago. He had added dimension and inventiveness among satin pillows in Egypt, on velvet covered courtesans' couches in Brazil, and in a variety of soft beds in sunny Mexico. She would profit from them all.

If, that is, he were in truth the scoundrel rumor painted him to be.

He would savor her a few minutes more, Garrett promised himself, and then release her to fly away, virtue yet intact.

A soft moan of desire escaped her lips as he pressed a final kiss into her captive hand. She reached out, brushed the spilling, tangled locks of his hair back from his brow in a motion that was tender and loving. "Why?" she whispered so softly he nearly took the words to be a caprice of the wind. "Why did it have to be you?"

Garrett wasn't sure how it happened. One moment they stood still, barely touching, their eyes locked, seeking answers. Then Wyn altered the script, no longer following the directions he thought fate had written for them. Slowly, ever so slowly, she raised her arms and slid the hood of her cape back off her glorious mane.

He stood frozen to the spot, seemingly forgetting to breathe as the provocative implications of the simple action dawned on him. She had only bared her head to him, but in doing so, she had implied a further unveiling, of her body, her soul. She had surrendered to him.

Moonlight gilded her flaxen locks a gleaming silver, turned her eyes into shimmering dark pools. Showed him that her lips were slightly parted and waiting. The flirtatious breeze teased her cloak open, tantalizing him with a glimpse of her square-cut, low neckline and the slight rise of her creamy breast above it.

Not trusting himself to accept the sweet invitation, but unable to resist touching her, Garrett gathered Wyn close, enfolding her protectively. She flowed into his waiting arms, nestling against him, her cheek pressed to the hard breadth of his chest.

"Dear God," he murmured. "Why did I have to meet you now? Why couldn't it have been a year ago when my life was still my own?"

Wyn tilted back her head to look up at him. The action displayed the long, graceful length of her throat in a gesture of trust and submission. "Y-you're married?"

He hugged her tight. "Lord, if it were only that," he said. "I'm bound in a far less pleasant indenture. One not as easily gotten rid of as an unwanted wife."

A shadow crossed her face, causing Garrett to wish he could read her mind. It was gone in a moment. Wyn bent her head again, resting against him. "I know so little about you. This can't be love," she whispered.

Love. A word he associated with women. A word they frequently mouthed, frequently asked to hear. He'd never said it to anyone but Sybil and she had rejected him in favor of his brother.

"I thought, perhaps, lust," Garrett said.

Wyn sighed softly. "In good measure," she agreed. "What should we do about it?"

He took a deep breath, hoping it would clear his mind, allow him to think clearly. The scent of her flowery perfume filled his head instead. "If I were a gentleman, I'd say we do nothing."

"Nothing," she repeated, her voice forlorn.

"But I'm not one," Garrett said. He tilted her face up. "Shall I prove it to you?"

The brightness of her eyes was all the answer he needed. Tenderly he drew her away from the rail, back into deep shadow and lowered his mouth to hers.

She murmured deep in her throat, a small cry of pleasure that he swallowed joyfully. He gathered her closer, forcing her head to fall back on his supporting arm as he deepened the kiss. She gave him back measure for measure, her mouth open and greedy, her tongue entwining with his in an intimate, ancient dance of passion.

When he tore free to taste the curve of her cheek, the line of her jaw, the sweet curve of her throat, Wyn clung to him, her nails biting into his shoulders as her breathing escalated. The ties of her cloak broke the path he charted but briefly. Garrett pushed the heavy fabric aside, gathered the fullness of her breast in his hand. Wyn's gasp of delight urged him to take even more liberties. The buttons of her long-waisted basque presented little resistance. He dispensed with them quickly, brushing aside the emerald silk to display the ribbons that decorated her corset, the lace-edged lawn of her camisolette peeping just above it.

"You're perfect," he said. "Beautiful and perfect."

"Mmm," she moaned, drawing his lips back to hers.

There was an urgency, a desperation, in her kiss that accorded with his own frustrated need. As he angled his mouth over hers, Garrett dipped his fingers inside her clothing to tantalize the budding tip of her breast. Wyn's response was all that he could wish. She moved closer to him, wordlessly insistent that he continue to caress her.

He did as she wished, dragging the fragile fabric away to replace it with his mouth. This time she moaned sweetly and buried her fingers in his hair, cupping his head, holding him in place as he teased, licked, suckled her.

"Wyn, Wyn, Wyn," he whispered. "I want you so."

"I want you," she murmured. "Make love to me. Please, make love to me."

But he couldn't, and live with his conscience.

It took a Herculean effort to release her, to draw the folds of her cape around her, covering the sweet, intimate delights he had only moments before savored. It was impossible to totally break the physical link they'd shared, though. His hands lingered, resting on her shoulders. "No, my sweet," Garrett said. "Bounder that I am, I will not leave you with a reason to regret this night."

She stared up at him in wonder. "I could never regr—"

"Hush." He leaned forward, brushed a tender kiss across her lips to silence the promise he knew she should not make.

Wyn's mouth clung to his. She raised on tiptoe to continue the caress when he tried to break it. "But we may never see each other again."

Garrett grazed her cheek tenderly with his knuckles, tucked an errant lock of her hair back. "Which is why—"

This time it was she who stopped him, pressing her fingers gently to his lips. "Then leave me with memories, Garrett," she said.

For what felt like an eternity he simply stood there, searching her face for a hint of vacillation. He found only need that matched his own.

In answer, he gathered her close once more.

From the shelter of shadows, a lone passenger paused to watch the tender scene. The moonlight was a whimsical stage manager, choosing to cast uneven light over the performers. Veiling clouds created cover for the lovers, shielding them from overt scrutiny. But the watcher had seen enough.

For all that the baron and the heiress appeared to skirt each other in public, the passionate embrace they were now engaged in left no doubt as to the depth of feeling that drew them together.

The watcher cursed silently, yet lingered, eyes trained to every move the couple made. When the baron swept the captain's belle up into his arms, the shadow trailed at a safe distance, taking special note of the way Blackhawk's dark head bent near her fair one to whisper.

Words of love, no doubt, the watcher decided and showed considerable surprise when, rather than carry his prize to his luxurious stateroom, the baron pushed open the hatch that led to the dark and deserted ladies' saloon.

Creeping nearer, moving slowly so as not to attract attention from the ship's night watch, the passenger glided to a porthole only to find the drapes drawn across it. The watcher stepped back, evaluating the chance of discovery should the couple notice the hatch being pushed slightly open. Was further knowledge of their clandestine affair worth the risk?

A faint glow of lamplight appeared at the previously unnoticed gap at the joining of the drapes. The watcher's lips curled slightly in an appreciation of the fickleness of the Fates before pressing an eye to the convenient opening.

The baron had deposited his lovely burden on one of the low couches. She posed there, watching as he turned the wick down on the single lamp to soften the light. When he rejoined her, he wasted no time but quickly unfastened the heiress's cloak, allowing it to slide, forgotten for the moment, to the deck. She sat before him unashamed, the bodice of her gown gaping open. She smiled, blatant encouragement clear to read on her face.

The watcher stayed long enough to see the heiress place her hand on the baron's chest, run it up his weskit, along his shirtfront. He said something, but only the heiress knew the words he spoke. The sound of his rumble barely reached the sharp ears of the interested passenger. Whatever had been said, it brought a brighter smile to the heiress's face. She dipped her lashes in a flirtatious ploy then slipped her fingers into his hair and drew him down to her spilling, displayed cleavage.

The one outside the cabin stepped back from the porthole. Leaned back against the bulkhead.

Deceivers were they both. Fools. *Enjoy this moment,* the shadow wished them silently before stealing quietly away. There were plans to be made. Revenge to be taken. All would come together soon, the grand plan falling finally into place. Tomorrow the *Nereid* would make land and the long awaited destiny would take shape. The reckoning, at last, had come.

Chapter Fourteen

The days after the *Nereid*'s arrival on English shores went by in a blinding flash for Wyn. She was glad of the frantic pace set. It left her little time to dwell on the all-too-brief hour she had spent with Garrett their last night at sea. On his restraint in not asking for or taking the one gift she would have regretted giving later. Hildy had insisted upon shopping for notions before leaving Liverpool, which necessitated their staying over in a hotel. They managed to catch an early train two days later, but the succession of transfers from one railway to the next that were needed to reach Much Wenlock made for a long and extremely tiring journey.

Sir Alston Loftus, Hildy's brother-in-law, had met the train himself, prewarned of their arrival by a wire sent from Shrewsbury. His welcome was warm; that of his tearfully happy wife even warmer. Wyn had fallen thankfully into bed that night sure that she would be too tired to dream of Garrett. But she had. Fitfully.

As a result she was far from rested when Alston walked into the breakfast parlor the next morning and dropped what amounted to a bomb.

Hildy had kept to her chamber, pleading weariness, so it was only Wyn and her hostess at the table. Alston arrived, yet in his riding clothes, pausing only to hand his top hat and riding crop to the butler before joining them. He was a handsome if unassuming young man, his hair a sandy brown, his stature not above average but well proportioned.

"You'll never guess who I ran across on my ride a bit ago, Rachel. The Changeling. Seems to have made his prodigal return a couple days ago," Alston said, then turned to peer at Wyn's breakfast plate. "That can't be all you're eating, my dear. Beacham, fetch Miss Abbot another rasher or so of bacon and some of those coddled eggs," he instructed the butler.

Wyn hastily refused the offer, accepting only a second cup of coffee from the elderly retainer.

"The Changeling!" Rachel exclaimed. Her hair was a darker shade of brown than her sister's although they shared the same vibrant shade of blue eyes. "Oh, I do wish you wouldn't call him that, Lofty. He can't like it."

"Doesn't," her husband agreed, taking his seat at the head of the table. "Never has, but it hasn't stopped a soul from calling him it, including his brother, Ellery, although not to his face, naturally. He's been away, what? Three years?"

"Two," Rachel said. "I never would have met him if it had been longer. He was one of the more welcoming of our neighbors when I first arrived. Apparently," she confided, turning to Wyn, "the neighborhood expected me to be a wild savage or something simply because I was an American. But Garrett was willing to overlook any shortcomings I might have as an apprentice English lady."

Wyn froze, her coffee cup poised in the air. Garrett? Surely, it couldn't be…

"Ha!" Alston snorted. "Flirting with the prettiest girl in the countryside, more like. That's always been his style."

"Nonsense," Rachel insisted, but she blushed prettily at his compliment. "You know quite well that he had eyes for no one but Sybil then."

Sybil? Hadn't that been the name of the young woman

Hildy claimed Garrett Blackhawk was accused of murdering?

"Such a tragedy Sybil's dying as she did," Rachel murmured. "How did he look?"

Alston dug with relish into the coddled eggs the butler set before him. "Brown as a nut. You'll see for yourself. Told him we had visitors with us. Said his mother had mentioned your sister was expected and that she wanted to pop over for tea to welcome the girl."

"Tea? Oh, dear. He didn't say when, did he?" Rachel fretted.

Alston swallowed a mouthful before answering. "I understood they'd troop over today."

"Today!" Rachel jumped to her feet. "I'll never be ready in time. There is so much to be done! I wonder if Cook has any of Lady Antonia's favorite cakes made?"

"Lemon cakes?" Alston asked hopefully.

Rachel frowned. "Almond. How did you ever go on before you married me?"

"Poorly," he said, and grinned, "as you often remind me, my dear."

With a hasty apology to Wyn, Rachel flew from the room for a consultation in the kitchen.

Alston savored a slice of bacon. "You'll have to excuse my wife, Wyn. Lady Antonia is our nearest neighbor to the east and quite fond of Rachel. But, just because she's the daughter of a duke, Rach worries whenever she entertains her. I've told her she has nothing to worry about since Lady Antonia chose to marry a mere baron rather than someone from her own rank."

Wyn set her coffee cup down, no longer trusting herself to hold it and not spill it. "Her surname wouldn't be Blackhawk by any chance, would it, Lofty?"

His brows rose in surprise. "Yes! How did you—?"

"Garrett Blackhawk was aboard the *Nereid*."

"Then you know what a ripping chap the new baron is," Alston said. "If you're the least interested in husbandry, get him to show you over Hawk's Run. I hate to admit it, but the estate is far better managed than my own. I've tried to lure his man of business away but the fellow's confoundedly loyal. Are you sure we can't tempt you with these coddled eggs? You don't know what you're missing, Wyn," he said, motioning to the butler to refill his plate. "They're delicious."

Wyn declined once more, her mind whirling with this new portrait of Garrett Blackhawk and the realization that she had maligned him in error by refusing to believe his title was real. That his fortune was real.

"What was it you called Lord Blackhawk a moment ago?" she asked.

Alston took a swallow of ale and leaned back in his chair. "The Changeling?"

"That was it," Wyn agreed, nodding. "However did he come by such a strange sobriquet?"

"Acquired it in the cradle," Alston said, and smiled brightly as the butler placed a freshly filled plate before him. "Ah, thank you, Beacham. Wyn, would you mind passing the preserves? Thanks awfully."

Wyn moved a silver bowl of dark currant jam closer to her host. "I don't understand."

"Superstition, my dear. At times Salopians are riddled with it. Garrett's a year or so older than I, but the tales were still being whispered when he reached his majority. You'll see why when the Blackhawks arrive en masse for tea. Lady Antonia is as fair haired as you are, and the late baron was fair, as well. Ellery, their second son, takes after them, but Garrett was a bit of a shock. At least to the nursemaid, who felt any child of Stewart and Antonia's should be golden haired. Well, as you know he isn't, quite the reverse, in fact. The idiot woman would have it that the pixie folk had stolen the true heir and left one of their own in his place. A changeling, if you will."

Alston took a moment to refortify himself with a forkful of food. "The whole concept was ridiculous, of course. And not simply because pixies don't exist outside of children's tales. If the nursemaid had ever taken a stroll down the family portrait gallery she would have known the family name was well deserved. One fiercely black hawklike visage after another. The fairer-haired offspring are relatively new additions. Started turning up about a century or so back when the barons began to acquire golden-haired wives. Still, I fancy it isn't his appearance that keeps the name alive anymore. He's proven himself time and again to the locals as a good and honest landlord. He's a changeling now simply because a chap never knows which Garrett he'll meet, the dashedly good fellow or the infernally aloof stranger.''

Wyn was still musing over their conversation an hour later as she gazed out over the landscape visible from the window of Hildy's room as she waited for her friend to finish her toilette.

The view showed a distant patchwork pattern of planted field, pasture and wooded coppice. Everything was much greener than the countryside outside of San Francisco, and pleasantly foreign. On the drive through the village the day before, Wyn had enjoyed the bucolic sight of pigs and chickens roaming the streets, jostling with the townspeople for the right-of-way. Sheep had dotted the meadows around the town.

Loftus Manor itself was a fanciful structure of red brick barely a century old, the family being relative newcomers to the area. While the main building was Palladian in design, a Gothic tower had been added to the northernmost corner. Hildy had been so taken with this whimsy, she had asked to be given the tower's suite of rooms, despite the fact that a scaffolding blocked a portion of the view. A lightning strike the week before had damaged tiles on the roof and workmen were busy seeing to their repair. Wyn's room was down the corridor from her friend's tower aerie and looked out to the formal garden that lay to the back of the house. While the carefully groomed expanses of lawn beyond it were beautiful, it was the more distant view of woodlands that appealed most to Wyn.

Hildy had barely given the vista a glance, preferring her

richly appointed bedroom and attached dressing room to the lush landscape. Hildy's room was a fitting setting, for it framed her friend's beauty well, Wyn thought. Deep blue, swagged, velvet drapes, their color a near match to Hildy's eyes, hung at the windows and around the gilded, lion-footed canopy bed. Deep-piled Oriental carpets covered the floor, their designs a passionate blend of jewellike tones. The ceiling featured a frieze of tastefully rendered figures from Greek mythology frolicking in an ancient grove. Above an ornately carved mantel, the portrait of a brown-haired lady in a pale blue Empire gown had dominated the room until Hildy supplanted her, stamping her own personality on her surroundings. A discarded nightgown and robe now lay draped over the back of one of the pair of darkly upholstered chairs pulled up near the hearth. Photographs and personal trinkets covered the tops of each of the many draped tables in the room. As she turned away from the open window and glided idly back into the room, Wyn noticed her amethyst brooch among the scattered items.

Hildy sat at the dressing table fidgeting with a wayward curl, tweaking it until it hung to her liking.

Wyn picked up her brooch and traced a finger along the intricate filigree of the setting. "You knew, didn't you," she said.

"Knew what, dearest?" Hildy asked. She pinched her cheeks to put color in them.

"That Baron Blackhawk's estate bordered Lofty's."

"It does?"

Wyn wasn't convinced that Hildy's artful surprise was genuine. "To the east, I believe."

"How wonderful! We won't have to go to London after all, will we?" Hildy declared.

"You already knew that," Wyn insisted, continuing to play with the brooch. It was one of the few things she had managed to keep when her other jewels were sold. Now she wondered if Hildy would ever return it to her. "Rachel told me she has mentioned the Blackhawks frequently in her letters.''

Hildy shrugged elegantly. ''Perhaps she did. I can't say I committed her epistles to memory.''

It had hardly needed that, Wyn thought. From what she had gleaned from Rachel and Alston, the Loftuses were quite fond of the residents of Hawk's Run. Especially the new baron. ''The baroness is coming to tea today, you know,'' she said.

''The baroness?'' Hildy's face stiffened briefly, then relaxed into a cream-pot smile. ''Don't tease me like that, dearest. I suppose, since we know him to be a single gentleman, that you are referring to the baron's mother. Will he accompany her, do you think? Surely tea's rather paltry entertainment. I'd much rather Rachel throw a dinner party or perhaps a ball for us and invite him.''

Wyn put the brooch back down on the table and wondered if there was anything that would discourage her friend. Hildy was blind to everything and heading for disaster, if not emotionally when Garrett rejected her, then socially because she was determined to push the limits of society's conventions.

''A ball?'' Wyn repeated. ''Oh, Hildy, it's too soon. Your attending the evening events aboard ship could be excused because of the circumstances of being at sea but I sincerely doubt anyone would consider it good taste for a family in mourning to—''

''Oh, that's easily taken care of,'' Hildy announced, getting to her feet. She smoothed her palms down over her ribs and waist, erasing invisible wrinkles in the snug fit of her deep violet bodice. ''I simply won't be in mourning anymore.''

Stunned, Wyn stared at her friend. ''But Oswin—''

''Has been gone only a few months?'' With a careless gesture, Hildy dismissed her late husband's importance. ''No matter. With the exception of Rachel, no one here knew him. Not even Lofty. Oswin was always too busy to attend any social functions with me, even family ones. If you'll remember, he was conveniently away on business when Rachel married Lofty.''

"Hildy, just because Oswin never—"

"Dearest," Hildy murmured, her voice ill concealing a trace of underlying amusement and steel. "I never realized how conventional you are! Believe me, Oswin's horrible offspring are mourning nothing more than the passing of his fortune, so why should I be any different?" She moved over to the table, picked up the amethyst brooch and, without bothering to apologize for not having returned it to Wyn, pinned it in place on her gown. "I've worn a widow's weeds quite long enough," she said. "I've a fancy for something lighter. A cream-and-gold-figured fabric maybe. What do you think?"

"I think you're rushing things," Wyn said.

"Pish," Hildy insisted. "I intend to marry Lord Blackhawk and cannot afford to wait a full year or more simply because Oswin wasn't thoughtful enough to pass away years ago. Rachel is my sister. She'll agree with me even if you don't."

Wyn doubted Rachel would. Once perhaps, but in her position as Lady Loftus, Rachel was now bound by a social code which Hildy refused to recognize. "This isn't San Francisco," Wyn reminded, "and Garrett is an English peer, not a man who made his fortune in silver or railroad stocks."

Hildy's brows arched. "Garrett?" she repeated. "You're awfully familiar with his Christian name considering you profess to dislike him."

Although she could feel color rising in her face, Wyn forged on. "I do," she lied, "but Deegan calls him by name. I suppose I've simply come to think of the baron as Garrett because of that."

"Of course," Hildy murmured, apparently satisfied with the hastily concocted answer. "And you've demonstrated that you know little of Lord Blackhawk since his wealth was, in part, built with mining and railway stocks." She smiled thinly. "While there were those who decried my

interest in him during our voyage, I did learn all I needed
to know about him from our talkative companions.''

But were the stories true? Wyn wondered. Alston decried the charge of Garrett's bastardy in the same breath
he called his neighbor a changeling. Rachel was visibly
fond of him and his family. Would she feel such a bond
if she believed him a murderer?

The answer was simple. No, she would not.

''Hildy.''

''My mind is made up, Wyn. Perhaps I'll find Rachel
and make my request immediately. That way we can an-
nounce our plans for a ball when Lady Blackhawk comes
to tea this afternoon.'' Hildy beamed happily, unconcerned
that Wyn did not share her enthusiasm. ''Do you suppose
we have time to run into town to look for gloves before
then? I'm thoroughly sick of these black lace ones.''

Garrett waited patiently in the gig while his mother settled herself at his side, fussing over the arrangement of her
mourning veil, making sure that it completely blanketed
her head and shoulders. It was a beautiful day for a drive.
Summer at its most perfect. A few picturesque clouds hung
in a blue sky. The sun shone brightly, charging the very
air they breathed with life. He could feel the eagerness of
the hitched bay mare like a jolt of electricity through the
reins. It was more through the offices of the groom at the
horse's head than through his own hands that the Thor-
oughbred was still rather than prancing like his brother's
and Deegan's mounts nearby. Not for the first time did
Garrett wish he hadn't given in to his mother's request to
drive her. The restlessness he'd hoped to cure with a ride
that morning remained; the chance for a mad gallop on the
way home from Loftus Manor had been sacrificed to please
his fond parent.

''It's a shame to hide that fetching bonnet,'' he commented.

The veiling bobbed as she nodded. ''Yes, I know,''
Lady Antonia agreed lightly, at long last satisfied with her

appearance. "But, having driven with you in the past, darling, I thought it wise to take extra precautions against getting bugs in my teeth. It so puts one's hostess off."

Garrett snorted at the slur on his driving skills. "You have only to request a sedate pace as befitting your bereaved state, madam, and I will be happy to comply."

"No, you wouldn't," she said, the lilt of her voice indicating her amusement. "You're just like your father and would have been itching to give the bay its head so that we might fly down the road at the most spanking pace."

"Never," Garrett vowed.

Lady Antonia laughed softly. "I know better than to believe that tone of voice. If I'd wanted to arrive at Lofty's at a funereal pace, I would have requested Ellery to drive me."

"I heard that," Ellery Blackhawk said, drawing his black gelding up alongside the carriage.

Next to his brother, Garrett felt even more foreignly dark than in the past. Ellery's golden hair gleamed even brighter in the sunshine. He sat his horse easily, his finely boned form looking ill equipped to control the beast, the strength in his hands belied by the foppish cut of his clothes. A wide grin of eager anticipation curved Ellery's lips, a clear indication that he was looking forward to the outing.

"I'm hurt, Mother," Ellery insisted, laughter barely banked in his voice. "You should have told me you wished to be landed in a ditch. I would have been more than willing to comply."

"So kind of you to offer, darling," Lady Antonia said. "But I'm afraid we're giving Mr. Galloway a terrible impression with such talk."

Deegan chuckled and let his borrowed gray stallion dance in a tight circle. "Not a bit, my lady. In fact, should Garrett's driving be found stodgy, it would be a pleasure for me to take his place at your side."

"Don't take him up on it, madam," Garrett warned.

"I've seen his driving. It would be an affront to your dignity."

Lady Antonia chuckled softly. "And how does my dignity at the moment? Do I look presentable?"

Dressed completely in black, it was only his mother's willowy figure that kept her from being a reflection of the Queen, who still favored mourning nearly two decades after the death of Prince Albert.

Garrett gave her a wry grin. "You look more like the ghost of a chimney sweep, all covered in soot," he said, and signaled the groom to release the horse. Rather than set off at a trot, Garrett let the bay meander down the long driveway at a sedate pace. Ellery and Deegan drew their horses into place behind the gig.

Lady Antonia folded her hands in her lap. "Such pretty compliments as you give, darling. I do hope you'll do better this afternoon when you meet Rachel's guests. It isn't often that two eligible ladies are delivered into our midst. Do be on your best behavior, won't you?"

Garrett flicked the reins, allowing the mare to pick up speed. "That sounds suspiciously like you have a reason for dragging me along."

"I do," his mother admitted. "And a reason for asking you to drive me. I wanted to speak with you privately where we would not be overheard."

When the humor dropped from her voice, Garrett knew he wasn't going to enjoy the conversation.

"I know things have not always been pleasant for you at home," she said. "Stewart meant well, but he wasn't the best of fathers."

If Stewart Blackhawk had indeed been his father, Garrett mused. The rumors concerning his birth had persisted and been believed because Stewart Blackhawk had never spoken out against them.

"He did love you in his own way," Lady Antonia continued. "And I know he felt remorse when you were forced to shoulder responsibilities for the estate, responsibilities that were his."

Garrett took the turn out of the estate gates. What could he say? That he forgave the late baron his failings? How could he when they had goaded him into becoming a success? They had pushed him to prove that, even if he wasn't a Blackhawk by blood, that he deserved to be one through achievement. He had saved the estate, and had made the family a tidy fortune.

He had become the Baron Blackhawk only to find it was not who he wanted to be.

His mother's next words only proved that the trap he had helped fashion had in truth closed behind him. "You are head of the family now, Garrett. You have a responsibility to marry, to provide heirs."

Garrett nearly laughed out loud. How well he had succeeded! Generations of Blackhawks were no doubt spinning in the family crypt at the very idea. In one fell stroke their bloodline was to be wiped clear, replaced by that of a man whose name even he didn't know.

"Ellery's my heir," he said. "When he marries—"

"Don't be ridiculous," Lady Antonia recommended. "I doubt Ellery will ever marry again. Haven't you noticed that he no longer smiles with his eyes? He misses Sybil. I believe he always will."

"We all miss Sybil," Garrett insisted.

"But she was his wife, not yours." When he didn't comment, Lady Antonia touched his arm. "Were there no exceptional women to be found in your travels, darling? Not one who could capture your heart?"

A pair of darkly lashed forest green eyes flashed in his mind. "No," Garrett said shortly. "Not a one."

"Oh, Garrett," she said quietly. "Let the past go."

Such a simple request, he thought. A shame it was impossible to do.

"It wasn't your fault, darling. You did all that was humanly possible to save Sybil. You did save Ellery's life, for which I will always be very grateful."

Briefly Garrett relived the hell that had been Cairo, saw again Sybil's wan, sweat-drenched face, heard again the rattled sound of her breathing. He had been running from such memories for two years and had still not been able to outdistance them.

"I only thought you might form an alliance with Rachel's sister because you've always been fond of Rachel," Lady Antonia continued. "I don't mean to push you into matrimony with undue haste, although she tells me her sister Hildegarde is very lovely."

Garrett glanced at his mother sharply. "What did you just call Rach's sister?"

"Hildegarde. Now don't tell me you dislike her name! It's a fine old Teutonic name, and—"

Garrett cut her off. "Is she a widow?"

Lady Antonia's head turned sharply to face him. "Why, yes."

"And she's from San Francisco?"

"Well, naturally, darling. Rachel's family is from California. She's brought a friend with her to visit. Well, Hildegarde couldn't travel on her own now, could she?"

Garrett stared out over his horses' heads. "I wouldn't bet on it," he mumbled beneath his breath. Considering the way she had hung on his every word, why hadn't Hildegarde Hartleby ever mentioned she was bound for the Loftus estate? Why hadn't Wyn?

Wyn.

Without conscious thought, Garrett whipped up the bay to a faster trot, anxious, now that he knew Wyn was so near, to see her again. Would she be just as glad to see him?

Next to him, Lady Antonia put a hand to the crown of her head, holding her veil in place as it fluttered in the wind. "Of course, I would quite understand if you would prefer not to court a woman who is the relict of another man, however, there is always Hildegarde's companion. Rachel says that the girl is a considerable heiress, which is always a consideration."

"Is it?" Garrett asked shortly.

"Well, to many of our set it is." Lady Antonia sighed

softly. "It never was with your father and I. He took me despite the fact that I hadn't a shilling to my name. And do you know why he did?"

"You're the daughter of a duke."

She sighed once more. "You really never knew your father, did you?"

Garrett glanced over at her. "Did I ever meet him, madam?"

He wished the words back immediately.

His mother's back stiffened visibly. Her gloved hands turned to tightly balled fists as they lay in her lap. "I thought better of your intelligence, Garrett," she said at last. "Do you truly think I would betray Stewart?"

"Mother, I—"

"I loved him," Lady Antonia said. "With all my heart. And he loved me."

"He loved his damn books," Garrett corrected. "Don't try to tell me differently."

His mother sighed softly. "All the same, he was your father. There was no other, Garrett."

"Forgive me if the evidence indicates otherwise, madam. I have had to live with a more believable truth," he said stiffly.

"Truth? A lie, rather."

"I have but to look in the mirror to—"

"Don't be ridiculous," Lady Antonia said. "You have only to look at the faces in the surrounding countryside to know that you are a Blackhawk."

Garrett frowned. "I can't argue that my features are similar to those of many of the tenants, but that is exactly why—"

"The fourteenth baron," his mother said quietly. "Eamon Blackhawk. He was your great-great grandfather, if you'll recall. He buried three wives and planted more than grain in his fields."

Thoroughly shocked at the allusion, Garrett stared at her, speechless.

"You are Stewart's true son and a Blackhawk, darling.

A stronger one than either your father or your brother could ever be." Lady Antonia folded her hands in her lap, the motion clearly indicating that the subject of his parenting was closed. "Oh, look, we're nearly to Lofty's. Do you suppose Rachel will have remembered my fondness for almond cakes?"

Chapter Fifteen

He wasn't a bastard. He'd just been acting like one.

"You're disgraceful," Rachel Loftus said with a teasing moue. "Not one letter in two years." She handed Garrett a delicate china teacup and turned back to the tea tray to pour a cup for Ellery.

Garrett glanced down at the creamy liquid and wished briefly that he'd accepted Alston's offer of stronger spirits. To keep Hildegarde Hartleby at a distance, he'd taken a seat next to her sister on the settee, but having the young widow and his mother across from them on the other sofa, engaged in what appeared to be a comfortable coze, was enough to put his teeth on edge. He was further annoyed by the fact that Wyn Abbot's greeting had been cool and detached, that she preferred Deegan's company to his. Or so the warm welcome she'd given Dig seemed to indicate. Apparently the lady regretted the sweet madness they'd shared their last night aboard ship. He had not been able to forget it, and because he couldn't, it was nearly impossible to keep his gaze from drifting to where she stood by the open terrace doors, Deegan close by her side as Alston pointed out various landmarks.

Damn the landmarks. Damn the company. He wanted nothing more than to sweep her into his arms. To once again bring forth her quivering response. Remind her of the all-too-brief passion they had shared.

The quiet grace of his hostess's movements and the low hum of polite conversation around him made Garrett feel confined. Trapped. Rather than the ardent lover he would by far have preferred to be at that moment, his present role called for a relaxed, languid air—the Baron Blackhawk at home with friends. It was a part he had not played in years.

"I had no idea you were pining away for me, Rach," he drawled. "If only I'd known, I would have flown back to your side in an instant."

Rachel made a slight sound. With another woman he would have called it a snort of disbelief, but English ladies, she would have patiently explained to him, never were so rude. "We worried about you, Garrett."

"There was no need. You should know by now I'm too disobliging as to cross the Stygian ferry," he said.

"Well, if you had died, how would we have even heard of it?" she demanded. "No one, not even Lady Antonia or Ellery had the slightest idea of where you were. If I remember correctly, it was you who told me the British were always polite, even when they were planning to stab one in the back."

He grinned, remembering the occasion well. It had been on an evening soon after Rachel's arrival in England, when she had been near tears of frustration as she tried to cope with her new status as Lady Loftus and with the attitude of the local gentry toward one they considered a colonial upstart.

"In not contacting anyone, you were far from polite," Rachel insisted as she added equal measures of cream and sugar to his brother's tea. "Isn't that right, Ellery?" she asked as she handed the cup to him.

"Dashed impolite," Ellery agreed, leaning forward from his seat in an adjacent chair to accept the fragile piece of china. "It also meant I had to deal with the invasion single-handedly."

Garrett glanced up quickly. Had his long absence nearly

cost him the prosperity of the estate? Granted he had not looked forward to returning to his home, but after the years of labor it had taken to make the lands profitable once more, losing even one harvest, one flock of sheep, would have hurt. He'd been surprised at the welling of pride he'd experienced riding over the estate his first day home, at the warmth he'd felt when the tenants had welcomed him back.

Garrett put his cup aside and frowned at his brother. "Invasion? You didn't mention it before. What kind? Poachers in the woods? Swarms of insects in the fields? You didn't have to go to a moneylender for any reason, did you?"

"Far worse than such paltry things," Ellery insisted. "Lofty was sneaking around trying to make off with Parkinson."

Garrett relaxed. If there was one thing he knew he could count on, it was the loyalty of Parkinson, his steward and man of business.

"I understand," Ellery continued, "that our despicable neighbor had the audacity to offer the man double his wages to abandon Hawk's Run to my far-from-tender mercies."

"Then we were fortunate, indeed, that you managed to repulse the scoundrel," Garrett said. "Dare I ask how much you raised Parkinson's stipend?"

Ellery's handsome face registered mock surprise at the question. "Certainly not here in enemy territory, old boy."

"We're not the enemy!" Rachel exclaimed.

"Of course you aren't," Garrett assured her. "Only your husband is. The rogue tried to steal my steward. It seems you've married yourself a blackguard, my dear."

Rachel pouted prettily. "How cruel of you to say so, Garrett."

Ellery chuckled. "And how correct. Look at Lofty over there, flirting outrageously with Miss Abbot."

Garrett wished his brother had not directed their attention to the threesome at the terrace door. The smile Wyn

had turned on Alston was radiant. As she tilted her head
to peer at something he had indicated on the far side of
the garden, she touched Deegan's arm, directing his attention to the view, also. The familiar gesture was enough to
make Garrett wish he'd purchased a ticket back to America
for his friend immediately rather than invite him for an
indefinite stay at Hawk's Run.

"Has Lofty no sense of decency?" Ellery asked flip-
pantly. "He can't even wait until his wife is out of earshot
to flirt outrageously with another woman."

"Yes, he is a villain," Rachel said, not sounding the
least bit disturbed by her husband's performance. "He's
cut poor Mr. Galloway out of the conversation very neatly,
has he not?"

"Don't sound so proud of the rascal," Ellery said. "Although I can hardly fault Lofty's actions, considering the
hoydenish way you threw yourself into my prodigal brother's arms the moment he walked in the door."

Rachel smiled impishly. "I was simply pleased to see
him."

Ellery arched one aristocratic golden brow theatrically.
"Never that dashed pleased to see me," he noted before
taking a sip of his tea. "Perhaps I should try my hand with
Miss Abbot. She's quite lovely, don't you agree, Garrett?"

Wyn was even more beautiful than he remembered, and
he'd left her but a few days ago. The willpower that kept
his eyes from following her every move was weakening
by the minute. "Yes, she is," he said, any hint of interest
stripped free from his voice.

Ellery looked at him thoughtfully a moment, then put
his china cup carefully aside on the table at his elbow.
"And an heiress, as I understand it. Just the type of woman
a younger son should latch on to, don't you think?" He
stood up, straightened his shoulders and shot his cuffs.
"Wish me luck?"

"You don't need luck," Rachel said warmly. "You're
a charming fellow, Ellery, as any woman in the neighborhood knows."

"True," he agreed, and flashed them both a rather rogu-ish grin. "The question is, am I charming enough to dis-tract Miss Abbot from her current admirers?"

Garrett stared at Ellery's back as his brother ambled across the room to join the group at the open doors.

"Careful," Rachel murmured softly. "You'll burn a hole in his coat, which would be a shame since he looks so well in it."

Garrett yanked his gaze away, concentrating on his host-ess. "Don't be ridiculous, Rach. With Ellery's panache he would look just as well in tatters."

She leaned closer to him on the settee, a plate in her hand as if she were offering him one of the delicious al-mond cakes her cook had provided. "But if you don't take care, someone will tumble to your secret," she warned.

"What secret?"

Rachel waggled the plate until he took a pastry from it. "Wyn," she said quietly. "The way you look at her. Or rather, try not to look at her."

Her words were like a dare, goading him into glancing Wyn's way. Ellery had taken her hand and was raising it to his lips. She smiled at him, then laughed delightedly at some nonsense he uttered.

The almond cake crumbled beneath Garrett's fingers.

Rachel handed him a linen napkin. "I think she'd make a lovely baroness."

Garrett concentrated on brushing crumbs from his trou-sers. "Would she? Someone else's then. In case you haven't noticed, the lady doesn't much care for my com-pany."

From the corner of his eye he saw Wyn tuck her hand in the crook of his brother's arm, allowing him to lead her from the room and out into the garden.

"Doesn't she?" Rachel smiled secretly. "Dearest Gar-rett. Outside of Lofty, you are the most kind and intelligent man I know, but you are without a doubt the biggest nod-cock I've ever met. You don't even know why you're act-ing this way, do you?"

He frowned at his hostess, hating with every passing minute the turn their conversation had taken.

Undeterred by his expression, Rachel's grin widened. She placed her hand over his affectionately. "You're in love with her, Garrett, and I, for one, find it quite delightful."

It didn't feel delightful. In fact, it felt like hell. There was no way around it, though. Rachel was absolutely right. He was in love with Wyn Abbot. Had been from the moment he saw her standing at the rail that first day, silently communing with Neptune.

Now all he had to do was decide what to do about it.

It wasn't something he wanted to deal with, not considering he was still struggling with the idea that everything he'd ever thought about himself appeared to have been grossly wrong.

What if he was wrong as well when it came to how he felt about Wyn Abbot?

Garrett sat in his study late, feet on his desk, leisurely enjoying a bottle of brandy that his grandfather had purchased not long after Wellington's victory at Waterloo. *His grandfather.* It was still amazing to think he was a Blackhawk. A true Blackhawk. Although he still saw little resemblance between himself and the fierce features of the ancestors whose portraits hung in the family gallery, his mother's words had given him a sense of belonging that he'd never experienced before. Or hadn't recognized for what it was before.

All the years he'd stayed away, he never once realized that the reason he kept on the move was not because he was looking for something, but that he was trying to distance himself from something he loved but didn't believe he deserved. Hawk's Run. Even the swell of emotion he'd experienced upon his return in viewing the well-maintained country house and prosperous farms had not enlightened him. He'd thought the feeling based in pride of having saved the estate through hard work and careful planning. He knew differently now.

He hadn't wanted to return, had cursed the need to do so. Now he was glad that duty, and Deegan, had forced his hand. He was the Baron Blackhawk, the master of Hawk's Run, and nearly at peace with himself over all that the title entailed.

There was a slight rap on the study door before it was pushed open. "I heard you'd scandalized Spears by making a raid on the wine cellar," Ellery said, strolling over to take a chair opposite Garrett. He reached over and picked up the still slightly dusty bottle, examining it. "Hmm. The sixteenth baron's contraband? And not in a proper decanter? Careful, old chap, you'll wound Spears's butlerly dignity if you continue to go on in this slapdash manner."

"I was abjectly apologetic when he caught me," Garrett said, "so I ought to be forgiven in a year or two."

"Only if you mend your ways," Ellery cautioned, his lips curving in a smile that belied his serious tone. "Mind if I join you?"

Garrett reached back for one of the extra goblets he'd instructed the butler to leave on the sideboard and passed it to his brother. "Where's Dig? I thought you were trying to skunk him at billiards."

"Skunk him?"

"One of the more colorful American colloquialisms I picked up," Garrett confessed.

"If you mean I was trying to trim his pockets at the game, you're quite right," Ellery admitted, pouring a generous portion of brandy in his glass.

Garrett grinned. "So, how much did he take you for?"

"Fifty pounds sterling."

Garrett laughed.

"It's good to hear you do that again," Ellery said.

"What? Laugh? Perhaps I've had little reason to be amused."

Ellery savored the aroma of his brandy before taking a

sip. "Isn't it about time you found a few more reasons to do so then?"

"Meaning?" Garrett asked.

"I've asked Wyn to go riding with me tomorrow," Ellery said.

Despite himself, Garrett frowned. To cover his reaction, he lifted the glass to his lips. "Wyn, is it? You're awfully familiar with her name considering you met her only today."

Ellery set his goblet on a corner of the desk and stretched his legs out. "Yes, aren't I? However, such a shocking lapse of manners on my part can be forgiven as I fully expect her to become one of the family."

Caught in the act of swallowing, Garrett choked.

"You are going to marry her, aren't you?" Ellery asked, his lips curving in a satisfied smile.

"The matter hasn't arisen," Garrett said, clearing his throat before taking a healthy swig of brandy. "As I never intended to marry, it never will, either."

"Don't be ridiculous," his brother murmured, comfortably slumping further into the cushions of his chair. "One of us has to wed, and I've already done it once. In the spirit of fair play, I really think it should be you who steps into the parson's trap this time, old man. Besides, the lady is quite exceptional and dotes on you."

"As she clearly showed in giving me the cold shoulder earlier."

Ellery closed his eyes, but the cat-in-the-cream-pot smile lingered on his pleasant features. "I repeat," he said, "she dotes on you. Why do you think I made an appointment to ride with her?"

Knowing he was going to need it, Garrett reached for the decanter and splashed a generous portion of brandy in his glass. "I would think a frippery fellow like yourself made it a habit to dance attendance on beautiful women."

"Yes, you would," Ellery agreed. "But in this case, it is a blind. You see, I sense an air of *Romeo and Juliet* about the two of you. For some reason the lady wishes to pretend she doesn't care a fig for you, yet her eyes quite frequently flicker to rest on you. Rather fondly, I might add. What I propose to do is turn her over to your excellent care the moment we ride out of sight of Loftus Manor. Which mantle do you think Lofty and Rachel have assumed? Montague or Capulet?''

Since Ellery was intent upon giving his life a Shakespearean twist, Garrett decided he needed more than just brandy to fortify himself and reached into the pocket of his coat for his tobacco and cigarette papers.

"It isn't Alston or Rach but Mrs. Hartleby who is the stumbling block," he said, long habit allowing him to build the cigarette by rote. "She seems to have staked me out as her next matrimonial victim before we even left Boston Harbor." A quick lick along the paper's edge sealed the smoke.

Ellery stopped him from enjoying it by reaching across and claiming the cigarette himself. "I say," he declared, studying the neatly rolled tube, "you must teach me how to do this. There's a certain rugged panache about it. Perhaps now that you're home, I'll do a spot of traveling abroad and see what eccentricities I can acquire." He struck a match and drew contentedly on the cigarette while Garrett rolled another. "So Mrs. Hartleby is the rub, hey? Yes, I can see how that might be. Her attitude toward Rach is patronizing, even though, as I understand it, our darling Lady Loftus is the elder sister."

"She is that," a new voice contributed. "A darlin', that is," Deegan added. "Is this a closed meeting or are other thirsty men welcome?"

Garrett palmed another goblet while Ellery dragged an adjacent armchair forward with his foot in welcome. "You knew Hildegarde in Frisco, didn't you, Dig?" Garrett asked, and passed his friend the second freshly rolled cigarette.

Deegan accepted it and the light Ellery offered, drawing deeply, clearly enjoying the rich quality of the tobacco. "Passing acquaintance only," he admitted. "Enough to know she's a harpy, which means she isn't much like her sister, is she?''

"Wyn's close to her though," Garrett pressed. He pushed the bottle of brandy forward so that Deegan could help himself.

"Girlhood friends," Deegan supplied. "I take it old Hartleby kicked the bucket not long before you and I reached San Francisco and Wyn got hoodwinked into feeling sorry for the widow. Ten to one it was her idea for the two of them to visit the serene Lady Loftus. Probably thought Hildy was in need of familial comfort, which the lady was most definitely not getting in Frisco—not familial or any other kind."

Busy building yet another cigarette, Garrett paused in the act of sealing the paper. "Not long before we got to Frisco?" he repeated. "Are you sure, Dig?"

"Absolutely. When I met her, Wyn was still writing Hildy's notes of appreciation for letters of condolence," Deegan said. "Seems the widow was too done up after putting the old man to bed with a shovel to be bothered with her own correspondence. Why?"

Garrett lipped his cigarette thoughtfully a moment before striking a match. "If that's so, Hildegarde's trying for a mining camp mourning period."

"I don't understand," Ellery said.

Deegan blew a smoke ring ceilingward. "Women aren't terribly plentiful in the mining camps," he explained. "A widow is wooed practically from the moment her husband draws his final breath. A good many women have remarried within a week or so, although there are those who wait a while longer. Say, six months?"

"Sounds like the time limit Hildegarde has set for herself," Garrett mused. "Mother was under the impression that the late Mr. Hartleby had passed on well over a year ago because the widow mentioned Lofty and Rach would be throwing a ball in her honor in a fortnight or so."

"That soon?" Ellery exclaimed. "Awfully short notice, isn't it?"

Garrett nodded thoughtfully and drew deeply on his cigarette. Usually the euphoric taste of tobacco on his tongue was soothing but this time it failed to ease his building tension.

"I doubt Rach even knows she's giving a ball," Ellery said. "She's never hosted one before so I would expect her to balk, then get in a tizzy over it and ask for Mother's guidance."

"My thoughts exactly," Garrett said. "When do you think the widow will break the news to Rach?"

Deegan swirled the brandy gently in his glass, to all intents and purposes enjoying the heady bouquet. "Knowing Hildy, I'd say she struck while the iron was hot and delivered the news before we'd all rattled out of the driveway. I'd even put money on it."

Ellery reached into his coat pocket and extracted his wallet. "This sounds like an excellent chance to win back my fifty pounds. I say Mrs. Hartleby waits until morning to do it." He smacked another fifty on the desk top.

A soft rustle of silk announced that another visitor had joined them. "You're both wrong," Lady Antonia said, gliding into the room. All three men got hastily to their feet and stubbed out their cigarettes.

"Why do you say that, madam?" Garrett asked, offering her his chair.

His mother smiled complacently as she arranged her skirts. "Mrs. Hartleby will create a circumstance where neither Lofty nor Rachel can take exception to her proposal, thus she will have popped it on them during dinner when there were servants present."

While Ellery and Deegan sank back into their chairs, Garrett leaned against the desk. "I was under the impression that you found the widow's company pleasant."

"Cloying, really," the baroness corrected. "Manipulative. If it weren't for a certain similarity of feature, I'd find it difficult to believe Mrs. Hartleby is dear Rachel's sister."

"Does that mean you think neither of these scoundrels has a chance of winning the bet?" Garrett asked.

"Not a prayer," Lady Antonia said. "Did I hear correctly that the wager is fifty pounds? How paltry. I have a hundred that says you're both wrong."

Wyn felt herself fortunate to have an engagement that took her away from Loftus Hall the next morning, if but for a short while. Maids bustled about, pushed to scrub and polish as never before by a stern-faced, disapproving Mrs. Beacham, the housekeeper. Despite Hildy's belief that she could simply adjust the length of her mourning period at will with none the wiser, Wyn had chanced to overhear a whispered phrase or so that indicated that the staff, if not the countryside, knew to the day how long it had been since Oswin Hartleby's death, and were scandalized by his widow's lack of proper feeling over his demise.

Although she had not said a word of reproach at dinner the evening before when Hildy confessed to having invited the Baroness Blackhawk to a ball, Rachel was far from happy. At breakfast, Wyn had noticed circles under her hostess's pretty eyes, a testament to a sleepless night. While Rachel was still gracious, she was distracted and patently hurt by her sister's action.

Wyn couldn't blame her. Rachel had worked hard to be accepted by her neighbors, an approval she risked losing in giving in to her sister's dictates. But, torn between position and family, Rachel had wavered very little before agreeing to the ball. Even Alston had raised no argument to the proposal, exchanging little more than a silent glance with his tense wife before calmly asking if Hildy had mentioned a precise date when speaking with Lady Antonia.

No one had proposed simply calling on the baroness and withdrawing the invitation.

Wyn was alone, wondering if the Loftuses had withheld the suggestion for the same reason she had, when Ellery Blackhawk arrived.

"You quite rival the sun in glory this morning, Miss Abbot," he declared in greeting. "Such dazzling beauty quite blinds me."

Although she knew the military cut of her navy blue riding habit and the rakishly curled brim of her plumed hat enhanced her natural assets quite well, Wyn shook her head in mock disapproval. "We have a word for such untruths where I come from, Mr. Blackhawk. You are fortunate that I'm far too much a lady to speak it."

"Dashed uncivil, is it?" he asked. "No doubt my brother or Galloway can supply it, should I ask. Shall we go?"

Wyn picked up her riding crop and accepted the offer of Ellery's arm. He covered her hand with his.

"By the way," he drawled, "Galloway says you're a bruising rider so I brought along a spirited little minx of a mare from Hawk's Run. I hope you don't mind. Rach is a timid rider so the horses familiar with a ladies' saddle in Lofty's stable are little more than plodding hacks. Not in your class at all."

The mare was a delight, a trim Arabian with a glossy black coat and a white blaze beneath her forelock. When Wyn spoke to her, the mare gave a coquettish toss of its head and blew softly against Wyn's gloved hand. Ellery's steed had like breeding and was black in color, also, a tall gelding with two white stockings on its forelegs. After Wyn had communed with the mare briefly, Ellery offered his linked hands to throw her up into the saddle.

"Have you seen much of the Loftus estate yet?" he asked, swinging onto his own steed.

"Very little. Hildy prefers carriages to horseback," Wyn said. "What I'm really longing for is a long gallop. Is there a possibility of indulging in one today?"

"More than just the possibility," Ellery answered. "I can guarantee one. In fact, since the horses are fresh, how about a race? See the gap between the trees in the copse at the top of that hill?"

Wyn didn't let him finish. With a touch of her heel, she

urged the mare forward and was soon reveling in the feel
of the wind tearing at her hair.

The mare's stride was long and strong. She stretched
forward, intent upon outdistancing the gelding, eager to
reach the designated finish line first. Wyn let the Thor-
oughbred have its head, if but briefly, not bothering to
glance back to see how far behind Ellery lagged. She was
fairly sure he would allow her to win despite the fact that
the tall gelding quite obviously had a longer stride.

The mare rushed at the copse, closing the distance all
too soon for Wyn. She drew back on the reins, slowing
the mare's headlong rush. There was a path through the
trees, she saw, a wide riding trail dappled with sun and
shade. Entering the woods, the mare pranced along the
cleared track, head tossing in eagerness for yet another
gallop, and whined, calling to the gelding in challenge.

Only it wasn't the gelding that answered.

In fact, Wyn realized, glancing back over her shoulder,
Ellery and his black were nowhere in sight.

The mare tugged at the reins, urging Wyn to move toward the pure ebony stallion standing in a patch of deep
shadow to the side of the trail.

"Still a hoyden, I see," the man standing at the stallion's head commented as he led his mount forward into
the ride.

"Hopelessly so," Wyn said, not bothering to brush back
the loose lock of hair that now trailed over her shoulder.

As the stallion arched its neck toward the mare to nuzzle
a greeting, the man tucked the powerful animal's reins
beneath a stirrup then turned to Wyn.

"I've missed you," he said quietly.

"I've missed you," Wyn whispered, and slipped easily
out of her saddle and into Garrett's arms. When their lips
met, she felt as if her world had at last righted. Even if it
was only for a brief period. For the moment, time stood
still—until the sound of horse's hooves intruded upon
them.

Chapter Sixteen

Cut short by Ellery's arrival, Wyn felt their embrace was too fleeting.

"Don't mind me," he drawled as he pulled the gelding to a halt and dismounted. "I'll simply study the flora and fauna and mind the horses. Time is brief though, so do make the most of every second. I am supposedly showing Miss Abbot around the Loftus estate so we really should run into Alston at least once to make the story believable."

"He's helping rebuild the stone fence along the lane between his land and Tilbury's," Garrett said. "Knowing you'd want to make sure he saw you, I did a brief reconnaissance on my way here. Dig's keeping a covert eye on him, and will join us here should Lofty cut his stay short."

Ellery smiled at Wyn as he gathered up the mare's trailing reins. "My brother is always deucedly thorough." With all three mounts dogging his steps, Ellery moved farther down the path, giving Wyn and Garrett a modicum of privacy.

"Yes, I am," Garrett agreed, and gathered Wyn close again. He dropped but a brief kiss on her mouth before guiding her toward a fallen log a few strides into the woods. Once she was seated on the rough surface, he propped one boot on the makeshift bench and leaned forward, his forearm resting on his upraised knee. "I have a couple questions, my love, and I hope you're willing to answer them.''

Wyn unpinned her hat and placed it in her lap. "Only if you will answer one of mine in return," she said.

"One or a hundred," Garrett promised. He lifted the straggling lock of her hair and played the strands through his fingers. "Would you like to go first?"

She shook her head. Although the carefully arranged clandestine meeting was a balm to her soul, their whole relationship had consisted of such meetings. It would be best to discover why he had arranged this particular one. "Tell me what you want to know," Wyn said.

"All right. This ball your friend mentioned to my mother. Are the Loftuses actually giving it?"

Wyn wrinkled her nose. "I'm disappointed," she claimed. "I expected something far more earthshaking. But, yes, from the state the household is in, I would say there will be a ball, although going ahead with it will cause a good deal of talk. Oswin Hartleby has only been dead—"

"A handful of months," Garrett finished. Carefully, almost tenderly, she thought, he released the lock of her hair, allowing it to drift to rest on her breast. "Galloway told me."

"Oh. Of course."

The wind ruffled his dark hair, running invisible fingers through it. As usual, he was hatless though otherwise dressed impeccably. Nearly the complete gentleman. She knew better than to believe the controlled facade, though. She'd seen glimpses of a restless spirit in his eyes. Experienced it in every kiss they shared.

Because she wanted to touch him, and felt she shouldn't, Wyn busied her hands by removing her gloves. Once her fingers were free, she felt for loose hairpins and gathered up her trailing tresses. "What was your next question?"

"The next one," he murmured. Wyn waited while Garrett delayed a moment, as if lost in a reverie of his own. "All right." He tossed back the tails of his tan riding coat and seated himself at her side. "That last night on the ship," he said. "Why didn't you tell me you were coming here?"

Wyn rammed a hairpin back into place. "Is that really what you are asking? Or is it, did I know you were the Loftuses' neighbor that night? The answer is, no, I didn't."

"Yet you didn't look surprised to see either Deegan or me when we arrived yesterday for tea."

"Only because I'd stumbled on the truth from things Alston and Rachel said earlier at breakfast," Wyn explained. "You didn't look surprised to see me, either."

"Yes, well, it was very nearly a shock," he assured her. "To all concerned."

Wyn dropped her eyes to her lap, ran the tip of her finger along the spine of the feather gracing the crown of her hat. "Not to everyone. I think Hildy knew all along that your estate bordered the Loftus one."

"The widow again," Garrett muttered. He pulled a long, tasseled weed free and lashed idly at a lone wildflower with it. "I suppose she's the reason we have to keep meeting like this?"

"Like this?"

"Secretly," Garrett said. He struck at the flower a final time then tossed the weed away. "Why do you keep me at arm's length whenever we are in public, Wyn? Why can't we let the world know I'm courting you?"

Wyn stared at the purple petals that drifted loose over the toes of her boots. "I didn't think you were. Courting me, that is."

"I didn't realize that's what it was myself," he admitted. "Does this mean I'll be welcome if I put in an appearance at Lofty's door to take you driving?"

Rather than look at him, Wyn stared off into the woods. A bird was chirping somewhere in the leafy canopy overhead, the sound cheerful. Sadly her own mood could not be in accord with the avian melody. "No," she said quietly.

There was a long silence before Garrett answered. "I see."

Wyn's heart contracted sharply at the hurt in his voice. She turned, sliding her hand over his, allowing their fingers to entwine intimately. "No, you don't." She took a deep breath, marshaling her thoughts. "Deegan told you he was courting me in San Francisco, didn't he?"

"Not in so many words, but I surmised that you were one of the two heiresses he was dangling after there," Garrett admitted.

"Then you know most of the story. Deegan meant much more to Leonore than he did to me, but she couldn't forgive either him or me for something she perceived as totally my fault. It wasn't, but she refused to listen. She was too hurt to face me." Wyn paused, unable to continue while their hands were joined, the heat of his warming hers. She pulled free, got to her feet and put the length of the fallen log between them. Preferring to concentrate on an idle occupation rather than face him, she placed her hat on one of the remaining branches of the fallen tree, playing with it until it sat at an angle that satisfied her. "I swore that day that I would never, even inadvertently, come between another woman and the man she wanted and yet, I have."

"It isn't the same, Wyn," Garrett said. "You should know by now I have absolutely no interest in Hildegarde. I never did."

It changed nothing to hear him say it. She had known all along.

Wyn bowed her head. "Do you remember that first day aboard the *Nereid,* Garrett?"

"How could I forget it?"

"I thought you were a fortune hunter," she confessed. "That you were like all the other men who have ever danced attendance on me. But you weren't. I suppose I realized it then, even if I refused to acknowledge it. Why else would I continue to…to…"

"Allow me to seduce you?" he suggested.

She looked up, met his eyes. "Yes."

As if he read her look as encouragement, Garrett got to his feet and closed the distance between them. "I'm glad you did."

When he tried to draw her into his arms, Wyn stepped away again. "I shouldn't have, Garrett. How you feel about Hildy doesn't matter here. My failings are what do. I knew that she wanted to attract your attention. Yet every evening I spent with you meant that I was undermining what she believed was her chance for happiness. Only this time, I wasn't doing it unaware and my actions were hurting the woman I considered my best friend."

He caught the subtle nuance of her admission. "Considered? Mrs. Hartleby no longer holds that honor?"

Wyn shook her head. "She's changed. Perhaps she was like this before and I simply didn't notice. But do you understand now why I can't let you court me? Why this must be the last time we see each other alone?"

Garrett tipped her face up to his. "No, I don't. But I will honor your wishes for a while longer. A very brief while longer, Wyn."

This time when he drew her to him, she went readily, nestling against the broad width of his chest. "I believe you had a question for me," Garrett prompted, gliding the backs of his fingers in a tender caress along her cheek.

Wyn leaned into his touch, hesitant to voice her query. He wasn't the man she had once believed him. He certainly was not a man in need of a wealthy wife. Both Alston and Rachel had verified the prosperity of the Blackhawk estate, and the diversity of Garrett's investments, without being asked. His title was real, not invented. And he intended to court her. If she asked the one question that still hung in the balance, would she lose him? She loved him. She knew it with the same certainty that she had always known she was not in love with her other suitors. So why couldn't she trust him without reserve?

The answer was simple. For too long she had been ruled by her mind, not her emotions, and logic told her to mis-

trust the mystery that hung about Garrett Blackhawk.
There were still far too many questions she needed answered before she could freely give him her heart.

"Tell me about Sybil Tilbury," Wyn requested quietly.

Garrett's hand stilled against the softness of Wyn's skin.
He had thought she intended to ask if he loved her. He
had been phrasing his answer so that she would not be
insulted. He wanted her, in his bed, in his life. He wanted
to see her lovely face first thing in the morning; wanted it
to be the last thing he enjoyed seeing every night. His
mother and his brother had reminded him that it was his
duty to marry, to produce the next generation of Blackhawks. To do so with Wyn Abbot would convert the duty
to delight. But did he love her? He wasn't sure what love
was.

She hadn't asked the expected question, though. She had
asked one that was even more difficult to answer.

Garrett drew Wyn closer so that she cuddled against his
chest, her cheek pressed to the soft fabric of his weskit.
"I suppose you've heard the stories," he said. "That
you've wondered if they were true."

Wyn nodded tightly.

"In essence they are. I did kill Sybil," he said. When
Wyn gasped and pulled back to look up at him in shock,
Garrett gentled her with his voice. "Hush. It didn't happen
in quite the way the rumor mill would have it." Not entirely.

He had guarded himself so well against the memory that
journeying back was painful, yet he forced himself to mentally relive the final days he'd spent in Cairo. Days when
he had thought to lose Ellery, and Sybil, to the fever.

"What I'm about to tell you isn't generally known,"
Garrett cautioned, "and it's best if it remains a secret."

"Is it so horrible then?" Wyn asked.

He ran his hand up her spine and back down again.
"No. More..." He paused, searching for an appropriate

word. A perfect word with which to remember Sybil. "More precious."

"You really loved her, didn't you?" Wyn said softly.

"Everyone did. She was bright, beautiful, and there wasn't a young man in the region who didn't weave fantasies about winning her hand. The man she chose was not favored by her father."

Wyn stirred against him. "Was it you?"

Garrett grinned, pleased that her voice sounded a slight bit jealous. "If you keep interrupting, we'll never finish this story."

"Was it?" she persisted.

"No, it wasn't me."

Wyn sighed contentedly at his answer.

The gentle sound had a strange effect on him. As if his heart had swelled. His chest felt tight, his head a bit dizzy. Desire curled through his veins, driven by the new sensation as much as by the feel of Wyn in his arms. He wished their time wasn't limited, that they were not forced to steal moments alone together. He would by far rather lay her down among the wildflowers and make love to her. The scent of her filled his head, the texture of her hair caressed his cheek. It would be so easy to forget his responsibilities, to lose himself in her.

Wyn tilted her head back against his arm, staring up at him, the look in her eyes patient and loving. "Garrett?"

The lady wanted her answer. One he owed her if they were to have a future together.

On the far side of the ride Garrett could see Ellery relaxed back against the trunk of a tree, the reins of the horses dangling loosely in his hand. The story was his brother's more than his, yet Garrett knew Ellery would refuse to relate it. He harbored his memories close inside, keeping her memory his and his alone.

Because Wyn's nearness made it hard to concentrate, Garrett released her, indicating she should perch on the log once more. As she complied, sunlight spilled in a golden ray over the flaxen coils of her upswept hair. He watched as she arranged the flowing skirts of her riding habit, a fussy, very feminine occupation. One he doubted he would ever tire of watching her perform.

She looked up at him then, her dark green eyes a reflection of the heart of the forest. "Go on," she urged.

Garrett plucked her hat free from the branch where she'd placed it before regaining his seat next to her. "The story. All right. It should come as no surprise that Sybil was the local belle."

Wyn nodded. "She was beautiful, you said."

"She was also a very talented artist. A painter, as was her lover," Garrett explained. "Together they hatched a plan to elope. Each took one confederate into their confidence. With Sybil, it was her former governess, a woman of middle years and a romantic heart. With Ellery—"

"Ellery!"

"...it was me," he finished. "My brother hasn't offered to show you his studio yet? He does landscapes and is quite good. But, as I was saying, the lovers cloaked their elopement in fine detail. So much so that two years later, Sybil's parents still do not realize that Ellery is their son-in-law." Garrett's brows nearly joined as he scowled in his brother's direction. "If he let it be known, he would stand to inherit Tilbury's lands and fortune, but the stubborn fool refuses to use their marriage lines for personal gain."

It came as a surprise to find Wyn smiling at him when he turned back to her. "I like Ellery very much," she said. "After the hordes of men sniffing around my fortune, to hear of one who refuses to claim his bride's inheritance is refreshing. Sweet."

"Sweet?" Garrett grimaced wryly. "Lacking in common sense, rather. Sorry, but until he comes to his senses, I'm afraid I'll remain rather virulent over the matter. Where was I?"

Wyn continued to smile warmly at him. "Being protective and concerned about your brother's future, I believe."

Since he wasn't quite sure his reasons were that honorable, Garrett returned to his story. "I believe I had mentioned an elopement. They chose Egypt over Gretna Green, although God alone knows why," he said. "Sybil and her companion left a week earlier so it would not appear that we were all to travel together. My role called for me to act the stunned and smitten suitor and dash off after her—with her father's blessing, I might add. Ellery announced he was bound for a spot of fishing in Scotland, then headed south, joining us hours before the ship sailed.

"They were married at sea by the captain. We were all quite jolly upon landing, and, because we were no longer needed, the governess and I left them to their newly-wedded bliss. She joined a friend whose husband was something or other at the embassy and I went off adventuring."

Although he'd hoped to hold them at bay, memories of Cairo rushed back with a clarity he would have preferred to forget. The heat of the desert, the calls to prayer from the mosque, the stench of the streets. "I was gone barely a month, but when I returned it was to find Ellery deathly ill with a fever and Sybil nursing him. It wasn't until the embassy doctor declared my brother on the road to recovery that Sybil collapsed. She hadn't let us know she was ill. Whenever we commented on her pallor or lack of appetite she blamed the heat."

"Oh, Garrett," Wyn murmured. She reached over and gently squeezed his hand—a hand tightly clenched in a fist he had no memory of making.

Garrett stared ahead. Forged on, determined to rush through and finish the tale before his courage failed. "Ellery was in no condition to take care of her, so I did. She was so frail, Wyn. So weak. She never had a chance. I stayed at her bedside three hellishly long days before she died, and when she was gone, I knew I'd killed her."

Wyn's hand on his tightened. "No. You tried to save her."

Garrett hung his head. They were the same words Ellery had said the day they buried his young wife, words that

were only a balm. Garrett was the man who never made
a wrong move in business yet he'd been unable to protect
one he loved. Sybil's death had been tragic because he'd
failed her and for that reason he couldn't forgive himself.
"I should have realized she was ill. I should never have
left them to their own devices. I should have talked them
out of sailing to Egypt when it was first mentioned, but I
didn't."

It had been impossible to look directly at Wyn during
the telling, but he turned to her now and found a single
tear coursing down her cheek. "Don't cry, love," he murmured, brushing his thumb tenderly across the damp track.

A second tear joined the first, but she was far from sob-
bing. Her eyes glittered with fury as well as unshed tears.
"I can't help it," she insisted hotly. "When I think of
how those...those...*biddies* aboard the ship took such
delight in painting you as a blackguard when the true story
is—"

He kissed her to quiet her, meaning only to touch her
mouth lightly with his. Wyn's lips clung, the taste of her
response pushing the past firmly from his mind. Garrett
deepened the kiss, needing Wyn's warmth and passion to
remind him that, while Sybil was gone, he was most definitely alive.

The rattle of a bridle as one of the horses shook off a
bothersome insect broke the spell. Garrett leaned back,
pulled his pocket watch out to check the time. "You'd
best finish your tour," he said, "else your hostess will
begin to worry about you."

Wyn reclaimed her hat, and pinned it back in place at
a jaunty angle. "Yes, but not until you tell me the end of
the story."

"There isn't much else to tell," he insisted, offering her
his arm for the short stroll to where his brother waited
patiently. "I arranged passage for Ellery back to England
and had Sybil interred in the English cemetery in Cairo as
she'd asked. Then I hopped on the first ship bound for

foreign shores with little intention of ever returning home."

"But you did," Wyn said. "Why?"

How often had he asked himself the very same question? Garrett grinned ruefully. "I suppose because, in the end, I wanted to."

He was still musing on how right the answer was when Wyn and Ellery rode out of the copse.

Wyn had a chance to both meet Sybil's mother and witness firsthand the difficult road Rachel traveled in her adopted land when Eleanor Tilbury came to call that afternoon.

The woman was elegant, her graying hair arranged in a sophisticated upsweep, her high-collared gown a muted silver. When she smiled there was no answering light in her cold blue eyes, just as there was no sign of softness in her rigid carriage. She was the antithesis of Lady Antonia Blackhawk, who had bubbled with life and goodwill when Wyn had met her.

Eleanor accepted a cup of tea from Rachel as if it were her due but barely sampled it before turning a censoring look upon her hostess. "Some rather distressing news reached me from the village, Lady Loftus," she said. "I could scarcely credit it."

"Really?" Rachel asked, concentrating on pouring tea for her sister and Wyn. "You must be referring to the coming loss of our dear rector, but we must all be happy for him in gaining this new living. I understand the house alone is well worth the move considering it is far larger and he has such a growing family."

The visitor's gaze grew colder. "That is not what I am referring to," Eleanor insisted. "I heard that you are preparing to give a ball to introduce your sister to the neighborhood."

Wyn wished she could do something to ease the tension she knew Rachel must be feeling. Her hostess's lips were pressed thinly together when she passed Wyn a cup of tea.

Before she could answer what was clearly a rebuke, Hildy rushed to grab center stage. "Am I not fortunate to have such a thoughtful family, Lady Tilbury? Although the invitations have yet to go out, I do hope we can look forward to seeing you there."

Eleanor's carefully shaped brows rose in affront. "Surely your bereavement negates the appropriateness of such a thing, Mrs. Hartleby. I was under the impression that your widowed state was but recently acquired."

"Not that recently," Hildy said. "Besides, the party is not for me alone, but for my dear friend, Miss Abbot, as well." Wyn thought the smile Hildy turned on her was rather cloying and insincere. "We've traveled so far to visit Rachel and Lofty."

"Indeed?"

Having just heard the tragic tale of Sybil Tilbury's death, Wyn had intended to be sympathetic over Eleanor's loss of her only child. She quickly changed her mind, her sympathy redirected to the woman's daughter. Garrett had painted a picture of a girl with spirit, one who had a mind of her own. While Wyn liked Ellery Blackhawk very much, she doubted if the elopement had been his idea. Or even the journey to Egypt. Sybil had not only been marrying the man of her choice, she had been fleeing her cold, unfeeling family.

"And you, Miss Abbot," Eleanor said, turning her piercing look on Wyn. "Are you as lost to decency as Lady Loftus and Mrs. Hartleby?"

Rachel flushed at the cruel words but Hildy gave little sign that she had been insulted.

Wyn took a sip of tea without tasting it. "I'm sure you would not think us so caught up in plans for our own amusement if you had had the pleasure of knowing Mr. Hartleby, Lady Tilbury. His last request was that his wife not mourn him. He wanted her always to be happy, never sad."

The late Oswin Hartleby was no doubt whirling in his grave at such untruths, but Wyn cared little for that. The grateful glance Rachel gave her forgave the lie, even if it was far from white.

Eleanor's expression remained arched—frozen in disapproving lines long ago, Wyn decided—but she said no more on the inappropriate timing of the forthcoming ball.

Rachel offered a plate of freshly made cakes to her far-from-welcome visitor. "I, too, heard some news that distressed me, Lady Tilbury. Have you indeed let Miss North, your dresser, go?"

"Yes, I did," Eleanor answered, politely accepting a cake. Rather than sample it, she set it aside on a small plate.

"But I thought Miss North came highly recommended," Rachel persisted.

"She did, however, I was quite deceived in her. Her former employer neglected to inform me that the woman had little sense of her own station."

"Oh?" Rachel murmured, her voice pleasant but noncommittal.

Wyn was quite proud of her hostess's ability to bite back the anger, far from dampened, that burned in her cheeks.

"Tilbury found North with the head groom," Eleanor announced. "There was nothing to do but turn the two of them off immediately."

"You did give them references though," Rachel said.

Their visitor's face darkened dangerously. "Certainly not."

Fortunately, Lady Tilbury's visit was brief, yet Rachel was fretful long after her unwelcome guest had departed. Hildy showed no sign that she recognized, much less understood, that her sister was upset. She immediately proposed a jaunt into Much Wenlock to visit the drapers and choose fabrics for her new gowns.

Before following her friend from the room, Wyn took a seat next to Rachel. "I'll try to restrain her spending spree," she promised, giving her hostess a fond smile.

Rachel chuckled. "You know, as I do, that is impossible," she said. "Dear Wyn. Thank you for being here. I don't know that I could bear up under the avalanche of demands without you.''

"I knew it. Hildy is expecting too much of you," Wyn declared.

"She's my sister. Besides," Rachel admitted, "I hate to see anyone suffer. Do you believe that woman? Turning off her ladies' maid simply because the woman fell in love with another of the servants?" She busied herself arranging the teacups on the tray, an office Wyn was sure Rachel's own housemaid usually performed. "Will you do me a favor when you are in the village?" Rachel asked.

"Anything."

"Ask after Miss North. If she hasn't left for London yet, leave word that I am interested in hiring a dresser."

Touched by Rachel's kindness, Wyn hugged her. "I hope Alston appreciates what a special lady you are."

Her hostess grinned impishly. "He had better, hadn't he? I suppose I would be pushing my luck to offer Tilbury's former groom a position, as well, though. Besides, he would probably sneer at Lofty's preference in horse-flesh."

"Do you think the man will have difficulty in being taken on elsewhere without references?" Wyn asked.

"Not with the stable I have in mind," Rachel assured. "If you see Beacham on your way out, would you ask him to send a message to Baron Blackhawk? I believe it is past time for Garrett to interest himself in the neighborhood, don't you?"

Chapter Seventeen

Once she reached the town, Wyn had no problem discovering Miss North's direction. The distraught dresser had accepted the dressmaker's hospitality while marshaling her resources for her reluctant return to London. She was delighted to learn Rachel wished to take her on, declaring she would visit Lady Loftus immediately. Hildy forestalled her, considering Miss North already in her sister's employ and thus available to give her invaluable advice on the fabrics and patterns to be chosen for her new wardrobe.

Finding herself no longer needed, Wyn excused herself and went to explore the town. Half-timbered Elizabethan homes sat cheek by jowl with cottages constructed of gray limestone and topped with equally gray thatch. Market day was in progress and the streets bustled with activity. Men and women hawked, bartered and joked together. Children, dogs and chickens were everywhere underfoot, their shrill laughter, barks and squawks adding to the calliope of sound.

Wyn strolled deeper into the hustle and bustle, enjoying the noise and confusion. She neatly avoided offers to buy fresh fish, meat pies and a gosling. A vendor selling bouquets of freshly cut sweet pea flowers tempted her briefly but Wyn moved on. It was as she dodged a trio of boys chasing a squealing piglet that she nearly came to grief by tripping over a running toddler. A firm hand on her elbow held Wyn upright as the child's mother caught up to the little one.

"Does this mean we are well met, Miss Abbot?" Deegan murmured softly in her ear.

Regaining her balance, Wyn stepped away from him quickly. "What are you doing here?" she asked, unable to keep a touch of irritation from her voice.

Unfazed by her far from cordial greeting, Deegan tucked Wyn's hand in the crook of his arm, covering it with his before leading her down the cobbled street, away from the crowd. "Same as you, sweet. Seeing the sights. Have you taken in the abbey yet? I understand it's a delightful sight. We might give it a look-over together."

There had been a time when to do so would have been her greatest delight. That time was past. While she had planned to visit the ruins, being alone with Deegan no longer held any appeal for her.

Wyn declined. "I'm due back to meet Hildy at the dressmaker's."

"Readying herself for the upcoming shindy, I take it? Another time then?" he asked.

"You know there won't be another time, Deegan," she said softly.

"Suppose I should," he agreed, "but that doesn't mean I need stop hoping. You will save a dance for me at the Loftuses' ball, won't you?"

He knew it would be ill-mannered for her to refuse. Rather than commit herself, Wyn prevaricated. "I thought perhaps you would have left by then, and have moved on to London."

"I doubt it," Deegan said. He touched the curled brim of his top hat in greeting as they came abreast of a couple of bright-cheeked young serving maids. One dipped her eyes shyly, a timid smile curving her lips. The other batted her lashes in a blatant invitation. Deegan's lips curved in a rakish grin. "Not quite yet at any rate. I find there is quite a bit to entertain me in this neighborhood presently."

Wyn was fairly sure he alluded to the flirtatious maids.

"The fact is, Garrett's got me fairly buried in paper-work," he said, surprising her.

"Do you mean to tell me you actually *are* his secretary?"

"Please," Deegan pleaded, grimacing. "Have some thought for my tender sensibilities. Of course not. I'm simply helping him catch up on things. A temporary situation, the action of a friend for a friend." He paused, then added, "Even if he is paying me.

"And what of you, Wyn? Is the ball only the first in a string of whirlwind social engagements? I doubt that, having dragged you this far, Hildy will be content with life in Shropshire. Are you London bound?"

Given her choice, Wyn admitted she would not rush off to the city. There was so much beauty to be appreciated in the countryside. So many things she would enjoy seeing. Alston had suggested a visit to nearby Bridgnorth to climb the long series of steps that led up the sandstone ridge to the Hightown and the ruins of a Norman castle. Or to Ironbridge to the northeast to view the iron bridge constructed nearly a hundred years before over the Severn River gorge. Hildy had made acceptance of the offers impossible by vetoing all such excursions. She asked instead to be escorted to the forthcoming local assemblies. Outside of shopping and dancing, there were to be few entertainments.

"We're with Lofty and Rachel for the next few weeks at any rate," Wyn answered. "You?"

"Actually," Deegan admitted, "I don't believe London is ready for me. I'd much rather jump on the next ship and head home."

Home, Wyn thought. Where thoughts of her family and San Francisco had once warmed her, she was now torn. Part of her belonged back in the mansion on Nob Hill, but another part of her would always stay with Garrett at

Hawk's Run, a place she had not seen, yet already loved because he lived there.

"The dressmaker's is just over there," she said, easing her hand from beneath Deegan's. "I really must go."

He sighed. "Been given my marching papers again, hmm? I'm sure we'll meet again. Give my regards to Lady Loftus, won't you?" Then with another tip of his hat, Deegan melted into the bustling traffic.

Wyn looked after him a moment longer, wondering what would become of him. Despite his treatment of her in San Francisco, she was fond of him. Deegan had changed since then. Not drastically, but subtly. She liked him better for helping Garrett. Perhaps, if he accepted the opportunity the baron was obviously offering in giving him employment, Deegan would discover there was more to him than just being a charming companion. If he ever discovered his true self-worth, the combination of both charm and dignity would make him a very dangerous man for a woman to know. Few hearts ever managed to withstand such a double-barreled broadside.

She was about to turn away when she caught a glimpse of another familiar face in the crowd. One she had not thought to see.

It was gone so quickly, Wyn wondered if she had been mistaken. Although she had not believed him when he had claimed to be en route to visit relatives, she doubted that even the most glib of con men could convince her that the way from Liverpool to Ireland lay through the heart of Shropshire. That left Wyn with a single question.

Who was Magnus Finley following?

Deegan flung into the study and reached for the decanter of whiskey on the side table.

Garrett put down his pen and watched as his friend tossed off a dram and immediately refilled his glass.

"Do you know who I saw in town?" Deegan demanded, slumping into a chair on the opposite side of the desk.

"That damn Pinkerton. What the hell do you suppose he's doing here?"

"Following the *Nereid*'s elusive thief, I would suppose," Garrett drawled. "You wouldn't happen to be him, would you, Dig?"

Deegan scowled. "Very funny. Of course, I've known for a long time that you believe me capable of being the fellow."

"Very capable," Garrett agreed.

"Yes, and I suppose that's meant as a compliment, too," Deegan said dryly. "But the fact remains, I didn't touch Suzanne Carillo's pearls, nor did I nip the other sets during the voyage. Jewel theft has never been my style. I've never aspired to be more than a penny-ante thief, and then only out of necessity."

"I know that, too," Garrett assured him. "I had a friend of mine in Liverpool look into your personal history."

Deegan's brows shot skyward in surprise, disappearing beneath his fall of tawny hair. "Did you now."

Garrett picked up a sheet of paper and tossed it across to his friend. The surface was crossed with close-set lines written in a precise yet spidery hand. "I had to be sure, Dig," he said. "According to this, you've led a rather colorful life."

Deegan glanced quickly down at the list of his sins before replacing it on the desk. "Colorful is not the adjective I would have chosen. Are you going to call Finley in to take me away?"

"Why should I? He isn't looking for you, is he?"

"I bloody well hope not," Deegan said. "But if not me, then who is he after?"

Garrett swung his feet to the desk top, relaxing back in his chair. "I have a few ideas," he allowed, "but why prolong the guessing game? Why don't we simply ask the good detective?"

Breakfast at Loftus Manor the next morning was disturbed by the arrival of the local constable and Lord Croyden Tilbury.

Tilbury was very like his wife, although Wyn was not surprised to find it so. He held himself stiffly, as if affronted by the necessity that had brought him to Alston's table. Rather than demean himself by making an accusation, Tilbury refused invitations to breakfast and to take a seat, and prodded the hapless constable into speaking for him. Something the villager looked quite unwilling to do.

"Pardon the interruption, m'lady, m'lord," the constable mumbled, tugging on his forelock respectfully. He glanced aside at Wyn and Hildy. "Ladies," he added. "Hate to bother you but it's come to my notice that you took on a woman who once worked for Lady Tilbury?"

Rachel nodded. "Judith North. Just yesterday in fact. Why?"

The constable cast a sidelong glance at Tilbury, hoping, Wyn decided, that his lordship would deign to answer the question himself. It was a foolish wish.

"We'd...that is, *I'd* like to ask her a few questions," he said.

"And search her belongings," Tilbury added, glaring at the constable.

"Search her things?" Alston exploded. "Whatever for?"

"Yes," Rachel declared, jumping to her new maid's defense. "Miss North has done nothing."

Tilbury redirected his scowl at her. "We'll just see about that."

Wyn decided she disliked Sybil's father very much. "Perhaps if you simply tell us what has happened, we can be of more help," she suggested.

"Yes, spit it out, man," Alston urged. "What's occurred to put you in such a taking?"

If possible, Lord Tilbury's demeanor stiffened even further. "You should be warned, Loftus," he growled. "The woman's probably cleaned out your wife's jewel box as well by now and left on the sly."

"Don't be ridiculous," Rachel snapped. "As I understand it, Miss North's only *crime* was to fall in love."

Tilbury's nostrils flared. "I would expect a person of your sort to side with a servant, madam, but I am sure your husband would not have allowed the woman in his household had he been apprised of her conduct."

"Her conduct?" Hildy laughed softly. "My dear sir," she chided. "You act as if poor North is amoral, which I can assure you, having spoken with her in great detail, she is not."

Rather than answer Hildy, Tilbury acted as if she hadn't spoken. "You can accompany us if you wish, Loftus. Whether you do or not is no concern of mine but I mean to return home with my wife's diamonds."

Rachel's hand flew to her lips. "Eleanor's diamonds are missing?"

Tilbury glared at her and motioned for the constable to follow him. "Will you show me the woman's room, Loftus, or must I find it myself?" he demanded.

With a snarl of irritation, Alston threw down his linen napkin and got to his feet. In the silence that followed the men's removal, Rachel stared at her barely touched breakfast. "I must go to Miss North," she said at last, pushing her chair back. "She will need to feel we do not mistrust her as Tilbury does."

Left alone with Hildy at the table, Wyn tried to eat her own breakfast but found the meal had lost its taste.

Her friend did not share her concern. Hildy's expression was one of delight as she savored a bite. "Do you think she did it?" she asked, eyes glowing with excitement.

"Of course not," Wyn said. "How can you even think such a thing?"

"Well, someone had to take them. Who better than North?" Hildy sampled a slice of toasted bread. "I wonder in what manner the diamonds were set?"

"Hildy!"

"Diamonds suit Lady Tilbury, you know. Although they have always been my favorite stones, you must admit diamonds are cold and colorless, just as she is,'' Hildy continued. ''Naturally, I know how she feels, having lost my own diamonds. You know you felt bereft when Pierce sold your jewels, Wyn.''

Since it had been at her own suggestion that her brother do so, Wyn remembered feeling nothing but relief that she could help him in an hour of need. Hildy would never believe her though. Collecting possessions, especially jewelry, had always been her passion. ''A few pangs,'' Wyn said.

''You really should have kept the aquamarines,'' Hildy said. ''I always liked them best. Do you know, I believe I saw a fabric exactly that shade! You really should speak to the draper about it. If you'd like, I could have him put the bolt on Lofty's account when I go into the village later. Would you like that?''

Wyn pushed back her chair. ''I believe I'll go see how Miss North is.''

Hildy surged to her feet. ''North, North, North!'' she snapped. ''I'm quite sick of hearing her name this morning. One would think she was a member of the family rather than one of the servants the way you all go on about her.''

Rather than say another word, Wyn stood absolutely still, stunned at how unfeeling her friend could be.

''I might as well come with you,'' Hildy said. ''We can all take turns holding her hand. Unless, of course, Lord Tilbury has found his wife's diamonds in her possession, in which case we can all wave our kerchiefs at her as she is driven off to jail.''

The sound of men's footsteps on the main stairs gave Wyn the excuse to fly from the room. She had never seen Hildy in such a temper before. It only showed her how little she really knew the woman anymore.

Tilbury led the way down the staircase, the constable trailing at his heels, looking rather relieved.

''I told you we wouldn't find anything,'' Alston insisted angrily. ''North is guiltless in the matter.''

"Is she?" Tilbury demanded, whirling on him. "She's probably passed them to her lover. If he's left the county, we'll know they planned the robbery together."

Rachel and Miss North had followed the men, but now the ladies' maid broke free of her new mistress's comforting arm. "We've done nothing," she cried, desperation making her voice sharp. "Nothing."

Tilbury barely glanced at her tearful face. Instead he looked to Beacham, waiting for the butler to open the main door for him. The man had barely complied when Tilbury stomped out to the portico and back to his coach.

Miss North wrung her hands. "You believe me, don't you, my lord?" she pleaded of Alston.

He glanced past her to Rachel before answering. "Of course, I do, North. Try not to let Lord Tilbury's actions upset you too much. I'm sure they'll find the real thief soon and all will be forgotten."

Wyn doubted it.

"Shall we send word to your young man that you are all right?" Rachel asked, slipping a comforting arm around the maid once more. When Miss North nodded, Rachel looked at her husband. "I sent him to Hawk's Run," she said. "Will you send word to him in the stable there?"

Alston turned to Beacham. "I'll see to it, my lord," the butler promised, forestalling the request. "Immediately. Perhaps Miss North would like to accompany me to the kitchen? Mrs. Beacham sets great store by a cup of tea when something upsetting has occurred."

"Capital thought," Alston agreed.

Wyn's mind was no longer on the maid's plight. The mention of Garrett's estate had brought him all too clearly to mind. Not just the beloved hawklike quality of his face, but the fact that she had not learned enough about him to acquit him of all the things she had believed him to be. One of which was the hand behind the thefts aboard the *Nereid*.

She needed to go into the village and find Magnus Fin-

ley, Wyn decided. Until she spoke with him, she would
find no peace.

Forcing her voice to be light, Wyn turned to where
Hildy stood in the doorway of the breakfast parlor. "I
believe I'll go into Much Wenlock with you after all," she
announced brightly. Rachel and Alston both looked at her
as if she'd gone mad. Perhaps she had. "Hildy was telling
me about the most lovely length of fabric. I feel I simply
must have it."

And, she thought, if they believed that, then she was a
better con woman than she had thought possible. But from
whom had she learned the trait? Deegan? Or the ever-
masked Baron Blackhawk?

Garrett scowled at Magnus Finley and drummed his fingers against the rough-hewn table. Rather than send for the
Pinkerton, he had tracked him down to the inn where he
had taken a room. So they would not be overheard, he'd
asked the landlord for a private room, but all that had been
available were the innkeeper's own quarters. Garrett had
taken them, paying generously for the honor.

The accommodations were far from those usually enjoyed by men of his station. And a step up from many
he'd occupied during his years of nomadic wandering. Finley didn't appear to notice the lack of comfort, although
he did appreciate the cool pitcher of ale their host had
thoughtfully provided.

He helped himself to a refreshing dram before pinning
Garrett with an intent look. "You find fault with my conclusions, my lord?" the Pinkerton asked.

"Far from it," Garrett drawled. "In fact, they concur
with my own. But it appears we haven't a fact between us
to prove those conclusions in a court of law."

"Sadly so," Finley said, "although, having heard that
there was a new robbery in the area leads me to hope such
will not be the case for long."

Garrett snorted shortly. "With Tilbury handling the
case, I wouldn't put much trust in that. A more inept mag-

istrate would be hard to find. The man's a bloody fool. Shall I tell him you are available and eager to solve this mystery for him?''

"I think not," Finley demurred. "I'm already serving a number of masters in this matter."

Garrett tapped the side of his tankard, deep in thought. "You're quite sure on all this?" he asked at last.

"Very sure," the Pinkerton said. "Beginning with the theft of the Hartleby diamonds in San Francisco, there has been a pattern developing. Each theft has been accomplished with more risk, and yet our culprit appears not to care whether capture is imminent or not. The danger of being caught is apparently as thrilling as the acquisition of the jewels."

"The false-sided case can be used as evidence," Garrett said.

"It isn't against the law in either of our countries to own such a piece of luggage," Finley reminded. "And, when I discovered it, the secret compartments were empty. I'm afraid we have no case, my lord."

"Bloody hell," Garrett growled. "Where do you think the items are hidden then?"

"I was hoping you had some suggestions," Finley said, and smiled faintly. "Short of breaking and entering, I can see no way to search for the jewels, can you?"

Garrett's scowl darkened. "Blast it, no. The first chance I can see where it might be possible to get into the house is when they are entertaining, and that's well over a week away."

"I would rather not wait that long," the detective admitted. "The more time there is to dispose of the jewels, the less chance we have of proving the culprit's identity."

"Don't you think I know that?" Garrett snapped. "But, damn it all, the man isn't going to just open up his house to us. He'd think us mad—me mad—to even suggest such a thing." Garrett stared across the room, turning over the problem in his mind. He and Finley had discussed the matter well over an hour already and had gotten nowhere. To aid his thought processes, Garrett lifted his tankard, planning to enjoy a cooling draft of locally brewed ale.

Instead, he smashed the tankard down against the sturdy tabletop. "Damn, but I've been a fool!"

Caught in the act of savoring another swallow himself, Finley put his own cup down. "You have an idea?"

Garrett grinned widely. "A glimmer, but a dandy one, Finley. Who, other than our thief, did you suspect earlier of the crimes?"

The detective smiled warily. "Well now, my lord, I'm not sure you really want to know that."

"My name was on the list, was it?" Garrett said, amused by the idea.

"Among others."

"And did all your suspects have a history of past crimes?"

"Some," Finley allowed. "Most were under investigation because they were known to be in the city—"

"San Francisco?"

"At first just there, but later in other cities, as well. Salt Lake City, Chicago, Boston, and then aboard the *Nereid*."

"And now in our little corner of Shropshire," Garrett finished. "And who among us meets all those qualifications?"

Finley's smile widened. "You do, sir, Miss Abbot, Mrs. Hartleby, and—"

"Galloway," Garrett said. "I have him working as my secretary currently. Quite a waste of his natural talents, don't you agree?"

The detective's smile faded. "I don't think I like what you are suggesting, my lord."

"Then forget you even heard me allude to it, Finley," Garrett suggested. "Just hope like hell that the plan works."

Chapter Eighteen

Wyn found it impossible to sleep that night. In the aftermath of Lord Tilbury's visit, the household vibrated with tension. Even the surprise arrival of a messenger from Alston's mother in Brighton had not alleviated the mood. When presented with a velvet-lined box, Rachel had merely sat staring blankly at the lovely antique necklace and earrings that nestled inside. "Bless me," Alston had murmured. "She's finally accepted you, Rach. Believe it or not, these are my great-grandmother's rubies. The most exquisite of our family heirlooms."

Hildy, of course, had appreciated the gems. She seemed to be the only resident of Loftus Manor immune to the undercurrents, for her spirits remained unusually high. They would sink soon enough. Having witnessed her friend's brief tantrum earlier, Wyn hated to think what Hildy's reaction would be when she finally realized that Garrett was lost to her. It wouldn't be pleasant.

And it would mean she had lost yet another friend.

If Hildy had ever truly been her friend.

Wyn struggled free of her tangled sheets and got out of bed. She was restless, a result of the day itself and the full moon, she decided. She felt its pull as strong as did the tides.

Because the night was warm, she had pushed the casement window open and left the drapes undrawn. Earlier she had been able to see a galaxy of stars but now that the moon had risen, the glittering array was somewhat dimmed in its glow. Nearly as bright as daylight, moonlight spilled like liquid silver through the window and across the patterned carpet, bleaching the richly woven colors from the wool.

The moon had been bright the night before, Wyn mused as she leaned against the casement and stared unseeing at the nightscape. Is that why the thief had struck?

She knew from the gossip she'd heard in the town that the last robbery involving precious gems had occurred in the neighborhood more than two decades before, and then it had been at the hand of a highwayman who'd stopped one of the peers' coaches. The villain had been shot dead by his next prospective victim and peace had settled over the community since then.

Wyn wished the episode had gone down in history as the final robbery in the area. She had heard of far too many jewels being stolen lately. Beginning with Hildy's ofttimes-mourned diamonds, tales of similar thefts seemed to have followed her. A tally that stretched the width of a continent and beyond an ocean.

If she didn't know Deegan as well as she did, she would suspect him of the deed. He had had the opportunity, had been in each of the locales where robberies occurred. But so had another.

It wasn't the first time she had suspected Garrett of the crime. She wished she could absolve him of it, yet she couldn't. Even if he didn't need the funds from the sale of the stolen jewels, she could see him taking them simply for the adventure of the game. For a game it truly was, the thief pitting his wits against the odds.

Not for the first time that day, she wished she had been able to locate Magnus Finley. To discover why he was in the area, to learn whom he watched. Hildy had been most insistent on her constant attendance when they drove into the village so Wyn had not had a chance to slip away to speak to him, even briefly.

Sleep was clearly impossible. There were too many fears preying on her mind. She needed distraction, Wyn decided. A book from Alston's library, preferably a tedious one. Warm milk would be an excellent sleep aid, also.

Rather than venture forth in her nightwear, Wyn stripped off her nightgown, tossing it across the foot of her bed. She pulled a dark walking skirt and a simply cut basque from the wardrobe and stepped into a comfortable pair of low-heeled shoes. Without the aid of her corset to mold her figure, the jacket's fit was a bit snug. Without the buffer of fine lawn undergarments, the fabric was rough against her skin. She felt decadent to be so ill dressed, but the brief time she would spend in the kitchen and library hardly merited a full toilette.

Loftus Manor was well maintained. The hinges were silent as Wyn slipped into the darkened hall and closed the door to her room behind her. The moonlight was diffused in the corridor, the angle at which it entered the narrow windows tempering the glow. Fortunately, there was sufficient for her to see her way without the aid of a candle.

The way was ghostly, especially in the close quarters of the servants' stairs, but, since it led directly to the kitchen, Wyn chose it over the more elaborate main staircase. Because her family's household was run in a far less class-conscious manner, she was familiar with the chores involved in building up the fire in the iron stove and in raiding the larder. Within minutes Wyn had found all she needed.

The coals in the stove had been banked for the night, which meant she had to wait while the stove warmed sufficiently again. The delay offered the perfect opportunity to choose her book.

Alston's library was one of her favorite places in the house. The room was airy, two stories high with a double tier of book-filled shelves, the upper accessible from a wide mezzanine reached via a circular iron staircase. Small-paned terrace doors opened onto the south lawn, a vista that rolled gently toward a heavily wooded coppice. Since the library windows faced the same direction as those in her bedroom Wyn had little need of a candle to guide her selection for moonlight flooded the room. Although, she mused, it would be better to pick a tome blindly, to guarantee it would hold little of her interest and put her to sleep quickly.

Wyn had barely slid a book from the nearest shelf when a movement on the lawn outside caught her attention. Could deer have strayed from the woods to enjoy a late-night feast of tender blades of grass? She smiled softly to herself, remembering how thrilled she'd been as a child to see wild deer grazing early in the morning on the lawn of her parent's country house. Drawn by the memory as much as by the fleet shadow she'd glimpsed, Wyn put her volume down on the desk and drifted over to the terrace doors.

The shadow hadn't stolen from the forest; it was stealing away from the house toward the forest.

And it had two legs, not four.

All thoughts of hot milk and dull books forgotten, Wyn released the lock on the terrace door. The man wore shape-concealing trousers and jacket, and a cloth hat tugged low over his face. He had already gained the safety of the coppice by the time she reached the lawn and could dash after him, anger driving her in a headlong rush. She'd known immediately who the intruder was and why he had come— word of the arrival of Rachel's rubies had spread quickly, fueled by Alston's pleasure over the event. It had taken Rachel far too long to gain the prized Loftus heirloom for her to lose the jeweled set so quickly to an unconscionable thief, Wyn thought as she gathered up her skirts and ran. And when she caught up with the blackguard who had stolen them, she was going to give Garrett Blackhawk the dressing-down of his life for taking them!

* * *

Garrett pressed back against the red brick of Loftus Manor, his dark clothing and coloring making him invisible in the shadows. Not an easy task with the moon undimmed by even the haziest veil of cloud. Given the choice, he would have preferred the threat of a downpour to clear skies this night.

The moonlight did make it easy to spot his prey when the figure slipped from the house, moving quickly across the brightly lit lawn, making for cover near Beggarhill Brook. Garrett's muscles tensed, preparing for the moment when he could safely follow, his longer legs crossing the expanse of carefully groomed grass in what amounted to an infantry charge.

His private army was spread out, each ordered to keep watch in a different sector should their quarry be successful in slipping by one of them. He only hoped that Deegan managed to play his part and depart before the thief arrived at the fence's rendezvous and recognized him.

Dig hadn't liked the idea of becoming a covert operative—a phrase favored by Finley—but Deegan had not only been the perfect man for the job, he'd been the only man for the job. He was a newcomer to the area, an agile pickpocket and a convincing liar. It had simply been a matter of his hanging around the more disreputable inns to make contact with the local criminal element, waiting to overhear the snatch of conversation that would alert Garrett's vigilantes. Word had arrived sooner than any of them had expected.

"We shouldn't be surprised," Finley had said upon hearing Deegan's report. "The gems taken in San Francisco were too well known in the area to be sold successfully there and our felon has been on the move ever since. By now, there is quite a tidy cache to be disposed of and keeping them hidden can't be easy. The fox is most likely getting desperate to sell them."

Based on the list Finley had given him, the pile of stolen articles resembled that found in a pirate's treasure trove. Not only were there gemstones of every known size and

variety, the most precious ones appeared on the tally time
and time again. Particularly diamonds. Their thief had been
most greedy, Garrett thought as he watched the culprit trot
surefootedly across the sod and into the trees.

He waited, allowing his prey to put a good bit of distance between them before following. It wouldn't do to be
seen should his light-fingered foe glance back. Mentally
Garrett counted off the steps the person ahead of him had
yet to take and still not be lost to him. A half dozen. Three.
One...

A furious rustle of sound froze Garrett in his blind. He
pressed farther into the shadows until the rough texture of
the brick bit through the sturdy fabric of his dark shirt to
score his back.

Footsteps sounded against flagstone steps, loud in the
quiet night air, then a whirlwind rushed by him, silken
skirts raised to display pale, shapely calves. Her long
flaxen braid bounced against her back as Wyn flashed by
him.

Beneath his breath, Garrett swore and launched himself
in pursuit. He hoped Ellery was alert to their quarry's presence when the dark-clothed figure left the coppice and entered Lingham Dingle. It would be darker in the dell and
easy to miss a person intent upon escaping attention. His
own hands would be full keeping Wyn from inadvertently
alerting the thief of their hastily arranged trap. On this
particular fox hunt, he would no longer be around for the
figurative kill.

Wyn was faster than he'd expected, reaching the edge
of the coppice before he caught up to her. She was so
intent upon pursuing the thief's shadow that she didn't
realize she'd become quarry herself. Pausing to get her
bearings, Wyn was still for a fraction of a second. Garrett
seized the moment and, covering her mouth with one hand,
he scooped her off her feet with the other and away from
the narrow path the thief had taken.

The element of surprise kept her still for the space of a
single heartbeat before she began struggling. When her

flailing fist connected with his jaw, Garrett nearly dropped her. His grip punishingly tight, he forged on to put enough distance between them and the path. Based on Deegan's information, there were bound to be others abroad that night, all headed for the tumbledown cottage outside of Shirlot. Men who would think little of dispatching an inconvenient witness to their midnight business.

Garrett headed north, deeper into the trees. Wyn was losing strength quickly, burning herself out. When her foot connected with the trunk of a sapling, he thought the sound reverberated as loudly as a shot. It wasn't until he identified the peaceful gurgle of the brook that he stopped, spilling Wyn onto the ground and covering her nearly exhausted form with his body.

She lay sprawled on a bed of golden broom, the scent of the crushed wildflowers when combined with her natural scent heady enough to make the danger of the night pale. Flyaway strands of her fair hair curled around her face; her flaxen braid trailed away, the color alone making it seem like moonlight. Garrett brushed back the straggling locks, luxuriating in their silken texture. Her breast heaved with exertion as she fought to tear his yet-restraining hand from her mouth. Her struggles caused a shifting in their bodies, her legs spreading slightly, his dropping into more intimate contact with hers.

Wyn stilled immediately, her eyes widening as his body responded naturally to the juxtaposition. His groin tightening with desire, Garrett slid his hand away from her mouth, trailing his fingers sensuously across her lips in retreat. Gasping at the cool night air in an effort to catch her breath, Wyn pressed her hands against his chest. "Damn y—"

He swallowed the last word, covering her mouth with his in a bruising kiss. She whimpered, though whether in protest or passion he was unsure until her hands moved, sliding across his shoulders and into his hair. Her lips parted, her tongue greeting his, sliding, entwining with it in a heated welcome.

And with her surrender, the last vestige of his sanity
fled. Never had he wanted a woman so badly, never in his
past had he been so lost as to desert honor. It went by the
wayside now, need that was no longer his alone triumphing
over it.

When his mouth tore from hers it was to travel the
length of her arched throat. His hands preceded his lips,
tearing free the straining buttons of her jacket, drawing the
lapels aside until she lay beneath him displayed, her warm
womanly flesh surprisingly unhindered by the constraints
of corset or camisolette. Tenderly he molded her breast in
his hand, savoring the gentle weight of it. Then his mouth
covered the blushing tip, tasting, as well as feeling, her
response.

Wyn arched toward him, her hands slipping back to his
shoulders, her fingers curving, clutching him in her ec-
stasy. Gasps of pleasure stole past her lips, sounds he trea-
sured all the more for knowing they were for him alone.

"You're so beautiful," he said against her skin.

"Garrett?"

He raised up, supporting his weight on braced forearms.
Her dark eyes were clouded with passion, dense as a sheltered lagoon.

"Let me see you," she murmured.

Her hands glided to the front of his shirt, slid down his
chest. He sucked in his breath when she reached his ribs
and extended her fingers, spanning them. Her touch was
gentle, awed as it traced the hard lines of his body. When
she attempted to unfasten the buttons of his shirt, her fingers fumbled with the closings.

No longer able to endure the sweet torture, he ripped
free of the shirt. Then they were heart to heart, bare flesh
to bare flesh.

He claimed her again, his kiss raw with hunger, his
thumbs brushing the extended tips of her breasts, causing
her to quiver with desire. She was his, not just for this
brief moment in time but forever. This night would seal
his fate to hers, for a gentleman he could no longer be.

Garrett tugged at Wyn's skirt, drawing the fabric slowly up, revealing the long satiny length of her bare legs. His palm slid from calf to thigh and ever higher until he reached the apex of her legs and felt her heat.

She jerked in surprise when he slid his finger between the silken folds. To further her acceptance, he kissed her deeply again, matching the strokes of his tongue across hers to the movements of his hand.

The sweet scent of woman mingled with broom and the rose-and-clove perfume she favored. Her body moved against his in unspoken need, her legs spreading naturally wider in welcome.

"Wyn," he whispered, his voice harsh with passion. "Let me love you."

In answer she raised her body against his hand. Her fingers clenched his hair, drawing his mouth back to hers in a greedy kiss. "Yes, oh, yes, Garrett," she murmured.

He hurt with desire, with the need to enter her, to spill his seed within her. Yet her response was too sweet, too innocently new to rush the moment. Rather than seek his own release, Garrett gathered the fabric of her skirt in his hands, pushing it clear to her waist, baring her body more fully to the moonlight and his greedy eyes.

"You are so perfect," he said, then showed her how much by lifting her hips and kissing her intimately. Wyn jerked in response, her nails digging into his skin. Throwing her head back, she rode the tempest of sensation he evoked, gasping his name as she peaked.

The taste of her on his lips, Garrett gathered her close, kissed her again as he eased free of his trousers. She quivered when he carefully probed the sweet entrance to her body. Slowly, so as not to hurt her overmuch, he slid inside.

Wyn tensed briefly then accepted him, her legs closing around him of their own accord. She lifted her hips in an innocent demand, drawing him deeper.

Garrett lost what little control remained and rammed

into her, breaking the last vestige of her maiden's existence.

A cry left her lips at the intrusion, then her body adapted, joined his in a rocking rhythm that quickened with each stroke as she sought once more the paradise of sensation he'd shown her existed. He was but a heartbeat behind when Wyn crested, her body convulsing around his.

Minutes passed with Garrett aware only of the rush of his own blood and the throb of Wyn's pulse beneath his ear. She was his as irrevocably now as he was hers. As he had always been hers.

He rolled off her, lying on his side, little caring that the coarse stalks of broom scratched his naked skin. "I'm afraid, Miss Abbot, that you have been compromised. Most thoroughly compromised." Unable to resist the temptation to touch her, he trailed his fingers above the waistband of her skirt, across her abdomen. He had done the unforgivable, and it was only now that sanity seeped slowly back into his veins that he could admit it. "How do you feel?"

She smiled beatifically at him. "Wonderful," she said, her voice a contented purr that was a balm to his troubled soul. "But far from compromised."

"I must strive to do better the next time then," Garrett teased.

Wyn ran her hand lazily up his arm, apparently as loath to end their intimacy as was he. Keeping her eyes on the path her fingers forged, she whispered, "I wanted this as much as you did. No guilt need be accrued."

"None tallied," he said. "However—"

Her fingers covered his lips briefly. "No. Don't say it."

Garrett leaned over, kissing her. Her mouth clung to his a moment. "I wasn't very circumspect, my love. There may be complications. A child." He trailed his fingers across her stomach again, wondering if even now she carried his son. His heir. A wave of tenderness washed over him at the thought. "This night will remain memorable whether fate has seen fit to interfere or not," he said. "In any case, you know I want you for my wife. I am, if you recall, courting you, albeit in a highly unusual manner.''

Wyn's lashes dropped, sheltering her eyes from his scrutiny. "Garrett, I can't."

All the warmth and pleasure he had been feeling drained away, leaving him cold and empty. The future suddenly stretched endless before him.

His hand dropped away from her. "I see," he said.

She touched his face. "Don't do that."

"Do what?"

"Don that mask. The man I love isn't the Baron Blackhawk."

The admission was like a slap in the face. She had let him make love to her, but it was to another man she gave her love. Deegan, no doubt.

Garrett sat up, reached for his shirt and shrugged into it. "Then you have my abject apologies for the evening, madam. I trust your inamorato is not unduly upset that I've anticipated him in enjoying your favors."

When he made to stand, she stayed him with a brief touch. "How could I ever love the cold, impossible man you become when playing the baron? I love you, Garrett. I always have." Her fingers brushed tenderly along his cheek. "I always will."

He caught her hand and turned his face into it, placing a kiss in her curved palm. "Then—"

"Hush," she murmured, raising herself slightly from the bed of golden broom. Her lips were parted, alluring. "Don't speak of it," Wyn urged. "Simply love me tonight."

It was a request he was more than willing to grant.

The darkly clothed figure crouched silent in the shadows, watching as the couple came together in a passionate embrace.

It had been a near thing this evening. Alerted by native cunning that the woods harbored hunters, the rendezvous had been avoided. While disappointing, delaying the sale

of a select few of the stolen jewels was not unwelcome.
They could be admired, fondled a while longer. And they
could be used in gaining a much sought vendetta.

The wounds of numerous slights had been assuaged
through the theft of favored gems in the past. Now one
particular set of those jewels would make revenge possible.
A most satisfying revenge.

The couple were attuned only to each other. His sun-
darkened skin was exotic-looking against her moon-white
complexion as he held her, the tenderness and passion he
showed her far from the cool exterior he showed to the
world.

Or to me, the shadow thought bitterly.

The moon had begun to set, the shadows to grow longer,
before the silent watcher slipped back toward the path and
away from the lover's glade. Tomorrow would be their day
of reckoning. A small smile of satisfaction curved the
thief's lips. A day to be enjoyed to the fullest.

At least by some.

Chapter Nineteen

Although she had barely slept, Wyn was up early the next morning. So much so that she had eaten in solitary splendor, neither her hosts nor her friend joining her. By the time Alston strolled into the breakfast parlor with Deegan at his heels, the plate before her on the table testified to a very healthy appetite and she was enjoying a second cup of coffee.

"Ah, you're in luck, Galloway," Alston drawled. "Your lady of choice is available. Now if you'd come to call on my sister-by-marriage it would be another case entirely. She's never abroad till midday, if then."

Deegan smiled. "Morning, Wyn. I've come to beg your company on a ride this bright morn."

"A ride?" Wyn's already high spirits soared even more. Had Garrett sent Deegan for her? Was he as anxious to see her as she was to see him again?

"If it tips the balance in my favor," Deegan said, "I've made off not only with that frisky little mare, but the good baron's prize stallion. I thought, a race, my dear?"

Thoroughly seduced by the offer, Wyn pushed back her chair. "Just give me time to change," she said, and flew from the room.

She had barely taken her riding habit from the clothes-

press when there was a tap on the door. "Come in," Wyn
sang out, too rushed to slow her pace.

She was pleased when Miss North stepped into the room
and closed the door. "Pardon me, Miss Abbot. Mrs. Hartleby would like to know if she might borrow a lace jabot."

Considering the maid had been hired as Rachel's
dresser, since arriving at Loftus Manor she'd been at Hildy's beck and call nearly constantly. The only aspect of
her arrival that surprised Wyn was that Hildy was actually
asking to borrow something from her wardrobe rather than
simply helping herself. Perhaps because she was unfamiliar with Hildy's propensity, the maid's voice held a note
of uncertainty.

Busy with the closings of her morning dress, Wyn
tossed a smile back over her shoulder to reassure the
woman. "Of course, Miss North. They are in that—" Wyn
broke off and spun to look more fully at her visitor. The
maid's left cheek was bruised. Her eyes were red veined
and swollen from crying.

Fury over the abuse the woman had suffered lit Wyn's
eyes. She could think of only one person who could have
abused Miss North so. The arrogant and ignorant Lord
Tilbury. He had obviously felt physical violence would
produce his wife's missing jewelry when questioning
failed to do so. "Are you all right?" Wyn asked softly.

The maid raised her chin in a show of pride. "Perfectly,
miss. You were about to tell me where I might find the
jabots?"

"Not until you tell me who struck you," Wyn insisted.
Once Miss North verified her suspicion, she would go to
Alston with the story and if he could not force Tilbury to
recompense the maid for such treatment, she would go to
Garrett. He, she thought proudly, could bring down lightning from the skies if necessary—or what passed for the
equivalent in social ostracism—to smite the offender.

Miss North turned her face away. "I deserved it," she

said. "I went beyond my specified duties in attending to Mrs. Hartleby's wardrobe."

Wyn stared at the maid, stunned. "Hildy struck you?"

"I did not realize she wished to keep the gowns she brought with her as they were," Miss North said. "I really must return, Miss Abbot. The jabot?"

"Not until you tell me exactly what happened," Wyn declared. Taking the maid's arm, she drew her over to the stool before the dressing table and forced her to sit down. "Please, Miss North," she requested quietly, kneeling at the woman's side.

The softly spoken request brought fresh tears to Miss North's eyes. "I thought I was helping her," she whispered, and fumbled for a handkerchief to stem the fresh flow. "You see, the jet cording on her violet gown would go so well on the amber walking dress Lady Loftus kindly gave Mrs. Hartleby from her own wardrobe. I'm making a few alterations to it and thought Mrs. Hartleby would appreciate having it retrimmed."

"It was thoughtful of you," Wyn said.

Miss North kept her lashes lowered. In her lap, her hands twisted the damp handkerchief, mangling it. "She didn't feel so, miss. I was working in her room yesterday, the afternoon light being better for close work there, when she discovered me about to remove the trim. I barely knew what was happening." The maid looked at Wyn, her expression bleak and confused. "Mrs. Hartleby's been so eager for my help since I arrived here, to see her in such a taking quite frightened me. Before I could explain what I was doing, she yanked the violet gown from my hands and struck me."

Angry over the treatment the maid had been given, Wyn's lips thinned tightly. "Did you tell Lady Loftus of this?"

"Oh, no, miss. Cook tended to me, but we felt it best to tell anyone who asked that I had tripped and hurt myself."

"But you didn't lie to me," Wyn said.

Miss North's eyes dipped again. "No, miss."

The admission warmed Wyn. She placed her hand over the maid's tightly gripped ones. "I'll speak to both Mrs. Hartleby and Lady Loftus."

When Miss North's eyes flew open in consternation, Wyn squeezed her hands lightly in encouragement. "I won't tell Lady Loftus what happened if you don't wish me to," she promised. "I'll simply ask her to give you other duties that allow you little or no time to devote to Mrs. Hartleby. Now, what was it you came to borrow?"

"A jabot," the maid said quietly. She swiped at her eyes a final time before getting to her feet and squaring her shoulders. "Thank you, Miss Abbot."

Wyn indicated the chest where she kept the lacy frills and had just turned back to her riding habit when the door flew open and Hildy sailed into the room. While her soft brown hair was already neatly arranged in an attractive spill of sausage curls, Wyn noted that her friend wore little beneath the clinging folds of her scarlet dressing gown.

"Dearest," Hildy cooed, totally ignoring Miss North's presence. "I realized I hadn't returned your amethyst brooch to you." She glanced to the dark blue habit laid out on the bed and grinned. "Ah, another assignation with the baron's handsome brother, I see."

"With Deegan, actually," Wyn said, her voice cool.

Hildy didn't appear to notice the lack of warmth. "Either way, I won't keep you. I'll just drop your pin in with your other trinkets, shall I?" Without bothering to ask where Wyn kept her modest cache of jewelry, Hildy moved over to the dressing table and drew open the shallow center drawer. There was a theatrical pause before she turned back to Wyn. "Oh, my dear! I thought Pierce left you without a decent gem to your name, but this is quite exquisite."

Before Wyn's astonished eyes, Hildy tenderly lifted a diamond necklace from the drawer. She held it so that a beam of sunlight struck the stones, bringing them to life.

Behind her, Wyn heard Miss North's gasp of surprise.

Hildy glanced over to the maid. "Yes, North?"

The woman wasn't looking at Hildy though. She stared at Wyn, her eyes narrowed, her expression suddenly malevolent. "So it was you," she said flatly.

Wyn glanced from the maid back to Hildy in time to see her friend hide a brief but triumphant smile.

"What do you mean, North?" Hildy asked, her face registering nothing more now than concerned confusion.

The maid's hand shook as she pointed to the necklace that dangled from Hildy's hand. "That is not Miss Abbot's," she announced in ringing tones. "It's Lady Tilbury's."

Lord Tilbury sat ensconced behind the desk in Alston's study, his eyes never leaving Wyn's face. Ousted from his natural place of authority, Lofty leaned against the mantlepiece, his back to the proceedings. The local constable stood near the door, alert to any attempt Wyn might make to flee. Rachel sat alone and still on the nearby settee, her eyes lowered, reluctantly but dutifully lending her countenance as a chaperon. Hildy had not evidenced any desire to bear her company during the interview, Wyn knew. In fact, her erstwhile friend had been only too ready to believe her capable of the theft.

"A highly unlikely tale," Tilbury snarled. "I'd like to hear the truth now."

From her place in the armchair set directly before the desk, Wyn faced him, determined not to show the fear that gripped her heart tighter with each passing minute. It was the third time she'd told the story, and still the magistrate had not believed her. "I have no idea how Lady Tilbury's diamonds found their way to my room," she said, forcing her voice to remain calm, her expression to remain serene. "They were not there earlier when I dressed. Someone must have put them in the drawer while I was at breakfast."

"Who?" Tilbury snarled.

"I have no idea," Wyn answered. "Whom do you suspect?"

"Yes," growled a deep voice from the doorway. "Whom do you suspect, Tilbury?"

Relief washed over Wyn. The fear receded slightly. She twisted in her chair to find Garrett striding purposefully to her side, her private Galahad come to rescue her. His hand closed around hers, the strength of his grip alone instilling her with confidence and renewed hope.

Lord Tilbury scowled even more fiercely. "There's no call for you to interfere in this matter, Blackhawk."

Garrett arched a single dark brow in patient disbelief. "Is there not?"

Wyn had never been more pleased to hear the hard-edged drawl he affected as the Baron Blackhawk.

Slowly he drew her to her feet, and raised their joined hands to brush his lips across the backs of her fingers. "Come, Tilbury," Garrett chided without looking at his now red-faced neighbor. "Why would Miss Abbot need to pilfer another woman's diamonds when, as my wife, she will soon have as many as she wishes? Personally, my love," he added, tipping Wyn's face up to his, "I think emeralds would suit you far better."

"Your wife!" Tilbury choked.

Behind him, Alston turned hastily, nearly knocking the figurine of a hunting dog from the mantel with his elbow. Rachel's already pale complexion blanched still more.

"We haven't announced it yet," Garrett said carelessly. "As Miss Abbot's parents are in San Francisco, obtaining their blessing is a tedious business." He swept the gathering with a single warning glance. "I trust our secret is safe?"

"Naturally," Alston said, casting Rachel a hasty look. She nodded, her head barely moving with the action.

"You can trust me, yer lordship," the constable assured nervously.

Not as easily subdued, Tilbury blustered. "The fact remains, Blackhawk, your affianced wife was found in possession of stolen goods.''

Taking courage from Garrett's staunch presence at her side, Wyn lifted her chin. ''Which I have explained I did not take, nor did I secret them in my room.''

''Dashed imprudent thing to do considering you were on the lookout for them, wouldn't you agree, Tilbury?'' Garrett demanded. ''Rather than waste our time with incessant questioning, why don't you look into discovering who might have had the opportunity to plant the diamonds in her room?'' He drew Wyn's hand to the crook of his arm. ''And now, if you don't mind, gentlemen, I've come to escort my betrothed on a visit to her future home.'' Without waiting for permission, he turned to lead Wyn out of the study.

Wyn dragged her feet. ''Garrett. Wait,'' she requested quietly. When he paused, Wyn gathered her remaining courage and faced her hostess. When she spoke, she felt her voice sounded harsh and stilted. ''Would you prefer that I remove from Loftus Manor, my lady?''

Rachel exchanged a speaking glance with her husband before rising and crossing the floor to where Wyn and Garrett waited. She touched Wyn's hand. ''Only if you wish.''

''You believe I'm innocent then?'' Wyn pressed.

Rachel glanced at Alston again. ''Yes,'' she said, her voice barely audible.

Garrett leaned over and brushed a kiss to Rachel's cheek. ''Thank you, Rach.'' A minute later he handed Wyn into the closed carriage that waited before the portico. As the driver gave the horses the office to start, Wyn buried her head against Garrett's chest and gave in to her tattered emotions.

He let her weep, soothing her with his hands and his voice. Then his lips brushed hers and the tempest in her turned from fear to longing. At last, she clung to him, emotionally spent. ''How did you know what had happened?''

Garrett brushed a hand tenderly over her hair and folded her closer to his heart. "Dig. I believe he rode *ventre à terre* to fetch me. Rather dashing of him, don't you think? Gave me the devil of a time concocting a way to outdo him."

Wyn smiled weakly against his waistcoat. "Stop trying to cheer me."

"Done," he said. "Now do something to cheer me. To fortify me, shall we say, for the coming battle." He tilted her face up to his and placed a light kiss on her lips.

She frowned over his choice of words. "Will it be a battle, do you think?" she asked.

"Only if we don't flush our bird from cover," he said.

Wyn looked at him is surprise. "You know who the thief is?"

Garrett didn't answer immediately. When he did, his expression was guarded. "Yes," he said quietly. "And I believe, my love, that you do, too."

The following day there was a change in the weather. Gone were the pleasant sunshine-filled days. The skies were gray and threatening, and a far better match to the atmosphere that prevailed within Loftus Manor.

Wyn wished she had not refused the invitation Lady Antonia had issued the afternoon before to remove to Hawk's Run. But to leave Alston and Rachel's now for Garrett's home would have fueled the gossip mill, something Wyn had no wish to do. Although he had requested that the betrothal be kept secret, the countryside was already abuzz with word that he would soon wed.

Perhaps he would, Wyn thought. But it should not be to her.

How cruel fate was. In her eagerness to escape the attentions of fortune hunters, she had beggared herself and now could not follow her heart. While their love had been consumated in the moonlight, in the bright light of day the reality of her situation held sway. She knew how society would view her should she give in to temptation and wed

Garrett. The gossips would term her one of the breed she herself so despised: A fortune hunter. Pride would force her to remain a spinster for she would not marry without a dowry to offer a wealthy man such as Garrett.

And so she sat silently as one group of ladies after another came to call on Rachel and bandy the names of other young women as possible brides for the man she loved. If only she'd thought of leaving days ago, of boarding a north-bound train, of booking passage on the next ship leaving Liverpool for home.

Home.

After having visited Hawk's Run, it was difficult to associate the house on Nob Hill with home. She'd been enchanted with the ancient gray walls, so like those found in the village or in the ruins of Wenlock Abbey. During her brief visit at the Run, she'd learned that the land upon which it stood had been in the family for over eight hundred years. The name, Lady Antonia had said, dated to the Norman conquest when a black-bearded Saxon had tricked his new overlord into granting him the lands that fell beneath a wild hawk's shadow during its soaring territorial run. The Saxon had often watched this particular hawk and knew the bird swept a wide circle during his hunt. The disgruntled Norman, so the tale went, had not only stuck by his bargain, he had dubbed his vassal with a new name: Blackhawk. A subsequent marriage between the families had resulted in the baronage.

There was little to be seen of the original fortified house in the sprawling structure of Hawk's Run now. Additions had been added at the whim of various generations, the only prerequisite appearing to be the use of the local gray limestone as a building material. Wyn found the caprices of Garrett's home very much to her liking.

It would have been impossible to stay there, knowing she could not remain.

Staying with Alston and Rachel had not been much wiser. While her hosts continued to go out of their way to be kind to her—their attentions based, Wyn felt, on their mistaken belief that she would soon wed their nearest neighbor—Hildy's attitude remained one of cool reproof. She had not requested Wyn's companionship on her daily drive to visit the dressmaker, nor did she seek her out to trade confidences. To all intents and purposes, Hildy treated her like an ill-met stranger.

If it had not been for Ellery and Deegan's escort about the various rides of Hawk's Run and the Loftus estate, Wyn was sure she would have gone mad. Unfortunately, she did not see Garrett. Business kept him from her side. Magnus Finley appeared to have left the region. Perhaps he had been en route to Ireland after all.

Thus, when she awoke to find the heavens overcast, Wyn was inclined to believe the weather a reflection of her own spirits. They would sink even further when next she saw Garrett.

There was an unaccustomed tightness in her chest at the realization that it was time for her to leave England, time for her to tell Garrett goodbye. She had lingered far too long already. With his wife's diamonds returned, Lord Tilbury had withdrawn the accusation of theft. There was nothing to hold her. Nothing but love.

Wyn took up her pen and hastily scribbled a note to the Shire Line office in Liverpool requesting passage on the earliest possible ship, then she asked that her trunks be brought to her room. When the rain began that afternoon, she had nearly finished packing.

The cloudburst continued well past the dinner hour. Rachel sent word that dinner would be delayed, but Wyn cared little, for she had lost her appetite days ago. While she waited, Wyn stood at her bedroom window staring out at the steady drizzle as she thought back over all that had happened.

Garrett claimed that she knew the identity of the thief, but he was mistaken. She had suspected him and been wrong. She knew that now. Perhaps had known it all along.

She tried to picture her family, her life in San Francisco.

Instead Garrett's beloved features lingered in her mind's eye. And another's.

Hildy's.

Would her heart ever find its ease over the loss of her friend? They had shared so much—their childhood, their hopes, their dreams. Surely a single misunderstanding should not be allowed to end a relationship meant to last their whole lives.

She wouldn't let it, Wyn decided. She would seek Hildy out, now, before dinner, so that she could leave the next day with a lighter heart.

The decision made, Wyn slipped from her room.

Chapter Twenty

Garrett returned home from yet another visit to Finley in the village just as the clouds broke. While the weather was inhospitable, he found that the sight of lamplight spilling from the windows of Hawk's Run was not. In the past week there had actually been times when he found it hard to remember how much he had once hated the thought of returning home. Now the only improvement he envisioned making to the manor was having Wyn there to welcome him back.

It took but a moment to locate where his family had gathered. The sounds of laughter echoed in the hall, coming from his father's book-lined study. It was his mother's favorite room but he rarely could enter it without expecting to see his father bent over the desk, his attention so bound up in an ancient Greek text that his wife and sons ceased to exist. One day Garrett hoped the specter would fade. Unfortunately, that day was far in the future if it even existed.

A fire burned in the grate, warming the room as it had always done. Because Lady Antonia enjoyed the sight and sound of rain, the heavy drapes had not been drawn across the windows. Reflected in the glass was the soft glow of flickering candles. At the sight of the burning tapers, Garrett grinned. His mother detested oil lamps and refused to use them. He wondered if she would feel the same way about the gas lighting he had long ago ordered installed in the town house in London. If, that is, she ever visited there. Without even having been to the city yet himself, Garrett knew that Blackhawk House had lain empty the entire two years he'd been gone.

"Garrett!" Lady Antonia cried happily, spying him even before he stepped into the room. "You must congratulate me. I've managed to do the impossible."

"And what is that?" he asked, bending to kiss her cheek.

"Ask your brother," she said. "It is, after all, a giant step forward for him."

Both Ellery and Deegan had risen from their chairs at his entrance, Deegan going immediately to the sideboard to pour him a whiskey.

"You intrigue me, madam," Garrett said, and turned to his brother. "Don't tell me you've finally agreed to a showing of your work in London, old chap. It's about time. The gallery has been after you to lend them a handful of your landscapes ever since you came down from university. And with good reason."

Ellery's fair complexion colored faintly at the praise. "No, although I suppose that is the next leap I should take. Care to contribute your own diabolical refinements to my current campaign?"

Deegan put the glass of spirits in Garrett's hand. "You may need this once you hear what he's up to."

"And you'd better sit down, as well," Ellery added. "You see, at my mother's urging, I've decided to lay claim to Sybil's portion."

"Lord, I do need this," Garrett declared, taking a swig of the whiskey. "Or better yet, champagne to celebrate. It's about time you came to your senses and pushed for what is rightly yours."

Lady Antonia beamed happily. "What about congratulating me?" she asked. "I'm the one who managed to discover the necessary pinprick to set your brother in motion.''

Garrett took a seat on the settee next to her. ''Then congratulations are most definitely due, madam. What exactly was this *pinprick?*''

His mother's smile widened even more. ''Miss Abbot,'' she said.

''To be more precise,'' Ellery corrected, lounging back against a corner of the desk, ''Tilbury's treatment of her. My suing for Sybil's portion will irritate him to such a degree it will be an excellent way to avenge Wyn.''

When Garrett's brow clouded, Deegan pulled his chair closer to the sofa and sat down once more. ''Relax. Tilbury hasn't harangued her today. We've seen to that,'' he said, glancing aside at Ellery. ''In fact, considering Wyn has the two of us dancing attendance on her, she's no doubt the envy of the local belles.''

Garrett's expression didn't clear at the news. If anything, it darkened. It should be him protecting Wyn from the rumors that had no doubt spread across half the county by now. Who better than he knew how harmful such whispers could be?

''Odds are jealousy will run rampant when the three of us fill up her dance card at Rachel's to-do next week,'' Ellery said.

Jealousy already raged unchecked, Garrett thought. The thief's unsuccessful attempt to frame Wyn for the theft of Eleanor Tilbury's jewels had shown that. The failure would only fuel the hatred directed toward Wyn.

With the thought, a feeling of unease settled over his heart. He should never have allowed her return to Lofty's Garrett realized. He and Finley had made a mistake in waiting for their thief to make the next move—especially when the next move might well be against Wyn.

Garrett bolted the rest of his whiskey. ''I'm bound for Loftus Manor,'' he announced, getting to his feet.

The others caught the sense of urgency he had been

unable to strip from his voice. His mother's face grew pale with worry, but she made no move to stop him.

Deegan's expression hardened. "Not without me to cover your back," he said quietly.

Garrett nodded shortly in acceptance of his friend's offer. "Ellery, would you have Spears send a man into town for Finley? To hell with waiting for the woman to make another move. It's time we forced her hand."

"Send some men for Tilbury and the constable," Ellery suggested. "I'll collect the good detective and meet you at Lofty's."

"Be careful, all of you," Lady Antonia urged. "I'll have a room prepared here for Winona. If you must, Garrett, carry her away against her will."

"Gladly, madam," he promised. Moments later he was striding purposefully toward the stable, his brother and his best friend staunchly at his side.

Wyn paused outside Hildy's room, rehearsing one final time the words she felt needed to be said. For so many years Hildy had been a part of her life. Perhaps they had not been as close in the last years, but the blame for that could be equally divided. Marriage to Oswin Hartleby had meant Hildy's social round had been in a different, older circle, one that Wyn had not cared to enter. Those events where they had met tended to be arranged by Wyn, never Hildy.

Once again she was the one putting forth the effort, Wyn thought, and she had no idea of what her reception would be like.

Taking a deep, courage-gathering breath, Wyn knocked on the door.

Never fully closed, it creaked open.

Wyn peered around the panel. "Hildy?"

Her friend spun from a contemplation of her reflection in a cheval mirror, one hand flying to her collarbone to shelter the necklace that rested there. "Wyn! Dearest, how you did startle me," Hildy declared.

"I'm sorry. The door was open."

"Was it? That wretched North neglected to close it then. Did you wish something?" Hildy asked.

Where should she begin? None of her prepared lines appeared sincere enough. "I wanted to—" Wyn began, then broke off. Hildy had not dropped her hand. She had, in fact, turned so that her shoulders were in shadow. But Wyn had seen the necklace her friend had worn too many times before not to recognize it.

The Hartleby diamonds.

The reason for her visit was forgotten, replaced by a new and more disturbing unease. "You had them all along," Wyn accused.

"La, my dear, this is the paste copy," Hildy said lightly. "I simply could no longer appear with little more than a paltry ribbon around my neck. My new gown called for something more. Do you like it?" She twirled about once, letting the deep red satin skirt flare slightly. Her diamond drop earrings caught the light, demanding attention.

"I know the difference between paste and a diamond, Hildy," Wyn insisted. "Why did you lie and claim the set stolen?"

"But I didn't lie, dearest," Hildy insisted. She moved around Wyn and firmly closed the door and locked it. "You see, I stole them."

Stunned over the admission, Wyn stared at her friend. "But why?"

"Such a silly question," Hildy murmured. Rather than face Wyn, she moved to the window and, despite the falling rain, pushed it wide open. "Oswin's horrible offspring, of course. He'd had the necklace made specifically for me and they wanted to take it away."

Wyn sank down onto the dressing stool. "I realize that, but to steal it, and then report that an intruder had taken it!"

Hildy preened as if she'd been given a compliment. "A true stroke of genius, was it not? And exciting. So very exciting. There was no one the wiser," she said. "And those fools of Pinkerton's never suspected the grieving widow of the theft.''

Perhaps they had, Wyn thought. Magnus Finley had followed them from San Francisco. It seemed a long way to travel to recover but a single diamond necklace.

''Is that why you decided to add other jewels to your collection, Hildy?'' she asked. ''How did you select your victims?''

Her friend didn't bother to correct the assumption that she had stolen other items. ''Dearest, you are so clever! Though I would hardly call them victims. After all, they deserved to pay.'' Hildy picked up her reticule, turning her attention to finding an item hidden deep within the fabric.

''Olympia Stokes? I believe you took her opals,'' Wyn said.

''Mmm,'' Hildy agreed. ''A frightfully common woman, although I chose her because I was miffed at her husband. Now, your cousin's wife in Boston? I took her sapphires after she had the affront to suggest I should spend my time in charitable acts rather than to gad about Britain.''

Wyn eased off the stool and took a cautious step toward the door. She had been blind, purposefully overlooking Hildy as a suspect because it had been inconceivable that her friend might be a thief.

''You wouldn't be thinking of telling anyone of our little secret, would you, Wyn?'' Hildy asked, and drew a derringer from her purse. Wyn recognized the gun, recalled far too well the occasion when she had helped Hildy purchase it years before. ''Because I really can't allow that,'' Hildy said.

Finding the barrel of the tiny pistol pointed at her, Wyn froze in place.

''In fact,'' Hildy continued complacently, ''the time has come for you to pay for your own sins, dearest.''

When Wyn didn't move, Hildy raised her gun. ''Come, come. I've seen you with Lord Blackhawk. Aboard the

ship. In the woods the other night. I was quite shocked at
your behavior, dearest.''

There would be no reasoning with Hildy, Wyn realized.
An insane glitter lit her friend's eyes.

A rain-chilled gust of wind swept into the room, stirring
the hem of Hildy's scarlet dress. ''You knew he was meant
to be mine,'' she said. ''And, once you have been removed, he will be and I will have no reason to horde
these.''

As Wyn watched, Hildy lifted a loosely wrapped bundle
and spilled a fortune in set gemstones over the top of the
dressing table.

''It has been such a chore to keep them hidden,'' Hildy
declared with a sigh over the effort. ''When I decided to
add sweet Suzanne's pearls to my collection, I knew a
search for them would in time uncover my clever little
trunk's secret.'' She smiled, proud to be at last boasting
of her cleverness. ''You thought me so diligent in altering
my wardrobe when I was really doing nothing more than
keep my treasures from being discovered.''

''Which is why you struck Miss North,'' Wyn said,
fighting to keep fear at bay. There could be no reasoning
with her childhood friend for she was clearly no longer
sane.

Hildy nodded graciously. ''Naturally. If she had removed the trim from that particular gown she would have
found the pearls and mentioned them to someone. I
couldn't have her recalling the exact nature of the questions I'd asked about her former mistress, either, although
the answers she innocently gave me made it quite easy to
steal into an unfamiliar house. Arranging that North be
present when I discovered the Tilbury witch's diamonds
in your room was truly brilliant, don't you agree?''

How blind she had been, Wyn thought. Purposefully
blind, not wishing to see the changes in Hildy.

''But why?'' she asked.

Hildy moved back toward the open window and glanced
outside at the rain. The muzzle of the derringer in her hand

dipped slightly to the side. Wyn wondered briefly what her chances would be if she leapt forward and tried to knock the gun from Hildy's hand. Not good, she decided. The door was locked. Even if the pistol discharged harmlessly, there was yet another bullet primed in its chamber to spill her blood before she even managed to turn the key.

"Don't be ridiculous, Wyn," Hildy urged. "You know as well as I do that retribution was merited by everyone from whom I stole. They snubbed me, looked down their long noses at me, acted as if I was not their equal. They deserved to lose a bauble or two. But you—" her eyes narrowed in hatred "—you never treated me so. At least not to my face, did you, dearest? No, you went behind my back and stole the future from me. And, as you have no jewels with which to compensate me for the loss, I must arrange for you to pay with something else of worth. Come here, Wyn."

Reluctant, Wyn hung back, hesitating until the muzzle of Hildy's small gun swung back up, centering on her heart.

"You see," Hildy explained patiently, "there will be a tragedy tonight. Realizing that once Lord Blackhawk discovered that you are indeed the thief Mr. Finley seeks, he will end his relationship with you. Bereft of his protection and in danger of being arrested, you will decide to end it all."

It was a story that only Hildy in her dementia could believe. Wyn knew Garrett would never believe she was the thief.

"I will grieve for you, you know, dearest," Hildy continued. "But the punishment must be given. An unfaithful friend is, I believe you'll agree, the worst kind of sinner. Now, come here to the window."

Her mind whirling, looking for a way out of what had become a nightmare, Wyn surreptitiously slipped out of her shoes. "Please, Hildy. It doesn't have to be this way. If the jewelry is returned—"

Hildy cut across the suggestion. "Of course it will be

returned,'' she assured. "With your passing, I shall be in
a position to comfort your lover. He is so delightfully
wealthy, is he not? And thus able to provide all the jewels
I could wish. I do fancy the title of baroness, as you've
known all along. Do hurry,'' she urged, gesturing with the
derringer.

Knowing it might be her only chance, Wyn knocked the
tiny pistol from her friend's hand and gave her a violent
shove. As Hildy screeched in surprise and fell, Wyn gathered her skirts and plunged toward the open tower window.

The drop to the ground was dizzying but the workers'
scaffolding remained as it had been days before, a web of
interlocked boards reaching from the flagstone terrace below to the steeply sloping roof above. Reaching for the
nearest handhold, Wyn stepped out onto the rain-slicked
platform.

The rain had eased to a light mist, yet it soon soaked
her gown, making her skirts cling, dangerously hindering
Wyn as she tried to climb. One hand grasping a crossbar,
the other sliding along the cold, damp brick of the building, she worked to put as much distance as possible between herself and the open window. It would not take
Hildy long to recover the derringer and come after her,
Wyn knew. Sane or not, Hildy had never relinquished any
quest.

A moment later, a bullet slammed into the brickwork
barely an inch from her hand. Wyn screamed.

The sound of a shot so close at hand sent both Garrett
and Deegan into a defensive crouch and the storm-skittish
horses rearing in fright. With a hastily bit-off expletive,
Deegan dashed to the Thoroughbreds' heads, joining the
footman who held their reins in trying to calm them with
his voice and hands.

Garrett ignored the ruckus behind him, the echo of a
scream tightening the fear in his chest into a tight ball.
"Did you hear that, Dig?" he demanded. "It sounded
like—"

"Wyn," Deegan answered. He abandoned the horses and grabbed Garrett's arm when he tried to rush off. "Don't be a fool, man. Take this." Where his hand had been empty a moment before, a small single-shot pistol now rested in his palm. "Take care of yourself."

Garrett nodded shortly then disappeared into the night, Deegan's gun in his hand.

Hugging the rain-slicked crossbar, Wyn slipped down it and felt with her stockinged foot for the next step. She could hear the rustle of Hildy's gown as she followed, climbing out onto the scaffolding. She felt the structure shift slightly at the added weight.

"Dearest," Hildy called. "This is quite foolish. You are ruining everything."

Wyn shut her ears to the sound of her friend's voice. She was one level lower than Hildy and temporarily out of sight beneath the platform. But she was still far too close should Hildy fire another shot, far too high should she lose her footing. Although Wyn knew the movement of the scaffolding would give her away, it was imperative that she continue moving. And to do so safely, she had to get rid of her clinging skirts.

"Wyn!" Hildy snapped angrily. "I insist that you come back here."

Fingers fumbling with the catches, Wyn freed her skirt. As the rain-weighted silk dropped around her ankles, she tore free the front closings of both her basque and corset. Clad only in drawers and camisolette, Wyn scrambled more easily among the web of boards, working her way ever downward.

One step at a time. Don't look down. Just look up. Feel for the next foothold. Above all, don't think, Wyn ordered herself. As it was she was far too conscious that with each handhold, each footstep, she was no longer sheltered from Hildy's sight.

"You really leave me no choice, Wyn," Hildy warned. Wyn knew her old friend had spotted her and was taking careful aim. Forcing herself to concentrate only on the climb, Wyn felt lower for the next crossbar. When the expected shot came, the scaffolding shook violently and her foot slipped. With a cry she grappled for a handhold.

Garrett watched helplessly as the warning shot he'd fired in the air distracted the widow, nearly causing her to lose her balance. Lunging against the scaffolding's frame, she sent the structure swaying dangerously so that it appeared to snap Wyn free from her perch over two stories above him.

Heart in his throat, he watched as the woman he loved caught hold, saving herself if but for a brief time.

Without further thought, Garrett threw the empty pistol and his coat aside and began climbing.

"No, Garrett, don't!" Wyn cried. Her dangling feet found purchase, allowing her to hug the scaffolding tightly as she regained her breath.

"Yes, my lord," Hildegarde called. "Don't bother with her. She's a thief. She has to die in atonement."

He pulled himself up higher, quickly closing the distance between himself and Wyn.

"I told you to stop!" Hildegarde shouted.

Ignoring her, he pulled himself to within a few feet of Wyn and reached out to her.

The bullet took him totally by surprise, slamming into his shoulder with a force that virtually spun him free of the scaffolding. Before he could fall, a hand caught at his, closed firmly around his wrist. Wyn's hand.

"I can't hold you," she said, each word a gasp for breath.

Garrett gripped her wrist, strengthening the slender bond between them as momentum swung him back into the fragile wooden frame. His greater weight jolted the scaffolding, tipping it away from them. The scream of wood tearing free from nailed joints was loud in the night, then lost as another cry rent the air.

His arm locking protectively around Wyn as he found

a foothold on the tilting structure, Garrett watched in horrified silence as Hildegarde Hartleby's form dangled a story above them, the scarlet fabric of her gown caught on a jagged, jutting support.

"Hildy!" Wyn screamed, seemingly unaware of their own danger as the scaffolding swayed.

It seemed forever before the sound of slowly rending silk was heard, heralding the end. For the space of one drawn-out heartbeat, the widow swung above them, not even making an effort to save herself.

The next she was falling.

Epilogue

Wyn stood by the grave site alone. They had buried Hildy a week earlier but she had delayed saying farewell to her friend until now.

The weather had remained damp, the skies cloud-laden since the day of Hildy's death, but today the sun spilled forth once more, warming the gentle breeze and promising a better tomorrow. Birds chirped happily in the hedges and trees. Sheep grazed in the next pasture. Perhaps here Hildy could at last find peace, Wyn thought.

She bent to lay a single rose on the fresh mound of earth. It would be the last time she visited the grave. Soon she would begin the first leg of her journey home to San Francisco with both Magnus Finley and Deegan as her escorts.

Or rather as escorts for the fortune in gems that she carried with her to return to the anxious owners. Despite the circus the newspapers had made of Finley's recovery of the stolen items, few would know about her mission. While she was pleased to have the taint of an unsolved mystery removed from the *Nereid*'s reputation, she wished the process had been accomplished quietly, that word of Hildy's deeds had been kept secret. She had been overruled to that end by both Shire officials in Liverpool and by a cablegram from Pierce in California.

Whether Oswin Hartleby's children minded having their

family name bandied about, no one seemed to care. Based on the brief word they'd sent, the Hartlebys' only concern was for the return of their diamonds. They did not mourn Hildy's demise.

But Wyn did.

"Come, my dear," Rachel urged, stepping up beside her and slipping an arm around Wyn's waist. "You'll miss your train."

Wyn nodded. "I just wish that—"

"Hush," Rachel soothed. She was drawn and pale, but the strain had receded from her face since the funeral. "The fault is not yours, Wyn. My sister had not been herself for the past year. My parents wrote that Mr. Hartleby had spoken to them about placing her in a sanitarium. His death simply delayed what might well have been the only solution. One you and I know Hildy would have disliked very much."

"But if I'd known, surely I could have done something for her," Wyn insisted. "She was my closest friend yet I betrayed her."

"You fell in love," Rachel said. "It would be a bigger betrayal to turn away from that now."

When Wyn didn't answer, Rachel drew her away from the grave and back through the cemetery toward the road where Alston's carriage waited. "Have you seen Garrett to tell him you're leaving?" Rachel asked.

"He knows," Wyn said flatly.

"But you didn't tell him why you rejected his proposal, did you?" Rachel sighed. "I won't say another word, even though I think you are making a big mistake."

Wyn squeezed her hostess's hand and followed her into the waiting carriage. It wasn't until they were on their way to the train station that Rachel pulled a slip of paper from her purse. "I nearly forgot, but this came for you just before I left the manor."

Wyn frowned at the folded sheet. "Another cable. From Pierce, I suppose."

Rachel nodded. "I believe so. He's turned into quite the

protective older brother. A welcome change from the scandalous rascal I remember him to be.''

There had been nearly daily word from Pierce lately, brief sympathies and more detailed instructions on Shire-related business. The now internationally known tale of the *Nereid*'s maiden voyage had generated interest from investors, as well as passengers eager to travel on the notorious ship.

Reluctant to learn the latest, Wyn opened the cablegram slowly. Her lassitude disappeared as she read, replaced by a spurt of anger. ''I can't believe this!'' she stormed. ''He's sold the liner! At a profit, no less!''

''But that's wonderful, Wyn!'' Rachel insisted. ''It means you have your dowry back.''

It came too late, though. She had already refused Garrett. Her pride would not allow her to go to him. As the Baron Blackhawk, his would keep him from asking for her hand again.

''I'm not sure whether I would term this wonderful news or not,'' Wyn said. ''Pierce says the new owner will be sailing with us on the return voyage and he wants me to be particularly nice to the fellow.''

Rachel smiled softly and shrugged. ''You know how men are about business, my dear. Humor him.''

''Pierce?''

''The new owner,'' Rachel said. ''Who knows. He may be dangerously dashing and well able to make you forget this sad visit.''

Wyn recalled her hostess's words three days later as she waited for the moment when the *Nereid* would steam out of Liverpool Harbor. Although she had promised herself she would not leave her cabin until they were well away and at sea, the warming throb of the engines and the lure of the salt-scented breeze wafting in the open porthole were more than she could resist. Hastily pinning her Gainsborough hat in place, Wyn headed for the far rail.

The shouts and calls of the crowd on the dockside competed with the cries of various seabirds, but she paid either little heed. It was the touch of the wind in her face, the warmth of the sun on her shoulders, the feel of the ship rocking ever so gently in place that she sought. Wyn closed her eyes to the harbor sights, standing quietly alone, remembering another time when she had lingered so and met a man who was both dangerous and dashing.

There was a tug on her hat, a pull stronger than she expected from the wind while still in port. Wyn's eyes flew open, but before she could grab the flamboyant picture hat, it sailed free, spinning out over the water, leaving the breeze to whip tendrils of hair loose from her hairpins.

"Much better," a beloved voice murmured at her side.

Wyn stared up at Garrett in wonder, half afraid that she was dreaming.

"I've always liked you better like this," he said and, burying his fingers in her falling hair, covered her mouth with his.

Sweet wildfire raced through Wyn's veins and swelled her heart. Clinging to him, she kissed Garrett back, telling him with her response how much she had missed him.

"I love you," he murmured against her lips. "I want you. Marry me."

Wyn brushed a strand of hair from her eyes and blinked at him. "What did you say?"

Garrett grinned and kissed her hungrily once more. "Marry me," he urged. "Today. Kittrick would like nothing better than to perform a ceremony at sea, and, as you know, my family has a penchant for such things."

It took her a moment to catch her breath, to realize that she was not dreaming, although she surely had not heard him right. "What are you doing here? The ship will be leaving and—"

Garrett cut her off in a most satisfactory way. It was minutes later before either of their heads were clear enough to continue the conversation. "Ellery claims he's become quite used to looking after Hawk's Run without me and I needn't return if I don't wish to."

"Oh, but you love the estate," Wyn said, content to stay close within the curve of his arm. "You've been gone far too long already."

"We can always return there."

Her eyes glowing softly, Wyn looked up at him.

Garrett's lips curved in a rakish smile that made her knees weak. "There are distinct advantages to be gained in marrying me, you know. For one thing, it would eliminate the hordes of fortune-hunting rascals you seem to have a talent for attracting."

Her cheek resting against his chest, Wyn grinned softly.

"It would allow you a continued interest in this ship," Garrett said.

Wyn looked up in surprise. "You mean, the *Nereid?*"

"Your brother set a high price, but I felt it was worth paying it, for the memories alone. And then, of course," he murmured, tilting her face up to his once more, "there are the innumerable opportunities marriage allows for doing this—" he kissed her brow "—this—" his lips brushed lightly over her eyelids "—and—"

When he didn't finish, or kiss her again, Wyn's eyes fluttered open once more.

His dark hair was tousled by the wind to hang in attractive disarray over his brow. "You do love me, don't you?" he asked.

She brushed back the falling lock of hair. "Very much so."

"And you do intend to marry me?"

Wyn's eyes traced over his harsh features lovingly. "If the good captain is willing to perform the ceremony, yes," she said. "But until we steam free of British waters…?"

Garrett grinned wickedly down at her. "Yes?"

She looked at him through lowered lashes. "Perhaps you could simply compromise me?"

And so he did. Most thoroughly.

* * * * *

HE SAID

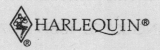

SHE SAID

Explore the mystery of male/female communication in this extraordinary new book from two of your favorite Harlequin authors.

Jasmine Cresswell and Margaret St. George bring you the exciting story of two romantic adversaries—each from their own point of view!

DEV'S STORY. CATHY'S STORY.
As he sees it. As she sees it.
Both sides of the story!

The heat is definitely on, and these two can't stay out of the kitchen!

Don't miss **HE SAID, SHE SAID.**
Available in July wherever Harlequin books are sold.

HARLEQUIN®

Harlequin® Historical

Coming this summer from
Award-winning author
Theresa Michaels

The Merry Widows
A heartwarming new Western series

"Michaels at her poignantly moving best."
—*Affaire de Coeur*

"Pure magic!" —*The Literary Times*

"A true gem…" —*Rawhide and Lace*

"Will hold you spellbound." —*Rendezvous*

"Emotionally charged…" —*Romantic Times*

**That's what reviewers are saying about
Mary the first book in the Merry Widows trilogy**

Coming in June to a store near you.
Keep your eyes peeled!

Harlequin® Historical

If your tastes run to
terrific Medieval Romance,
don't miss

The Bride Thief

by Susan Spencer Paul

The exciting conclusion to her
Medieval Bride Trilogy

Look us up on-line at: http://www.romance.net

MBT797

And the Winner Is...
You!

...when you pick up these great titles
from our new promotion at your
favorite retail outlet this June!

Diana Palmer
The Case of the Mesmerizing Boss

Betty Neels
The Convenient Wife

Annette Broadrick
Irresistible

Emma Darcy
A Wedding to Remember

Rachel Lee
Lost Warriors

Marie Ferrarella
Father Goose

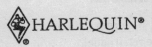 

KAREN HARPER

She would risk everything for love....

Brett Benton came to America to claim her inheritance:
one half of Sanborn Shipping. The other half belongs to
Alex Sanborn, a man who awakens the dormant passions
within her—a man committed to a cause that is about to test
his courage, his skill...his very life.

Forced to make a devil's bargain, Brett must betray Alex in
order to protect him. Now, only the hope of love can see them
through to...

DAWN'S EARLY LIGHT

Available in June 1997
at your favorite retail outlet.

MIRA The brightest star in women's fiction

Look us up on-line at: http://www.romance.net

MKH1